A SMOKE FILLED HAZE

REBEL VIPERS MC BOOK 4

JESSA AARONS

A SMOKE FILLED HAZE

This book is a work of fiction. The names, characters, places, and incidents are all products of the author's imagination and are not to be construed as real. Any similarities are entirely coincidental.

A Smoke Filled Haze Copyright ©2023 by Jessa Aarons. All rights are reserved. No part of this book may be used or reproduced in any manner without written permission from the author, except in the case of brief quotations used in articles or reviews. For information, contact Jessa Aarons.

Cover Designer: Charli Childs, Cosmic Letterz Design

Editor: Rebecca Vazquez, Dark Syde Books

TABLE OF CONTENTS

WARNING	VII
DEDICATION	IX
PLAYLIST	X
PROLOGUE	1
CHAPTER ONE	17
CHAPTER TWO	29
CHAPTER THREE	43
CHAPTER FOUR	53
CHAPTER FIVE	63
CHAPTER SIX	77
CHAPTER SEVEN	87
CHAPTER EIGHT	109
CHAPTER NINE	117
CHAPTER TEN	133

CHAPTER ELEVEN	147
CHAPTER TWELVE	161
CHAPTER THIRTEEN	173
CHAPTER FOURTEEN	187
CHAPTER FIFTEEN	207
CHAPTER SIXTEEN	221
CHAPTER SEVENTEEN	243
CHAPTER EIGHTEEN	257
CHAPTER NINETEEN	279
CHAPTER TWENTY	293
CHAPTER TWENTY-ONE	309
CHAPTER TWENTY-TWO	331
CHAPTER TWENTY-THREE	345
CHAPTER TWENTY-FOUR	363
CHAPTER TWENTY-FIVE	371
CHAPTER TWENTY-SIX	377
CHAPTER TWENTY-SEVEN	387
CHAPTER TWENTY-EIGHT	395
CHAPTER TWENTY-NINE	403

CHAPTER THIRTY	411
CHAPTER THIRTY-ONE	421
CHAPTER THIRTY-TWO	431
CHAPTER THIRTY-THREE	441
CHAPTER THIRTY-FOUR	453
CHAPTER THIRTY-FIVE	467
CHAPTER THIRTY-SIX	481
CHAPTER THIRTY-SEVEN	491
CHAPTER THIRTY-EIGHT	497
CHAPTER THIRTY-NINE	507
EPILOGUE	513
ACKNOWLEDGMENTS	520
ABOUT THE AUTHOR	522
OTHER WORKS	525

WARNING

This content is intended for mature audiences only. It may contain material that could be viewed as offensive to some readers, including graphic language, dangerous and sexual situations, murder, abuse, and extreme violence.

Love comes in all shapes, sizes, and colors. No person should ever define themselves by a check mark in a box. We weren't born into this world in a box, so we shouldn't have to live in one.

Color outside the lines, jump in a puddle, dance and sing like no one is watching, be who you truly are. The world is your oyster. Crack it open and see what shines inside.

Stay strong and shine on, you crazy diamonds!

PLAYLIST

CLICK HERE TO LISTEN ON SPOTIFY

ABBY – Travis Denning
Loving You Easy – Zac Brown Band
Drunk (And I Don't Wanna Go Home) – Elle King, Miranda Lambert
I Could Use a Love Song – Maren Morris
Break Stuff – Limp Bizkit
Soul – Lee Brice
Kiss the Girl – Brent Morgan
Kiss Me I'm #!@'faced – Dropkick Murphys
Fancy Like – Walker Hayes
I'm Not for Everyone – Brothers Osborne
At the End of a Bar – Chris Young, Mitchell Tenpenny
Steal My Love – Dan + Shay

Lil Bit – Nelly, Florida Georgia Line
Beauty in the Struggle – Bryan Martin
Sugar – Maroon 5

PROLOGUE

JACOB

NEW YEAR'S EVE – NINE MONTHS AGO

It's New Year's Eve and the party is in full swing. I'm sitting on a stool, back to the bar, shooting the shit with Ring. Duchess and Whiskey just disappeared upstairs, but no one is fooled by what they're going up there to do.

"What about one of them?" Ring points at Stiletto and Jazz, two of the club girls, dancing naked on the coffee table in the middle of the main room. He's been trying for ten minutes to find me someone to hook up with for the night.

But it's who's behind the girls that really catches my eye.

Sam, another club Prospect like me, is staring me down. But the second he realizes I'm watching him watch me, he diverts his attention to the girls between us. His eyes snap to their long, naked legs, trying to ignore that I just busted him.

I've been crushing hard on Sam since we both started Prospecting, and based on the few other instances when I found him looking at me, I've wondered if he's felt the same.

Too bad every time I look at him, he looks away. Something tells me he's in denial, or maybe he's not even aware of what he's doing. But if he's going to pretend I'm not sitting here, just as interested in him, maybe it's time to move on from my stupid crush.

I spin my stool toward the bar and take a swig of my beer before answering Ring's question. "Nah, they're not my type."

Ring almost spits out his beer. "How are naked women not your type? They're club girls. That's why we have them here."

"I don't know." I shrug, trying to brush off the conversation. "Club girls just don't trip my trigger."

"Then who does?" Ring persists.

"I'm waiting for the right person." I toss my empty beer in the trash can behind the bar and pop the top on the second bottle I grabbed earlier.

I've been around the club for a few years, and I'm so close to earning my full patch, I can feel it. Is it so wrong to want someone to share that with? There's no rule that Prospects can't be with the club girls, and I have a few times, but it was never for more than just the physical release. If I never slept with any of them ever again, I wouldn't bat an eye.

"Do you have a certain lady in mind?" Ring nudges me, wiggling his eyebrows, trying to get me to spill my secrets.

I chuckle. "Not tellin' you nothin'."

"Damn, Jacob." Ring rolls his eyes. "You're a buzzkill."

I shove his shoulder. "What are you razzin' me for? You don't have a woman either."

"I will soon. I just know it." Ring nods, almost like he's trying to convince himself.

Sensing I'm not in a female hunting mood, Ring turns to his other side and starts talking beer stuff with Buzz. I mostly zone them out when, in the mirror hanging behind the bar, I notice a reflection of Sam slinking around the edge of the room. My eyes follow him as he tries to be inconspicuous.

Whether it's by luck or just plain chance, Sam looks my way before he starts up the stairs. The way he's looking at me is like he's begging for something. But then why would he need to run away?

If what I think I see in him is even half of what I feel, maybe this isn't all one-sided. Could he feel for me what I feel for him? I guess there's only one way to find out.

Chugging the rest of my beer, I decide to follow.

I slide off my stool and slap Ring on the back. "Goodnight," I say to whoever hears, then try and not run to chase Sam.

"Wait," Ring calls out, "where you goin'?"

At the top of the stairs, I head straight, then hang a right at the end of the hall. First door on the right is the Prospect bunkroom. The door's open a crack, so I shuffle in, shut it behind me, and flip the light on. That's where I find Sam, sitting on the end of his bed, head in his hands.

Either he's too in his head or he's ignoring me. Too bad, so sad for him, because I want answers.

I skirt around a few bunks and stop six feet in front of him. "Are you okay?"

"No," Sam mumbles.

"What's wrong?"

That gets his attention. "You," he growls, looking up at me.

"Me? What'd I do?"

"Nothing." He sneers, squinting at me like I'm a bug.

What the hell? Who pissed in his Cheerios this morning?

"And that's a problem, why?"

Sam's anger flares and he snaps. "Because I don't know if I want you to do something or not. And that pisses me off even more."

The tenacity and aggression flying makes me take a step back but not for long.

I think I know what's going on here—he wants me, but at the same time, he doesn't *want* to want me. Well, too fucking bad for him because I want him too. I use his admission of uncertain feelings as a sign.

Watching as his eyes grow wide, probably from the shock of what's happening, I start moving. Closing the distance between us, I lean down and then I'm kissing him. I set my hands on his shoulders, push him onto his back, and only when I'm kneeling over him do I close my eyes.

And much to my surprise, our kissing intensifies. Sam doesn't try to push me off. Oh no, he wraps his arms around my neck, pulling me closer.

My arms bracket his head, so I unlock my elbows and let him pull me down.

But my shock turns to confusion when I feel myself start to fall to the side and I realize he's trying to roll us over. Oh no, I don't fucking think so. I'm not letting the hottest kiss of my life end this quick.

My tongue is wrestling with his, so I lick the roof of his mouth and growl. Our teeth clash against one another's, and somehow, he gets the upper hand . . . or is it lip? Sam bites down on my lower lip, and I gasp. And he uses my shock to his advantage.

Sam's arms are now around my torso as his legs move beneath mine. Next thing I know, he gives another heavy shove and rolls me over on my back.

Now looking up at the ceiling, I feel Sam begin to kiss down my neck, then down my t-shirt covered chest. It takes a few seconds for my brain to come back online, then switches start flipping when Sam's lips hit the bare skin of my stomach. My t-shirt has ridden up in our rolling, so his wet lips press against my suddenly hot flesh.

What really wakes me up is the popping of the button of my jeans and the sound of Sam lowering my zipper.

I sit up fast, knocking him back onto his knees. "What're you doing?"

But this doesn't stop him. Sam sets his hands on my thighs and slides them up toward my hips. Pushing my shirt up farther, he finds the open flaps of my jeans, and before I can stop him, he pulls them apart.

Right away, my cock feels the freedom from his denim cage and springs into the air.

"Sam, you don't need to do this," I practically whine as I look down at him. My hands are balled into tight fists at my sides, trying not to touch him. Because I know the second I do, there's no turning back.

"No, Jacob." Sam looks up at me with determination. "I need to know."

I don't know what's gotten into Sam, but now that it's happening, I can't find a real reason to stop it. He seems to want this... I want this... so why am I trying to stop him?

Here goes nothing. As long as he's the one pushing for it, bring it on. I wasn't going to force myself on Sam, but if letting him take the reins will get us a step in the right direction, I'm game.

"If this is really what you want," I say, trying to make sure one last time.

Sam nods. "I need to."

With that, I let the last bit of resistance fall.

Lifting my hips, I allow Sam to pull the denim down my legs. Not bothering to undress any more, risking Sam backing out, I settle my bare ass on the comforter and wait to see what he has planned next.

It doesn't take but two seconds to figure it out.

Sam wraps his left hand around the base of my cock before he opens his mouth, sticks out his tongue, and licks me from balls to tip. My cock jerks hard, but he keeps at it, doing it again, then licking the bead of precum from my tip.

He takes another lick, but this time when he reaches my quickly turning purple head, he wraps his lips around it and proceeds to swallow me fucking whole.

"Holy fuck!" I shout, letting my eyes roll back. I prop myself on my elbows, so I can look down and watch what's happening below.

No warning, no holding back, Sam breathes in through his nose, and the heat and wetness of his mouth surround my hardness. He begins his slow slide up and down my manhood, and the gentle suction almost sends me straight through the roof.

Now, don't misunderstand me, I've been on the giving and receiving end of plenty of blowjobs in my teenage and adult years, but none of them had felt like this.

This blowjob is a masterpiece. Sam is a magician of phallic fuckery. Either he has beginner's luck or someone taught him how to suck a dick very well. What brain cells I have left firing really don't like that second option AT ALL!

Watching as his lips make my cock very happy, I try to push that anger to the back of my mind. I'll worry about that another time when I'm not about to explode after two minutes in heaven.

Sam looks up at me and groans. "Mmm."

The vibration from his throat reverberates through my dick, into my hips, and makes my entire lower half come alive. That's definitely a sensation I've never felt before. I'm immediately so close to coming, if I didn't know better, I'd say Sam did that on purpose.

Maybe he did, and if that's the case, he asked for it.

Pushing up to sit again, I grab Sam's head with my left hand. Threading my fingers through the few inches of hair he has, gripping as tight as I can, I stop his bobbing. If he keeps going, I'm not going to last.

I start pumping my hips up and forcing myself even further down Sam's throat. His eyes bug out, but he doesn't stop me. His hands latch onto my knees as he lets me use his mouth and throat as my personal toy.

The tingling in my legs comes rushing back up, and as soon as it hits my spine, I know I'm a goner.

"You . . . ready?" I grunt, still thrusting.

With his mouth too full to answer, Sam scrapes his teeth against my flesh on the next slide up, so I take that as a yes.

One . . . two . . . three . . .

Four more grunts and I explode. My leg muscles go taut, and I can't move even if I want to. Though right now, I have no interest in going anywhere. My abdomen is tight and my orgasm has reached its boiling point.

I hold Sam's head in place as I blast rope after rope of my seed into his mouth. I feel his throat constrict as he swallows everything I force him to take.

Only after hearing him choke, do I let up and allow him to take a breath.

Looking at Sam kneeling before me, I rest my hands on my knees and take in his haggard appearance. His lips are dark pink and swollen, his cheeks and chin are shiny with his saliva, and his eyes are closed, his head tilted down at his lap.

Needing to see what he's feeling, I tip Sam's chin up, hoping to get him to look at me.

He takes a deep breath and his eyes finally open. But what I see staring back at me is anything but good. He looks defeated. That's the last thing he should feel, because nothing we just did is to be ashamed of.

"What's wrong, Sam?" I whisper.

"I don't—"

"Stop." I cut him off before he can go there. Now isn't time for doubt.

I reach down for his hand and pull him up as I stand. Maybe if I show him how I feel about him, he'll see this isn't a bad thing.

I reach for his waist, but before I can get ahold of his zipper, Sam pushes me back and turns away. With my jeans around my ankles, boots still on, I almost trip but end up sitting back on the bed.

Sam starts pacing the end of the row of bunks, mumbling to himself as he runs his hands over his head.

Grabbing my jeans, I pull them up but leave them open, then step into his path. Not looking up, he runs into me, and I stop him with my hands on his shoulders. He takes a big step back out of my reach.

"No!" Sam shouts.

Raising my hands, I stay where I am. "What?"

"I can't." Sam shakes his head. "You can't touch me there."

"Why not?" I ask.

"I don't know if I'm ready for that." He's panicking.

Any softness or tenderness I had for him is gone in a heartbeat. My anger flashes to the forefront and I snap. "You can suck on my dick, but I can't touch yours?"

Sam looks at the floor, kicking his boot against the hardwood. "I'm not sure. My head's all messed up."

"Why are you being like this now?"

I'm stunned. I know I liked what we just did, and based on the vigor and groans coming from him, I thought Sam did too. I've been with other men before, and I've gotten several blowjobs since I accepted my sexuality at sixteen, but they never made me feel like this when they were done. And no woman has ever turned away my offer of going down on her.

I know I'm bisexual, but maybe Sam doesn't know what he is yet. And I'm not about to be someone's social experiment, no matter how much I like him.

"What's the big deal? It was just one make-out session." Anger flashes from Sam as he gets defensive. He sets his fists on his hips and stares at me like my cock down his throat is a normal occurrence for us.

"Newsflash, Einstein, you just swallowed my cum. That was more than a make-out session," I taunt him back with a smile.

"This can't happen again," Sam declares like it's a law.

Too bad for him, this can't be swept away, or hidden in the closet like I guess he still is.

"I don't care how much you wanna deny this, but you sucked my cock. I can't forget about that," I retort.

"This," Sam steps into my personal space, waving a hand between us, "wasn't supposed to happen. Do you really think the Brothers will allow two Prospects who are fucking each other to join this club?"

I shrug, standing my ground. "I don't see why not."

"IT CAN'T HAPPEN!" Sam shouts.

"What the FUCK are we supposed to do now? Ignore what happened?" My voice raises with every word, and my anger has just about met its boiling point. One more degree higher and my lid will pop off, blasting this whole room with my steam.

"Yes," Sam answers, like he doesn't have a care in the world.

And there it goes—my last string has snapped.

I grab his biceps and slam his back against the wall. Pressing my chest into his, I get in his face, nose to nose. But that's not the only pointy part of us that's touching.

With my jeans still wide open, my dick is rubbing against the bulge in his pants. I can feel his hardness between us, and there's no hiding how his cock is twitching. My dick can feel every move of his.

I move my hands from his arms to the wall on either side of his head. Sam leans his head back, trying to get away from me, but I close in that much more. Moving my lips to his ear, I feel his puffs of air against my cheek.

"I won't give up on this. I know you feel what I feel. You're hard as a rock," I purr, nipping at his earlobe.

"Whatever. It's never gonna happen again." Sam finally touches me, pushing me away.

"If you need time to straighten your head out, fine. I'll step back." I give him a little space but keep my eyes on his, hopefully showing him how serious I am. "But know this. One day, when you least expect it, you'll need me. And when that day comes, watch the fuck out, because when I get you underneath me, there will be no more running away."

"I'm not running," Sam tries to say with gusto, but it comes out more like a whine. "I just don't feel like that toward you."

"Your earlier words say differently. And so did your mouth on my dick. Never mind the fact your dick is probably leaking cum, begging me to swallow it. But say whatever you think you need to say to push me away. Just be careful because I'll only take so much from you before I walk away for good."

I tuck my now deflated dick back into my jeans, buttoning and zipping myself up. I head for the door, pushing past Sam, and he asks where I'm going.

Not bothering to look back at him and ignoring his sudden need to know my whereabouts, I give him enough that hopefully he won't follow. "I'll find somewhere else to sleep for the night." With the whiplash he's thrown at me in the last half-hour, I don't know why he cares.

Pulling the door shut behind me, it slams, and I stomp my way down the hall, around the corner, and back downstairs.

At the bottom, I hang a one-eighty and head for the back patio. Pushing the screen door open, my intention is to sit outside in the freezing winter air until my body is too numb to feel anything. Then I'll find a bottle of whatever shitty alcohol I can find, drag myself into one of the empty cabins, and drink myself into an oblivion that won't let me wake up until at least noon.

But I make it no more than three steps before I hear a voice calling my name. Looking around the yard, I see the porch light is on at the second cabin. A body appears from the shadows, and I see Brick standing from a chair on his porch.

"It's too cold out here for whatever grovelin' you're tryin' to do. Come on in," Brick calls out.

My feet start moving, and before I know what I'm doing, I'm inside his cabin. "Thanks."

Brick shuts the door, then leans against the kitchen island. "Everything okay?"

I tuck my hands in my pockets and rock back on my heels. "It will be, one day."

Brick winks. "Knowing the both of you, you'll figure it out."

"What?" I'm confused. Both of us? What's he talking about?

"Never mind. The couch is pretty comfy, feel free to crash on it. Good night." Brick nods, then disappears down the hall.

Between Sam, the whirlwind of emotions from our encounter, and now Brick's cryptic comment, I'm suddenly exhausted. My eyelids are getting heavy, so I flip a few switches, shutting off everything but the light over the kitchen sink, and carefully make my way to the couch.

Sliding off my Prospect cut, I lay it on the coffee table and kick off my boots, then I flop on my back and stretch out on the couch. Brick wasn't kidding—this couch is comfortable.

Letting myself sink into the cushions, my whole body starts shutting down.

If Brick knows about me and Sam, I wonder whether anyone else in the club does too. Not that I have anything to hide about liking another guy, I just hope it isn't a problem with anyone.

CHAPTER ONE

ABBY

FEBRUARY – SEVEN MONTHS AGO

How in the world did I get here? I'm in my car, six hundred miles from home, and about to take a step back in time. I've been on the road for two days, and I'm ready to be done driving.

Lord knows this is a trip I never thought I'd have to take, but with the events of the last six months, I needed to get away from him. I couldn't do what he suddenly expected of me, so I planned and plotted and built myself a way out.

My escape may not have gone down like I originally thought, but when your plans go to hell in a hand basket, you grab what you can and run.

And that's what's led me to where I am right now.

It's the middle of February and cold as shit. Luckily for me, and my car with no functioning heat, it's not snowing. But if the slowly growing clouds peeking through the tree branches above are any sign, a winter storm is brewing.

Right now, the words I'd use to describe the snow on the ground are slushy and dirty. So even though the sun isn't super bright, any light reflecting off what is on the ground makes it just bright enough to wear sunglasses.

That's a good thing too because if anyone saw me right now, they'd be asking questions I don't have answers for.

I'm driving to my grandma's house in Tellison, Wisconsin. Grandma Harris doesn't know I'm coming, and I hope the surprise won't be too much for her. I haven't seen her in almost six years, and that's one hundred percent my fault.

When I got married, I listened to the wrong person and eloped to Las Vegas. And since no one had any notice, none of my family attended. All of his did, though. I guess that's what happens when you marry into a family who has too much money and no care for others.

I follow the curvy roads, slowing down when I see something strange ahead on the right. A super tall chain link fence topped with barbed wire seems to grow out of the ground, and I can't help but stare as I roll by.

A group of people are standing in the parking lot behind the fence, and they're all wearing black vests. *How strange.* Even though I don't see any motorcycles, it is mid-winter after all, my guess is they're some sort of biker gang.

Looking further, just past the fence, I see a sign reading 'Rebel Repairs' on top of a garage.

Before I can blink again, the road curves to the left and I drive past.

That's what I get for only relying on a paper map. I have no idea what kind of area I'm driving through. Had I known I'd be driving by a scary den of bikers, I would've chosen a different route.

But the closer I get to town, the more I remember driving along this stretch with my mom.

It's another ten minutes before I see the 'Village of Tellison' sign.

I turn right at the stoplight.

Left on Knoll Road.

Grandma's is the second house on the right.

I see the sidewalk and driveway are clear, so I pull in and park. Turning the key, my car sputters and shakes a little. Ignoring the fact it may not start again if I have to leave in a hurry, I open my door, get out, and nudge it shut with my hip.

I walk to the bottom of the porch steps, but before I can take the first one, the screen door opens.

"Whatever you're sellin', I ain't buyin'" is hollered out at me.

"Hi, Gram," I say with a wave.

She lifts her hand, shading her eyes. "Abby, honey, is that you?"

Pushing my sunglasses up into my hair, Gram gets her first look at my face. I watch her jaw drop as she steps out onto the porch.

I take the steps up to stand in front of her. She looks at me from head to toe, taking in the purple, blue, and yellow bruises I know are on my face and arms.

"Oh, my lord almighty. What happened to you?"

"He did, Gram," I whisper as my tears start falling. "He did."

"Do you need help burying the body?" Gram asks with a stoic expression. Her lips are pinched, her eyes squinted, and it's almost as if I can see the thoughts rolling through her mind like a movie. My feisty Gram is ready to fight.

All my tension floats away, and I can't help but laugh at her straightforwardness. Her tenacity shows me that coming here was the right choice. "I took care of him myself. I think he got the message."

"That's good," she replies with a satisfied nod. "Now, let's get you inside and out of this shitty cold weather."

"Sounds good to me." I let Gram grab my hand, and she leads me inside.

Her house is exactly like I remember it. It may have only been six years, or maybe seven, since I was here last, but it feels like a lifetime.

The wall in the foyer is lined with hooks, and I shrug off my coat, hanging it on the farthest right hook. I toe off my tennis shoes and slide them under the bench.

The silence is quickly broken by the jingling of metal and a continuous rumble that's getting closer. I turn and see a giant ball of golden fur running down the hall.

"Sampson, NO!" Gram calls out, but the dog doesn't listen.

The four-legged pooch is headed straight for me, but I don't mind it one bit. As he gets closer, he tries to stop, but his paws slide on the hardwood and Sampson collides with my legs.

Kneeling to his level, my face is immediately slobbered with wet kisses. He barks as I start scratching and petting him everywhere his constantly moving body will let me reach. "Oh, aren't you such a good boy."

"He's a menace is what he is," Gram scolds. "Sampson, sit."

And this time, he listens. I keep loving on him as his tail wags so hard, his whole body moves side to side.

"How long have you had this cutie?"

"Comin' up on four years. He wandered into my yard, and no matter how many times I tried to shoo him away, he just kept comin' back. So, I convinced him to get in my car with a leftover T-bone and took him to the vet." Gram walks and talks as we make our way into the living room and sit on the couch. "I intended on leavin' him there, but when the vet tried puttin' him in a kennel, he started whinin' so loud, I caved."

Sampson sets his big head on my knee, and I lean down to kiss his forehead. "Who could say no to this face?"

I open my eyes when I feel Gram's warm hand surround the top of my knee as she squeezes it. "It's time to spill the beans. Not that I don't love you bein' here, but you didn't even call."

I place my hand on top of hers and look down, trying not to see the disappointment in her eyes when I tell her what I'm about to say. "I'm sorry for cutting everyone off, but it had to be that way. He wouldn't let me call."

From the second Toby proposed to me six years ago, he did everything in his power to seclude me from anyone I'd ever known. He moved us from Madison, Wisconsin, to Kansas City, Kansas, his hometown. He came up with every excuse in the book to not come back to Wisconsin for any reason.

I had graduated at the top of my high school class and gotten accepted into the University of Wisconsin - Madison on an academic scholarship. When I was born, my mom, Diane, was on husband number two, but he wasn't my father. My father, she said, was a one-night stand whose name she didn't remember.

I was born here in Wisconsin, in Henderson, but we moved away when I was little. We bounced around the Midwest, moving wherever Mom could find a man to support us and anywhere away from the only family we had.

But no matter our vagabond location, I always managed to focus on my studies, and as soon as I graduated, I moved out.

I'd always had some sort of part-time job while in high school, and I stashed away every penny I could. I worked at a few fast-food joints, a car wash, a couple restaurants, even cleaned horse stalls on weekends at our neighbor's farm when we lived in a double-wide trailer in the middle of bumfuck country nowhere.

But when I got to college and moved into my dorm, I was swept off my feet by my roommate's older brother. Looking back now, it was bad from the start. Toby never wanted me to go to any parties, even though he did because he was in a fraternity. And after my freshman year was over, he asked me to come to Kansas City to meet his family.

What I didn't expect was to see my mother sitting on the couch when I walked into Toby's parents' home. I hadn't seen her since the summer before, and had no intention of visiting her because I didn't know where she was living.

She apologized profusely about ignoring my calls until she was blue in the face. Being the lovestruck nineteen-year-old I was, I soaked it all up. I never did make it back to school.

Now, at twenty-five, I see the manipulation from all sides and am building myself up to be stronger and more independent. Crawling back to Gram's house may not seem like I'm trying to strike out on my own, but sometimes, you need to ask for help to keep moving forward.

"No one's gonna come for you, are they?"

Her voice snaps me back from memory lane, and I wipe a few tears I didn't realize were rolling down my cheeks. In a way, her question shocks me, but it really shouldn't. I don't know why I was so afraid of coming here, I had no reason to be. I was just more afraid of what would happen to me if I got caught calling my family.

"I don't think so. The ink is dry on the divorce papers. That's why he did this to me." I use my pointer finger to circle my face.

"Well, don't you worry. You're safe here with me." Gram leans forward and opens a wide, skinny drawer on the front of the coffee table.

The drawer is filled with envelopes and pens and a few spools of thread. But when she shifts aside a *Better Homes and Gardens* magazine, I understand what she meant by being safe. Gram has a gun in her living room!

I sit back fast and look at her like I've never seen her before. This isn't the Gram I know. She's always been a spunky lady, but never in a million years would I expect her to have a weapon.

"What are you doing with that?"

"One can never be too safe these days." She waves me off like I'm the crazy person. "I took a concealed carry class down at the VFW and learned all about how to handle a gun. Not that I need it. We've got one heck of a scary biker club just outside town. They take care of any riffraff that tries to come around."

Remembering the crowd of leather inside the tall fence, I wonder if that's who she means. "I think I drove past their hangout on my way here. Aren't gangs supposed to be a bad thing to have close by?"

"Oh, honey," she shushes me with a waging finger, "those boys ain't no gang. They're a full legitimate club. They have officers and everything. There's not much around here that they don't have a finger in. They may look scary, but they keep us all safe. Heck, their President has a girlfriend who owns the bakery around the corner. She's the sweetest little thing you've ever seen. I bet you and she would be great friends."

"I don't know, Gram. I just got away from trouble. I don't need to be knocking on some biker lady's front door, asking her to teach me how to bake muffins."

Gram waves me up, and I follow her into the kitchen. "Kiana doesn't make muffins. She's a cupcake queen."

Sampson follows us and heads for a doggy bed in the corner by the back door.

And sure enough, sitting on the kitchen peninsula is a package of six cupcakes, all decorated like they belong on one of those baking competition shows.

"Those look delicious." I can't take my eyes off them.

"That's 'cause they are." Gram reaches into a cabinet and sets two small plates in front of us. "Let's have a snack while you fill me in on what's been goin' on. Then we can figure out what your next step is."

Before I attack a cupcake, I reach across the counter and lay my hand on Gram's arm. "I missed you, Gram."

"I missed you too, Abby-Bear," she says with a wink.

I can't help rolling my eyes at the childhood nickname, but I secretly love it. "You'll never stop calling me that, will you?"

"Not 'til you're as old and gray as me," Gram retorts.

I wave her off. "You'll outlive me."

"I prob'ly will."

Gram opens the box, and we each grab a cupcake. I choose a chocolate frosted one with vanilla drizzled over top. "What kind is this?"

"I never ask. I just get an assortment so each one is a mystery."

We take our first bites, and my eyes almost roll back into my head. "This really is heaven."

"Told you," she mumbles around a mouthful. After chewing, she locks onto me and gets straight to business. "Now, tell me what brought you home."

Setting my cupcake down, I wipe my hands on my jeans and lay it out, straight to the truth. "I found Toby in bed with Francesca."

"Oh no, he didn't." She gasps. "Your sister?"

"Yes, unfortunately, he did."

"Your husband was havin' an affair with your little sister?"

"He doesn't seem to think it was an affair," I reply.

Gram has her cupcake in front of her mouth, about to take another bite, when she drops it and it falls to the counter, frosting side down. "And what in the name of Jesus, Mary, and Joseph does that mean?"

"That story may require more than sugar." I rub my forehead, feeling a headache coming on.

"Got ya covered." She reaches to the cabinet to her right and pulls out a bottle of rum. "We ain't got nowhere to be. Spill the beans."

It may have been years since I've seen her, but Gram picks up just like it was yesterday. This is exactly where I need to be.

It's time for a brand new start.

CHAPTER TWO

SMOKE

SECOND TO LAST WEEK OF JUNE – TWO AND A HALF MONTHS AGO

What an interesting last couple of days . . .

First, Sunshine was kidnapped by Bullet and the Chaos Squad misfit club.

Then, when we found her, they shot and killed Brick, our club Secretary and Mountain's younger brother.

And now, because of his actions that day, chasing and capturing Bullet, Sam is getting his full member patch and road name this weekend.

We're finally going to be on equal footing in the club, and that means his reasoning for us not being together is no longer valid. His concerns that the club would have an issue with two Prospects being together, especially because we're men, will no longer matter. He can't use other people as an excuse.

Now, I just have to find the fucker and try to get him to see my side of things without telling him he's getting patched in. Earlier in Church, it was ordered that he's not supposed to know until the day of, so it can be a surprise.

When I was brought in as a member a few months back, I moved out of the Prospect bunkroom and into the bedroom Whiskey and Duchess vacated when they moved out to their cabin. I enjoy not having to share a large room with half a dozen other smelly guys, but the quiet is something I'm still getting used to.

Growing up with two older brothers, then moving from my childhood home into the clubhouse bunkroom, privacy has never been something I've had.

After checking the bunkroom, I head downstairs to find Sam. It's the middle of the night, so I know he can't have gone far. I notice the back doors are open, so I head that way. Maybe he's on the back patio.

Before I push the screen door open, I see his silhouette sitting at one of the picnic tables. He's out there in the dark, so I flip on one of the outdoor lights, then step outside. His head pops up. The second Sam sees it's me, he stands up and heads in my direction, trying to get around me to go inside.

Leaning on the door, I block the path, forcing him to stop in front of me.

"Move," Sam growls.

"I'd like to see you make me," I reply, hoping to get a reaction out of him.

Ever since our encounter on New Year's Eve, he's done everything in his power to only be around me if other people are present. I've even seen him walk the long way around the clubhouse to avoid encountering me alone.

But too fucking bad for him, he's not getting away so easy this time.

Sam steps back and crosses his arms, like he's trying to build a wall between us. "What do you want?"

"I wanna know why you're ignoring me."

"I'm not," he says defensively.

"Yes, you are. But we aren't children, so we shouldn't fuckin' bicker like we are. You won't even look at me if you can help it, and I wanna know why." I didn't find him to argue, but now that we're face to face, my anger is building quickly. "You can't blow me off every time you're within ten feet of me."

"I already blew you once. What more do you want?" Sam snaps, his upper lip curled in a sneer.

His childish response makes me roll my eyes. "I didn't mean it like that, and you know it."

"Coulda fooled me." He's now leaning back against the table.

"And that night started all our problems. We worked together so well as Prospects, but as soon as you let your true feelings peek out in the open, you snapped the lid down so fast, I never even got a chance to know the real you."

"That night wasn't the real me," Sam tries to insist, but I can see in his eyes it's a lie.

"I'm not sure who you're trying to convince more, me or yourself." I step toward him, but when I get too close, he circles around me, forcing me to turn with him. "I know you liked sucking my dick. I tried to tell you not to, but you insisted. *You* unzipped my pants. *You* pulled them down. *You* swallowed my cum. It was only when I tried to return the favor that you freaked the fuck out. What the hell was that about?"

Once I get rolling on my rant, I can't stop until all my points are made.

Sam looks to the left, out at the backyard, anywhere but at me. "It was a mistake."

"What?" I push more. "Has no one given you a blowjob before? Do you not know what it's like to have another man go down on you?"

The way his eyes bug out when he about snaps his own neck looking back at me tells me I hit the nail on the head. Somehow, some way, Sam has never let a man touch him that way.

Does that mean he also hasn't been intimate with another man? At all? Because if that's the case, I want him even more now.

"Have you ever been with another man?"

"Yes!" he barks. "Of course, I have. Yours isn't the first dick I've sucked."

"I don't know if you're trying to make me jealous, but it's not fucking working. You took me down your throat way too easy to be a newbie at that," I reply. "I wanna know if you've done other things. Because if I get to teach you, I'm gonna be in fuckin' heaven." I force my eyes not to roll back, or let my mind drift off into happy sexy dream land.

"Not that it's any of your fuckin' business, but since you won't leave me alone, I've sucked and fucked a few guys before, women too. I've let chicks blow me, but never another man. I just can't do that yet."

"See! You said yet!" Whether he meant to say that out loud or not, I don't know, but he did, and I won't forget it. "That means you want someone to."

"Why can't you just drop it, Smoke? I'm not a member yet. I can't be in a relationship with a Brother. It's not done like that."

"Just because it's never happened before, doesn't mean it's not allowed," I retort. "You and I know this club's bylaws backward and forward, and there's nothing that forbids Brothers from being in a sexual relationship."

"Well, there fuckin' should be!" Sam yells in my face.

"All I'm hearing from you is excuses," I yell back. "I've yet to hear a logical reason as to why we can't even talk about being in a relationship. I'm not saying we need to start humping each other in the main room in front of everyone tomorrow. I just want the chance to get to know the real you."

"No one would accept us."

"That's bullshit and you know it."

"How do you know they'd be okay with two guys fucking?"

"Because they're our Brothers. We're closer to them than we are our real families." How can he even think they wouldn't accept us? What we do behind closed doors is no one's business.

"So, you think no one would give us shit for sucking face like the other couples do around here? You think we'd get away with attacking each other like Whiskey does to Duchess, or how Ring and Steel do to Sunshine?"

"I don't think they'd care." I throw my hands in the air. I feel like a broken record talking to a damn wall. "And you just further proved my point. The club doesn't care that Sunshine has two guys. Ring and Steel share her just fine. What's the difference?"

"Ring and Steel don't fuck each other, that's what." Sam runs his hand over his head, making his hair stick straight up. "And what about the fact that we both also like women? How would that work? I'm not gonna give up ever being with a woman just because you wanna be with me. That's not negotiable for me."

"Sam," I whisper, stepping closer to him, "I know you like men and women. And you know I'm exactly the same."

"You are?" he asks, like the thought never crossed his mind.

"You've seen me with women. What'd you think I was doing with them? Crossword puzzles?"

"I thought you were just hiding who you were so the Brothers didn't know."

"I've never hidden who I was since I turned sixteen and realized I liked looking at dicks just as much as I liked tits. I told my parents, and they said they're happy as long as I'm happy. I've just never felt the need to raise my hand in Church and tell the Brothers what my sexual orientation is. It's not like there's a job application with a box you have to check for them to let you in the door."

Just when I think I've gotten through one of Sam's locks, he turns another deadbolt, trying to push me back. "You wouldn't be happy with me. I'm not your equal. I don't know if or when I ever will be."

"That's bullshit and you know it. Just another excuse."

This time, I turn away from him. I wish I could tell him to wait until the weekend and his reason will be invalid. A few more days and he'll be a full member.

"I've never been with just a man. I don't even know if I'd know how. I'd only disappoint you, then be stuck in a club with someone I could never have. I don't even wanna risk it. You know this club is all I have left."

"I know your family situation, Sam. We discussed this when we started Prospecting." I turn back to defend myself. "And don't try and tell me how I'd be with you. You don't know me *that* well. You won't let me close enough."

"Hey!" Sam gets defensive. "You don't know what I want."

"That's because you won't let me find out." Insufferable, stubborn, sexy ass man, he's going to make me lose my damn mind. "I'd be happy with you. Just thinking about you makes me happy. Why isn't that good enough?"

"We talked about this on New Year's Eve. I said no." And he keeps bringing up the past.

I ignore that jab and move on to another point, hoping to move the conversation along. "Why does it need to be just me? Ring and Steel are sharing Sunshine. If you wanna be with a woman, why can't we find one to share?"

"What? Are you crazy? Where in the world would we find a woman who's gonna be okay with two men fucking each other?"

"I don't know. But I'm sure there's a woman out there who's right for us."

"We live in the middle of the boonies. This ain't no big city where there's a million people to choose from."

"You and your damn excuses. Damnit, Sam, are you gonna be alone for the rest of your life?"

"Of course not. I'll find a woman who wants to be with me and start a family just like everyone else in the history of the world has done. I don't need to upset the status quo just because you can't take no for an answer."

"So, you're gonna ignore your need for a man because you think society, which we already say *fuck you* to by being in an outlaw motorcycle club, won't accept you? You'll live a lie and settle for what you think everyone else expects of you? That's fuckin' stupid!"

"You're not getting it, Smoke," Sam replies. "What Steel and Ring have is different than what you're talking about. They don't fuck each other!"

"If they can share, why can't we?" I toss back before noticing the screen door opening behind Sam.

As soon as I look past him, Sam brushes me off one more time. "It's just not enough. You need to drop this." And with his parting words, he turns and heads inside, skirting around Steel.

Knowing the conversation I'd hoped to have isn't going to continue tonight, because Sam will shut me out again, I feel myself deflate. And now, I have a headache. Raising my hands to my head, I massage my temples, trying to stave it off.

"Is everything okay?" Steel finally asks.

I didn't even notice he was still out here, so I jump a little when he speaks. Seeing his concern, I sink onto one of the picnic table benches. "I'm not sure."

Steel leans against the porch railing. "If you need to talk, let me know."

I glance up to see him looking a little haggard himself. "Thanks." I nod, then rest my hands on the table. I don't think this headache is going away for a while. "Can I ask you a question and it stay between us?"

"Of course. If you don't want me to repeat it, my lips are sealed."

"How do you do the three people in a couple thing? How does it work? Don't you get jealous?"

Steel joins me at the table, sitting across from me. "Not where I thought this was going."

"Sorry, you don't have to answer," I reply. I know this isn't what he came out here for. I don't want to unload my problems on an officer if he doesn't want to hear them.

"It's not a problem." He shakes his head. "I don't know your specifics, but since Ring and I don't like each other sexually, our feelings for Sunshine are separate. I'm sure there are couples out there who do have jealousy issues, but it's something he and I talked about before deciding to really pursue her."

"What about the other guys in the club?" I ask, curious about their circumstances, even though his are a bit different than what I'm looking for. "Do any of them give you shit for being in bed with another man, even if you're not really with him?"

"I'd like to think our Brothers wouldn't have a problem with whatever you decide to do with your personal life. But for us, other than a few funny jokes, no one has given us any real grief about it."

"That's good." Hearing that makes me a little less nervous.

"I'm gonna say one last thing, then you need to do a lot of thinking. Okay?"

A serious look crosses Steel's face, so I lean in to listen. "Throw it at me."

"If you have feelings for Sam, you gotta give him time to figure himself out first. If you push too hard, he's likely to buck back and never give you a chance." Now, there's a truth bomb I didn't expect. I don't know how much of our conversation he heard, but seeing Sam outside must have clued him in to who I'm talking about. "And if you're thinking of adding a woman to the mix, don't do it 'til the two of you have your shit straight. You can't use a woman as a Band-Aid to help you stay together. That wouldn't be fair to any of you. Does that make sense?"

"It does. Thank you, Steel."

He's given me a lot to think about. As much as I'd like to find Sam and get answers now, maybe Steel's advice is what I needed.

Leaving Steel alone to deal with whatever brought him out here, I make my way inside.

I shut myself in my room and hang my cut on its hook, still a little in shock that I've got one. After taking a leak, I brush my teeth, then tie my hair up. And since I hate wearing anything to bed, I strip down and climb in butt naked.

I hate the feeling of anything tight against my skin, which is one of the reasons I don't like wearing underwear. I'm not a boxers or briefs kind of guy. Sleeping with just a sheet covering me is plenty.

Staring at the ceiling, I think about what I want. Someday, I want a family. I want kids.

I want Sam. I want someone he and I can share.

There's so much I dream of having, maybe I need to give Sam time to catch up. If he's never been in a relationship, he needs time to adjust.

How can I expect him to give in when I don't give anything in return? A three-sided relationship, one woman and two men, would be new for me too. It's not something for the faint of heart, and I know it'll be a lot of work to get there.

One day, we will. I know Sam is the man for me, so if he needs time and a little space, I need to let him have that.

But when we get there, he better watch out . . . because when I'm all in, there will be no way out. They'll be mine forever.

I just hope it doesn't take him long. I know it's selfish to think this way, but a man can only be so patient.

CHAPTER THREE

HAZE

LABOR DAY WEEKEND – PRESENT

It's party day, but I'm not in a very celebratory mood. In fact, I'm pretty damn surly, and I know it.

The club has been celebrating for three days, but now that it's Monday, the actual holiday, the front gate is open for friends and family to join the festivities. And let me tell you, the party going on today isn't what most would think of as a normal biker club party.

In fact, the front parking lot looks like a carnival had a baby with a petting zoo and invited the county fair to join the special occasion. There are people everywhere.

Because of the number of shitty things that have happened over the last year, and since all our known enemies have been taken care of, the club officers thought it was safe to finally let everyone celebrate. To let our hair down, so to speak.

And while I'm not usually one to be a party pooper, I'm not in the mood for funnel cake or cotton candy. But that doesn't mean everyone else isn't in the party spirit.

Based on the number of screeching kids running around, and the laughter I hear from everyone, the only person not having fun is me.

And they should be having fun. This is a joyous time for several of the club members.

Duchess just had a baby a week and a half ago. The day after the club got back from Sturgis, Duchess went into labor. Whiskey freaked the fuck out because she had to be put on bed rest to stop the baby from coming too early, but a few days later, their son, Krew, was born.

Then, two days later, Hammer discovered he also had a son, a three-year-old named Taren.

While at the hospital to see Krew, Angel encountered a nurse friend who filled her in on a newly orphaned toddler and his newborn baby brother. Turns out, their birth mother used to be a club girl who left almost four years ago without telling Hammer that she was pregnant with his baby. But with a rush DNA test, and a small paperwork miracle, Angel and Hammer now have two boys of their own, Taren, and the baby they named Ace.

Things couldn't have been crazier if I'd made this all up.

Walking around the parking lot, I see the future I want for myself. I've really taken a deep dive inside myself these last few months to figure out what I want in life, and everything I want is right in front of me.

I got my cut and club name almost two months ago. Haze wasn't the name I was expecting, not that I got to choose it, but I like it.

When a Prospect gets to a point in his journey, the voting members get the final say as to whether he'll be allowed into the fold. The Brothers have a vote in Church, and it needs to be unanimous. There has to be a one hundred percent vote of 'ayes' or you're booted out for good.

Somehow, by the grace of the MC gods, I was welcomed in. I'm now finally a fully patched Brother in the Rebel Vipers MC.

That weekend was one for the record books. I received my patch one night, then Sunshine got her Property patch the next. After drinking for two solid days, I didn't wake up for another two. I barely remember crashing into my bed, so when I woke up and looked at my phone to see it was

Tuesday, let's just say surprised isn't a strong enough word to describe how I was feeling.

There's just one thing that's been chewing on my brain since then, and it hasn't always been a good thought.

It's the way I treated Smoke.

I'm not proud of it, but I know I acted like he was a piece of gum on the bottom of my boot. I said everything I could to push him away after what we did on New Year's Eve. Or I should say, what I did to him that night.

I gave Smoke a blowjob. I sucked his dick like it was the tastiest lollipop I've ever had, then backed away from him like he was a leper. But it was me who was the big scaredy cat. The second I felt his fingers on my zipper, I panicked.

Because even though I'd gone down on guys before, I've never allowed any of them to return the favor.

Then, when Smoke cornered me again the week before I got my cut, I had to admit my shortcomings. That even though I'd been with men and women, having had sex with both, and that I liked both genders, I'd never let a man give me a blowjob.

But what I failed to reveal to him was I'd never let a man fuck me in the ass, either. I almost said it, but the words got caught in my throat and I ended up running away.

I hate being a fucking chicken. I'm a goddamn biker, for fuck's sake. I'm not weak. My time to be weak was when I was a kid, but that's not who I am anymore. My stepdad tried to beat what he thought were my shortcomings out of me, but I fought back and got away.

Starting to get to know the Rebel Vipers as a hangaround at eighteen was my clean slate. I became a new man. I hid my true feelings away and embraced the biker life. None of the other members were interested in men like I was, so I assumed it wasn't allowed. And since I didn't want to be tossed back out on the street, I never said anything about my sexuality. It never came up ... until Smoke.

But now that Smoke has opened himself up to me, something I couldn't see coming from a mile away, I have no choice but to face this shit head-on.

I've been attracted to Smoke since the day I met him, back when he was just Jacob, another hangaround like me. It seems weird to think we've known each other for years already, but neither of us was around full-time, so those first few years almost don't count.

Jacob had been a Prospect for a few months when I fully moved in at twenty-two. He's also a year older than me, so I always kind of looked up to him. But I had to hide my crush.

It's not like I could just walk up to a fellow Prospect, thread my hands through his long, wavy hair, and kiss him in front of everyone. Those things don't happen between men around here.

If he was a woman, and I did that to her, the Brothers would be congratulating me for landing an Old Lady. But with another man, I didn't think it was a possibility.

But now? Now, I could give zero fucks what anyone says or thinks. I want what I want and need to figure out how to get it.

Too fucking bad for me, the man I want won't give me the time of day. Payback really is a fucking bitch.

I've circled the parking lot and clubhouse three times now, and Smoke is nowhere to be seen. Where is his stubborn ass? He hasn't said one word to me outside of club business since I got my patches. That's karma for you.

On a whim, I decide to step into one of the open bay doors of Rebel Repairs to see if he's hiding in here. I push my sunglasses to the top of my head and let my eyes adjust from the brightness. Looking around, it doesn't take me but two seconds to spot him . . . and the two tight, round globes of his denim-covered ass cheeks.

Holy mother of Moses, can he wear a pair of blue jeans.

Smoke is squatted down, working on a motorcycle, while everyone else is outside having fun. If he's not hiding from me in here, I'll be a monkey's uncle. And while I'd love to look at his fine ass all day, I need to get this show on the road.

A bike backfiring in the lot snaps me out of my trance. "Why are you working on the holiday?" I call out.

Clang! A wrench slips from Smoke's hand and crashes to the cement floor.

"Fuck!" he calls out as he falls back. Smoke turns his head and his eyes go wide when he realizes it's me. His face drops to a scowl before he turns away. "Oh, it's you."

He's gripping his knuckles, and I rush forward when I notice the blood running down his fingers. "You're bleeding."

"No shit, Sherlock. What was your first clue?" he snaps, looking around.

I follow his eyes as he looks for something, and when I spot a pile of clean shop rags on one of the benches, I grab them before kneeling next to him, trying to help. Smoke yanks a few from my outstretched hand, then tries to push me away, but I don't budge.

"What do you want, *Haze*?" He says my name with an almost sneer. Like me being a Brother now is something against him.

I think it's time for me to eat some crow. Knowing my words spooked him and caused him to get hurt, I decide to go with the truth. No better time than the present, when we're just inches apart. "I wanna know why you've been ignoring me since I got my patch."

His head pops up, looking at me like I'm crazy. His eyes are squinted like he's in deep thought. "I thought that's what you wanted."

Getting back to my feet, I hold a hand out to help him up. "Just because I said we couldn't be together doesn't mean we can't be friends."

He pushes my hand away, hops up on his own, and walks over to a utility sink along the wall to wash the blood and dirt from his hands. After patting his still bleeding knuckles with a clean rag, he wraps it up, then turns to face me fully for the first time in months.

"That's exactly what that means. If you can't accept us for what we could be, then we need to be nothing at all."

"What? I'm trying to tell you I want what you want. I want us." I run a hand over my head, exasperated. "Isn't that what you wanted me to say?"

"That's what I wanted six months ago. Hell, it's what I wanted three months ago. But you were too good for me. So, why should I want you now?" And with that, Smoke stomps toward the open garage door, heading away from me. Leaving me behind.

I turn to see his back getting farther away from me with each step. "Where are you going?" I call out.

"I'm walking away," he calls out, not once looking back. "You should know what that looks like. You've done it to me plenty of times."

He's right. I've done the exact same thing. But I won't lie—I don't like the way it feels coming back at me.

Fuck me with a pogo stick. Maybe I really did fuck things up. So, how do I fix it?

I think it's time I take another step back and make a real plan. I thought I did by waiting these two months to approach him, but I'm starting to think I might've just made things worse.

Knowing I'm not going to enjoy the party, I head inside and make my way up to my room. Well, it's technically not my room. When I became a full patch Brother, I was offered any empty room I wanted but still haven't picked one. I don't know what's holding me back, but none of them feel right.

Closing myself inside the bunkroom, I flop onto my bed and stare at the ceiling. I shut my eyes and all I can see is the hurt radiating from Smoke's brown eyes staring back at me.

I seem to cause that look on him a lot. I really need to figure out how to turn this train around.

Otherwise, I might lose Smoke forever. As a friend, and maybe even more.

CHAPTER FOUR

ABBY

It's the first Monday in September, Labor Day, and The Lodge is filled to the brim. I push through the swinging doors from the kitchen, into the bar and restaurant area, and there are people everywhere. Every table, booth, and bar stool is occupied.

From a manager's point of view, I see dollar signs flowing through the air. But from an employee standpoint, I already feel the phantom pain my feet will be feeling by the end of the night, even though I haven't clocked in yet.

It's only noon, but I can tell it's going to be a late one for me.

And while I'm not on the schedule for today, coming into work was my excuse to get out of the house and not go to the party I was invited to.

My boss, Ring, a member of the Rebel Vipers Motorcycle Club, invited me to their clubhouse for a party they're throwing today. The club owns this place and the brewery next door.

After a couple weeks of healing, both mentally and physically, I decided I needed to get into the working world. My bruises were finally gone, and I had no reason to hide out anymore. Gram supported my decision to stay living with her for a while longer, so I began looking for jobs locally.

I saw a posting on the bulletin board at the grocery store for a job at The Lodge and thought it sounded too good to be true. Gram told me the place was owned by the motorcycle club she told me about the day I arrived and encouraged me to give it a shot, so I did.

Since I never went back to college or worked outside the home after moving to Kansas with Toby, I don't have any recent references on my resume. But I definitely lucked out getting this job.

Ring barely looked at my resume before he invited me into his office for an interview. After talking a bit about what kind of job I was looking for, he gave me a tour of the bar and brewery. I was introduced to a few bartenders, kitchen staff, and some brewery employees, and as we walked, Ring explained what my expected day-to-day tasks would be.

Apparently, the woman who had the job before quit with no notice, so they were in need of someone reliable. I could tell by Ring's excitement to show me around that he was stressed with all the work thrown in his lap. But the more he told me, the more excited I became too. Being the face along with running the bar and restaurant front end is a big responsibility, but I was up for the challenge. Frankly, I needed something to occupy my mind and time.

Before I left, he offered me the manager position.

I have restaurant experience from working part-time jobs in high school, then my first year in college, but never anything this all-encompassing. I knew it'd be hard work, but I dove in and have been loving it.

Working directly under Ring has been a breeze. He's hands off with my responsibilities unless I ask him for something, and since The Lodge obviously has beer from the brewery, I deal with Brewer, the manager over there, more than anyone else. He's a nice guy, but he tends to stay in his work bubble too.

But that's as far as I involve myself with the club side of things. I know a few members by name because they come in occasionally, but I don't interact with them outside these walls. I like to keep my professional and personal lives separate.

I've been working at The Lodge for six months now as the front-end manager. I'm in charge of scheduling the employees' hours, ordering supplies and alcohol, bookkeeping, planning special events, and anything else that pops up. I'm basically the go-to person for anything in the bar area. The restaurant has its own manager.

When Ring told me a few days ago about the party at the clubhouse, I told him I'd think about stopping by, but when I woke up this morning, I realized I still wasn't ready.

I have no reason to not like any of the bikers, but because of my past, I'm skeptical of socializing with strangers. Especially strangers in places I don't know. So far, I've kept my club interactions to inside The Lodge and Moraine Craft Brewery.

I peek my head outside and see the patio is busy but running smoothly, so I hop back behind the bar to assist the other bartenders.

After greeting a couple regulars and getting their orders, I grab a few glasses to make their drinks.

A shiver crawls up my spine, so I turn to see what's behind me. When I don't see anything or anyone out of place, I shake my head and try to concentrate on my work. For some reason, I feel like someone is watching me, but with a room full of people, that comes with the territory.

It's probably a combination of my brain not being fully in work mode yet and a crowded space, but I tell myself to buck up and keep going. Now is *not* the time or place for a breakdown.

I haven't had a panic attack in almost a month, and I'd like to keep it that way. Taking a deep breath, I truck on.

Completing the drinks and sliding them across the bar without spilling them, I take a second to shake my hands out and push my worries away even more.

"You okay, Abby?" Stiletto, one of the bartenders, asks as she shimmies behind me to grab a bottle from a high shelf on the back wall.

"I'm good." I nod. "Just didn't sleep well." I lie because I don't need to burden her with my silly worries.

"I know the feeling," she replies with a giggle and a wink. "With the club party going all weekend, last night was a late one."

"Thanks for working, though. It's crazy here today."

"I'll be happy for the tip money." And she's gone.

One thing I learned early on in dealing with a motorcycle club is that everyone has a place in their hierarchy. The first major holiday that came around after I started working here was Memorial Day. When I asked Raquel, another bartender and club girl, why none of the club members were at The Lodge on the holiday, she explained that they celebrate holidays and big events partying at their clubhouse.

Then, when I asked why none of the club girls were at the party, she explained the difference between a club party and a family party. Apparently, when the club has family and public parties, club girls aren't allowed to be there. So, in addition to the civilian employees, Stiletto, Raquel, Jazz, Cinnamon, and Toto are working here today.

While I get along with mostly everyone here, the only club girl I've ever had a problem with is Toto. It's not that I've had any major confrontation with her, it's just her attitude is always a bit off. She's been nice to my face, but something about her rubs me the wrong way. Anytime she says anything nice, it comes across as snarky at the same time.

Toto seems to think she's the queen bee around The Lodge, but it doesn't fly with the other girls. As the newest of all the club girls working here, when she tries to tell the others what to do, they push back and put her in her place.

"Why are you workin' today?" Toto asks as she starts typing an order into the computer. She's got a slight accent that sounds partially southern, but it's not a full drawl, so

I'm not sure where she's from. I do know it's not from around here, though.

I continue to pull ingredients and pour them into the glasses I have lined up in front of me. Two whiskey Old Fashioneds sweet, a rum and Coke, and a Long Island iced tea for the two couples at the end of the bar.

While I'm technically her boss, and she has no right questioning me about being here, I'm not in the mood to argue, so I just go with the flow. It's easier to catch flies with honey, so I smile at her. "I was bored and didn't feel like going to the party."

Toto spins so quick, her long braids whip around and hit her in the face. "What party? The one at the clubhouse?" she asks as she flips the plaits behind her shoulders.

"Yea." I skeptically give her a side-eye glance while skewering fruit for the drinks' garnishes.

"You were invited to that?" she asks, squinting her eyes like she thinks I'm lying.

That look right there totally rubs me the wrong way. But I try to ignore the goosebumps that run up my arms and walk away to serve the now finished cocktails.

Not that it's any of her business, but once I'm near her again to add the drinks to the customer's tab, I respond.

"Ring invited me to the clubhouse because I've never been there."

"Oh girl, you need to go sometime." Toto moans as she lets her eyes roll back. It's so loud and lewd, I'm almost embarrassed for her because of the nasty looks she's getting from customers within ear range. Whether she doesn't see them or just doesn't care what others think, she continues, "The Brothers there are hot as fuck."

The woman is practically drooling because of some men who do god knows what with how many people. How is that attractive? Personally, I think the idea of being a club girl is gross and demeaning to women, but to each their own. It's another reason I'm not sure about going to the clubhouse and being around the members.

Her abrasiveness makes me lose it, and I snap at her. "While you're here and on the clock, please refrain from acting inappropriately. What you do at the clubhouse has nothing to do with what you're being paid to do here."

"But I—" Toto's eyes bug out, but I cut off whatever lame excuse she tries to lay on me.

"You may not like it, but I'm here today." I cross my arms and give it to her straight. "So, unless you want me to call Ring and tell him what you just did in front of paying customers, I suggest you clean up your act and get back to work."

"Whatever." Toto rolls her eyes as she stomps away.

Talk about childish behavior. I know I'm supposed to have some say in who does and doesn't work here, but I've tried to stay away from causing a stink about anyone affiliated with the club. Toto is the only employee, from the club or regular joe, that I've had a problem with, but I've let her attitude go on a bit too long. Right here, right now, I decide she's already earned her two strikes. One more problem and I'll stick to my threat to report her behavior to Ring.

"Don't let her push your buttons." Cinnamon startles me as she snaps me out of my half angry funk. "She's just mad she can't be at the clubhouse today."

"Is the party really that big of a deal?" I ask as I start to refill the napkin holders.

"Depends on who you're asking. For someone like her, it's the end of the world not being there." Cinnamon rolls her eyes, making me chuckle. "For the rest of us, it's just another day. Those of us who know our place are just fine with letting the Brothers have their family time."

"Then what's her issue? Shouldn't she be happy she's here making money?"

"Yes, she should be," Cinnamon says, grabbing a tray full of drinks and hoisting it over her shoulder with one hand. "She'll learn eventually that her shit isn't really as great as she thinks it is. Otherwise, she'll be gone just as fast as she appeared." And with that, she heads for her tables.

I think it's time I start implementing my outside of work ideals to inside work.

No more being a pushover. No more letting others make me feel small. I'm in charge of me.

It's time to get back to work and hope the day continues with no more unnecessary drama.

CHAPTER FIVE

HAZE

September is a busy month for the whole club. I'm meeting with Whiskey in his office to go over some things for the salvage and recycling yard. It's closed on Mondays, so today's the perfect day to get office work out of the way.

Fall keeps us super busy because people are clearing out their garages and sheds, preparing for the upcoming winter. And since we don't have any runs scheduled this month, we need to organize storing the metal we get in until we're ready to use it to camouflage the guns we run from Canada to Chicago.

Midway through some weight forms, Whiskey gets a text from Duchess and leans back to check his phone, while I keep reading.

"I gotta head to my cabin," Whiskey says before setting his phone down. He rubs his eyes while groaning. "I swear, this baby never sleeps. I'll be right back." He gets up and heads to find his Old Lady and kid, leaving me to wait in silence.

Never one to sit still for long, I stand to stretch my legs and start looking at the picture frames on the bookshelf lining the wall to my right.

My brain is constantly running at full speed, only slowing when I'm sleeping, and sometimes not even then. I think my mind doesn't know how to shut itself off. Between my knowledge of math and my photographic memory, I always have some problem tumbling around up there.

Maybe that's why I'm having such a hard time figuring out this situation with Smoke. I think my biggest problem is, when I realized I had real feelings for him, and him in return for me, my systems went on the fritz. I need to have a clear plan before I approach a new situation.

I focus on the largest picture, which is front and center on the bookshelf. It's of the original five Rebel Vipers members.

Mountain, Brick, Bear, Butch, and Skynyrd are standing in front of what is now the clubhouse. The building looks a bit worse for wear in the photo, and there's no front porch yet, but they all look young and ready to take on the challenges ahead. I wonder if they had any idea things would turn out like they did.

Two pictures sitting side by side make me chuckle. They're of Whiskey, Hammer, and Buzz as kids. One is of them as babies, sitting in the grass, while the other is them wearing their blank Prospect cuts, arms folded across their chests. They look like they're either not thrilled to be having their picture taken, or they're scowling to look like badasses, probably a mixture of both.

The three of them are the only kids of the original five members who grew up here. Sunshine didn't find out Mountain was her dad until earlier this year, after her mother passed away. She took the discovery of her unconventional family in stride, and she's now in a relationship with two Brothers.

Maybe Smoke is right about it being okay for three people to be together within the club. While Ring and Steel aren't attracted to each other like Smoke and I, it doesn't seem to be causing any problems. Hopefully, that's a good sign.

Looking at more pictures, I see several group shots from club rides and parties over the years. There's even a new one from the weekend I was patched in. The day after I got my cut, Sunshine got her Old Lady Property cut, and the whole club was gathered for a group photo. We're all standing in the backyard, in front of Brick's cabin, where Ring, Steel, Sunshine, and their daughter, Opal, now call home. I wonder if I'll have a family like that one day.

As I continue to look, something on the bottom shelf catches my eye. I squat down and find an envelope on top of a brown leather photo album that's laying on its side. There's a sepia-toned photo sticking out of the envelope, and my curiosity is piqued.

I don't know why, but there's a voice taunting me to pick it up, so I do. As soon as it's in my hand, I instantly want to put it back, but it's too late.

Forgetting about the envelope, I absentmindedly set it back on the shelf.

I feel myself slowly standing up, as if my body is moving on its own. I have no control of my limbs. My eyes are glued to the picture because I recognize it. I have the same picture in a frame on my nightstand. Why is this in Whiskey's office?

Every detail of the photo is engrained in my brain. It's the only one I have from my childhood, a faded Polaroid picture of my mom and me that was taken when I was a baby. She told me someone at the local church took it the day I was baptized. Having been born in Ireland, my mom was super religious and took her faith very seriously.

The more I look at this picture, the more questions I have. Then suddenly, for the first time in my entire life, every gear and sound and puzzle running through my mind grinds to a screeching halt. I drop back into the chair just as Whiskey comes walking back into the office.

I track his movements as he circles his desk and sits in his chair.

"Sorry about that. Duchess needed a hand with Krew so she could shower." He picks up his pen, then looks across at me. He must see something in my face because he leans forward and asks, "Are you okay, Haze?"

I hold the picture up. "Why do you have a picture of my mom and me when I was a baby?"

Whiskey's eyes almost pop out of his head. My question causes him to look as shocked as I feel. Then, with no words, he picks up his cell phone and taps the screen a few times. It's only when I hear a familiar voice coming through the speaker that I realize he called Mountain.

"What's up, son?"

"Pops?" Whiskey croaks, his eyes still locked on my hand.

"What's wrong, Whiskey? Is everything okay? Is Krew alright?" If I weren't so numb, I'd probably feel the panic in his voice more.

"Krew's fine, Pops." Whiskey runs a hand through his shoulder-length hair. "I need you to come to my office. We've got a situation I think you need to see."

I hear movement in the background while Mountain keeps talking. "You're freakin' me the fuck out, kid. I'll be there in thirty seconds." Then the line goes dead.

Still staring at each other, Whiskey and I don't say another word until Mountain comes hobbling in. I hear some strange clomping, so I turn in my seat to see him standing in the doorway on his crutches.

Whiskey rolls his eyes. "Jeezus fuckin' Louise, Pops. We coulda waited 'til you put your leg on."

"Your call sounded urgent." Mountain nods at me, then scoots around the chair next to me before sitting in it, setting his crutches to the side. "What's with the S.O.S. call?"

Whiskey points at me. "I think Haze has something to show you."

Mountain looks my way, and I become mute. Any question or thought I was having disappears, and all I can do is hold out the photo in my hand.

His eyes find what I'm trying to hand him and he grabs it. "Why do you have this?" His brows furrow as he looks between me and the picture.

"I found it on the bookshelf over there," I answer, pointing to the wall. "I should be asking why a picture of my mom and me is in here. I have this same one upstairs."

"Your mom?" Mountain's eyes bug out, very similar to how Whiskey looked before. "This is you and your mom?"

"It sure is." My brain is slowly starting to fire back up and my questions start flowing. "Why do you have a picture of me? I know the club ran a background check, but what does that picture have to do with it? I thought I had the only copy. Where'd you get it? Can I have it?"

"Hold on a minute. Let me wrap my brain around this." Mountain hands the picture to Whiskey. "Do you remember Sunshine finding this?"

Whiskey looks down at it. "I remember you showing it to me, then asking me to put the photo album in here."

"What photo album? The one on the shelf?" I ask the room. I don't care who answers, but someone better start talking.

Mountain turns in his chair to face me. "Did you read the letter?"

"What letter?"

"The one in the envelope this picture was in."

"No." I shake my head. "I saw the picture, then zoned everything else out."

Taking a deep breath, Mountain closes his eyes and rubs his hands over his head. After what feels like several minutes but is really only seconds, he finally looks at me with what has to be the saddest expression I've ever seen from him.

"I'm not even sure how to say this."

"Say what?" I ask.

"Haze, I think Brick was your dad."

"WHAT?" I bark. "Brick? Like as in your brother, Brick? How's that even possible?"

"Whiskey, grab that envelope," Mountain orders, pointing at the shelf. "When Sunshine was going through Brick's cabin, she found a bunch of old Hill family photo albums. While flipping through them, she found a letter tucked between the pages. She opened it to see what it was, but as soon as she started reading it, she knew it was private and set it aside for me."

"But what does Brick supposedly being my dad have to do with a letter?" For a self-proclaimed smart person, I'm feeling pretty dumb right now. The gears may be moving, but the machine isn't running at full speed.

"Is your mother's name Erin?" Mountain asks.

"Yes," I draw out.

I watch Mountain take the faded envelope from Whiskey. Just looking at the paper, I can tell it's been handled a lot. I imagine at one point, it was stark white, but over time, it's turned a faded tan.

Mountain gently pulls a piece of lined notebook paper out and hands it to me. Folded in thirds, I take the paper and unfold it. There are only a few paragraphs on the page, and I'd recognize the handwriting anywhere.

It's from my mother, telling someone named Andrew that he has a son.

It goes on to explain that she doesn't expect anything from him and that she'll raise me alone.

There are more words, but I can't force myself to comprehend them.

If what this letter says is true, Brick really is my father. I've known him for six years and never had a clue we were related.

"Oh shit!" I lean back and brace my hands on the chair's armrests. My eyes flick between Whiskey and Mountain, almost not sure where to look. "If Brick's my dad, that means you're my uncle and cousin. And Sunshine, too."

"It sure does." Mountain nods, a smile slowly growing on his face. "Just when I thought I'd lost my brother, he sends me a piece of himself. And to think, you've been here this whole time."

I know what he's saying is true, and also that he's trying to find the light in a dark time for himself, but I'm over here still trying to find the floor. I can feel myself spinning out of control.

"This is crazy. Did you know this was me?" I ask Mountain. I'd like to think he would've told me had he known, but with Brick recently passing, I know his emotions are still a bit raw.

Mountain shakes his head. "I had no clue. There was no return address, and the only name was *Erin* signed at the bottom. If I knew you were blood family, I never would've kept it from you."

"Me neither," Whiskey voices. "I hope you know that."

My heart is pounding so fast, it feels like it's trying to jump out of my chest. And now that my mind is firing again, there are so many thoughts jumbled up, all trying to race to the front for attention.

The walls are closing in, and I need to get out of here.

Standing, I set the letter on Whiskey's desk, then head for the door.

"Wait," Whiskey calls out, "where are you going?"

One hand on the door frame, I look back to see both men standing. "I need some air."

I hang a right into the hallway and push out the back door, already running at full speed. I have no clue what stops me from continuing across the backyard and into the woods surrounding the compound, but I slow my steps and stop, bending over to place my hands on my knees.

Dragging deep breaths into my lungs, the ringing in my ears lessens and I can hear a voice calling my name. Figuring it's either Mountain or Whiskey who followed me out, I turn to tell them I need more time.

But it's neither of them...

It's Smoke.

He's standing on the back patio, under the porch overhang, leaning against the railing.

"Haze, are you alright?" he calls out.

I don't know what causes everything to snap into place, but I finally see him for everything he is. I really see him for the first time.

Smoke steps onto the grass, about to head my way, but my feet move faster.

I jog in his direction, and before I can blink, there's barely two inches between our chests. I close the distance and kiss him. I kiss him right there in the open for anyone to see.

And I don't care.

That's not what's occupying my thoughts.

I'm focused one hundred percent on the man standing in front of me, who now has his arms wrapped around my shoulders.

At first, he's frozen, but the second I open my mouth and trace the seam of his lips with my tongue, he thaws and starts battling with me. His movements are soft but firm at the same time. He doesn't necessarily try to control the kiss, but Smoke is in it as much as I am.

I slide my hands up under the leather of his cut and grab two handfuls of the back of his t-shirt, trying to pull him even closer.

One of his hands moves over my shoulder, and his fingers start playing with the hairs at the back of my neck. It's a tingly feeling, but I like it. His other hand moves to the back of my head, holding me to him, like he's afraid I'm going to wake up and realize what I'm doing is wrong.

But he's wrong—I have no need to run. I'm exactly where I want to be. I may not know why it happened now, but I'm done running.

The only thing that stops our kiss is someone whooping and hollering behind me. It sounds like a monkey has gotten loose from the zoo and is having the time of his life.

Amid the noise, Smoke has lightened up on me too. After one last gentle meeting of our lips, I open my eyes and see his gaze is focused on me . . . and he's sporting one hell of a smirk.

"It seems we've found ourselves a cheering section," Smoke comments. I can tell he finds it a little funny. Letting go of Smoke's shirt, I back up a step so I can turn to see where the ruckus is coming from. When I see that it's Steel, my boldness seems to falter.

Even from across the yard, I can see the huge smile on Steel's face, but my heart skips a beat and jumpstarts, making me breathless.

I feel myself start to panic, and my brain is trying to send a message to my legs to run, but before I can, Smoke appears in front of me again.

"I know you wanna bolt, but let's get you inside." He threads his fingers through mine and pulls me with him.

And like they know where to go, my feet follow right along behind. My eyes may be open, but I don't see where we're going. I simply follow like a lost puppy.

I try to make sense of what just happened, but I need time to reboot. So much has happened in the last hour, I can't think.

I know I've kissed Smoke before, but something about today feels different. It's like my insides were a powder keg full of dynamite exploding on the Fourth of July. The second I heard him call my name, and saw him standing there, the fireworks went off.

Maybe that's what happens when you really open yourself to someone else for the first time. Is this what it's like when your true vulnerabilities come to the surface?

Minus the freak-out I'm experiencing right now, I'd say the kiss was worth it.

If this is what being with Smoke is going to be like, I need to hold on and never let go. But after the way I've treated him, I hope he's still on the same page.

Combined with the news of finding my father only to realize he's already gone, I don't think I could survive being pushed away by Smoke. The possibility of our future is what's holding me together.

I've never considered myself a weak man, but right now, I need all the support he can give me.

CHAPTER SIX

SMOKE

"I know you wanna bolt, but let's get you inside."

Based on the panic I see in Haze's eyes, I know I need to get him in private before something happens that he may be ashamed of later. I don't want him to regret anything he doesn't remember happening.

I imagine there's a bit of embarrassment flowing through Haze right now, so I think us being alone is a good idea, especially after Steel's little cheerleader act. As far as I know, he's the only Brother who knows there's even an idea of us, but I guess it's not a secret anymore.

I grab Haze's hand and tug him back inside the clubhouse. Just when we reach the stairs, I see Whiskey appear at the end of the office hall.

"Is he okay?" Whiskey calls out. Something happened, and I can see his uncertainty, but I'm not sure what's going on. Hopefully his hesitation isn't about the fact that Haze and I are holding hands.

"He will be" is all I can think of to say. Because I'll do anything to protect Haze.

"Take care of him, please." And with that, he's gone again.

As my President, I'd never want to disappoint Whiskey, but even if he hadn't asked it of me, I'd still be right here for my Brother.

I lead Haze upstairs, and once we're in my room, I pull him to sit next to me on the couch.

When I got my patch, I originally moved into Whiskey's old room. But when Cypher needed a room change to accommodate his computer set-up, and Ring and Steel moved out to their cabin, I switched to Ring's old room.

Haze is still gripping my hand tight, but I could care less. I think I'm in shock myself from the sudden kiss ambush that I have no interest in letting him go. Even if a few of my fingers end up as causalities.

I wait for Haze to say something, but he's just staring off into space, so I use my free hand to turn his chin. "What's going on?"

His eyes finally meet mine, and what he says knocks me off my rocker even more. "Brick is my dad. Was my dad. I don't even know."

My body jerks in response. "What? How?"

"I found a picture of me and my mom in Whiskey's office."

"Where'd he get it from?"

"Details are still a little fuzzy on that," Haze replies, rubbing his eyes, like he's trying to clear the fog. "Something about Sunshine finding a letter in a photo album in Brick's cabin."

"And who wrote this letter?"

"I just read the beginning of it, but it was from my mom." Haze turns sideways to face me. "She wrote Brick a letter to tell him that he had a son, but that she was gonna raise me alone."

"So, let me get this straight. You found out Brick is your dad because of a picture of you and your mom in a letter she wrote to him?"

He nods, still looking stunned. "Yup."

"Does Mountain know about this? Brick was his younger brother after all."

"He did. They had no clue it was a picture of me. The letter didn't have my name on it, only my mom's first name."

I can see that Haze is in need of support, and he's got it from me. I'll be with him through whatever he needs.

Of course, that's easy to say now, but I still have a tiny bit of self doubt in my mind. What about the kiss? Was that real or just Haze feeling overwhelmed and reaching for anything he could grab onto?

"I'll be there for you for whatever you need. And I hate to change the subject, but the elephant in the room is getting a little obvious. I gotta know . . . what was that kiss for?"

"I hafta confess, I've been thinking about what you said about us for a while now," Haze admits, sheepishly looking down at his hands. But I see him shake off some sort of heavy black cloud, and when he looks back up, his eyes are clear and his focus is all on me. "And even though I'm still not sure how we can really make this work, I'm willing to try."

"Willing to try what? Being together? The two of us?" While the thought of that makes me happier than I think I've ever been, based on things he's said before, I don't know if I'm enough for him.

"Yes," Haze responds, but it sounds more like a question than an answer.

"Are you asking me or telling me?" I question with what I know is a dopey grin on my face. I try to lighten the mood, hoping his answer is what I want it to be.

"Telling," he replies with a smirk. "I wanna see if we can make a go of us. But the more I think about what I said about still being attracted to women, your suggestion of sharing someone in the future does make me wonder if that's really a possibility."

"It's definitely a possibility. We can make a relationship anything we want it to be."

"A relationship, huh?" Haze's smile is now full force, and I'll do anything to make him smile like that again.

"I want us, if that's what you want."

"Then I guess we're a thing now." Haze grabs hold of both my hands and scoots even closer. "It may make me sound like a damn pussy, but I'm happy you found me outside. I almost beelined it into the woods. Who knows where I would've ended up."

His words make me happy like you wouldn't believe. Knowing he wanted me is more than I can ask for. "You may have come outside on instinct, but me being there was fate.

We're supposed to be together, Haze. I was exactly where you needed me to be right then," I tell him.

A quick flash of doubt makes his face turn a bit pale. "Do you really think the club will accept us? Even without a woman in our lives yet?"

"I know they will. Didn't you hear Steel's victory cry when you kissed me?"

"I was so out of it, I didn't even know he was outside 'til he started hootin' and hollerin'. Why did he do that?"

"Remember the night I found you sitting in the dark out on the back patio?"

"Yea," he mumbles. "Not my proudest moment."

"After you stormed inside, I had a conversation with Steel about relationships with more than two people. Like he and Ring have with Sunshine."

"You asked him about being with me?" Haze asks, shocked. "So, he's known this whole time?"

"Not at first. I didn't tell Steel why I was asking. It just so happened it was him who walked into the middle of our conversation, so I took the moment and ran with it."

"I didn't know you did that."

I shrug. "You weren't supposed to. It's not like I searched him out to talk. He could sense something was off and asked what was wrong."

"You told him you liked me?"

"Not directly," I reply. "I asked a vague question about three people being in a relationship and if there's any jealousy. It was him who put the clues together and figured out it was you."

"We did kinda make it obvious when I ran away from you." Haze rolls his eyes. "But he's not a bad person to ask. He's got a bit more experience in the sharing department than we do."

"I know a little about how you and your magic jumble brain works. You need all the facts before you make a decision." I wiggle one of my hands free to push a stubborn piece of hair behind my ear. "Things may have been rough for us since New Year's, but I was still processing it all myself."

With his now free hand, Haze traces the skin peeking through the hole in the knee of my jeans. Just feeling the touch of our skin connecting sends a buzz through my veins. I try to push the physical feelings I have for him aside and get back to our conversation. If I have any say in it, there'll be plenty of time for touching later.

"I think it'll take us both more time to figure everything out, especially with maybe adding someone else down the road, but I don't wanna waste any more time." Haze is sounding so much bolder about his wants. "I think this was the sign I needed that I can't take time with someone for granted. You need to take all you can get."

"That's right," I nod, "and now is our time."

"Maybe that's what me finding that picture now was, my wake-up call pulling me out of my own doubts."

Now, it's my time to touch him. I slide my hand up his thigh and feel his muscle shift under my palm. My gaze locked on his, I lean closer to him. "Whatever happens, I'm just glad you're here now."

Just before our lips meet, his eyes close, and I take that as his silent 'come and get it', so I do.

But unlike our kiss earlier, I take a more dominant role in this meeting of our lips.

He may be expecting soft, based on his gentle sigh, but I press my whole body forward, forcing him to adjust and lie back. I work my right knee between his spread legs and kneel on the cushion, applying the slightest pressure against his dick.

Haze's sigh turns to a groan as his head tilts back and he raises his hips, trying to gain traction against me, but I only let him press so hard.

I set my left boot on the floor to hold myself up, then bracket his shoulders with my hands. Lowering my head to his, this is where things turn hot.

I dip down and attack his soft lips with mine. I'm on a mission to get this show on the road. Now that I have him, I won't let him get away. This is our future, so there's no going back.

I'm determined to prove that I'm worthy of him. My movements are determined and undeniable. His lips mold to mine, and he kisses me back with a vigor I've yet to see from any partner.

"Fuck, yes." Haze gasps when I bite down on his lower lip, tugging it a pinch.

His breath allows me the opening I need to kick things up another notch. Sliding my tongue against his, I dive deeper. We demand so much more of each other like this. It isn't a feeling I expected, but damn if I'm going to complain.

I feel Haze shifting under me, but I pay no mind until his hands slide up the sides of my neck to cup my cheeks. He doesn't try to stop me or steer me in another direction—he's just holding me in place, as if I'd go anywhere.

I give him entrance when I feel his tongue press against mine, and I feel the tip slide across the roof of my mouth. Fuck, that's hot.

There's nothing I can do but keep kissing him back . . . until an even better idea pops into my head.

I lift my head, and his lips chase mine until I'm back too far and we separate.

Haze's eyes open. "Why'd you stop?" he practically whines.

"What do you say we move this somewhere a little more comfortable?"

"I like the way you think." And with that, Haze pushes on my chest, and I sit up, him following behind.

He works his way to his feet, then reaches out his hand. I take it and let him pull me up. "Now what?"

"Now, we really get to know one another."

CHAPTER SEVEN

HAZE

"You sure about this?" Smoke asks as I kiss his neck, pushing his cut off his shoulders. He catches it behind him before it hits the floor.

"Fuckin' positive," I groan as I lick a sensitive spot behind his ear. "Couldn't stop . . . even if I wanted."

Tugging on the back of my cut, I let my arms go loose so Smoke can pull it off me.

He steps out of my reach and backs toward the door. With our cuts in his hands, he lifts them, like he's showing me what he's doing, then he turns to hang them on a hook.

As he turns back, he looks over his shoulder. "They look good hangin' next to each other, don't they?"

Looking at the two leather cuts, with their identical skulls and green vipers, I have to agree. "It's like they're meant to be together."

"I agree." Smoke chuckles. The next thing I know, he yanks the front of my t-shirt and pulls me to his chest. "Now, where were we?"

Working my fingers under his shirt, I press my hands flat to his abdomen, then slide up his chest. "Right here."

When one of my fingers touches his nipple, Smoke inhales quickly, gasping. "Fuck." He reaches behind his head and yanks his shirt up and off. I'm standing here, hands still flat on his pectorals, and the man has no fucking t-shirt on. I'm staring at his tan skin . . . tan skin and tattoos.

Holy fuck. How did I not know Smoke was inked like this? But again, holy fuck, is he hot!

"When'd you get all this ink?" I question as I trace the dark lines. There's a ghost surrounded by swirls of smoke on his right pec. The design on the left looks like his skin is cracked and peeling away, so you can see inside his body, and a green snake is slithering in and out of him. "I like this one."

"The snake is recent. Got it after I patched in." Smoke looks down, laughing lightly. "Funny thing about the ghost, though, is I've had it for two years. The smokey fog just so happens to go with my road name."

Enough of this talking... I need more. I slide my hands to his belt loops and pull him closer. Starting at his shoulder, I pick up where I stopped kissing before. My lips graze his warm skin as his chest rises and falls with every breath.

I trace my tongue along an inked crack on his chest, then circle around the bud of his nipple before taking it between my teeth, giving it a light bite.

"That's it," Smoke barks out. "You bite me like that, I need to get my hands on you."

Smoke grabs two handfuls of my shirt and jerks it up. Raising my arms, it disappears from my body, and he tosses the cotton to the side, paying it no mind. His eyes are glued to my chest.

"Y-y-you," he stutters, "you're pierced."

"I sure am," I reply, pushing my chest out like a proud peacock. I never had a reason to hide them, but it's not like I walk around with my shirt off just for people to see.

I got them for me, and with the hope of someone in the future toying with them. I knew I'd get something out of them one day. Can't blame a man for liking his nipples played with. It turns me the fuck on.

Smoke is stunned. "And you have chest ink too. What does it mean?" He lifts a hand to touch the black lines.

"It's a Celtic cross, a nod to my mom. She was born in Belfast."

Smoke looks up and meets my eyes. "I didn't know that."

"I guess we've got things to learn about each other, huh?" I reply with a smile.

"We sure do." And with that, he flicks the barbell just below my ink, causing the metal to jiggle, sending a jolt of electricity through my chest.

The sensation causes me to close my eyes and lean my head back. I wasn't kidding when I said my nipples were my hot button.

"You like that?" Smoke asks, tugging on the metal.

"Yea," I grunt.

"I think I'm gonna like playing with these," he says as he gives a bar a light twist, causing me to rock up on my toes. My hips sway forward, rubbing against his. "Especially if it makes you do that."

"Please, Smoke," I beg, grinding on him, my eyes still shut. "If you're gonna tease, do more."

"Well, since you asked so nicely."

Smoke tugs my button open, then unzips my pants, and with no delay, pushes them down. Seeing that he's going all in, I toe off my boots and kick them behind me.

Once my jeans are around my ankles, he comes back for more. His fingers send chills through my body as he grips the waistband of my boxer briefs, sliding them down my legs.

And as they fall, so does Smoke.

I watch the top of his head get lower as he kneels before helping me out of the last of my clothes. I rest one hand on his shoulder for support as I lift each foot. My socks are last to go, then I'm naked.

Smoke looks up, and I feel his hands slide up the front of my thighs. He's doing absolutely nothing wrong, but something in my brain freaks out when his fingers brush against the side of my cock. It causes me to back up a step.

The hunger in his eyes disappears in a flash.

"I'm sorry," I croak out. "I'm not ready—"

Before I can finish my thought, he's up on his feet and cradling my face in his hands. "It's okay. If you're not ready for that, there's plenty of other things we can do."

I press as close to him as I can. "I want you to touch me there." I need him to know I do. "I'm just not ready for you to go down on me yet."

I loosen my balled-up fists, then place my hands on Smoke's waist. I slide them around to his back and hug him.

He lets go of my face and wraps his arms around me too. We stand there in each other's embrace, and I soak in the warmth he offers as he holds me, rubbing his chin into my neck.

"I'll never do more than you're ready for." Smoke nudges my cheek with his nose, forcing me to meet his eyes. "Are you sure you wanna keep going?"

"Of course," I insist. Grasping his shoulders, I walk him backward toward the foot of his bed. "How about we get these jeans off you and see where things go."

"I can handle that." Smoke grins. "I'd like to see what you feel like inside me."

With his words, I freeze mid-step. My fingers are on his jeans, the button already undone, when his backward momentum causes me to lose grip of the zipper pull. Smoke pauses when he notices I've stopped.

I knew at some point both Smoke and I would take the lead on our sexual encounters, but for some reason, me topping him right now never crossed my mind.

"You want me to top you?"

"Haze," Smoke runs a finger down my cheek, "if you're not ready for me to give you a blowjob, and you've never let a guy fuck you, something tells me you're not ready for my dick yet. And I'm okay with that."

"So, you want me to fuck you?" I know he said it once, but I need to be sure.

"Do I have to beg you?" He chuckles. "'Cause I will. If I have to get on my hands and knees and beg you to put your dick in my ass, I will." I watch his eyes dilate like he's dreaming of what he's saying.

I take his word for it and get my fingers back on his zipper. If he wants me to fuck him, I'm going to do it until we both pass out from exhaustion.

He's mine now.

I falter one more time when I push his jeans down and see he's not wearing underwear. I look up and down, from his face to his crotch, and he laughs again.

"I don't like being constrained."

"Easier access for me," I reply before pushing the denim down.

Now in reverse of earlier, I'm on my knees ridding Smoke of his boots, socks, and jeans. When all the material is thrown to who knows where, I stand and push his chest, causing him to sit.

"Do you want something, Haze?" Smoke taunts. He grabs hold of his hard cock and starts stroking it slowly.

I watch as the head grows a deeper purple color, then lick my lips when I see a bead of precum appear at his tip.

He smears the off-white liquid around his girth with his thumb, using himself as lubrication.

"I want something alright," I growl. "Now, slide back and lay the fuck down."

And Smoke does exactly what I say. He scoots up the bed, then lays his head on the pillow in the middle. "Like this?" he asks as he gathers himself in his hand again, continuing where he left off.

I lean one knee on the bed, grab hold of his ankle, and squeeze. His eyes go wide, but I don't relent. "Hands off my cock."

Smoke releases himself on an upstroke, so his cock is standing straight up like a damn flagpole. Only when he lays his arms down, hands flat on the comforter, do I move.

Careful not to place my hands or knees on any important parts, I crawl up, kissing Smoke's skin as I get higher.

His shin. Left knee. Right thigh. And again. Left hipbone. Then closer to his center.

Hands on each side of his hips, I lower my head and lick his cock from base to tip. Again, the precum bubbles over, and with my lips, I suck just his tip, collecting what he's giving me.

"Haaaaaaze," he drawls my name. His hips buck when I lick the underside of his dick, hitting a sensitive spot. "More."

"I'll get there," I assure him. "Be patient."

"I'm done with patience." And he's not kidding.

Before I can do anything, there's a hand in my hair and I'm fumbling to keep up as Smoke pulls me up. He's relentless until I'm where he wants me. My hands are gripping the edges of his pillow, and my knees are spread open, kneeling over him as best I can.

But let's face it, Smoke isn't a small guy. Frankly, neither am I, but I'm a little leaner in the muscle department, so the bulk of his legs and waist have me more sitting on him.

I feel the hardness of his cock along the crease of my ass, and surprisingly, I'm not freaked out about it. Smoke rocks his hips, and I take the fact I'm not panicking as I allow him to rub against me as a good sign.

Moving my left hand so it's flat on the sheet, I cup the back of Smoke's neck in my right. Sliding my fingers into his long hair, I gather the strands, moving the length to the other side of his neck. Then I lower my head and dive in for a kiss, still holding his head.

Smoke's lips are aggressive. We battle and bite and lick, not letting up. What seems like forever passes before his hands on my back distract me from what my lips are doing to his.

Smoke grabs hold of my ass cheeks, then with speed and agility, he flips us so I'm underneath him. I didn't see it coming, so I just let him drag me around like a ragdoll.

He sets his forehead against mine, and I swear he looks into my soul. "If you want to get inside me, you need to tell me how you want me."

My mind runs through the rolodex of possible positions I'd like to put him in, but once one idea pings, I know it's perfect for our first time. But there's one thing we need to discuss before going any further. Because if I need supplies, I'm going to need to run to my room.

Lifting my arms, I tuck Smoke's hair behind his ears. I need to see his face when I ask this. "I hate to be a buzzkill, but when's the last time you were with someone?"

His smile grows so big. "I haven't touched another man in over a year. And as far as the club girls, I've always wrapped it up. But I got tested right after New Year's and haven't done anything with anyone since you gave me that killer blowjob."

Hearing that makes my heart explode. "No one?"

"Since I realized my feelings for you, I knew I was done with anyone else. They were just a distraction anyway. Something to sate my needs 'til I found the right person."

"And you waited?" I can't believe it. "For me?"

"Haze, when I saw you sitting across the main room, it was like I woke up. I knew my feelings for you were real, and I was going to do whatever it took to get you." Smoke ducks down and pecks my lips. "And now that we're here, it's gonna be you and me 'til the day we find our woman."

"Then we'll be with her and each other." I don't know where the words come from, but they're so true.

I finally get what he's tried so hard to get me to see. We can do this. We'll travel our journey together, and once we find that special woman, we'll both battle to make her ours.

"Yes, we will, Haze."

"I can deal with that." I smile.

"But until then, I think I know what you're asking." Smoke slides to my right and stretches himself out beside me. I roll to face him, our heads sharing one pillow. "I'd understand if you want to, but I don't need you to wear a condom. Honestly, I'd rather you don't. Just the thought of you inside me, skin to skin, is making my dick so damn hard, it might break off."

"I want that too. I just didn't wanna assume."

"Now that you know my recent history, are you gonna tell me yours? 'Cause I need to know whose ass I gotta kick for being near my man."

That makes me chuckle. "I haven't been with another man since last November. And that was just some random hook-up at the bar. I've never been with anyone in the clubhouse."

Smoke props his head on his fist. "No one? Not even a club girl?"

"Nope. Never touched any of them. None of them tripped my trigger."

"Damn," he mutters, but the corner of his lip curls up. "I find that kinda hot. I'll be your first clubhouse fuck. Shit, I need you bad." And he kisses me. Hard.

"And you'll be . . . my last . . . for as long as it takes . . . to find her." I roll him onto his back and kneel at his side, kissing him between words. "But first, do you have lube? I'm gonna need to get you ready for me."

He rolls out of my reach and rifles through the nightstand drawer. A bottle comes flying at me, and I catch it midair.

Smoke lies back down and rests his hand on my hip. I stay kneeling for a few seconds, soaking in his gentle touch, but when his hand begins moving, sliding low enough for his fingers to graze the length of my dick, I move.

I pop the top of the small bottle with one hand, and wrap the other around Smoke's cock. I tip the bottle just enough to let the clear liquid drizzle out, down into the gap between my palm and his hardness. Once I have enough to make my fingers slick, I close the bottle and lay it off to the side but still within reach for later.

"You like that, Smoke?" I ask, using both hands in tandem as I twist my wrists and tug the tight skin of his member up and down.

"Fuckin' heaven," he moans out with a long groan. "But you need to be putting that damn lube on your cock so you can fuck me. You can tug on me more later."

"Why don't you do it?" I ask, needing him to touch me.

"You don't have to ask me twice." Smoke reaches out, opens the lube, and pours a puddle in his hand. "Now, get over here," he orders as he bends his knees and spreads his legs, feet flat on the bed.

I crawl over and park myself between his thighs. Sitting up to reach me, Smoke wraps his hand around my girth, causing me to flinch. The liquid coating his hand is still a bit cold, so it takes a few seconds for it to warm up.

In the meantime, I take my still-coated fingers and tease him back. As he pumps my dick, I use one hand to hold his up against his stomach and rub it with the flat of my palm. My other hand starts exploring the underside of his balls.

Starting with one finger, I trace the seam of his ass until he adjusts his hips, spreading himself open for me. Once I can see the pucker of his hole, I use the tip of my finger and circle the rim.

Smoke makes a sound from his chest that's like a rumble of thunder. "I need more. Put your finger in."

So, I do what he says. With little pressure, I push my finger into his ass and feel the ring of muscles flex around my digit.

"More," he pants.

And again, I do. This time, I use my pointer and middle finger, sliding both in on the next pass. I feel his insides relax, and this time, I'm allowed in all the way up to the third knuckle. I pump them in and out of his ass, wishing it was my dick.

Smoke begins to grunt each time my fingers sink all the way inside of him, so I keep going.

Reaching for the lube with my left hand, I squeeze more out into the valley of my fingers and push the cool liquid inside him.

Meanwhile, he hasn't let go of my cock. He's squeezing me tight in his grip, and I'm starting to feel tingles at the base of my spine. And while I'd love to let him jack me off, letting my cum fly out to coat his chest, now's not the time. He wants me inside him, so that's where I need to be.

"Let me go, Smoke," I groan out as I push on his wrist.

"Only if you fuck me, Haze. I can't take it anymore. You're hitting a spot inside me, and I need more."

"Well, you're making my back tingle, so unless you want me to come on you, you need to roll over so I can get behind you."

"You can come on me anytime you want, damnit. Just after you fuck me in the ass!" Each word comes out harsher as he glares at me like I'm the one doing him wrong.

"Roll over," I snarl, slapping my wet hand on his hip. "Lay flat on your stomach. Hips up and knees spread wide."

"Yes, sir." The smartass salutes me before doing what I say. Once he's flat out in front of me, ass in the air, I maneuver myself forward.

One more palmful of lube and I grab myself and slick my cock, then use my fingers to tease his now puckering hole. I kid you not, the thing is blinking at me.

"You ready for me?" I ask one more time.

"Yea." He turns his head so I can see his profile.

I slide my dick between his cheeks, letting the tip nudge his opening a few times, before pressing forward on the third pump of my hips.

I could feel the beads of sweat rolling down my forehead as I push into Smoke for the first time. They slide down my neck, and my chest is starting to perspire. It feels like the temperature in the room has gone up twenty degrees.

The sporadic tightness of his hole is like nothing I've ever felt before. He may not be my first sexual conquest, but he'll definitely be the last man in my life.

With each slow rock of my hips, I push inside him farther, until my groin bumps into the meat of his butt cheeks.

The second I bottom out, Smoke rocks back and, I swear, lets me in even more. I didn't know I had more to give.

"Fuck me," he moans. "Harder. Fuck me harder."

If he wants me to go to town on him, I'm going to need him closer to me than this. Our first time, I need to touch and kiss him and feel his body against me.

I slide in all the way and press my chest to his back. I link my fingers with his beside his head, and lay my whole body on him. Once I'm wrapped over him like a damn heating blanket, I tell him to roll to his left.

Using both our momentum, we're lying on our left sides, and I have my arms around him. I'm essentially the big spoon to his little spoon, and my cock is buried in his ass.

"Fuck, that feels good," I say out loud.

"You should feel it in here. Your dick is right up against my prostate, and I feel like I'm sitting on the edge of the cliff, about to come any second."

"I think I can help with that."

Adjusting my right leg, I set my foot on the bed, opening my hips. Sliding my right hand down his flank, I hook my hand under his thigh and lift his leg to lean against mine. This opens him so his legs are apart, and I can reach down and grip his cock tightly.

Smoke lifts his free hand and cups the back of my neck, holding me close so he can kiss the underside of my chin and neck.

"Smoke," I sigh as I start moving, sinking into his tightness again, until our hips are flush with each pump. "Fuck, you feel good."

Good isn't even a big enough word to describe this. He's tight. Wet.

Devastating.

The pleasure is mind-blowing, and my body shakes as I try to regain control of my thundering heartbeat.

Smoke rocks his hips back against me with each forward movement I make. "Move . . . please . . . right . . . there."

Kissing across his shoulder, to his neck, and up to bite down on his earlobe, I shift my arm under him to wrap over his shoulder and lay my hand flat across his chest. I keep thrusting into him, a little faster with each move, burying my dick as far inside of him as I can.

We're both gasping for air, filling the room with pants and moans and skin slaps.

Using the leverage of my right foot on the bed, I stretch my left leg out under Smoke and power through the sudden burst of energy that hits my body. I don't know what caused the boost, but I'm not going to let go of the throttle until both of us hit the finish line.

I slide my left hand up to Smoke's neck and lift his chin. Our lips meet in a messy tangle of tongue, teeth, and pure need. I bite his lower lip to keep him with me, but he slips away when his back arches suddenly.

As soon as he jolts, his ass bumps into my lap out of rhythm, and I snap.

Using all my strength, I push my chest against his back, rolling Smoke back onto his stomach.

I slide a hand under him, grasp his cock in my fist, and begin jerking him off between me and the sheet.

And my hips, seemingly moving on their own, pound my dick into Smoke's ass like a piston in an engine at full RPMs. The needle on the tachometer hits the redline and the race is almost over. We're both about to blow.

"Right there." Smoke gasps. "Fuck, Haze. Right fuckin' there."

"You close?" I gasp in his ear.

"Gonna come," he says over his shoulder before lifting his head.

I lower mine and kiss him sloppily.

I feel his dick tighten, so I know he's there. The crown is wet, and I use every drop of his now flowing precum to keep my hand sliding against him. He's practically rutting into my fist, so I let him take what he needs.

All of a sudden, Smoke stops moving. His entire body spasms, then tenses, before he groans so loud and deep, I swear there's an earthquake inside him.

"Fuck, fuck, fuck," he shouts, his head thrown back, and I feel his dick tense as my hand is coated with warm, sticky cum.

Holy hell is that a sight to see. Smoke is even more handsome when he comes. Every muscle I can see is rock hard, bulging like they're exerting every ounce of power they have.

Smoke's hips jolt once more, dragging me back to the present. I haven't stopped pumping against him, and now, it's my turn to rocket into space.

I untangle my arms from around him, push up a little, then slide myself out of his hole. One hand on his shoulder, bracing myself, the other around my still wet and lubed cock, I begin to jack myself off.

Not two pumps later, my body seizes. The pleasure floods up my spine and throws me over the edge. I thrust forward, pumping ropes of my cum up his back and into the crease of his ass.

"Smoke," I hiss out as I let my eyes fall closed. My head falls forward, resting on his shoulder.

Both of us lie still, panting, trying to catch our breath. And after a few minutes of clearing the lust-filled, post-orgasm fog, I roll to the right and flop on my back.

"Why the hell did we wait so long to do that?" Smoke chuckles through his gasps for air.

"HA!" I laugh. "Because I'm a dumbass."

I roll my head to the side and see Smoke's smile drop in a flash. He leans up on his elbows and puts his face an inch from mine. "I never wanna hear you say that again. Do you understand me, Haze? You are *not* a dumbass. You never were."

"But—"

He shuts me up with a hard, forceful kiss. There's no tongue, and our mouths don't even open. It's only his lips pressing against mine, stopping my words. "No buts," he whispers. "Not gonna lie, we could've done without the arguing, but we're here now. That's what's important."

"Thank you," I say through a cough. I've never been one to take compliments well but hearing something positive coming from Smoke makes me feel worthy of him.

"No need to thank me." He threads our fingers together and lifts my hand to kiss the back of it. "Let's get cleaned up and back in bed. I'm not ready to let you go yet."

"You want me to sleep in here?"

"I'll chase you down if you try to run from me ever again." One more kiss, on my cheek this time, then he shimmies himself off the side of the bed. "I need a quick shower. Wanna join me?"

No need to ask me twice. "Hell fuckin' yea, I do."

Careful to not press my still lubed and sticky hands on the comforter, I stand and follow Smoke into his bathroom.

We shower just long enough to soap up and rinse. After drying off, and me borrowing a pair of workout shorts to sleep in, we toss the cum-stained comforter on the floor to deal with tomorrow, and crawl under the covers.

Smoke lifts the sheet to rest at our waists, pulls me close, and I rest my head on his shoulder, one arm over his chest.

His arm under my head curls behind me and his fingers trace invisible shapes on my shoulder blade.

"Move into Steel's old room. You'll have your own space if you need it, but with the connecting door, we'll still be together," Smoke says out of nowhere.

I think about it for a second and almost argue, but something stops the words from coming out. I find I have no reason not to move into the room next door. In fact, it would be perfect for the future we're both looking for. "Then when we find her, she can have her own space too," I reply in reference to the woman we both want one day.

Smoke nods. "Exactly."

A sense of calm flows over me, and I let my eyes grow heavy. I'm content. This feels right.

"I'll move in tomorrow."

"Good night, Haze." I feel his lips press against the crown of my head.

"G'night, Smoke."

CHAPTER EIGHT

ABBY

It's bright and early Tuesday morning, and I'm ready to dive into my work for the day. I've got inventory to take before I start making the supply order for the next week, so I rifle through my file cabinet for the papers I need.

But before I can open the second drawer, there's a knock at the door.

"Come in," I call out. I normally don't shut my office door, but when I'm busy with paperwork, I'd rather not hear the clanking of pots and pans coming from the kitchen down the hall.

I look up and see Ring standing in the now open doorway, and he's not alone. There's a tall, leggy redhead beside him. She's wearing faded jean capris and a black Harley-Davidson tank top. Her long hair is pulled back into a tight ponytail that hangs over her shoulder. I have to admit, she's a very beautiful woman.

If it weren't for the huge smile she's sporting, I'd definitely be intimidated by her beauty. She looks like someone you don't want to mess with, and those are the women I usually try to steer clear from.

I do recognize her from being around The Lodge with some of the club members, but that's all I know about her. I don't even know her name.

"Hey, Abby," Ring says as he steps inside. "You got a few minutes?"

"Sure," I reply. "I'm about to start the order, but you caught me before I even sat down."

"I promise we won't take too much of your time," the redhead speaks for the first time.

"There's someone I want you to meet." Ring gestures to her. "Abby, this is Angel. She's my Brother, Hammer's, Old Lady."

Angel steps forward and wraps me in a hug, totally surprising me. "I heard from a little birdie that you need a new place to live." She pulls back, then makes her way to one of the chairs in front of my desk.

A little birdie? Who did I talk to that could've told them I was looking to move? I know Gram and I have discussed it a little, and I do talk to some of the club girls while we work, but I don't like the idea of people discussing my private plans behind my back.

"Who told you that?" I question.

"Let's all just sit and we'll tell you everything," Ring interjects. "If you don't like what Angel has to say, no harm, no foul."

Curious, I sit, then Ring parks himself next to Angel.

"Ring," I draw out, "while I appreciate whatever you guys are trying to do, you know I like to keep myself out of your club."

"I know. It's just I overheard you talkin' to Raquel about wanting to move out of your grandma's house." Oh, so it was him who heard me. Better him than some random customer, I guess. "And I thought Angel might be able to help you with that. I'm not tryin' to step on your toes. I just couldn't not offer a suggestion when the perfect opportunity popped up."

"I get the idea of being involved in the MC can be scary, but this isn't really a club thing." Angel scoots forward in her chair. "I've got a house here in town that's available to rent, and Ring thought you might be the perfect person to live there. It's got three bedrooms and two baths, and it's on a quiet cul-de-sac."

"It's actually only about two blocks from where you live now," Ring adds. "You'd be close to your grandma, but not actually live with her."

"I have been looking for a fresh start. Living with Gram has been great, but I need a place of my own," I say. "And I bet Gram would like her house back. She's a light sleeper, so I always feel bad for coming home from work in the middle of the night."

"See," Angel declares like it's a done deal, "this would be perfect for you. With a place of your own, you can come and go as you please."

"But isn't a house like that a bit too big for just me?" Three bedrooms to myself? I don't even have enough stuff to fill the one bedroom I'm using now, much less a whole house. "I was planning on looking for an apartment."

"You'd be doing Duchess and me a huge favor." Angel waves me off, dismissing my objection. "The house used to belong to our grandparents. They passed away a few years back and left it to us. But seeing as we both now live on the clubhouse compound, no one is living there right now. We don't really need the house, but aren't ready to sell it yet."

"I don't know. What would you charge for rent? I'm saving up for a new car, so I don't know if I can afford a whole house on my own." While the idea sounds nice, I'm unsure of the cost.

"We'll figure that out later. You living there will help keep the inside clean, and we won't have to come check on it all the time," Angel answers. "And you won't have to worry about any of the outside work like lawn mowing or snow removal."

"I know you said you don't like getting involved with the club, but we can have them come around when you're not home, if that works better for you," Ring offers.

"You can keep all your correspondence through me, if that makes you more comfortable. You could call or text me whenever you need anything," Angel adds.

"I have an idea on the money thing, if that's your biggest concern," Ring says. "Would you be open to having a roommate? One of the Brothers, Steel, his sister, Meredith, has been staying with us for a few months but just decided she doesn't wanna move away to college. She'll be working at the local daycare and can pitch in on the rent too."

"I've never had a female roommate outside of college, but I don't mind the idea." Living with another woman doesn't sound so bad. I enjoyed living with my college dormmate, even though she ended up introducing me to my worst nightmare. But the girl talk, movie nights, and just basic human interaction was nice. "I'd like to meet her first."

"Perfect." Angel smiles and claps. "When's your next day off? I can meet you and Meredith at the house to give the grand tour. Then we can iron out all the details like rent and such."

"I'm sure Sunshine will wanna be there too," Ring adds. "She's kinda taken Meredith under her wing since she's been with us."

I guess this is a done deal now. And now that the idea has settled in, my brain is ready to start planning. This will be good for me, I just know it.

"Any idea when I could move in? I need to tell my Gram the plan, so I can keep her in the loop."

"You can move in tomorrow if you want," Angel laughs, "but let's say October first. That's just over two weeks. If you need more time, that's fine. But Duchess and I need to do one last go through of the house to make sure all our stuff is out."

"Works for me." Like I said, I don't have much, so packing and moving in will be a breeze. Now, I need to think about what I have to buy. I've never decorated a place of my own. When I moved to Kansas City, the condo we lived in was decorated and furnished by some fancy designer. I wasn't even allowed to move a lamp without permission.

"Oh, and if you don't mind, it's mostly furnished," Angel says like she's reading my mind. "You'll need a new mattress for the master bedroom. But all the couches and tables and dressers, we left behind. Duchess and I started fresh when we moved out."

"I got a new queen size mattress shortly after I moved here, so I'm good there. But I've already got a list of things I want forming in my mind." Now, I'm excited.

"See, Ring, I knew she'd be perfect." Angel shoves his shoulder as they both stand up.

"You?" He laughs. "I'm the one who suggested Abby to save you from renting to some stranger."

"Whatever you need to tell yourself," she says. "Don't make me tell your Old Lady on you. She'll take my side."

"Woman, you're evil. How does Hammer handle you?"

"He handles me just fine, thank you very much," she sasses back. "Abby, it was nice to meet you. I'll get your number from Ring and call you this afternoon to set a time to go check out the house after I talk to Meredith."

"Thank you so much," I call out as they disappear out the door.

And with that, they're gone.

I flop back in my chair and stare at the ceiling in shock. Lifting my arm to look at my watch, I realize I've only been here twenty-four minutes. What a whirlwind!

Ring and Angel's bickering was quite funny, but also kind of strange. I've never met two people, especially ones who aren't together romantically, who talk to each other that way. I never joked like that with Toby. Had I talked back to him, even in an attempt at a joking manner, he would've thrown a fit.

Maybe being around people in the motorcycle club isn't such a bad thing. It's too soon to judge based on one conversation, but if I'm going to move into the house they suggested, one owned by them, maybe opening my mind a little won't hurt.

One day at a time. I can do this, one day at a time.

CHAPTER NINE

HAZE

After spending a lazy morning in bed with Smoke, I decide to get up and start moving my stuff into the room next to his.

I knew these connecting rooms used to be Steel's and Ring's, but I recently learned they were Mountain's and Whiskey's before that. When the club started, and this building was renovated from a meat processing plant into the clubhouse it is today, Mountain put a door between these two rooms so he could watch over Whiskey when he was little.

And the setup also worked perfectly for Ring while Steel was in prison for two years. Ring looked after Steel's daughter, Opal, during that time, and the connecting rooms worked perfectly for them. But now they have an Old Lady, one they share, they moved out of the clubhouse and into one of the cabins in the backyard.

Now, the rooms have a third round of residents, and I couldn't be happier.

Just thinking about being so close to Smoke is a draw in itself. But being able to share the adjoining spaces with whoever we meet in the future is what makes this all perfect.

Knock knock.

I set a stack of t-shirts in the drawer and push it shut, then look up to see Mountain poke his head around the half-open door.

"Hey, Mountain."

"Hey," Smoke says as he walks through the connecting door to join us.

"Sorry to interrupt your moving day," Mountain says with a smile, "but Haze, I was wondering if you had some time to talk?"

"Sure," I reply. "Something wrong?"

"Not wrong, really. Things yesterday got a little overwhelming, and I was hoping we could sit down and dive deeper into the whole you being my nephew thing."

"Oh." I let out a huge breath and look at Smoke, who's moved to my side. His nod is all the support I need to march forward, so I turn back to Mountain. "Sure. There's lots of blanks we both need filled to figure out what's going on."

Mountain nods. "Exactly."

"You want me to come with?" Smoke grabs my hand as he asks me.

I look to Mountain, and he's nodding like a bobblehead. "Please do. You two are together now, I presume."

"We are," I answer, hoping it's not a problem with him.

"Then I have no issue with him joining." The look on Mountain's face shows no sign of lies or disgust. "Smoke being with us will save you from having to retell him everything later." He grins.

His gentle yet mighty presence has always put me at ease, and I wonder if something inside me has always felt the blood connection. Maybe our paths crossed for reasons even we can't explain.

"I guess I'm ready if you are," I say.

"Everyone's in Sunshine, Ring, and Steel's cabin, if that's okay?" Mountain asks. "Sunshine suggested meeting there since that was Brick's place. And the dining table would be more comfortable than being crammed in Whiskey's office."

"That's fine with me." I grab my cut off its hook and slide it on.

Smoke hands me my phone while pocketing his, and we head out.

Mountain leads the way downstairs and outside. As we walk across the lawn, I see Whiskey and Duchess appear on their front porch.

"Do you mind if we join you, Haze?" Duchess asks as she steps to my side. She's got Krew strapped to her chest in some kangaroo pouch contraption.

"Only if you bring this handsome devil." I chuckle as I smooth my fingers across the baby's bald head.

Duchess smiles up at me, then hooks her arm through mine. "I don't go anywhere without him these days."

"At least he's not cryin' anymore." Whiskey lets out a sigh. "Krew doesn't seem to realize yet that he's supposed to sleep at night time. He's a frickin' night owl, which means I get very little shut-eye."

"You were exactly the same way at that age, Whiskey, so shut your yapper." Mountain throws an arm over Whiskey's shoulders. "I told you this was your payback for being such a rotten kid."

"Well, if you're such a pro at fussy babies, why don't you come deal with him at three a.m.?" Whiskey knocks his arm away.

"I'd love to watch my grandbaby," Blue calls out. Everyone turns, looking for her, before the screen door of the cabin opens and she appears.

Ring and Steel follow her out before the tiny tornado on two feet barrels out behind them. Opal takes a running leap off the porch steps, heading straight for the playground jungle gym. And before you know it, she's climbing up the slide and cheering victory at the top of the platform.

"Watch her like a hawk," Sunshine yells from inside. "If she's anything like her uncle, she's due for a broken arm here soon."

"Hey, now," Whiskey stomps inside, "she'd look badass with a pink cast."

"Heaven help us." Duchess rolls her eyes.

"Heaven was no help with your Old Man when he was a child," Blue deadpans as she holds her hands out. "Now, give me that baby. I wanna smell his cuteness."

"Babies have a smell?" Smoke looks at me, eyebrows furrowed.

"They sure do." Blue now has Krew in her arms and she's holding him tight to her chest, nuzzling his head. "Just wait 'til it's your guys' turn for one of these. You'll know exactly what I mean."

"Our turn?" I cough. "Give us a few years before we go down that road."

"We've got a lady to find first," Smoke adds as we all head inside. "We kinda need someone to actually have the baby."

"Whoa, whoa, whoa! One step at a time here, people," I state. "We just got together."

"Oh my gosh." Duchess gasps, then grabs my hand and pulls me to the chair next to the one she chooses. "You two are gonna add a woman to your relationship? That's so cool! Do you have someone in mind?"

Seeing her excitement does something to me. I never in a million years thought I'd have this. Why did I doubt that the people around us would accept us? If this is what our President's Old Lady is saying, I hope everyone else feels the same.

"Are you sure nobody minds Smoke and me being together? I mean, this isn't exactly the norm around here."

"Haze," Whiskey calls out. I look across the table and see him and Mountain sitting next to each other. "As long as you two are happy, we could care less if you have a dozen partners."

"I agree," Mountain pipes up. "This club is a family. You being with a man and a woman isn't hurting anyone."

"You never answered my question." Duchess tugs on my sleeve. "Who's the lucky woman we get to welcome into the club as another Old Lady?"

"We don't know who she is yet," Smoke says from my other side. "We'll know when we find her."

"That's so sweet," Sunshine gushes from her chair at the head of the table. "I always wanted a sister."

"And what am I?" Duchess crosses her arms. "Chopped liver?"

"Haze is my blood family," Sunshine sticks her tongue out at Duchess, "so their lady will be a Hill too."

"Alright. That's enough outta you two busy bodies." Mountain laughs. "You're all Hills one way or another, so let's move on. We're here for a reason, ya know."

The room goes quiet and everyone zeros in on me.

"And I guess that'd be me."

I feel something rub against my jeans and look down to see Smoke's hand on my left leg. He squeezes my thigh, then I link our hands and set them up on the table. I have no reason to hide our connection, and by the looks on everyone's faces, they're happy for us too.

"How about we start with your mom, Haze?" Blue suggests. "What can you tell us about her? Do you have any clue how or when she might've met up with Brick?"

"I'm just as lost as you guys are." I shake my head. "I knew my stepdad wasn't my real dad, that was never a secret. I asked a few times who he was, but she always said she didn't wanna talk about it."

"Sounds familiar," Sunshine adds in, shaking her head. Duchess reaches out, and they squeeze hands before I continue.

"Her name was Erin. I know she was born in Belfast, Ireland, and moved here when she was fifteen. She had me when she was eighteen. I don't remember much 'til I was older, and she was already married to my stepdad."

"Hold old were you when she passed away?" Mountain asks.

"Fifteen. Car accident. That's when I went into foster care."

"If you had a stepdad, why didn't you stay with him?" Duchess questions.

"Because he didn't want me after I came out to him as bisexual."

Mountain's face blooms bright red and his fist pounds the table, making Krew whimper in Blue's arms. "He did what?" he whispers as she soothes the baby back to sleep.

I know it's not worth hiding any of the not so happy details from this group, so I lay it all out. "He said he was going to beat the gayness out of me, so I knew I had to leave."

"He hit you?" Describing Mountain as angry is an understatement. He's livid. "Please tell me he didn't."

"He tried," I answer, smirking, "but I blocked it and knocked him on his ass. He didn't try again."

"Good." I feel Smoke deflate at my side. His tight grip on my hand loosens and he slouches a little in his chair.

"I still think we should pay him a fuckin' visit," Whiskey growls, eyes squinted. "Teach that fucker a lesson about touching family."

While I appreciate the family support pow wow, there's no need. "He moved shortly after that, so I have no clue where he is. Last I heard, he was down south somewhere. He's not worth the hassle."

Blue hands Krew to Duchess, then starts rubbing Mountain's arm. "How'd you end up in foster care?" Her touch seems to be calming him a little, but I can still see the anger in the tightness around his eyes.

"After I packed my clothes in a duffle bag, I spent one night sleeping on a bench in the park. But I got picked up by the cops the next morning." Smoke is squeezing my hand again, so I use my free hand to unfurl his fingers from mine. "It's okay, Smoke. I'm okay."

"No, it's not okay. You shouldn't have had to be forced from your home." His eyes are locked on mine. "It's bad enough your mom passed, but for you to have to run away, I can't even imagine."

"I agree," Mountain comments. "You shoulda been with our family all along. It's not fair you had to miss out on the love and support we would've given you. You shoulda grown up knowing who we were your whole life."

"I know you know my story, about not knowing my dad either." Sunshine's words draw my attention to her. She's got tears in her eyes. "Our stories are a lot alike, so if you ever need to talk, I'm here."

"I just might take you up on that," I say back with a crooked grin.

She nods. "Good."

"Now, I know the basics from your past because of the background check we run on hangarounds," Whiskey speaks up, "but can you just lay it all out for everyone? I wanna know what you went through."

"Sure." I unlace my hands from Smoke's and rub my sweaty palms on my jeans. "I spent one day in a group home in Henderson, then was placed with a family back here in Tellison. Mark and Emma weren't able to have children of their own, so they opened their home to foster kids of all ages. When I moved in, I was the oldest of six kids living there at the time."

Duchess whistles. "That's a lot of kids."

"But I loved it there from day one." I think back to the day I met my foster parents. "They were so kind, considering I was the oldest kid they'd ever had up to that point. I had my own room, and they let me be a teenager for the first time in my life. I didn't get yelled at for asking for dessert. I never went without clean clothes. I always had money for hot lunch at school. I hit the jackpot with them."

"I'd love to meet them one day," Blue says through a sniffle. "Are they still in town?"

"They are," I reply with a smile. "They know about the club, but I haven't had a chance to fill them in on this news."

"It's been less than a day since you found out." Smoke chuckles. "But I'll go with you when you tell them, if you want."

"I wouldn't go without you." I turn in my chair and place my hand on his leg, giving him all my attention. "From now on, it's you and me."

"You two are so damn cute," Duchess says, giggling.

I wink at her, causing her to smile even bigger.

I face the table and ask Mountain, "Can you tell me again where you found the letter and picture? The details from yesterday are a bit fuzzy. All I remember is something about Sunshine and a photo album."

"Sunshine, you wanna fill him in?" Mountain asks her.

"I sure can." She smiles at him. "Well, as you may remember, I was going through Brick's things after he passed, helping the guys sort his personal effects. Mountain, Whiskey, and Brewer were in charge of all his Secretary stuff, so I focused on everything else. When I found a stack of photo albums, I got sucked into them. I was like a sponge, trying to learn all I could about the family I didn't know."

"I'd like to see those too one day, if that's okay?"

"They're all on the bookshelf by the fireplace," Sunshine points somewhere behind me, "exactly where I found them. You're welcome to look anytime you want."

"Thanks."

"But anyway, I got to the last album in the pile and found this envelope between the middle pages. I saw Brick's name written on it, the name 'Andrew' anyway, but thought nothing of it until I started reading the letter inside. I got a few lines in and immediately tucked it back in the envelope. I knew whatever it was, was none of my business, so I shut the album and waited a few days until I could talk to Mountain about it privately. He took it from there."

"And I looked at it before showing it to Bear, Skynyrd, and Butch," Mountain explains. "None of us remembered her, so we figured it was a dead end."

"Pops gave it to me to put in the office for safe keeping. Then you found it," Whiskey says. "Still blows my damn mind. What a fuckin' small world."

"Right?" I nod, still a bit dumbfounded myself. "I've been around the club since I turned eighteen and none of us had any clue."

"Did Brick ever say anything to you that now makes you suspicious of him knowing?" Duchess asks.

"Nope. Never." I remember back to the day I first saw him. "Does anyone know the story of how I started being a hangaround?"

"I vaguely do," Whiskey answers. "Something about a grocery store parking lot and an elderly lady's purse."

"Yup. I was seventeen and working at the grocery store. I was outside bringing in the carts when I heard shouting. I turned and saw these two dudes in leather chasing some guy across the parking lot. It was Brick and Skynyrd. I had no clue who they were at the time, but I saw them again a few weeks later when they were shopping. I knew about the club, but not much about what you did other than keep the bad stuff outta town."

"So, what made you come here and check things out?" Sunshine asks.

"I watched from a distance for a few months, then when I turned eighteen, I introduced myself to Whiskey at an open party. I liked what I saw and decided I wanted to be part of the club."

"I gave you the job at the salvage yard, and you've been here ever since." Whiskey chuckles.

"I met this yahoo," I nudge Smoke with my elbow, and he smiles back, "and had a huge crush on him ever since. It just took me this long to get my head out of my ass and figure out he felt the same."

"You didn't have any idea y'all liked each other?" Blue leans her chin on her fist, invested in our story.

"Nope," Smoke responds. "Not 'til I chased him down on New Year's Eve and told him how I felt."

"And then I pushed him away 'til yesterday," I continue. "Stupidest nine months of my life."

"That long?" Duchess's jaw drops. "You two have liked each other that long and never did anything about it?"

"I wouldn't say we never did *anything*," I say as I wiggle my eyebrows at her.

"Ooooooo!" She laughs. "Tell me more."

"That's enough outta you." Whiskey reaches across the table and grabs Duchess's hand. "You two can gossip all you want later. I have one more question for Haze."

"What's that?" I ask him.

"Do you wanna read the letter your mom wrote?"

Ah, shit. The letter. I read part of it yesterday but didn't finish it. It was too much.

"I'd love to, but not right now." Smoke reaches for my hand again. "One day, I will, but I need some time to unscramble first."

"I'll keep it in my office 'til you're ready."

"I don't want you guys to think I'm not grateful or accepting of you being my family," I say as I look around the table. "I'm thankful for every single one of you, whether we're related or not. I just need a little time to let my head realize it."

Mountain laughs, breaking the tension of my serious admission. "I don't know why I never saw it before. You sounded just like Brick when you said that. He was the same way, always needing to think things through."

"He sure did," Whiskey says with a chuckle.

"I'm just glad I got to know him, even if it wasn't like I should've."

"His memory will never go away. Anything you wanna know, just ask." Mountain smiles as he taps his finger on his temple. "I've got stories up here that he'd never want me to tell."

"I'm sure I've got a lot to learn."

"But we'll all be with you every step of the way." He leans his forearms on the table and looks me straight on. "Because that's what family does."

I couldn't ask for anything more. I'm finally finding my home.

CHAPTER TEN

SMOKE

If someone asked me a year ago what my life would be like today, I never would've said this.

I'm dating a man, one in the same motorcycle club as me, and I wouldn't change a thing.

Haze and I have officially been a couple for a month and things are going really well. I go to bed every night in the arms of the man I've chosen, and wake up every morning with a smile on my face. Sometimes, the reason for my smile is that man.

Hell, I woke up this morning to his tongue on my dick and thought I was dreaming.

Every day, Haze becomes more and more brave with his expressions of affection, and I'm never one to complain about feeling any part of him on me. Whether it be his hands or mouth on my body, or his cock fucking me in my ass, I'll take it.

He's yet to say anything about me returning the favor, as much as I want to, but I'm not going to push him. The most I've done to his backside is trace a finger over his hole while giving him a hand job. And based on the seismic spasm his entire body went into, I know he enjoyed the feeling. But when he didn't comment on it after, while we were lying in bed, sated after multiple orgasms, I didn't bring it up.

It's now the beginning of October and planning for the club's annual Halloween party is already in full swing. Duchess, along with club girls Stiletto and Jazz, has taken the reins on getting everything ready. They've started to hang a few decorations but don't trust us rowdy ones to not wreck anything else, so the rest of the stuff is staying in boxes until the day before.

Last year, after a few drinks and being hopped up on way too much sugar, some of us were in a pranking mood. Maybe Hammer and me placing the life-sized skeletons they had out in sexual positions was a bit much.

But one tradition that has carried over from last year has turned out to be torture for me—the surprise costumes.

I have the perfect costume in mind for myself, but Haze was undecided, so he went shopping with a few of the other Brothers. When he came home last night, I chased him up the stairs yelling at him to show me what he bought, but he refused to spill the beans.

Catching him when he had to slow down to enter his room, I tried to sneak a look in the bag, but he held it out of my reach. As soon as the door was open, he knocked me to the side and scurried over to hide it in his dresser.

Getting my footing back, I made one last attempt to get the bag, but he shoved it in a drawer, almost pinching my fingers in the process. He laughed and said that's what I'd get for ruining the surprise. Now, I have to wait. Fuck. It's not fair, but the fun I had messing around with him was worth it.

I'm looking forward to the party. I just hope that now we're patched in, our hazing is over. If our Brothers make us run around the clubhouse again, having us pretend to be racing imaginary motorcycles like they did last year, I'll be pissed.

It may have been Haze and me pretend racing last year, and he may have beaten me in the process, but I have a man to impress now. That same man kicked my ass in that foot race, and I can't be making a fool of myself again. I'd rather strip naked and sing the national anthem than run laps any day.

It's Friday night and we just got out of Church. There's not much going on club-wise other than a gun run mid-month, so it was a quick meeting. Once everyone involved in a club business gave their report, we discussed what team was up for the run, then Whiskey called Church to an end with the slam of his gavel.

The Old Ladies had ordered a pizza delivery for dinner, so as soon as the doors opened, the delicious aroma of sauce, cheese, and grease fill the Church room.

"Fuck yea," Gunner grunts, "I need to fill my face with as much pepperoni as I can."

"I didn't know you swung that way, Brother." Kraken tosses his arm around Gunner's neck, dragging him into the main room while giving him a noogie.

"Kiss my ass, octopus man," Gunner yells while trying to get away. "That's not what I meant and you know it."

The two continue to wrestle until their tangled bulk knocks into a side table next to one of the couches, resulting in a lamp toppling to the floor.

"Knock it off, you two," Duchess yells out from behind the bar. "Watch where you're going. You could've run into one of the kids with your roughhousing."

Kraken releases Gunner before picking up the lamp and inspecting it to make sure nothing is broken. "Sorry, Duchess," he replies, actually looking regretful.

Gunner, on the other hand, not so much. "Why do I always have to watch out for them? Maybe all your kids need to watch where I'm going and not get in my way," he growls, hands on his hips.

The room goes dead silent.

I watch as Duchess unstraps the harness from her chest, handing a wide awake for once Krew to Stiletto, then she marches her way toward Gunner.

She makes it halfway before Whiskey interferes, pulling her into his arms. "That's enough, Gunner. You know how things are around here during family time. Deal with it or go hide in your room."

"But—"

"I said that's enough!" Whiskey roars. "I don't care how rowdy y'all get when we're partying, but when the kids are just trying to eat dinner, you need to calm the fuck down. Do I make myself clear?"

"What the fuck ever." Gunner stomps off and disappears down the club girl hallway. I don't know who he expects to find down there, since all the girls are here in the main room, but that's none of my business.

"And with that, the show's over," Duchess mumbles with a grunt toward Whiskey. "I coulda handled him myself."

"I have no doubt you could," he replies with a half-smile she can't see behind her. "I just didn't wanna have to carry his carcass outside after you were done with him."

"Damn right." And with that, she stomps back toward the bar. "Now, I need a drink."

The sound slowly grows back to its usual level of half too loud, and things are back to normal.

Haze grabs my hand, and we make our way across the room toward the left hallway. After grabbing a full pizza box off the stack on the kitchen passthrough counter, we head for the double doors leading out to the backyard.

"Where are you two goin' with that whole pizza?" Kraken hollers behind us, laughing, as I push the screen door open.

Haze turns to face him so he's walking backward. "We're still growing boys, Kraken. We need our own food, otherwise, you'd eat it all before we got any," he jokes.

That causes a ripple of laughter as anyone within ear shot cracks up.

"Ohhhhhhh burn," Trooper calls out. "The kid got you good."

"Who you callin' a kid?" I call out, chuckling. Sliding my hand into Haze's back pocket, I use the denim in my grasp to pull him onto the patio. Haze tries to keep his footing as he almost trips over the door transition. "Haze is *all* man as far as I'm concerned," I continue as the screen door slams shut behind us.

And with that, we escape to the semi-quiet of the outside. We're followed by laughter and clapping and the sounds of pretend kisses from everyone inside. I'm glad the sense of fun and comradery didn't go away when Haze and I came out to the club. It's part of the reason this club works so well—we all genuinely like each other.

When we're further out onto the lawn, Haze swipes the pizza box from my hands and sets it on one of the chairs around the currently dead firepit. He grabs my hand and pulls me into his arms. "So, I'm man enough for ya, huh?"

Wrapping my arms around his waist, I slide my hands under his cut, feeling the cotton of his t-shirt. "You know you are." With his chest pressed against mine, I dive in for a kiss. It's hot and heavy and totally what I need right now.

Sitting across the table from him in Church was torture. As the two newest members, neither of us get to pick where we sit around the giant table, so I was stuck in an empty chair directly across from him. I'm forced to look straight at him but can't touch him, and I've been needing his lips on mine.

The Brothers have all been accepting of us. They also know Haze and I are looking for a woman to add to our relationship. A few have jokingly made suggestions of different women, but none have felt right.

Haze was skittish about public displays of affection at first, but he quickly came around to accepting my newfound need for touching. Because let's face it, my man is hot as fuck. Between his dirty blond hair, scruffy beard, and brown eyes that have a yellowish tint to them, he's irresistible.

After one night in bed with him, I realized I have an innate need to feel his skin against mine. It's important to me. Even sitting next to each other on the couch, or just standing around, I need to have a hand on Haze in some way. Whether it's wrapped around his waist, resting on his back, or in his back pocket, it's the way I truly feel connected to him.

After scarfing down the whole pizza, Haze and I lounge back in two Adirondacks with our legs stretched out in front of us. I've got one boot crossed over the other while Haze is sprawled out like a drunken sailor.

My right elbow is propped on my armrest, and I've got my trusty flathead screwdriver twirling through my fingers like a dancer's baton. Any time I'm sitting, either in Church or watching television in the main room with the club, I've got the tool spinning.

Shortly after becoming a Prospect, I found myself carrying this screwdriver around with me all the time. I slipped it in the back pocket of my pants one day while working in the shop, and I've had it on me ever since. It's now carried in a leather holster type of thing hanging from the right side of my belt, but it's always there.

Having my hand on something at all times might not be as new of a concept as I thought. Maybe that's why I carry this thing around everywhere I go.

But I have to say, as calming as the spinning is for me, feeling Haze's hand in mine is better. His right hand is linked with my left, resting on his armrest. I could hold his hand all night.

"Are you gonna talk to me," Haze looks at me with a smirk, "or just spend all night playin' with your tool?"

Flipping the screwdriver in the air one more time, I tuck it back in the holster at my side, then shift in my seat to angle my body toward Haze. "Don't be jealous. I'll play with your tool later."

Haze sits up. "Is that a threat or a promise?"

"Whatever you want it to be," I mumble before leaning in to press my lips against his.

We stay like this, letting our tongues swipe against each other's for a few minutes before breaking for air.

"I like this," Haze says with a lazy smile.

"What's this?" I ask, wanting to know what he likes. Needing to know, so I can do it again.

"I like the simplicity of us. Now that we're not arguing and running away from each other, we fell into *us* pretty easily."

"I agree." Leaning back in my chair, I rest my head on the back and roll it to look at him. "I've got nothing to complain about either. I'm glad the fighting is over."

"But I can't help but wonder . . ."

"Wonder what?"

"Is it always gonna be this easy?" I see worry in his eyes. "Will it be like this when we find the woman we're looking for?"

I squeeze his hand still in mine. "I hope so."

"Do you have a certain type of woman you're looking for?" Haze asks. "I don't think I've ever seen you with one type."

That makes me snicker a little. "That's 'cause you've probably only seen me with club girls. None of them look anything alike."

Haze lets out a harsh *harumph*. "I don't like thinkin' about that."

"I'm sorry," I apologize. "Had I known what you were feeling, I never would've wasted my time trying to bury my feelings for you. That's all any of them were."

"I know," he responds with a sigh. "I just wish we had some idea of who she was, ya know?"

"You sick of me already?" I squint my eyes and give him a mock glare. "I didn't know I bored you so much."

"That's not what I mean." Haze laughs as he tosses one of his discarded pizza crusts at my head.

"I'm not a duck." I chuckle as I lean to pick it up from the ground between my legs, tossing it in the firepit. "Don't be wasting perfectly good crust on me. I don't know why you don't eat it. The crust is the best part."

"You're so weird." Haze shakes his head. "The only time the crust is edible is if it has cheese in it."

"Talk about a conversation switch. We go from talking about what kind of woman we want to arguing about pizza crust. We're crazy." I laugh out loud, looking at the sky. "What woman is gonna want us?"

"As long as she's okay being with both of us together, and accepting the club lifestyle, I don't care what she looks like."

"Accepting the club is definitely important. We can't be with someone who isn't okay with our family," I reply. "Especially now that you've found out you're a Hill. There's no getting around that."

"I know the ladies here do it, but whoever we find has to be okay with us sometimes putting the club first." Out of my periphery, I see Haze stare up. "But maybe having the two of us will make her feel double protected. Kinda like how Sunshine has Steel or Ring. One of them always seems to be with her."

"But Haze?"

He turns his face toward me. "Yea?"

"I'll always need you too, not just her." I feel a little of my own insecurity slip out. I know right now it's just him and me, but whenever she comes to us, I don't want to lose him in the process.

"And you'll always have me, Smoke. I hope you know that."

"I do," I sigh, "I just don't want us to get lost in the mix."

Haze raises our hands and kisses the back of mine. "Are you in a hurry to find her?"

"Nope." I pull and bring his hand to my lips. "I just got you. I'm happy."

"But you're ready whenever we find her."

"Exactly. I know she's out there somewhere."

"No matter what happens, we'll be okay."

Settling ourselves back in our chairs, we relax and look up at the stars. There's no words. There doesn't need to be.

I think about what Haze just said. We'll be okay. Because for the first time in a long time, I believe it. Even though it took us a while to get to this point, maybe waiting for now is what we needed.

Time really is a funny thing.

CHAPTER ELEVEN

HAZE

It's bright and early Saturday morning, and I'm on my way into town. Last night, Whiskey asked if I'd mind helping him with some yardwork at Duchess and Angel's house, and I said sure. Smoke is spending the day at Rebel Repairs, so my schedule is wide open.

I grab a handful of throttle as I turn right at the one stoplight in Tellison, then roll down the main drag through town. I turn right into the cul-de-sac and coast to a stop at the curb. The house sits at the end of the road, so there's no missing it.

Not that I could anyway since Whiskey's truck and open trailer are parked in front of it. The ramp on the trailer is down, but the riding lawnmower he brought from the clubhouse is still on it.

Booting my kickstand down, I turn my Harley off and swing my leg over to get off. Grabbing a pair of work gloves from my saddle bag, I start my walk up the driveway. It's not a long driveway, enough for two cars to sit end to end, but currently, the only vehicle I see is in the garage.

The garage door is open and that's where I find Whiskey. He's talking to someone, but I can't see them in the shade of the overhang. I know Meredith, Steel's sister, is living here now, but I've never met the other renter.

From talk around the club, I know she works at The Lodge, but I can't remember her name. I'm sure I've seen or heard of her before, but I've never been introduced.

Whiskey waves as I walk up, then turns to the side to give me space in their tiny pow wow. The woman is leaning back against the bumper of what I see now is a rust bucket on wheels.

Does someone drive this hunk of junk, or is it a fixer upper? It really should be neither. This car looks like the next candidate for the crusher over at the salvage yard. I'd be more than happy to push the button on that job.

"Hey, Haze. Thanks for coming." Whiskey holds out a hand, and we shake.

Something about this stranger draws me in. I scoot a half step to the side, trying not to make it obvious I'm moving closer to her because I can definitely feel the fear pulsating off her. Something's not right, and I immediately wonder what her story is.

Since I stopped walking, I've noticed one thing about her—she's had her eyes darting in multiple directions the whole time, and right now, she's staring at her feet.

"No problem," I reply to Whiskey. Maybe talking will get her to acknowledge me. "You're the boss, so I go where you say." I make an attempt at a joke, but the only person who laughs is Whiskey.

"Very funny." He chuckles. "Haze, meet Abby." Whiskey turns to her. "He'll be helping me with the yardwork today."

Her name is Abby. Pretty name.

At Whiskey's introduction, she finally meets my eyes. And everything around me disappears. I can hear the drone of Whiskey's voice, but none of his words make any sense. My vision goes a little blurry around the edges, but I see her perfectly clear.

I swear, my heart stopped for a few seconds. And as soon as it starts beating again, it's in overdrive. Holy hell. Beautiful isn't even the right word to describe this woman. She's stunning.

Abby has straight, jet-black hair that goes all the way down to her waist. Her eyes are as black as coal, but not in a bad way. They're sparkling like the water across the lake after dark. You can see the movement and ripples, but the dark sky makes the surface appear black as an obsidian rock.

Where in the hell did I get that description from? I've never had words like that come from my mind before, and that's saying a lot for a constantly busy brain.

Her cheeks are flushed and rosy. And her lips... her lower lip is a smidge plumper than the top, and I'd give anything to kiss her to see how they feel against mine.

If Smoke's kisses drive me crazy, I can't imagine what Abby's would do to me.

Smoke! He's going to fall for this tiny beauty, I just know it. I can't wait to get back to the clubhouse and tell him all about her.

Shaking my head and snapping myself out of my way too long, silent stare, I hold out my hand to her. "Hi, I'm Haze. It's nice to meet you, Abby."

Even her name on my lips is amazing.

"Hi," she replies softly like she's afraid to talk too loudly. She sounds just as shy as her posture reads. Her hand slowly slips into mine, but a second later, she pulls back. Pointing at the door leading into the house, she starts backing toward it. "I'll just head inside and let you guys do whatever you need to. Just knock if you need to come in."

And with that, she's gone.

In the three minutes since I walked up, I feel like I was standing in front of a kicked puppy. I don't like it. All I want to do is rush after her and hold her in my arms. I want to take whatever it is that she's so afraid of and smash it in the compacter along with this car.

I turn to face Whiskey. "Is she okay?"

"She's a skittish one, ain't she?" He shakes his head. "Like a deer in headlights."

"I could almost feel how afraid she was of us."

"She's not always like that. I swear it took her a month before she would even look me in the eye." He chuckles. "Once Abby gets to know you, though, she'll open up more."

"I wouldn't mind getting to know her more," I mumble as I turn away and grab the ladder hanging on the wall.

"What was that?" Whiskey asks, still laughing a little.

"Nothing," I laugh back, "nothing at all."

"Don't think I didn't see the way you were looking at her, Haze. Your eyes almost bugged out of your head when she finally quit staring at the floor and looked at you." He nudges me to the side and grabs a stack of buckets before heading for the front yard.

"I have no idea what you're talking about, cousin," I say as I prop the ladder up against the side of the house. I slip on my gloves, then climb up a few rungs until I can see the inside of the rain gutters. They're full of leaves and pine needles, so I grab a handful of the soggy muck and let it plop to the ground, barely missing Whiskey's boot.

"Hey!" he shouts. "Watch where you're droppin' that. I don't need decaying shit in my hair."

"Oh, you poor thing," I goad. "Don't be tellin' me what my eyes were doin'."

"But they were," he insists. "Don't be tellin' me that you're not interested in her, 'cause I'll know you're lying if you try that bullshit. I know how these things work. I fell for Duchess the second her pink Converse dropped to the pavement."

"Hand me that bucket," I call out, another chunk of dead leaves in hand.

"Here." He passes one up, and I hook it to the top of the ladder platform.

"And, so what if I am?" I ask as I begin to fill the bucket. "Abby seems like a nice lady. Shy, but nice."

"Do you think she'd be okay with you and Smoke together?"

I pause, thinking about it for a second, then look down at Whiskey. "Do you think we're crazy wanting to be with someone together?"

"A year ago maybe." He leans an arm against the side of the house. "But knowing what kind of guys you and Smoke are, I have no doubt whoever you two end up with will be in good hands."

"Thanks," I reply, trying not to smile like a lunatic. Hearing that from him, my President, friend, and now cousin, means a lot.

I fill the bucket with as much as I can reach from my position, then start my climb down.

When I hit the grass, Whiskey takes the bucket and dumps it in the rolling trash can. Handing it back, he doesn't let go right away. "But remember this, Haze. Before you bring a woman around, make sure she's really the one. I don't allow Brothers in my club to toss around the 'Old Lady' title too easily. That patch has to be earned just like yours was."

"I know." I look him dead in the eyes, hoping he can see how serious I am, and nod. "There's just something about her."

Whiskey slaps me on the shoulder with his free hand. "And that's how I know you're a goner."

"Is that a good thing?"

"It sure is." He smiles, then lets the bucket go. "When we're done here, you head back to the clubhouse and talk to Smoke. I'm sure he'll be excited to hear what you have to say."

"I sure hope so." My heart skips a beat again, nervous about what he'll think. "Now, let's get to work. The sooner we finish, the sooner I can get the ball rolling."

"You finish the gutters, then rake out the floor beds. I'll mow the lawn, then we'll discuss what's left after that." Whiskey checks off his imaginary checklist. "If I go home and something's not done, my Old Lady is gonna have my hide."

So, we get to work.

An hour later, I look up just in time to see the front screen door swing open. I'm down on my hands and knees, trying to pull a stubborn root out of the flower bed, when I see Abby step outside with two bottles of water in her hands.

Standing up, I brush the mulch off my knees, then take off my gloves and tuck them in my back pocket. "Hey," I call out, "is one of those for me?"

Abby stops at the edge of the stairs. "One of them is. Is Whiskey around somewhere?" She looks around the yard.

"He's mowing out back."

Abby's yet to move from her perch, so I take a risk and move up one step. She doesn't run away, so I take that as a good sign.

One more step up, then another, and I'm a step below her, but we're finally eye level with each other.

This time, it's her turn to snap from her trance. She shakes her head a little, and I can see her long hair wave back and forth with the motion.

"Here," she hands one of the waters to me, "I hope it's cold enough for you. I just got it out of the fridge."

I take it, letting my fingers brush against hers. She doesn't flinch, thankfully. Maybe now's my opportunity to put out some feelers. If I can make sure she remembers me in a good way, when I get a chance to introduce her to Smoke, maybe things will move in the right direction.

I take a drink, then start out easy. "So, how long have you lived in Tellison?"

Abby immediately looks down at her shoes. The other bottle of water still in her hand starts shaking a tiny bit, and she grabs hold of her wrist with her other hand, steadying it. She doesn't comment on it, so I don't bring it up.

"I moved here in February," she says quietly.

Okay, so a simple question wasn't great, but at least she responded. I really don't like her being afraid of me.

"Abby?" I set my water on the railing and take the last step, moving to the side so I can be next to her. She glances up at me, but she looks petrified.

As gently as I can, I reach forward and trace my fingers down the side of her hand. Her pinkie twitches a little, so I hook mine around it and stay just like that.

Eyes still on mine, Abby exhales, and I see the tenseness of her shoulders drop. "Yes?" she whispers.

"I know we just met," I tell her, "but I want you to know you don't have to be afraid of me. I'll never hurt you. I promise."

Abby looks over my shoulder, shaking her head again. "You can't say that. You don't know me."

"Not yet." I try to meet her eyes with mine, but she's still looking away. "But I know me, and I'd like to get to know you."

"Me?" Now, her attention is on me. She steps out of my reach, but I keep my boots where they are. "Why would you wanna know me? I just work for your club, nothing special."

"Everyone is special," I reply. "I'm not gonna push, but I'd at least like to start as friends. Would that be okay?"

This is a woman I cannot push, not that I'd ever force her to do anything she didn't want to. But these last few minutes have pretty much confirmed my first thoughts—Abby has been hurt before. And based on her instinct to flinch and jump back, her pain was physical.

I feel the anger starting to rumble in my stomach, but that's not something I ever want to show her.

She obviously has a fear of men, and I hate it. Whoever hurt her, made her feel even the smallest amount of fear, is now on my list of people who will die. If I have anything to say about it, Abby will never be afraid of him or them or whoever it was ever again. The darkness of her past is over, and I want Smoke and me to be the light in her future.

It's now our job to protect her from whatever ghosts haunt her past. She'll never have a reason to be afraid of me . . . and I'll bet my patch on that.

"I don't know." Abby finally shows me her sparkling eyes again. "I don't have many friends."

"That's okay." I smile wide, trying to give her my best. "We all gotta start somewhere."

"I guess." This time, the right side of her mouth curls up in a small smile. Just a flash, but it's enough for me to know I'm slowly breaking down her walls. "One more friend won't hurt."

That makes me snicker. If only she knew what I have in store for her. She'll be getting more than just one friend, at least in the way I'm hoping. "By the time you get to know me, I promise I'll have lots more friends for you." I grab my water and chug the rest, then start backing myself down the steps. "But until then, I'm gonna get back to your yard. Thank you for the water. Now, you get back inside and out of this heat."

"Oh . . ." She scampers back a step, and there's the scared Abby again. "I'm sorry for interrupting your work. I'm sorry."

I pause my descent and march back up to stand in front of her. I grab both of her hands and draw her attention to me. "Never apologize for bugging me. You didn't interrupt anything. In fact, you made my entire day by bringing me something to drink. Okay?"

"Okay," she whispers, her voice cracking. I can see the start of some tears, so I know it's time for me to let her go.

"I don't know if I'll be able to say goodbye before I leave, so I'll say it now." I drop a gentle kiss on her forehead, then let her hands go. "Goodbye, Abby. I'll see you soon."

"Bye, Haze." And she's gone again in a flash, both the screen door and inside door slamming behind her.

I stare down at my hands, still feeling her tiny, shaking fingers against mine.

She's the one. She's the one for us. I just know it.

I want her more than the air I breathe. When I get back to the clubhouse, I'm going to tell Smoke all about her.

Last night, we agreed we were in no hurry to find her, but here she is. We said she'd come when the timing was right, but I never imagined it'd be like this.

But no matter what happens from here on out, Abby will be protected until the day I die, and even after that. I swear on my mother's grave.

CHAPTER TWELVE

ABBY

I fell in love with the charm of this house the day Meredith and I met with Angel to tour it. Angel told us all about the things her grandfather had built or added for her and Duchess's grandma, and I could almost feel the love within the walls. I knew it was the right place to move to.

I tried to argue with Meredith when she told me to take the master bedroom, but she insisted. She swore up and down that she was okay with taking one of the bedrooms upstairs, and when I tried again, she pushed me into the bathroom and told me to look at the bathtub.

Once I saw that giant soaker tub with the built-in headrest, all my objections melted away.

It's only been ten days since we moved in, but I've quickly learned that Meredith James is a force to be reckoned with. She gently bulldozes you until she gets you to agree with something, then somehow makes you think it was your idea to begin with. She may be single now, but God help any man who falls into her path.

I'm in my walk-in closet, finally breaking down my last cardboard box, when I hear a knock coming from somewhere.

Heading out of the bedroom and down the hall, I hear the knock again. It's coming from the door in the kitchen that leads out into the garage, and I briefly wonder if it's Haze.

I pull the door open, and there stands Whiskey. He's typing something on his cell phone, but he quickly looks up, then tucks it into his vest.

"Hey, Abby. Just wanted to let you know I'm about ready to head out. You can close the garage door after me if you want."

"Thanks, Whiskey," I reply, trying not to make it obvious that I'm looking behind him to see if Haze is still here. "Do you want something to eat or drink before you go? I've got a roast in the crock pot."

"I'm good." He shakes his head, thumbs tucked in his pockets. "I've got a baby and Old Lady at home waitin' for me."

"Oh, that's right. Congratulations on the little guy. I heard about his arrival from some of the girls at The Lodge."

"Thanks. He's growing like a weed and keeping us up all hours of the night," he replies with a deep laugh. "But I wouldn't trade him or his momma for the world."

"That's sweet."

"Well, it was good to see you, Abby. Don't be a stranger."

"I'll try." I wave as he takes a step back.

He waves back. "I'll tell Haze goodbye for you too, if you'd like."

"Oh, no, you don't have to do that." The words rush out. "We talked a little bit earlier."

"You did? Well, good. Have a good night now."

"You too. Goodnight."

I watch as Whiskey walks down the driveway, then I hit the button to close the garage door.

Back in the kitchen, I head to the sink and watch as Whiskey loads the lawnmower onto the trailer. His movements seem so seamless and easy. I noticed the same thing about Haze. Maybe it's a biker thing? While I've seen a bunch of them inside the bar, I've never watched any of them work until today.

As Whiskey jumps off the side of the trailer and circles around to the front of his truck, I see the back patches on his vest. The white patches stand out against the black leather, and the skull and green snake are strikingly vivid. It's almost like they're leaping off the material, ready to strike.

I tried to keep myself away from the front windows earlier, but peeks of Haze kept drawing me back. He climbed up and down the ladder countless times while cleaning the gutters. Then, as he raked the leaves out of the flowerbeds, laying out fresh mulch, my eyes went straight to his arms and flexing muscles each time I glanced out.

And when he ditched his vest to take off his t-shirt, I almost swallowed my tongue. I saw a flash of a tattoo on his chest but lost sight of it when he put the vest back on and kept working.

What a tease.

The beeping of the oven timer forced me to walk away, thankfully, before he caught me watching him, and by the time I looked back, he had disappeared from sight.

But the devil on my shoulder walked me right over to the fridge and directly outside to offer him something to drink. I went out there with two bottles, one for him and one for

Whiskey, but the angel on my other shoulder graced me with Haze's presence alone.

But now, here I stand, after probably making a fool out of myself, and Haze is gone. I know he said his goodbye earlier, but I had a small hope I'd at least get to watch him ride away when he left.

Before I even knew who he was, seeing him ride around the corner, then up to the curb, I was drawn to him. There was this halo of light that glowed around him as we walked up the driveway, and I had to force myself to look away. If he'd caught me staring, he probably would've thought I was an escaped mental patient.

Why would he want to be my friend?

Even in my shy, shutdown mode, I could tell Haze was trying to flirt with me, but I don't understand why. I never for even one second thought I'd be the type of girl to draw the attention of someone as handsome and rugged as him. He has the looks of someone you'd see in the movies, or on television, not of someone living in a town this small, trying to get the attention of a simple girl like me.

But his eyes . . .

The first time our eyes met, I felt a shiver. It was like he could see inside me.

His golden-brown eyes drew me in, and I had to keep telling myself to look away. I've never felt anything like that, not even with my ex-husband.

Toby.

Talk about a mood killer.

My eyes start to water, and I feel my way toward the table, finding a chair and sitting before I fall.

It's been eight months since I left him, but that day still runs through my mind like it was yesterday.

Francesca just left for the salon, so the house will be empty for a few hours. I should have enough time to pack my last few bags of clothes, then it's time for me to go.

How did my life end up like this? Where did I go wrong? What did I ever do to God to make him mad?

This isn't anything like I thought my life would turn out to be. When I got home from that women's weekend church retreat in Topeka, I hadn't expected to find my husband in bed with another woman.

His car was in the driveway, so I knew he was home. Walking in the side door, I called out Toby's name, but he didn't respond.

I checked the living room and his office, but he was nowhere to be found.

I dropped my suitcase in the laundry room on my way down the hall, then froze mid-step outside our bedroom door. The door was closed. It's never closed. Toby hates having the door closed, and I'd learned the hard way to never close it when he's home, so I never touched that handle again.

But it wasn't the closed door that caught my attention—it was the noises coming from the other side of it.

They were noises I didn't think I'd ever heard in that bedroom. Not even when I was in there myself.

Grunting. Slapping. Moaning.

I turned the handle and pushed the door so hard, it swung open and slammed against the wall.

That's when I saw my husband's bare-naked backside in-between the widespread legs of a woman who wasn't me. And then, when he jumped back, his dick waving in the wind, I saw the face of my younger sister, Francesca.

I screamed Toby's name so loud, even I cringed. I began hysterically crying at first, but his response killed my heart that instant.

He very calmly, still naked, sat on the bed next to a smirking Francesca and told me that under no uncertain terms was he going to listen to me screeching like a banshee. *Calm down or I'm not going to tell you what's going on.*

I was then informed that Toby would no longer answer to that name, and I needed to start calling him Tobias.

Not only that, but Francesca was going to be moving in with us, and she was going to be his second wife.

I stood there, jaw opening and closing like a goldfish. I couldn't believe what I was hearing.

When we started dating, I began going to church with him, but I had never heard of multiple wives being part of his religion. Was he crazy?

Apparently, the church had been going through leadership changes, ones I hadn't heard of yet because I was a 'lowly woman', and Tobias was now an elder for the congregation. And to gain and hold his new position as a leader, he needed to take another wife.

I wanted nothing to do with the changes, but no matter how much I tried to talk him out of it, tried to convince him that I was enough for him, he didn't budge.

With nowhere else to go, seemingly stuck in the mess that my life had turned into, I locked myself in the spare bedroom and cried for hours. I ended up falling asleep and waking up wondering where I was.

For those first few moments, I had no memory of the disaster of the night before. But when I saw the brown bedspread, not my white one, it all came flooding back.

I rushed out into the kitchen and there sat my sister on the lap of my husband, eating breakfast together like it was just any other day.

After one more desperate, yet unsuccessful, attempt at changing his mind, I knew I needed a plan.

I never hid the fact that I wanted a divorce, but he refused every attempt I made to get him to sign divorce papers when I asked. He ripped up three sets before I became desperate.

With some careful sneaking around, and the stack of papers mixed in with our normal monthly bills, I somehow managed to trick Toby into signing them.

After filing in a county almost an hour away, the ball was in my court. I had to keep everything hidden from him and the church, so I crossed my fingers every day that everything stayed on track until I got word the papers were in front of a judge.

Five months later, when Toby thought I was at an extra-long hair appointment and shopping trip, I stood in front of a judge and was told I was a free woman.

One week after that, I had to take my car in for an oil change, so I drove to the District Court offices and picked up my divorce decree.

Once I had it in my hand, step two of my plan kicked into action.

I needed to pack my things without anyone noticing, and it wasn't easy.

So, with Francesca at the salon and Toby at a church meeting, I saw my chance and took it.

I had stashed a couple suitcases in the trunk during the prior week, but that day, I made three trips out to my car, loading as much into the backseat as I could fit, before he came home early.

I was in our bedroom, zipping my last duffle bag, when I heard him yell my name. And before I could think of what to do next, his footsteps came thundering down the hall.

He entered the bedroom ready for a fight.

When he rounded the side of the bed, I tried to crawl over the top and get to the other side, but he grabbed my leg and pulled me back.

My face hit the mattress as he dragged me off the bed. I curled into a ball as my butt hit the floor, but it wasn't enough.

Toby hit and kicked anywhere he could before I managed to get out of his reach. I crawled over to a table we had set against the wall and pulled on the cord for the lamp. His fists were still hitting me, but the crash of the glass against the hardwood somehow made him stop.

And I used that split second to my advantage. I got to my feet, ignoring the throbbing pain all over my body, and I ran. I made it to the kitchen island before he caught up with me.

Toby grabbed for my elbow, but I swung it back at him, hitting him in the chest. His cry out was a tiny victory. Until he slapped me in retaliation.

I fumbled for my purse strap, trying to get my cell phone to call the police, but my hand found something I didn't expect until after it was swinging through the air. Time slowed to an eerie stretched-out few seconds as I watched myself hit my now ex-husband in the head with a cast iron frying pan.

You know when you watch those crime shows on television, and the wives insist they didn't mean to kill their husbands? I never believed them until that day.

I seriously thought I'd killed him.

But luckily for me, and for him, that's not what happened.

The pan only grazed the side of his head, but it did knock him over, and he fell to the floor. And in his stunned state, curled up on the linoleum, with his head in his hands, he didn't come after me again. So, I took off.

With one last run to the bedroom, I grabbed my duffle bag and was out the front door and in my car in seconds.

After my shaking hands dropped my keys on the floorboard numerous times, I finally managed to get the right key in the ignition.

And as I drove away, I felt nothing.

I didn't cry until I saw Gram two days and four states later.

I was finally free and ready to start over.

Tellison has been my home ever since.

I love my job. I've got an awesome roommate. And apparently, I've met a guy.

A guy in a motorcycle club that I didn't ever want to get involved with.

What do I do now?

CHAPTER THIRTEEN

SMOKE

"When is this heat gonna go away?" Kraken whines before taking a sip of his beer. "I'm sick of sweatin' my balls off in the shop. It's supposed to be fall."

"No clue, Brother," I respond, then polish off the rest of my first beer. Diego swipes my empty for a fresh one. "Thanks, Diego."

"No problemo," he says with a nod.

I'm half a swig into beer number two when the front doors open behind me and I hear a trample of footsteps. Turning to see what all the commotion is about, I see Haze jogging straight for me.

"Smoke," he pants when he steps between my spread legs, setting his hands on my knees as he catches his breath. "We need to talk."

Haze spent the last few hours doing yardwork with Whiskey at Duchess and Angel's house in town. They're renting it out, but the club has taken responsibility for the maintenance and such. And seeing what Haze looks like right now, I might volunteer him for all the housework.

Sweat dripping down his brow, Haze wipes his forehead with the back of his hand. When he raises his arm, it draws my attention to the shifting of his cut, revealing that he's not wearing a shirt under his leather. Damn, does he look good.

There are a few smudges of dirt on his chest, and even a small clump of dried mud on his stomach, but it's his arms that are killing me most. His tan is even darker than before, after hours in the sun, and his biceps are solid, rock hard, and flexing with his every movement.

But before I can speak, or even attempt to draw him in for a kiss, Haze starts talking a mile a minute.

"I met her. She's it. You have to meet her, Smoke."

Needing him to slow down, rewind, and start over, I set one hand on his shoulder and the other on top of his hand on my knee. Whatever happened while he was gone sounds important, and I want all the details. Especially if *she* is *our* she.

"Hold on there, hotshot. If you're about to say what I think you're about to say, let's take this upstairs. The main room ain't no place for this talk."

I jump off my stool and pull him along with me up the stairs to our rooms. His door is unlocked, so I push it open and lead us in. Sitting on the end of his bed, I yank him down beside me, but he trips over his own feet and lands on top of me. I take our current position to my advantage and get that kiss I wanted.

Haze's lips crash against mine, and we battle for dominance. His hands thread through my loose hair, tugging my head to an angle that's to his liking. I nip his lower lip with my teeth and suck it into my mouth. He kisses me back, his tongue playing with mine, as I feel his bulge rub against my hip.

I reach my arms around his waist and grab hold of his backside, pulling him down against me even harder.

Goosebumps rise all over my body as I feel a slight pinch on my dick from my zipper, but I could care less right now if I end up with a funky imprint on my skin. Feeling Haze rut his own hard cock against mine, denim to denim, is worth any discomfort or inconvenience.

"Fuck, you feel good," I groan as Haze's lips move down my chin, then onto my neck. He nips a spot that causes my hips to buck like a rodeo bronco. "Shit," I wheeze. "Again."

And he does. For a few more minutes, we move against each other, taking what we need while giving to the other. Nothing short of grinding each other into the mattress, we finally come up for air.

Hands braced on the mattress on each side of my head, Haze pulls back, panting. "Now, that was one hell of a hello."

"I can't help that I missed you." I sneak another quick peck before we untangle and sit up. Legs folded crisscross applesauce style, I get us back to the topic of importance. "Now, slow down and tell me what you're babbling about some woman for."

Haze takes a deep breath and folds his hands in his lap. He's got a super serious look on his face. "She's the one for us."

"Who's she?" So, I was right. He thinks he found our one.

Haze's eyes are locked on mine. "Abby."

"Abby who?" At first, I recognize the name but can't place it. But then I remember. "The woman who works at The Lodge. The one who moved into Duchess and Angel's house with Meredith?"

"Yes. She's ours. I just know it." Haze's words rush out like he can't keep them in.

There's a feeling of happiness and heat radiating off Haze, one I know so well even after such a short time together. It's hard to describe, but every time he and I are done being intimate, he gives off this aura of joy. Haze's smile is unending, his cheeks are flushed, and even his speech sounds a little bit deeper. And that's exactly how he is right now.

Everything about Haze is telling me that something good happened today, and I want to know it all. "Tell me everything."

"She's beautiful, but words aren't even enough. She's not tall, her head only comes up to my shoulders." While Haze is talking, his hands are moving like he's conducting a band. "She has long black hair all the way to her ass. Her eyes are so dark, they're almost black, and the way she looks at you, her eyes speak more than she does."

"What do you mean? Is she shy?"

"Extremely shy. She looked at the ground or over my shoulder the whole time I was talking to her. It's like she was afraid of me. Whiskey said she's a bit skittish when she first meets people. I have a feeling that she didn't have a good past back wherever she came from. Like someone hurt her."

That doesn't sound good. I like the way he described her physical attributes—she sounds like an attractive woman. But just the idea of her having anything bad happen to her makes my skin crawl. There's nothing in this world I hate more than a hurt woman. And if it was a man who put his hands on her, he's a dead man walking.

But as much as I like the good and hate the bad, what if she's not interested in getting involved with people like us? If she's not in a place in her life where she can handle one person, this could be a deal breaker. Haze and I are a package deal.

"While she does sound like a woman I'd like to meet, I don't want to intrude on her life if she's not ready. We're a lot to deal with, you and me. What if we're too much?"

Haze smiles. I think he can read my mind more than I can sometimes. He gets me. "I get what you're saying, Smoke. I know it won't be easy, but something in here," he taps his chest, "tells me that she's worth it. You just need to see her. See what I did. It's all in her eyes."

"If I agree to meet her, will that make you happy?" I reach out and grab his hand. I need to touch him. I need to feel his skin against mine.

"It will," he replies. "We can maybe go to The Lodge one night for dinner. If she's there, we can try and talk to her.

We won't be pushy or bring up a relationship, only just so you can try and get a read on her. I wanna see if you see what I do. And her skin is so damn soft, ugh! I'd do anything to hold her hand again."

"Talk about a conversation one-eighty." His switch from just meeting her, to telling me he touched her, makes my back straighten a bit. "What exactly did you all do with this woman while you were supposed to be doing yardwork?"

"Smoke," Haze's head tilts a little to the side, "please don't be like that. You have nothing to be jealous about. I may or may not have touched her hand, but that's all. Like I said before, she has this habit of looking at the floor when she's talking, so I brushed my hand against hers to get her attention."

"I'm not jealous, Haze. I'm just a little hesitant. This is all still so new." I sigh. "I haven't met her, and I hear you touched her. You're still mine."

"And I always will be." His free hand traces my cheek. "If you meet her and don't like her, we move on. But you and me are forever, right?"

"We sure are."

Haze closes his eyes as he leans in. We go back to kissing like earlier, except this time with no rolling around and humping each other like rabid dogs. This time, we stay seated, knees against knees, just savoring. But we're interrupted when both our phones start beeping. I feel my chest vibrate through my cut pocket.

We both let out a deep groan as we separate to dig our phones out. I wake up the screen and see a text message.

Cypher: Emergency Church NOW!

I look up at Haze. "You get the summons to Church too?"

"Yup. I guess we gotta go," he replies. "Rain check on the kissing?"

"I'll hold you to it." I finagle myself off the bed and adjust my t-shirt, pulling the bottom down to straighten it. "But would you mind putting a shirt on before we go down? I'd rather I be the only one to see you half naked."

Haze smacks me on the ass, shocking me as he gets up. "If you say so, boss."

He shrugs off his cut, hands it me, and grabs a clean t-shirt from his dresser. As we walk out the door and down the hall, he finally puts it on. I hand him back his cut at the bottom of the stairs, then we head into Church, side by side.

I take my seat and see mostly everyone is here. It's Saturday night, so most of the club is here for a night of drinking, hanging out, and a little bit of mayhem. Club party nights have a tendency to get wild and crazy, but the last-minute text tells me we won't be raising hell tonight.

Fifteen minutes later, Whiskey slams his gavel—*Bang!*—and everyone goes quiet.

"I'd say sorry for interrupting your evenings, but I'm not. We've got a problem."

"What's up, Prez?" Brewer asks from beside me.

"Cypher has detected a few breaches in our security system, one at The Lodge and the other here for the clubhouse. He's still up in his room diggin' through a whole shit load of zeros and ones to figure out who or what we're dealing with." He rolls his eyes. "His words, not mine."

"Someone hacked into Cypher's computer and is spying on us?" Trooper questions.

"From what Cypher said, it's not his computer directly. But with everything being wireless and floating around in the web," Whiskey raises a hand and swirls it through the air, "I guess nothing is impenetrable."

"Any idea what this mystery hacker is looking for?" Haze asks.

"It was security footage," Whiskey replies. "With whatever hidden tech magic he's got working, Cypher was able to see what the hacker was looking at."

"Any clues on what they were trying to find?" Ring asks. "Or if they found it?"

"Between The Lodge and here, it could be almost any one of us," I think out loud.

"Exactly, which is why I'm putting the clubhouse on soft lockdown," Whiskey continues. "Hammer and I discussed this, so we're reimplementing the buddy ride rule. No one in or out without another Brother. And the women are to stay on the premises at all times. Those who live in cabins must have a Prospect on their front porches at all times when someone is inside."

"I'd rather the cabins be used for sleeping only, so Whiskey's, mine, and Steel and Ring's kiddos and Old Ladies will be in the clubhouse during the daytime," Hammer adds. "Mountain and Blue have already volunteered their room as a daytime nap room. If anyone has a problem with the kiddos being around, too fuckin' bad."

Everyone looks at Gunner. "What the fuck? This is a lockdown. Why would I raise a stink?"

"Because you always do, man," Whiskey barks. "But if I hear one peep outta you about them, I'll tie you to a chair and lock you in a closet. With an unknown threat looming, I want peace in my clubhouse. Capiche?"

"Yes, sir." Gunner mock salutes and shrinks in his chair.

"Now that we have that covered, does anyone have people on the outside we need to call in?"

"Ray, Sara, and Jamie are in Illinois visiting family," Steel speaks up. "Do we need to call them back?"

"Give him a call and fill him in," Whiskey replies. "He's still a hangaround, so there's no need for him to be here, but it's his choice to jump into the fire or not."

"I have a feeling he'll be on the road before you hang up the phone." Mountain chuckles, making all of us laugh. "That man wants his Prospect cut way too bad to stay away from whatever mess seems to have found us this time."

"Fuck," Whiskey groans as he runs his hand down his face, tugging on his beard. "Shit just cleared from our last fuckin' adventure. Who the hell'd we piss off now?"

Just then, one of the doors opens and Cypher comes hustling in, laptop in hand. "I think I found something."

"Spill," Whiskey snaps, leaning forward in his chair.

Cypher skirts around the room until he's at the front, where he plugs a cord into his computer. Half the room goes dark as the projector screen behind Whiskey's head drops down. And just like we're all trained to follow the light, everyone adjusts their chairs and turns to face the square of white now glowing on the wall.

The image on the screen switches from a bunch of folder icons on his desktop screen to six separate security camera feeds.

"These are the times and dates that each camera view was accessed for the first time." Cypher points at each one with a red laser pointer. "There's still more to go through, but I wanted to give an update with this first big discovery. I haven't found any similarities between each set of times yet, but I've got hundreds of more hours to go through."

"I'll help," Gunner volunteers. "It'll keep me outta the way of the crotch goblins." He chuckles at his own comment, but it falls flat when no one else finds him funny. No response except one pissed-off father.

"What the fuck did you just call my kids?" Hammer roars as he jumps to his feet, his chair crashing back against the doors behind him. His hands are braced on the table, and if looks could kill, Gunner would be meeting Saint Peter at the pearly gates before being sent straight to hell.

"THAT'S ENOUGH FROM YOU TWO!" Whiskey roars. "Gunner, while I appreciate the offer to help Cypher, calling the little ones a name like that was unnecessary. Kinda funny, but unnecessary."

The room fills with coughs and snickers from everyone trying not to laugh too loud. Everyone but Hammer, that is.

He turns to glare at Whiskey. "You think it's funny he called our kids crotch goblins?"

"Oh, come on, Hammer." Whiskey leans back in his chair. "You gotta admit, it was pretty funny. Lighten up, man. We've got bigger fish to fry right now."

"Whatever," Hammer pouts. He turns to straighten his chair, then drops into it with a *harumph*. But his pissed-off glare never leaves Gunner, who, unfortunately for him, is seated directly in front of Hammer.

"You," Mountain points at Hammer from his seat at the far end of the table, "grow the fuck up. You're a dad now. Stop acting like a child yourself. Those days for you are over."

"I'll help keep an eye on the kiddos," Butch offers. "I wouldn't mind more time with my grandsons."

"Sounds good to me," Mountain says as he holds out a fist to Butch. They fist bump, then settle back in their chairs.

"Anything else, Cypher?" Whiskey asks. "Otherwise, we're ending this circus."

"Nope," Cypher replies. "I need to head back to my room and keep workin'."

"Let's set up a patrol schedule for here and at The Lodge and brewery, since that seems to be what whoever's out there is watching," Steel suggests.

"Good idea," Whiskey says. "Enforcers, y'all stay here and we'll work out a plan. Everyone else, get the fuck out, but don't go far. Assignments will be comin' your way shortly."

Bang! Whiskey slams the gavel, and most of us clear the room.

After snagging a couple sodas off the bar, Haze and I plop our butts on one of the couches and wait to be told our security duties for the night.

This isn't exactly how I thought the night would go, especially after Haze's announcement that he found the woman he thinks is meant for us. If Haze says she's the one for us, I believe him.

But like many things in our life, unpredictable seems to be the name of the game. For us, the club comes first. So, when this new threat is taken care of, I plan on finding out all I can about Abby. I just hope it's sooner than later.

CHAPTER FOURTEEN

ABBY

It's a crisp fall day, and the perfect start to what I decide is going to be a good day. Other than work, there's nothing special about this Sunday morning, but because I want to have a good day, I start it in a good mood.

Hot shower, check. Wearing my favorite holey blue jeans, check. Green tank top under my tie-dye hoodie with The Lodge logo, check. Hair braided and twisted back into a messy bun, check.

I loop my purse over my shoulder, grab my tumbler full of coffee, and head out the door. Or at least, that was my intention.

Door knob still in hand and one foot in the air, my forward momentum comes to a quick screeching halt.

The garage is empty. My car is missing. Where the heck is it?

Turning around, I set everything on the table, fish my phone out of my purse, then flip on the light before stepping out into the garage. A few steps forward and I'm standing exactly where my car is supposed to be sitting. This is where I should be opening the door, sliding in, and driving away to go to work. Where is it?

Spinning in a circle, I look around the open space, wondering if it'll magically reappear in a different spot. As if fairies snuck in while I was sleeping and hid it behind the snowblower.

"How am I gonna get to work?" I ask the empty garage.

While no one has confronted me about the state of my car, I've seen the looks people have given it. Everyone thinks it's a piece of junk, and that's because it is.

Any time I need to have the oil changed, the employees at the tire and oil change place stare at the car like it's about to explode. And some days, I myself wonder if it will. But since I'm so close to saving enough for a down payment on something better, I'm milking that car for every last mile it'll give me.

At least, I was.

Shit, I need to call Ring.

Back in the kitchen, I peek out the front window, just in case I mysteriously forgot to park inside when I got home from the gas station last night, but nope, no car in the driveway.

I hit Ring's contact icon and tap the speakerphone button.

"Hey, Abby. What's up?"

"Morning, Ring. I hope I'm not calling too early."

"Nope. I've been awake for a while. Everything okay?"

"Yea," I stall for a second, "about that . . . I seem to be having some car trouble and can't make it in to work today. Would you mind if I called someone to cover for me?"

This would be the first day I call in since I started back in February, so hopefully, it's okay.

"Is the battery dead? I can have someone come over and give you a jump start."

"Oh no," I mumble, trying not to sound panicked about a visitor. "That's okay. I'll just call a tow truck and see if someone can take a look at it."

"Abby, it's Sunday. Anyone you call is gonna charge you a fortune. Why don't I have one of the guys who work in the shop swing by? They won't charge you a penny 'til they figure out the problem."

"I can't ask anyone to do that. It's not their job to work on my car."

"Don't worry about it, I insist." I hear some talking in the background, then Ring comes back on the line. "Smoke here heard me talking about your problem. He's on his way out the door to you now. He'll be there in a jiffy."

"Ring, no." I panic. Shit, I'm panicking. If this Smoke guy shows up and sees I was lying, there's no telling what will happen. "I'll figure something out."

"Too late, Abby. He's on his way. Maybe he can give you a ride to work if he can't get it started. Call me back once you know what's what. Bye." And he hangs up.

He started talking, and before I knew it, he didn't stop until he hung up. What do I do now?

I can't hide in the closet and wait for whoever is going to appear at my door to disappear. I may not know the inside workings of the motorcycle club, but I've been around long enough to know they don't stand down from a problem. And rumor has it, they've had a few run-ins with the dark side lately.

It's not long before I hear the rumble of motorcycles outside.

Looking out the window, I see two guys roll across the cul-de-sac and up my driveway. I recognize one of them. The guy on the right is Steel, Meredith's older brother. He helped her move some of her things in.

Now, the other guy, I don't really know. I recognize him, probably from being at the bar or brewery, but we've never met. I'm guessing this is Smoke.

Steel stays seated on his Harley, but Smoke dismounts and starts up the front walk. I scramble to the front door and open it just as he raises his hand to knock.

I stare at him through the screen door, neither of us moving. Totally aware of the fact that he's checking me out, I stand in the foyer and gawk at him.

He's drop-dead handsome. Is that something you can say about a man? Too bad if you can't because this guy is fine.

His long, dark brown hair is tied back at his nape, and a short, trimmed beard covers his chin. A tight white t-shirt stretches across his chest, under the black leather vest all the club members wear. And his jeans should be illegal. Calling them normal blue jeans would be a sin. The faded denim hugs the front of his thighs and definitely doesn't leave much to the imagination in the zipper area. How can somebody ride a motorcycle when they're carrying a package like that?

What in the jumping Josephine am I saying? A package? I've never looked at a man's . . . private parts . . . and thought something like that. I think I need to get my head examined.

"Ahem," he coughs, "sorry to interrupt your perusing, but my name's Smoke. Ring said you might be in need of some help."

I feel my cheeks burst into flames. I know I'm blushing like nobody's business and need to get my act together. I've never met this man, so why am I acting like this?

"Sorry," I mumble. "Come on in."

Smoke opens the screen door but doesn't step inside. That's when I realize I still haven't moved.

"Oh, sorry. My brain's a bit mush today. Haven't drank my coffee yet." My feet finally get the message and spin around before marching into the kitchen.

"Are you sure you're okay? I can come back another time if you're busy," Smoke says as I chug my now lukewarm coffee. "But I promise I can look at your car and figure out what's wrong real quick."

"I'm not busy. It's okay. But you don't need to look at my car. I tried to tell Ring I'd figure it out, but he insisted on sending you. Then he hung up before I could say another word."

"That sounds like Ring." He chuckles. "He's a good guy, though. I'm sure you know that since you work with him."

"He's been great." I tuck my sweaty hands in the pocket of my sweatshirt and rock on my heels, while staring at my shoes. "The job's great. Everything's great." And now, I'm babbling.

I hear footsteps, then see two black boots stop in front of mine. A hand appears under my chin, and by instinct, I feel myself flinch when his finger touches my chin. With the slightest pressure, my face is tilted up and I look up into his dark brown eyes.

"Are you okay, Abby?" I see his lips move, but the static in my ears doesn't let the sound through.

All I can do is nod.

Before I can think, my body is being moved, and I'm sitting in a chair. Smoke is kneeling in front of me, rubbing my back as the static fades, and I start to get feeling back in my legs.

"Oh my god," I groan into my hands. As if I wasn't embarrassed before, I look up and see a sad smile on his face. "You can leave now if you want. You don't need to deal with whatever the heck craziness seems to have clobbered me this morning."

"Hey, it's okay." Smoke, I'm sure, is trying to reassure me, but it's not working. "How about you stay sitting here for a minute, and I'll go take a look at your car?"

He stands, but his words make me chase him. I jump up and grab hold of his forearm. "No!"

"Why not? I'll be in and out in no time."

"Because my car is gone," I spit out.

His eyebrows furrow. Crap, why does he have to look hot even when he's confused? "What do you mean gone?"

I let his arm go and walk toward the side door. I pull it open and wave my hand toward the vast empty space. "My car's missing and I don't know where it is."

Smoke walks around the table, and once he's right in front of me, chest to chest, he looks where I'm pointing. He looks at me, then in the garage, then back at me again a few times. "I guess you weren't kidding. Does your car have a habit of doing a Houdini when you need to go places?"

And that breaks the tension. I start laughing so hard, I snort. My eyes bug out as I look at Smoke, and I slap a hand over my mouth, but the laughs just keep coming.

"That wasn't even that funny, but I'm glad you liked my joke." Then Smoke keeps going. "How 'bout this one? Why does a duck have tail feathers? . . . To cover his butt quack."

His eyebrows start doing this up and down dance, and I lose it again. This time, I can't control the snorts, and they don't seem to stop until I'm bent over, hand on the table, laughing until my sides hurt.

"Oh my gosh." I chuckle as I wipe my fingers under my eyes, trying to clear the tears of laughter. "I don't think I've done that in years."

"Done what?" Smoke looks at me like he's trying to solve a puzzle. "Laughed? Everyone should laugh every day."

"Things have been a little rough lately." I shrug. "So, thank you for that. I don't feel like my head's gonna pop off anymore."

"Anytime you need a joke, I'm your man." Before I can stop him, he grabs my phone from where I left it on the table and starts tapping away. I hear a ding from somewhere, and he pulls his phone from somewhere inside of his vest. One phone in each hand, his thumbs click the screens a few times, then he sets mine back down. "There, now you can call or text anytime you need a giggle."

"You don't—"

"It wasn't a request, little lady." Smoke lifts my chin again. "You got my number. You can decide whether you use it or not. Okay?"

"Okay," I repeat.

"Now, back to the subject at hand." Smoke lets me go, steps back, and starts spinning his phone around in one hand. "Did you happen to leave your garage door open last night?"

I shake my head. "I know I closed it. I always do."

And I do. While I have no reason to be hiding in this town, I never leave my car where it can be seen from the street. When at work, I park behind the building, backed into a spot near the tree line. And when at home, my car is always in the garage with the door closed.

"Okay." He reaches for my hand, threading his fingers through mine. And again, when my instinct to flee kicks in, I try to back away and get my hand free. But this time, Smoke echoes my steps until my butt hits the edge of the dining table, stopping me from going any further.

"Can you let go of my hand, please?" I ask as I stare down at my hand curled inside his much larger one.

"No," he answers. "I think I like holding your hand."

"But I just met you." I look up but to the side, trying to pretend I'm not drawn to him.

Using his left hand, he turns my face to his. "Would it be weird if I said I feel like I already know you?"

"Yes!" I say, exasperated. I don't know what's happening to me, but mere minutes in this man's presence and I'm a light-headed, bumbling mess. Just like I was when I met Haze the other day.

Oh no! Am I floozy? How can I be attracted to two men only minutes after meeting them? This isn't like me at all.

"Look, Abby, I'm sorry. I won't bug you anymore, I promise." Smoke lets go of my hand and backs a few feet away, hands raised in front of him. "Let's start over and talk about what's going on. I do have another question about your car."

"Okay." Starting over, that sounds good to me. Clear slate.

"Do you have any ideas on who would want to steal your car?"

"I might." I didn't want to think this was a possibility, but if it would be anyone, it'd be him. He's the one who always refused to buy me a new car, but he sure held this one over my head. "My ex-husband."

Smoke looks shocked. "You were married?"

"I was. But I've been divorced for almost a year. I moved here to get a new start." I begin pacing back and forth, from the table to the couch, and back again. "But if anyone would do something like this, it'd be him."

I have no idea how he found me here. I don't recall ever telling Toby where my Gram lives, but that obviously didn't stop him. He probably used connections he has in that mess of a church congregation he swore had to become our way of life. There were members who were involved with the local authorities, so I'd bet anything he tracked me down and stole my car under the cover of night.

When Smoke doesn't say anything, I turn around to see what's wrong, but I end up bouncing off his chest because he's right behind me.

Luckily for me, he's got quick reflexes. Smoke grabs me by the shoulders, saving me from falling on my butt.

The shock of everything comes crashing down all at once, and I suddenly feel like a fish out of water. I can't breathe. I open my mouth to inhale, but my throat feels like sandpaper and my chest is burning. My eyes start to water and I cough, trying to swallow, but nothing happens.

"Let's just take a deep breath. In . . ." Smoke begins to talk, and I lock onto his voice. I look at his chest and see it rise, so I try to breathe again, and this time, I can. Another few breaths in, my head has stopped spinning and I start to feel better.

"And out." Smoke's exhale slides across my forehead and sends shivers down my spine. But not in a creepy way. Not in the way like every time Toby would yell at me about something in the house not being done to his liking.

No, these shivers, these are different. I don't know how, but they're different.

A few dozen more breaths assisted by my rescuer and I'm ten times better. "I'm good now." I force myself to step out of his grasp, then I cross my arms, trying to put my shield back up.

"Are you sure?" Smoke asks reluctantly.

"I'm sure." I nod. "I guess I just need to figure out how to get to work."

"Work? You wanna go to work after all that?" Smoke waves an arm at me.

"I have to go to work. I'm the manager, ya know."

"Let me make a phone call and I'll let you know what the plan is." He grabs his phone from the table—wait, when did he put it there—and starts tapping.

"What plan?"

"The plan to find your car." He's still tapping away. His phone dings a few times, but his thumbs keep moving.

"That's not your problem. It's mine."

Smoke's head jerks up. "Abby, if your ex knows where you are, we need to get you somewhere safe. I'm guessing he's not supposed to know where you are?"

"No," I mumble.

"Then let me make this call." He walks into the living room, phone raised to his ear.

I can't hear what he's saying, but he keeps looking out the front window. I dash to the window in the kitchen and see Steel still sitting on his bike, his phone out as well. I'm guessing they're talking to each other, but why wouldn't Smoke just go outside?

Steel taps his screen, tucking his phone in his pocket, just as Smoke speaks up from behind me.

"I'm gonna give you a ride to work today."

"But why?"

"Will you do it if I say 'cause I said so?"

"No," I reply. "I don't wanna leave my house if you say I'm in danger."

"I get that," he says softly as he approaches me with small steps, like I'm an injured animal he's afraid to spook. Maybe that's what I am. "But my VP out there says I need to get you to work, so that's what we're gonna do."

"VP? What's that?"

"Steel is the club's Vice President. After Whiskey, he's the man in charge."

"Oh."

"Yeah, oh, and he says we should take you to work, at least for now. That way, we can keep an eye on you. That place has cameras like a fortress. And with the amount of people around, you'll never be alone."

"I don't know if that makes me feel better or worse."

"I promise, you'll be much safer there." He grabs my hand again, and this time, I don't flinch. "I'll give you a ride to work, then be back at closing to bring you home, unless something changes. Sound like a plan?"

"It doesn't sound like I have much of an option, do I?"

"Not really," he laughs, "but I've got a spare helmet for you. Just hold on tight to me, and I'll have you there in two shakes of a lamb's tail."

"I've never ridden on a motorcycle before."

"Never?"

"Nope. Until I moved here, I never even knew anyone who had one."

"Well then, you don't know what you're missin'. Grab your stuff and let's get rollin'."

So, I do. I guess this is what I'm doing today, riding on the back of a virtual stranger's motorcycle and letting him take me to work. Is this what a good day is?

I lock the front door behind me, then follow Smoke down the steps and to the black and chrome machines parked in my driveway.

"Hey, Abby," Steel says with a wave. "I hear we're your escort today."

"Hi, Steel. I guess so."

"Let's get this helmet on you." Smoke is holding a black full-faced helmet, one strap in each hand. "I don't think you'll get this on with your hair up like that. Can you undo the bun?"

I reach up and untwist the hair tie holding my bun up, letting the braid fall back, and then tuck a few loose strands behind my ears. "That okay?"

If I could guess, I think Smoke might be choking on his tongue. Steel coughs to break the stare down Smoke is giving me, snapping him back into action.

It's truly a heady feeling to have. I've gotten it twice now in a matter of days, and I don't know how to handle it. So, I tuck it deep inside to deal with at a later time, maybe when I'm not near either one of the men who have barged into my life and thrown my axis off center.

After helping me slide the helmet on and clipping the strap for me, Smoke leads me to the left side of his motorcycle and shows me which foot pegs are mine.

Smoke swings his right leg over, straddling the bike like it's no big deal, like he does this every day. Oh, that's right, he does. He stands it straight up, balancing it with his legs, then tells me to climb on.

Placing my left hand on his shoulder, then my left foot on the back peg, I climb up and pull my right leg under me to slide over the other side. Once both feet are on their respective pegs, I lower myself to sit on the seat. There's a backrest behind me, so I slide my butt back as far as I can go, giving Smoke room to take his seat.

"You good back there?" he turns his head and asks, smiling the whole time.

"I guess we're about to find out."

"Alright, hold on tight, okay? When we go around a corner, just lean your body with mine and don't let go."

"Let's just get this over with." I close my eyes and sigh.

And that's when the butterflies kick in. Smoke starts the engine, and my entire body begins to shake like I've never felt in my entire life.

I feel like I'm riding on top of an earthquake. This feeling is insane.

But before I can decide to either go with the flow, or jump off and hide in the bushes, we start moving.

My arms instinctively reach around Smoke's chest and my hands grip the front of his vest like it's my lifeline. I feel his chest shaking with laughter, but I don't know what he thinks is so funny. This is scary!

A second roar of thunder comes from my left as I see Steel fly past us in the other lane. He swerves back in front of us, then we follow him the rest of the way.

A few hair-raising curves and two corners that made me scream of surprising joy later, we pull into the parking lot of The Lodge and Moraine Craft Brewery. The ride went so much faster than I thought, I almost don't want to get off the motorcycle. I want to keep riding.

The bike shuts down, making this weird tinking noise, and Smoke taps my leg. "And this is where the ride ends. As much as I'd like to ride with you all day, we've both got work to do."

Standing up, I manage to swing my right leg around and back to the ground without falling on my face. Smoke follows and reaches for my chin. He unsnaps the buckle, then lets me take the helmet off myself.

One look at me and I can see his thinly veiled attempt at not laughing. I can only imagine how crazy my hair looks right now, but I don't care.

I smooth down as much as I can with my hands but know I'm going to need to brush it out and re-braid it to settle all the flyaways.

"Thanks for the ride, Smoke. I'm sure I can find a ride home, so don't worry about me."

"I don't think so." He hooks his hand into my elbow as I try to walk past him. "I said I'd be back to pick you up, so that's what I'm gonna do."

"But—"

"Nice try, but no. I'll be here a little before closing. Have a good day. Bye now."

I make one more attempt to say no, but he silences me with his finger on my lips. He drops a kiss on my forehead, then turns to get back on his bike. Along with Steel, who I forgot was even still here, he fires up his Harley and rides away.

I stand there, outside the back door of the bar, dumbfounded. Smoke basically just bulldozed me. He didn't listen to a single thing I said. He refused to take any objection, and I allowed him. But unlike how small and belittled I felt after Toby denied me when I asked for things, I don't feel that way now.

In fact, I feel the opposite. For some reason, I'm not afraid at all. I'm still nervous as heck but am expectedly looking forward to seeing Smoke again.

I'll let him come back and take me home. I don't know what will happen after that, but much like my other problems, I'll tuck the thought of the long-haired, muscly biker into my back pocket to worry about later.

Regardless of how I had to start my day, I choose to march forward. I'll worry about what happens later, well, later.

CHAPTER FIFTEEN

HAZE

"Are you sure this is a good idea?"

"It'll be fine." Smoke threads his fingers through mine, pulling me into his chest. He kisses my cheek, then tugs on the front of my cut with his free hand. "She's gonna find out about the two of us eventually. We can't exactly hide it from her if we plan on convincing her to be with both of us, right?"

"I guess you're right," I admit.

"Say that again. I'm right?" Smoke pulls himself away from me and looks up to the dark, star-filled sky above us. "Is the sky falling?"

"Quit being such a smartass, Smoke. Let's just get in there and see what happens. Maybe she won't care."

"It'll be fine, I promise." Smoke heads for the door and pulls it open. "One step at a time, remember?"

"Day one of the rest of our lives." I slide my hand across his stomach as I walk past him, stepping inside.

"Watch where you put that hand. I may not be responsible for my actions if you start that here," Smoke says right before he smacks my ass.

As soon as I'm two steps in, I find Abby right away. The bar is empty of customers, so she's hard to miss. It's eleven-thirty, and the bar closes at midnight on Sundays, so it looks like we're the last ones here.

Abby is wiping down tables, and as soon as the door shuts behind us, she looks up. She's got a smile on her face, but it slowly turns to a confused look. Her eyebrows scrunch in this crooked way where the one on the left is a little lower than the right. Then there's two little vertical creases that form between her eyebrows, making her look even more adorable.

She looks completely thrown off, and I know why—Abby wasn't expecting me to be here.

"Damn, she's cute when she's confused. Where has she been all our lives?" Smoke whispers beside me.

"No clue," I reply. "But we're not letting her get far."

"Hi, guys." Abby unknowingly interrupts our whispers. "What are you both doing here?"

I walk toward her, and as soon as I reach her, I settle my left hand on her side and kiss her temple. Her face gets even more frazzled when Smoke steps to her other side and does the same. Her eyes grow as big as saucers.

"You look beautiful," I tell her. And she does. The dark green tank top she's wearing makes her tan skin look even deeper.

Abby takes a few steps back out of our reach and positions herself in front of us. I step closer to Smoke and hook two fingers in his back pocket.

Smoke looks at me with a big smile. "That's what I thought when I picked her up this morning."

"You've got good taste." I smile back and give him a wink.

"Great minds think alike," Smoke replies with his own wink.

During our tiny conversation, Abby has curled into herself, a serving tray that was on the table she was cleaning now clutched to her chest.

"I'm sorry, Abby. We didn't mean to go off like that," I apologize. "It's just we can't help it when we see a beautiful lady like you."

"He's right," Smoke adds in. "We're only here to give you a ride home, not get in your way. Don't mind us. Pretend we aren't here. We'll just sit at the bar and wait 'til you're done."

Our apologies seem to snap her out of her self-imposed hiding, and she spins around, her long braid whipping behind her. What I wouldn't give to wrap that thing around my fist as I plow into her from behind. I can just imagine her black, silky tresses brushing my thighs while she rides my dick. Giddy up, cowgirl.

"Can I get you two anything to drink?"

Now, it's my turn to snap out of a daydream. Smoke has already situated himself on a stool at the middle of the bar. He's smirking like he can see the dirty movie playing in my mind.

"Just water, please," Smoke says.

"No beer?" Abby asks, hand already on a pilsner glass. She sets it down and grabs two pint glasses from a different stack.

I join the conversation after settling myself to Smoke's left. "Thanks, gorgeous, but we have to get you home, so no beer."

"We?" Abby looks up, and at the same time, she loses grip of the ice scooper and it clashes back into the bin. Between filling our glasses successfully during her second attempt, she asks, "As in both of you?"

"Yes, ma'am." Smoke slides his left hand over my shoulder and rubs the nape of my neck with his thumb. "As soon as Haze heard I was giving you a ride home, he wanted to come along."

I can't help but lean into Smoke's grasp, but my attention is focused on a very puzzled Abby. I hope me being here is okay. "Is that alright? Me being here?"

"Oh, no . . . I mean, yes . . . I mean, it's fine. I'm happy to see you both." Abby sets our waters on coasters and starts backing away slowly. "I've got more closing stuff to do. I'll be ready in forty-five minutes."

"No rush from us, darlin'. Do whatever you gotta do. We'll keep each other company." Smoke's hand has moved down and is now resting on the back of my chair. His fingers are tracing my shoulder blade where the arm hole of my cut meets my t-shirt.

Abby spins around and disappears behind a door, into what I know is a stock room. I turn my stool to face Smoke, displacing his hand. "Are you touching me on purpose? You're confusing the hell out of her."

"So what?" Smoke takes a drink, then uses his boot to spin my stool back to face the bar. "Touching you isn't illegal. And she'll get used to it eventually."

"I know." I sigh and take a sip of my water. "It's just that . . . now that we're here, I'm kinda freakin' out a bit."

Until this very second, I didn't know I was. But now that I said it out loud, I am. I'm freaked. What if she doesn't really like us? What if she doesn't like us together? What if she likes one of us more than the other? That might kill me more than actually growing the balls to get Smoke in the first place.

Abby reappears through the swinging door, a dish rack full of clean glasses in her hands. She balances the tray on her knee and stacks the glasses under the bar, her hands moving faster than a bird's wings.

"You have nothing to worry about, Haze. It'll all work out like it's supposed to." Smoke rubs my back, and I feel myself start to calm.

"Thanks." I give him a lazy smile and set my right hand on his knee. "We don't even know her yet and I'm losing my marbles."

Smoke nudges me with his elbow and wags his eyebrows up and down. "You can lose your marbles with me anytime."

That makes me laugh out loud, drawing Abby's attention to us. She may be fluttering around behind the bar like a bird on steroids, doing several things at once, but I don't miss her continuous glances. She's trying to be stealthy, but it's not working. Abby's checking us out just as much as we are her.

"So," I try and turn our conversation away from bedroom talk, "what do you think?"

"I think you were right." Smoke slides his hand over top of mine on his thigh and lifts them onto the bar. He flips my hand over, cradling the back of mine in his palm, then tracing my palm with the tips of the fingers from his right hand. "I get what you were saying about just knowing after one look."

"I told you she was the one." I work my right hand free, giving him my left instead, then tuck a wild strand of his hair behind his ear.

"But I do think you're onto something about her past," Smoke says, his eyes following Abby.

"Yea?" I ask, using his distraction to drop a quick kiss on his cheek.

That gets his attention, and he turns to look at me. "I see the uncertainty in her eyes. She's got something goin' on that we're gonna have to break through."

"Do you think we should talk to Whiskey about this?" I question while running my fingers over the inside of his forearm that's draped on the bar in front of me.

"I filled him in on the whole missing car and ex-husband thing." Smoke shakes his head slightly. "He said he'll have Cypher run a search on him. But with the security system breach, I'm not gonna push it too much yet. We'll watch over her for now. Just hearing her talk about her ex laying a hand on her pisses me off."

I can feel the anger rolling off Smoke from that last bit. And I feel the same way. While I knew whatever it was she was hiding from wasn't good, an abusive ex-husband was my worst fear.

When Smoke came back from dropping her off this morning, I was gone on errands, so I didn't see him until just before dinner. I walked into the clubhouse and was almost knocked over when he barreled into me. He pulled me into the alcove where the pool table is and told me everything he'd learned that morning. About her car being missing. About the fact she's divorced. And to top it off, Smoke put the pieces together and suspected the ex had hurt her.

I hadn't wanted to think that when I talked to her, but it's starting to look that way. Part of me still doesn't want to believe it. What kind of man would hurt Abby? A fucking soon-to-be-dead one, that's who.

"I'm sure she wouldn't have been hired without Cypher running a background check on her, so it can't be anything bad, can it?" I try thinking of something not so bad to settle us both, but until we know all the facts, I have to stay calm. In front of Abby, at least.

Smoke turns, his knees settling on either side of mine. He grabs hold of my hands and leans into my space, forcing me to look at him. "No matter what it is she's going through, we'll help her through it. I promise."

I feel all the wind leave my sails. My shoulders slouch a bit and I look down at our hands. "Why did I wait so long to get you?" I think I'll always beat myself up on the inside for doubting our connection.

"Hey, now, none of that. I can see your thoughts in your eyes." Smoke tries to reassure me. "Things happened when they were meant to. Maybe our timing led us right here. We got together just in time to meet her. Look at her." Smoke lets my hands go before he turns his stool. I lean forward and rest my right arm over his shoulder.

"She's trying so hard not to look at us," I whisper, my head next to his.

"I think it's hot." Smoke looks over his shoulder at me.

"You're a dork." I use my boot and spin him to face forward. "Let the lady work, or we'll never get her home."

But Smoke is right—Abby's trying to look busy. Her nose is buried in receipts, but she's failing miserably because every time she sets one down, her eyes peek to the side, looking to see what we're doing. I'd hate to be a cocky man, but if I had to guess, I'd say a certain raven-haired lady is just as curious about us as we are her.

"Thank you." I brush the same stubborn piece of Smoke's hair back. For some reason, he doesn't have it tied back in a ponytail anymore. He did this morning. I remember distinctly that he tied it back when we were standing at the bathroom sink while I was brushing my teeth.

It's unusual for him to have it down, especially since he spent all day at Rebel Repairs. Long hair and moving motorcycle parts don't mix well. "You know, your hair is gonna be a mess when we get home."

Smoke just took a drink, so he sets the empty cup down and chuckles as he crunches a few ice cubes. "It'll be even more of a mess when I get done with you later."

His innuendo makes me snicker. "You promise?"

Smoke watches my hand disappear below the overhang of the bar. His eyes widen when my fingers slide across the denim of his thigh. His mouth opens in a soft gasp when my fingers keep moving, brushing against his inseam, then shifting up, my pinky feeling the bulge tucked inside.

"You know it," Smoke growls before bombarding me with a kiss. Not a long one, but definitely not a peck either. I hear something clatter as it hits the floor, so I pull back an inch and peek over Smoke's shoulder. "What'd she drop?" Smoke whispers.

"The napkin straw holder thingy," I whisper back.

"What'd you think she'd do if I threw you down on the floor and took you right here?" Smoke chuckles, eyes on me. He's not turning around on purpose, trying to see what I want to do.

"Let's not and say we didn't." I push his shoulders and force him back onto his own stool, then grab my water and chug it. "You promised me hair messing duties later. Let's leave that for our bed, not the bar floor."

"You said *our* bed." It's Smoke's turn to be shocked.

"What are you talkin' about?" I look at him like he's got two heads.

"You said *our* bed," he repeats. "That's the first time you've said anything in regard to something being an *our* thing."

"Oh," he's right, "you're right."

"HA!" Smoke cheers. "You said it again. I'm right!"

I roll my eyes and spin my back to the bar. From this position, I can look to the left and see Smoke, and Abby still at the far end of the bar. "You're never gonna let me forget that, are you?"

"Nope." Smoke crosses his arms. "You said I'm right twice now. That means I'm right for the rest of the night. You may get to put your cock in my ass, but I'm gonna be the one in charge later."

"Will you keep your voice down?" I punch Smoke in the forearm. "Let's change the subject to something more pressing. What are we gonna do about this asshole ex-husband?"

"I say we hunt him down, drag his ass back here, and hang him upside down in the barn." Smoke grunts. "That should teach him a lesson about hurting our woman."

"She's not our woman yet, Smoke," I remind him.

"But she will be," Smoke declares like he can predict the future. "Until then, I say we do all we can to get her to be our woman. That way, she'll never have to worry about him again."

"I like the sound of that."

"Me too."

Smoke and I both look, not hiding where we're looking, at Abby. She stacks a bunch of file folders, then slides them into a drawer under the cash register. She turns and sees us watching her.

"Everything okay down there?"

"Everything's perfect," I reply with a smile.

"Let me grab my purse, and I'll be ready to lock up."

"No worries," Smoke answers. "We're ready when you are."

CHAPTER SIXTEEN

ABBY

"Thanks, gorgeous, but we have to drive you home," Haze says as he settles himself on the stool next to Smoke.

"We?" I was only expecting Smoke, so it threw me for a loop seeing both of the guys I find myself attracted to walk in together. But hearing they're both taking me home throws me off my game even more. I'm in the middle of getting them some water when I drop the ice scooper and it lands back in the bin with a crash. Trying to save face, I pick it up like nothing happened and keep working. "As in both of you?"

"Yes, ma'am," Smoke replies. As I fill the glasses, I watch Smoke scoot a little to his left, closer to Haze, and put his arm around his shoulder. "As soon as Haze heard I was giving you a ride home, he wanted to come along."

And if I'm not mistaken, I see Haze's eyes flutter a little at Smoke's touch, like he's enjoying it. I feel my head tip to the right a little as I snap myself out of it. I can't stare at them. That'd be rude.

"Is that alright? Me being here?" Haze asks me.

"Oh, no . . . I mean, yes . . . I mean, it's fine." I set the glasses in front of them and back into the counter behind me, almost throwing myself off balance. But I correct my footing and continue backing down the bar, away from the distractingly hot men in front of me. "I'm happy to see you both. I've got some more closing stuff to do. I'll be ready in forty-five minutes."

"No rush from us, darlin'. Do whatever you gotta do. We'll keep each other company," Smoke comments like he doesn't have a care in the world.

The farther away I get, the faster I shuffle my feet. I need to get away from them before I say something stupid. At the end, I push my way into the stock room and lean against the wall.

Since when did I turn into a clumsy, staring, bumbling, crazy person? Ever since those two walked in, I've lost all my senses.

And they're touching each other! First, Haze put his hand in Smoke's back pocket. Then, they were almost holding hands while talking to me. Smoke had his hand on Haze, and Haze seemed to like it. He didn't brush him off. In fact, he was leaning into it. And they both kissed my cheeks!

I've never seen men touch each other like that before. Well, I have, but only gay men. Not that there's anything wrong with that.

Wait a minute . . . are Smoke and Haze gay? Have I been reading them wrong? Have they not been flirting with me? Is this just how they are? Do they do that with everyone they know?

"How the hell am I supposed to know?" I say out loud like I'm going to answer myself. Crazy person, table for one, please.

And what am I still doing back here? I'm pacing the stock room, getting none of my work done in the process. I need to put on my 'nothing affects me' face and get back out there. I need to focus on my closing tasks and get home.

Focus on the end goal—warm shower, clean clothes, a mug of hot tea. Sign me up.

I grab a tray of clean glasses and push the swinging door open, then begin stacking them behind the bar. After that's done, I refill the straw holders, dropping one when I catch them canoodling, then head to the register. Ignoring the two men across the room, I hit 'save' and 'print' on the day's receipts and wait for the printer to spit out a mile-long piece of paper.

But my eyes keep betraying me. Every turn I make to do something else on my checklist, I find myself looking at Haze and Smoke.

And every time I do, something new is happening. They don't seem to be able to stay in one position for long. Either one of them is shifting on their stool, touching the other's hand, laughing at something, or even leaning on the other. And they're constantly touching each other. It's never inappropriate, but I have to admit I did see one cute thing.

Smoke's hair is looking a bit wild, I'm guessing from riding his motorcycle, so Haze tucked a piece of it behind his ear. And then Smoke kissed Haze's knuckles. Totally swoon-worthy moment I feel guilty of intruding on. I feel like a peeping Tom.

But I have to admit that the affection they show each other is sweet. I wish I had someone like that.

Done sorting through this morning's delivery order sheets, I put the file folders away, and when I turn and look up, I see both of them staring at me with smiles on their faces.

They're both facing forward, hands clasped together on the bar.

"Everything okay down there?" I ask, trying to break the silence.

"Everything's perfect," Haze calls out.

"Let me grab my purse, and I'll be ready to lock up."

"No worries," Smoke replies. "We're ready when you are."

I grab my sweatshirt from under the bar and put it on, then get my purse from my office. I've got a satchel purse, so once it's looped over my shoulder, I head for the front doors, deadbolt them, and turn off the open sign.

"Need any help?" Haze asks as he and Smoke get up and push in their stools.

"Nope, I'm good." I take one last look behind the bar and start flipping light switches. "Follow me toward the back door so I can shut everything off and set the alarm."

And like the perfect gentlemen, they do. I shut off the lights in the kitchen, bathrooms, and server's prep area before hitting the 'arm alarm' button on the panel. As soon as it beeps, I push the back door open, and we all walk outside into the cool autumn night.

Once the door is shut behind us, I use my key to lock the deadbolt, then my work here is done.

Turning to face the parking lot, I see two motorcycles. Two men and two motorcycles . . . that's it. I forget for a second my car isn't here and realize just as fast I'm going to need to get on one of these motorcycles to get home.

"How am I getting home?" Apparently, my brain still needs to catch up.

"You can ride with whichever one of us you want," Haze says. "But we're both escorting you home."

"Both of you? Why?" I look back and forth between them. Thank goodness they're standing close to each other, or I'd get whiplash.

"How 'bout we discuss that more once we get you there. Okay?" Smoke throws an arm over Haze's shoulder and drops a kiss on his temple before climbing on his bike.

"Are you gonna get on, or just stand there and gawk?" Haze grabs my hand and pulls me with him toward his bike. Both guys are wearing smiles so wide. "Smoke got you on the way here, I claim you for the ride home."

And just like Smoke did this morning, Haze gets me situated with a helmet and helps me settle myself behind him on the tiny seat, then we're off. The ride home is much cooler, but it feels good. Riding in the dark is scary, but thankfully, it's quick.

Next thing I know, we're parked in my driveway and I'm climbing off. Two successful rides with no falling on my face, I'd say that's a win for me.

As soon as I pass the helmet to Haze, Smoke grabs my hand and leads me up to the front porch. He pulls me over to the giant log bench under the front window, and all three of us take a seat.

Haze to my left and Smoke on my right, I'm the middle of a leather biker sandwich.

"What's going on?" I ask, not caring who answers. This whole day has been a whirlwind. Definitely not how I thought my self-proclaimed good day was going to go.

Smoke turns to face me. "What do you mean?"

"Why are you both here?" Now, I feel like I'm getting whiplash, turning my head to look at both of them.

"Isn't that obvious?" Haze draws my attention to him. "We both like you and want to get to know you more."

"What? But you've only known me for a few days." I'm looking at Haze, who just smiles. "And we didn't say more than hi."

"And you," I turn to Smoke, "I just met you this morning."

Smoke shrugs like it's no big deal. "Sometimes that's all it takes."

"But aren't you two like . . . together?" I wave my hand between them.

Haze nods. "We are."

"So, you're gay?" I blurt out before slapping my hand over my mouth. "Sorry, none of my business."

"No, weren't not gay." Smoke chuckles.

"If you wanna get technical with titles, Smoke and I are bisexual." Haze goes on to clarify. "We like each other, but we also like you."

"You like men and women?" I lean back, realizing this is a better way to see both of them.

"Yes," they both echo.

"And you like me?" I point to myself, hand on my chest. They both like me? Can they do that?

"Yes." Now, both of them are chuckling, like I'm the crazy one.

"But why?" I don't get it. I'm no one special. I'm damaged goods. If they knew the real me, they'd be running for the hills.

Smoke reaches forward and tucks a loose strand of hair behind my ear. Oh my gosh, my hair must look a mess again. Damn helmet!

I try to smooth it out with my fingers, but Smoke grabs my hand and holds it in his. "I know this is a lot to take in. Like you said, you just met us. But in an attempt to be upfront and honest, we're gonna lay it all out for you, okay? Then we'll both say good night to you and let you think about everything."

From I don't know where, I grow some lady balls and speak up. "For honesty's sake, can I say something first?"

Haze pulls my free hand to him and links our fingers together. "Whatever you need to say, you can say to us."

"What he said." The right side of Smoke's face lifts in a smile.

"I have no idea what's happening here," I shrug, "but I'll admit I was attracted to both of you when I saw you separately. And that scares me a little."

"Why does it scare you?" Haze sounds worried. "We don't want you to feel like that around us."

I take a deep breath and say what I can. I'm not ready for them to know everything, not yet. "The root of it is something I'm not ready to discuss now, but I'm open to listening. But I make no promises, this is a lot to take in at once."

"And we get that," Smoke says with a nod. "But in the life we live, the struggles we faced to even get this far together, we agreed from the jump that any woman we were interested in, we'd be honest with her from the start."

"Smoke and I had our own battles to face to be together, but our goal as a couple is to find a woman to make our twosome into a trio." Haze adds, "Some people call it a throuple, but we don't feel a need to put a title on it."

A throuple? I've never heard that word before.

"Before we got together, we knew we were both attracted to women. And both of us are okay with sharing," Smoke continues.

So, not only do they want a third person in their relationship, they want to share her?

They want to share me?

Does that mean they wouldn't be together without a woman? But haven't they been together for a while now?

"So, you're saying you wouldn't be together if there wasn't a woman involved?"

"No." Haze shakes his head, a soft smile on his face. "We'd be perfectly okay if it was only the two of us forever."

"But that's not what either of us wants," Smoke says. "We want someone to share our lives with. Someone like you."

But what about their club? I've been around several club members since I started working for them and haven't ever seen anything like they're describing.

"Is this normal in your biker club? Does everyone share with each other? How many others do you two share with? Because I don't—"

"No." Smoke scoots forward, settling himself to face me again. "The sharing thing is actually very *un*common in the Rebel Vipers."

"There's only one other family that does it, and that's even different from us," Haze reveals.

"What do you mean?"

"Well, you know Ring and Steel, right?" Haze asks.

"Yea. Ring is my boss, and Steel is with Sunshine," I reply. "I've never met her, but Ring talks about her a lot."

"Have you ever wondered why that is?" Haze quirks his head, making me think.

"No. Maybe." Looking between them, I start to think. Now that they mention it, Ring does talk about Sunshine and Steel a lot in the same conversations. "I don't know."

"Abby," Smoke draws my name out, a smirk on his face too, "Ring and Steel share Sunshine. They're not together like Haze and me, but Sunshine is with both of them."

Haze drops the bomb. "Sunshine is their Old Lady."

Boom! My mind explodes. "They both sleep with her?" I gasp.

"They do." Haze chuckles. "They, along with Steel's daughter, Opal, are one family. They live together in a cabin on the club's compound."

"But the guys don't sleep with each other?" I feel like I'm a spectator at a ping pong game. My eyes are still back and forth between these two, volleying each time one of them gives another tidbit of information.

Smoke leans back against the bench's arm, relaxing like he's not part of throwing me for a loop with all this news. "While they may be intimate with her at the same time, Steel and Ring don't have sex with each other."

"But you two do?" I pull my hand free from Smoke and wag it between him and Haze. "You two are a couple? Is that what you're saying?"

Smoke laughs. "I think you're startin' to get it."

"And you want me to be with you both? You want to share me and all have sex at the same time?"

"Eventually, yes, but that's a little ways down the road." Haze turns to face us. "There's a lot we'd need to talk about and get out in the open first."

"Like what?"

"Well, the biggest thing is that you'd need to be one hundred percent sure you like both of us back. It might sound selfish, but we, Haze and I, come first right now."

The look on Smoke's face is suddenly very serious. This is obviously important to him, so I pay close attention. "If you were to decide you only like one of us, this wouldn't work. It's either all three of us, or just him and I. We won't be breaking up if the whole package doesn't work."

"And that's only if you don't think we're crazy for asking this of you." Haze draws my attention to him. "We're taking a huge shot in the dark bringing this up. We wouldn't have even attempted this had both of us not felt a spark when we were with you separately."

"Why do you think I volunteered to come rescue you and your supposedly broken-down car?" Smoke has a small smile, showing a little of his vulnerable side. I haven't seen this side of him yet, but I have to admit, it's awful sweet.

"You did?" I ask softly.

"You bet." Smoke's smile grows a little. "Haze told me about meeting you when he was here last weekend, and I had to meet you myself. And I gotta say, he was right. You opened your front door, and I could see what drew him to you. You're not only beautiful, but there's just something about you that calls to us."

I face forward and stare out at the road. It's probably close to one in the morning and pitch-black outside of the glow of the street lights. "This is a lot. I'm gonna need time to figure this all out in my head."

"And we totally get that." I hear Haze's voice but stay looking forward.

Smoke asks, "How about this?"

Him asking a question piques my interest, so I look to my right. "What's that?"

"Until we get your car situation worked out, you're gonna need a ride to work. So, 'til that's dealt with, Haze and I will be picking you up and dropping you off."

"That way, you have an opportunity to get to know both of us individually," Haze adds, so I turn to him. "I know both of us at once can seem overwhelming, so we'll start with baby steps. One of us at a time."

"But if at any time you begin to not feel comfortable with one or both of us, we need you to be honest. We don't want you to feel railroaded and just going along because it's what you think we want," Smoke says.

Haze shuffles so the side of his leg is pressed against mine and looks down into my eyes. "As much as this is about me and Smoke, a future for the three of us is what we're building toward. So, if at any point you can't see that as what you're working for, we would understand."

"This is a lot," I whisper, looking up at him.

Haze nods. "It is."

"I need some time." I knot my hands together in my lap and look down.

"We understand that more than you think," Smoke voices.

"Was it hard for you two to get to where you are?" I look at Smoke.

Smoke chuckles as his left hand slides across the back of the bench, settling on Haze's shoulder. "It took some of us longer than others, but we figured it out."

Haze looks over, smiling at Smoke. "We sure did."

"Can I ask one more thing?" I need to look at both of them at the same time, so I stand up. I lean my butt on the porch railing, hands propped up next to me on either side.

But before I can continue, I immediately notice how the guys gravitate toward each other. As soon as I stood up, they scooted closer together. Smoke's hand is now on Haze's knee, and Haze is leaning his shoulder on Smoke.

"Whatever you wanna ask, we wanna hear it." Haze's words draw me in.

Something about his gentle demeanor tells me Haze is the softer soul of the two. I can tell he's a caring one, and I feel like his heart is the one I'd need to be most gentle with. I'd never want to hurt either one of them.

"How long did it take you two to get here? As in being a couple, knowing that you wanted a third?"

Smoke answers first. "For me, almost a year."

"That's it?" A year doesn't seem like a long time.

"But Haze now knows I wanted to be with him almost since I met him, and that's been six years," he adds.

"And while I've liked him almost as long, it took 'til a month ago for me to wake up and see what I had all along," Haze says a little sheepishly.

"You've only been a couple for a month?" My mouth drops open, probably making me look like a cartoon character.

"Yes, ma'am." Smoke smirks.

The shock makes me rub my forehead. "But you've known each other six years and never said anything until a year ago?"

"That's what happens when two men are very stubborn and don't admit their feelings for each other," Haze says as he looks at Smoke with a small smile.

Smoke nudges Haze with his elbow, then looks up at me. "And even though it's probably crazy for us to bombard you with all this at once, we don't wanna beat around the bush with our feelings."

"We lost a lot of time by assuming things." Haze points to Smoke and himself. "We don't want that anymore. Not with you."

I pull the strings on my sweatshirt and sink back against the railing again. "That's a long time. What finally made you admit that you liked each other?"

"Believe it or not, it was New Year's Eve," Smoke answers with a snicker. "I caught this one checkin' me out from across the room."

That makes Haze laugh. "Then, when I tried to escape, Smoke chased me down."

"But then we fought for another eight months." That makes Smoke look a little sad. "It wasn't 'til last month that this one came running."

Haze leans back, playfully looking offended. "I didn't come running."

"Yes, you did." Smoke slaps Haze's knee. "You ran across the lawn and attacked me."

"I kissed you. That wasn't an attack." Haze folds his arms, keeping up the adorable, playful defense.

Is it weird to say I find their bickering to be cute? Cute? Can bikers be cute? Hot? Attractive? Sexy? Because all those words fit the bill for these two. I have a feeling if I do pursue whatever this is with them, I'm going to be in for some double trouble. But I kind of like it.

"Are you alright in there?" I look up to see Smoke standing in front of me. "You're smiling but look like you fell down the hole into Wonderland."

"You know *Alice in Wonderland*?" I ask, shocked. What man knows a story like that?

"It's my mom's favorite book," Smoke replies with a grin able to rival the Cheshire cat.

Before I'm able to dive into my love of the White Rabbit, Haze stands too, joining us. "Alright, you two, I think it's time for someone to go in and get some shut-eye."

"I think so too." Smoke grabs my hand. "What time do you work tomorrow?"

"Eleven thirty."

"I'll be here at ten forty-five. That okay?" Smoke asks, his thumb softly tracing the back of my hand.

"You don't have to." I try one more time to give them an out, but it's futile.

"Yes, we do." Smoke leans his head down and kisses me on the cheek. I feel his lips close to mine but not directly touching. They're gentle and soft but still warm.

As Smoke draws back, Haze grabs my other hand, then kisses my other cheek. His eyes meet mine. "And I'll pick you up after. Do you have our numbers?"

"Smoke put his in my phone this morning."

"Of course, he did." Haze chuckles. "Lucky man."

"Can I have your phone? I'll add Haze's." Smoke holds out a hand.

I dig it out of my purse and hand it over. He taps on the screen a few times, then I hear a muted ding.

"Now I've got your number." Haze taps his chest. I'm assuming his phone is in his vest pocket. "When you know what time you'll be done tomorrow night, call me. I'll be there in a flash."

"Okay." I accept my phone back, tucking it in the pocket of my hoodie.

Smoke still has my hand and he walks me to the front door. He tries the handle, and looks at me shocked when it opens. "Is Meredith home?" He looks into the house.

"I think so. The lights are on."

"I need you two to lock this door, even if you're home. Okay?" Smoke tugs on my hand, drawing my attention to his pinched eyebrows. He definitely looks worried. I'm not imagining things. I wonder why?

"But why? If someone's home, who cares?"

"We do," Haze professes, grabbing my other hand again. "We want you safe, that's all."

"Okay, I'll make sure to be more diligent." Hopefully, my agreement will appease their sudden care of my unlocked doors.

"Well, this is where we're gonna say good night." Smoke kisses my hand this time, and I can feel myself blushing as he lets go.

"Now, remember, no pressure," Haze says before kissing my cheek again. "Just think of what we said and we'll talk more soon. Okay?"

"I'll see you both tomorrow."

I don't think I'll be able to think of anything else. I can't stop the smile that seems to appear on its own when I look at these two. They may have dropped one hell of a doozy on me tonight, and I've got a lot to think about, but something about it all just feels right. Even though I feel a bit hypocritical at the same time.

"Good night, beautiful." Haze steps back, causing our hands to unlink.

"Good night."

Smoke grabs Haze's hand, then they turn to walk down the porch steps together. Once they get to the driveway, I watch as they kiss once, then separate to get on their bikes. They both wave that typical two finger man wave at me.

"Head inside, then we'll leave," Smoke calls out.

I give them a small wave back, then go inside.

Once the door is closed, I lift the edge of the lace curtain to watch through the glass inlay in the door as they back their motorcycles onto the street, then ride away. I close my eyes, lay my forehead against the glass, and let out a huge sigh.

"Sounds like you've got a whole bunch to be thinkin' about."

A voice behind me startles me, causing me to knock my forehead onto the glass. "Ow!"

I turn to see my roommate, Meredith, leaning against the stair banister, smiling at me.

"How much of that did you hear?" I ask, rubbing my forehead.

"Everything," she replies. "The living room window is open."

Her easygoing attitude gives me a sense of calm, and I deflate. "What am I gonna do?"

Meredith sets her hands on her hips and cocks her weight to one side. "Both of them, I hope."

That causes both of us to burst into laughter.

"I think you and I are gonna be great friends," I say as I flip the lock and deadbolt on the front door before kicking off my shoes and hanging my purse on the coat tree.

"I sure hope so." Meredith loops our arms together. "Let's get you your men, then you can help me chase down mine."

I look at her, mouth agape. "And who exactly do you plan to chase?"

"Do I have a story for you." She laughs as she leads us down the hall toward my bedroom. "It all started on July third."

CHAPTER SEVENTEEN

SMOKE

It's been exactly one week since Haze and I began giving Abby rides to and from work, and things couldn't be going better. Actually, I take that back. They could be better in the sense that she could already be our Old Lady, but unfortunately, that hasn't happened yet. But I have to say, things are moving in the right direction.

Haze and I trade off who takes Abby to work in the morning and who brings her home at the end of her shift. Since her schedule is fairly consistent, it's just worked out best this way.

The club is still on orders to always ride with another Brother, so depending on who needed to run somewhere off the compound, someone different has come along each time. As luck would have it, no one else needed to leave today, so Haze decided to join me this morning.

It's Sunday morning, and Abby has to be to work by eight, so we're currently on our way into town to pick her up.

Each day, Abby is opening up to us more and more. It took a couple days, but she no longer flinches when we hold her hand or kiss her on the cheek. Definitely baby steps, but I'll take it. She's even been initiating some text messages to ask for one of us to pick her up or tell us if she'll be running late.

I've learned that Abby loves using random emojis in her texts. Throughout the day, I'll send her funny jokes, trying to brighten her day, and she sends back the silliest things. Just this morning, when I texted her saying we were leaving the clubhouse, her reply was one of the tiny monkeys with its hands covering its eyes. This woman is a little quirky, but I like her that way.

Haze leads the way as we make the right-hand turn into the cul-de-sac, and I pull up on his right in the driveway. Just as I shut down my Harley, and Haze climbs off his, I hear a ding from my pocket. I pull my cell phone out and see a few missed text messages.

Whiskey:	Call me when you get this.
Whiskey:	Don't take Abby to work.
Whiskey:	Dammit Smoke. Answer me.

What the hell is going on? Before I can reply or call him, Haze's phone starts ringing in his hand.

"It's Whiskey," he says as he answers it. "Hello? ... Yea, we just pulled up ... Okay ... What's goin' on? ... Fine, we'll be ready." And he hangs up.

"What's happening?" I'm starting to panic. I don't like the look on Haze's face.

He starts jogging for the front steps. "Whiskey says we need to get both Abby and Meredith packed and ready to go back to the clubhouse."

I swing my leg over my seat and follow him. "Did he say why?"

"Nope," Haze answers as we stop in front of the door and he knocks on it. "Just said a few Brothers are on the way to provide backup and extra protection for the ride back."

"Something big musta happened in the last fifteen minutes, 'cause he looked perfectly calm before we left." There's no answer to Haze's knock, so I open the screen door and try the handle. The door opens with no resistance.

"Goddammit," Haze curses. "I thought we told her to keep this door locked at all times."

"We did," I reply as I barge in. "Abby! Where are you?" I yell out.

"What's all the ruckus?" Abby appears at the opening of the hall, hopping as she tries to put one of her shoes on. "I was in the bathroom."

I march forward and get in her face. "Why was the front door unlocked? Someone could've just walked in here and kidnapped you." I don't mean to sound angry and hurtful, but we've warned her several times about her safety. With what happened to Sunshine at her old house, no one can be too careful.

Abby's face drops and she begins to cry. "I . . . I . . . I'm sorry."

Her quick turn from sassy to sad flips my attitude just as fast. "Oh, honey, I'm sorry." I wrap my arms around her shoulders and press her to my chest. "Please don't cry."

I feel Abby's shoulders and chest heave and know immediately that I messed up. Looking around, panicked, I find Haze talking to Meredith at the bottom of the stairs. As soon as he notices me looking at him, he must sense my panic and rushes over. I slowly let go of Abby, and Haze steps in, leading her further into the living room and over to the couch.

Haze pulls her down onto his lap, and her feet settle on the cushion next to him.

Knowing I need to fix this, I kneel down in front of them and settle my hands on Haze's knees. As much as I'm dying inside to touch Abby, I don't want to spook her any more than I already did. As soon as they were sitting, she leaned her upper body on Haze's chest and turned into him, curling into herself like a cocoon.

"Abby," I whisper, "I'm sorry I yelled at you."

Her head turns my way, her eyes open, and she nods slowly, letting out a sniffle. She doesn't say anything, but I see the acknowledgment in her eyes. I've got some making up to do, but unfortunately, it'll have to wait.

"Smoke?" Meredith speaks up from behind me. "Can you help me?"

"One sec," I call out. Getting back to my feet, I drop a kiss on Abby's head, then one on Haze's forehead. "I'll be right back."

I follow Meredith down the hall and into what I know is Abby's room. I've never been in her bedroom until now, but being familiar with the layout of this house, I know this is the master.

"Haze filled me in a little," Meredith starts. "I don't know what's happening, but he said to pack some clothes for a few days. Any idea what Abby might want or need?" She asks this as she starts opening drawers and pulling out random items of clothing.

"I don't know. I don't know what she has. I've only seen her in work clothes."

"Typical man." Meredith rolls her eyes as she shoves me out of the way and tosses a duffle bag onto the bed. She's moving so fast around me, I have no clue where she pulled it out from. "Just stand there and look pretty 'til I have a few bags packed. Then you can carry everything."

"Works for me." So, I do. I stand back and watch her flit around the room, pulling out shirts and shorts, jeans and underwear, and shoes, then sorting them into three separate duffle bags.

Once Meredith zips the last one, she tosses it at me. "There. I'm gonna head up to my room. Be back down in a jiffy." She disappears out the door, and I hear her run up the stairs, then her footsteps above me.

I toss the bags' straps over my shoulder and do my job as a pack mule to carry everything toward the front door. I drop everything to the foyer floor just as I hear a rumble growing louder from outside.

It sounds like the cavalry has arrived. Through the screen door, I see six of my Brothers pull up at the curb in front of the house, and Angel's white Jeep Wrangler stops in the driveway next to mine and Haze's bikes. Whiskey, Hammer, and Steel meet up in the middle of the lawn and chat for a minute, then Steel and Whiskey head my way.

I step out onto the porch as they walk up the steps. "Is someone gonna tell me what's the emergency?"

"Nope. We'll fill everyone in at once when we get back to the clubhouse and have Church," Whiskey replies as Angel skirts around us and heads inside. "Are the girls ready?"

"Meredith is upstairs right now. Abby's bags are just inside."

We all walk in the house, and I make a beeline for the couch. Angel is sitting on one side of Haze, so I settle myself on the side where Abby's feet are. I lift them up and scoot myself so my hip is touching Haze's, then settle Abby's legs over my lap.

"Are you okay, Abby?" Angel asks.

"Yea," she mumbles as she nods.

She doesn't look up, but I can see her eyes open. Using my right hand, I tuck a long strand of onyx hair behind her ear, then trace my fingertips down the side of her jawline. God, she's beautiful.

If I were the jealous type, I would be possessive right now. While I wish Abby was in my lap, seeing her in Haze's arms is just as appealing. I know what it feels like to be held in his warmth, and I bet she's feeling all the care he has for her. Now that Haze let his walls down, he has so much to give, and we just happen to be the lucky ones he shows it to.

I find one of Abby's hands linked with Haze's and lift both of them to my lips. I kiss the back of her hand, then wrap my own around theirs, settling it back in her lap.

Someone coughing makes me look up. It's Steel. "I hate to be the bearer of bad news, but we need to get this show on the road. Angel brought her Jeep, so y'all three can ride back together, if you want. Diego and Hammer can ride your bikes back, if that's okay."

"That's fine by me," Haze responds. "Smoke, hop up and carry our raven outside. I'll grab her bags."

Untangling myself from them, I stand and lift Abby from his lap. With one arm under her knees and the other cradling her back, she settles into me with her face buried in my neck. I kiss her temple as I walk around the couch and step outside.

"Keys are in the bikes," I say to Hammer as I pass, and he opens the back door of the Jeep for me. I sit Abby on the seat and turn to see Haze leaning against the side. "Why don't you climb in with her? I'll drive back."

"Are you sure?" he asks.

"It looks like you're what she needs right now," I say as I nod. "Once we get her back to the clubhouse and figure out what's going on, there will be plenty of time for the three of us to cuddle together." I grab the front of his t-shirt in my fist and yank him to me. I kiss Haze hard, let him go, then slap him on the ass. "Now, get in before I put you in myself."

"I just might like that." Haze winks as he climbs in.

I laugh as I shut the door and come face to face with Angel.

"Be careful with my baby now, ya hear?" She holds out her keys but yanks them back as I reach my hand out. "If my Jeep has one scratch on it, I'll kick your ass myself."

Setting my hand over my heart, I give her my best attempt at a serious straight face. "Yes, ma'am."

Angel hands over the keys. "Just for that, I'm gonna ride on your bike with Hammer. If you hurt my baby, I'll hold yours hostage."

And I have no doubt she would. So, as gently as my rough self can, I climb into the front seat before sliding it back as far as it goes. My long legs and steering wheels aren't good friends.

Once we're back at the clubhouse, Whiskey calls Church, so Haze carries Abby inside and settles her on a couch next to

Meredith. As if on instinct, I lift Abby's chin with my finger and give her a quick kiss on the lips before I walk away.

It's not until I drop my phone in the box outside the Church doors and look back at her, seeing her eyes open wide and looking at me in shock, that I realize what I did. I kissed her. The first time I really kissed her was done purely on what I was feeling. It's like I've been doing it for years.

I smile and wave, then head inside the meeting room.

Bang! Whiskey pounds his gavel on the table as the doors shut behind me. I take my seat and wait for whatever news has caused such an uproar.

"There's been a development on the security breach, and it involves Abby," Whiskey starts. I whip my head forward to look at Haze and see him white knuckling the arms of his chair. It looks like he's ready to jump up.

"What does that mean?" I ask.

"It turns out all the times the footage was accessed match up with the days and times that Abby was working," Cypher answers from his perch at the table he has his electronics set up on in the front corner of the room. "I still don't know who accessed it, but seeing as I was able to trace the IP address to a coffee shop in Kansas City, my guess is it's her ex-husband."

"That's where she's from," Haze finally speaks up.

"Exactly," Whiskey says, "and since she thinks it was the ex who stole her car, I'd say he found her."

"Then why hasn't he tried to contact her?" I question, thinking out loud. "If he wants to talk to her, wouldn't it be easier to just call or drop by? What's with all the sneaking around?"

"That's what I'm trying to figure out." Cypher clicks a few buttons on his laptop, then a picture pops up on the screen behind Whiskey's and Steel's heads. "This is Tobias Moretti."

He's not what I would call an ugly fucker had I passed him on the street, but knowing the hell and trouble he gave my sweet Abby, he's a hideous monster. The image Cypher shows is of Toby's driver's license, and even here, he looks pissed off. I mean, who really enjoys the Department of Motor Vehicles, but the evil glare he's sporting is a bit much.

"Well, doesn't he look friendly?" Mountain says, sarcasm oozing from his words.

"I've searched high and low for the guy all around Kansas City, but he disappeared off the map two weeks ago," Cypher adds. "None of his credit cards have been used, but a shit ton of cash was withdrawn from his bank account just before he went dark."

"So, he just took his money and ran?" I slam my fist on the table. "And now, we don't have any clue where this motherfucker is?"

"Abby isn't leaving this clubhouse 'til we find this fucker and burn his body to ash." Haze growls, his eyes locked on the doors leading to the main room. I imagine he's picturing our scared woman on the other side.

"That's why I called Church," Whiskey announces. "Abby's in danger, and this is now officially a club matter. She's one of our employees, and we won't tolerate anyone hurting someone we care about."

"She's more than just an employee!" Haze jumps up and his chair makes a horrible screeching sound as the legs slide across the floor. He points at me and keeps talking. "She may not be our Old Lady yet, but she will be soon. This is family business."

"I'm glad to hear you say that, son," Mountain remarks. I look at him, and his eyes are volleying between me and Haze. "Haze is more than a Brother—he's my blood. And now that you two are together, the both of you are in charge of keeping that woman out there safe. She looks like a scared little bird who needs all the love and care you two have to offer. Don't let her go, ya hear?"

"Yes, sir," I reply.

"We won't let her out of our sight," Haze answers.

"We need to put this whole Tobias, Toby, dumbfuck, whatever his name is, thing to a vote," Brewer announces. "Especially since he hacked into the club security network, we need to make anything from here on out official."

"I motion we find this asswipe and mop the bathroom floor with his ugly face." Kraken cracks his knuckles, then lounges back in his chair.

"I second that," Saddle adds. "I think I'm due to give someone a good 'ol fashioned beat down."

The room erupts in *hell yea* and *let's go* and a bunch of ruckuses.

Whiskey slams his gavel to quiet the room. "All in favor of continuing to look for Tobias and keeping Abby safe, say aye."

"AYE!" everyone shouts.

"Motion passed." The wood of the gavel clashes against the grain of the table again, making a cracking sound louder than a bolt of lightning.

"Until Cypher finds Tobias, Abby isn't to leave the compound," Hammer says as the room quiets again. "And the women and kids are still on lockdown as well."

"What can we tell Abby about what's going on?" Haze asks.

"I don't see this as something we need to hide," Whiskey answers. "She can know whatever you two feel comfortable telling her."

"Then we'll fill her in once we're done in here," Haze responds.

"I agree," I say.

"With a security issue like this, everyone needs to know." Whiskey leans back in his chair and nods. "We'll have a whole clubhouse meeting in the main room in one hour. Pops, can you ask Blue to throw some pizza in for lunch for after?"

"Can do," Mountain replies.

"Main room. One hour." *Bang!* He slams the gavel one last time, and we all stand.

I find Haze waiting for me just outside the doors. "Let's take Abby upstairs. I think we should fill her in so she doesn't find out about all this mess from someone else."

"Good idea."

We grab our phones from the box, then collect our lady.

This is a talk we need to have in private. Abby needs to know everything we do. I just hope she doesn't want to run.

I hate it enough that we're about to drop the news on her that she's basically stuck here. I don't know how she'd handle us forcing her to stay if she doesn't want to, so let's hope it doesn't come to that.

CHAPTER EIGHTEEN

ABBY

"Are you okay?"

I look at Meredith sitting next to me and try to smile. "I think so. I just wish I knew what was going on. I mean, why did they need so many guys to come and pick us up? Couldn't they just call and ask us to come here?"

"Well, I'm glad you haven't gone mute." Meredith laughs, which in turn causes me to join in.

Once our giggles die down, I lift my feet up on the couch cushion and wrap my arms around my legs, resting my cheek on my knees. I let out a deep breath. "I don't handle confrontation well. I tend to try and shut out everything, and I guess that's what happened."

"Smoke did come into the house kinda on a rampage," she says as she rolls her eyes. "He was a little bit dramatic. I forgot to lock the door when I took out the garbage. It was only like five minutes before they got there. I knew someone was coming to take you to work."

"It's not your fault." I squeeze her knee. "I just overreacted like usual."

"Hopefully, they come out of Church soon." Meredith looks over her shoulder at the doors behind us. "I really wanna know what's up. Do you have any idea what it could be?"

"No clue." I spin on the couch and kneel to look behind us. "Whatever it is, they're taking forever."

"In my time around the club, I've come to realize Church usually goes down one of two ways." Meredith lifts her pointer finger. "One, if it's their weekly Friday meeting, it goes by fairly quick. Or two," this time, she's got two fingers up, "if it's an impromptu situation, it takes for-ev-er." That, she drags out to make the word sound super long.

Just as I'm about to sit back on my butt, the noise level from inside the closed room grows louder and the doors open. Bikers of all shapes and sizes pour out the double doors, first stopping to grab their phones from a black box sitting on a tiny table, being watched by a younger Hispanic man.

I found it quite weird that a few of the guys in leather weren't in the meeting, but when I see two walk past with a patch on the back of their vest that says 'Prospect', I figure it's a theme that whoever they are, aren't allowed in.

"What's a Prospect?" I ask Meredith.

"Prospects are bikers trying to earn their way into the club. It's like a probationary stage. They're the club's minions and have to do whatever they're told, like cleaning toilets, washing dishes, or anything the Brothers don't wanna do."

"Kinda like a glorified gopher?"

"Pretty much."

"Hey there, gorgeous." I look up and see Haze smiling down at me. He drops a kiss on my forehead. I got distracted watching all the other Brothers, I missed Haze and Smoke walking over.

"Are you feeling better?" Smoke leans on the armrest next to me and wraps an arm around my back, tugging me into his embrace. "I'm sorry for yelling at you back at the house. I didn't know what was all going on and panicked when the door was unlocked."

Pulling back, I rest my forearm on his shoulder and tuck a piece of his long, wavy hair that came loose from his ponytail behind his ear. Looking into his big brown eyes, filled with so much sadness, I try and ease whatever is bothering him. "It's okay. I'm okay now. I just freaked out a bit myself."

"I'll let you three be." Meredith pops up and gives me a half-hug. "Peace out, girl scout."

I can't help but chuckle at her goofiness.

Haze moves around to the front of the couch and holds my free hand to help me stand. "We've got some things to talk about. How about we head upstairs and fill you in?"

"Lead the way." One hand held by each of them, I follow Smoke and Haze around the maze of couches and chairs, then up the stairs.

It's a long walk up. This building used to be a factory or warehouse at some point, so the bedroom area is higher up than a normal home's second floor. Once we reach the top, we're in the middle of a long hallway with doors on both sides.

Haze walks to a door on the left, about halfway down, then pulls keys out of his pocket and unlocks it. He steps in, and Smoke and I follow. Smoke flips the light switch and the whole room comes to life.

A ceiling fan starts spinning and the four bulbs hanging from it brighten the whole room. I can tell there's a window on the wall straight ahead, but it has a black curtain hanging over it that looks like one of those light-blocking panels.

On the wall to the left of the door is a tall dresser. To my left is a king-size bed with nightstands on either side. Straight ahead under the window is a couch, and to the right is a closet in the middle with a door on either side of it. Both are closed, so I'm not sure where they lead. And tucked in the corner, behind where the door opens, is a desk and chair.

But even with all the furniture, what surprises me most is how sparse the room looks. There are no pictures on the walls, no magazines or books laying around, and no dirty clothes on the floor. If it weren't for the fact there's two pillows and a blanket on the bed, I wouldn't guess anyone sleeps in here.

"Let's have a seat and talk." Haze sits on the end of the bed and pats the spot next to him. I sit and fold my hands together in my lap.

Smoke rolls the office chair over and sits in front of us. "I hate to be the bearer of bad news, but it seems like your ex-husband has struck again."

Almost on instinct, my head jerks back and my mouth drops open. I'm shocked. I knew whatever this crazy day was about probably wasn't good, but I never imagined this.

I feel myself getting angry. Can't this man just leave me alone and let me move on with my life? "Wasn't stealing my car bad enough?"

"We still don't know if that was him," Haze turns, "but with what we've found, I have no doubt it was. But this time, he's pushed the club's buttons—"

"And that's not good news for him," Steel finishes Haze's sentence.

"What'd Toby do now?"

"A few days before we met you for the first time, Cypher, our club tech guru, discovered someone had accessed the security footage from both The Lodge and here at our clubhouse. He wasn't sure who it was at first, but after some dark web digging, this morning he discovered it was done from an IP address in Kansas City," Haze tells me.

I cover my mouth with the tips of my fingers, shocked. "That's where I'm from."

"We know. But that's not all." Smoke reaches forward, and on instinct, I give him my hand. His larger one dwarfs mine as he rests the back of his hand on my knee. "When Cypher was doing his digging, he found that Toby withdrew a bunch of money from his bank accounts and has seemingly fallen off the map in the last few weeks. We don't know where he is."

"Has this Cypher guy looked into Toby's parents? They're even more rich than he is. Hell, that's where he got most of his money from."

"I'm not sure if he did or not, but we can ask him when we go back downstairs in a little while," Haze responds. "We're just afraid that whatever his motive is, it isn't a good one. Especially now that we know why he broke into the security system."

"Oh my gosh." I know what he was looking for. They don't even have to say it. "He was looking for me, wasn't he? He was looking for me and he found me. That's how he found me and my car. Oh my god. I need to go."

I shake my hands free, displacing both men's grip on me, then try and stand. But I don't get far. Unfortunately for me and my attempted escape, Smoke is still sitting in front of me.

Just as I manage to find my footing, he stands, blocking me from taking a step in any direction. He's so tall and wide, he blocks any escape route to the door.

And we're suddenly as close as any two people can be with their clothes still on. Looking straight ahead, I'm face to leather with the patch on the left side of his chest. I'm looking at the name 'Smoke' embroidered on a patch that's sewn onto his leather vest. I knew he was tall, but holy crap, my five-foot-five height is nothing compared to him.

"Where do you think you're going?" I hear his voice rumble through his chest.

Slowly looking up, I see him smiling. "I have to leave. He found me. I gotta go."

"I don't think so," he says as he laughs. I don't know what's so funny. "You're exactly where you need to be, my little midnight raven."

"Your what?" What's a midnight raven?

I feel Smoke's hands slide along my sides, just under the bottom hem of my sweatshirt, settling on my waist. He lowers his head a bit, resting his forehead against mine. Our eyes are so close, I can see the tiny specks of gray mixed in with the brown.

"You're our little midnight raven. Your hair and eyes are darker than anything I've ever seen," he says, not quite whispering but still very quiet. "I don't know where the name came from—it just popped out that way."

"But why do you care about me enough to even think like that?"

"What do you mean?" I hear movement behind me, then feel Haze press his chest against my back. His hands span my ribcage, just above Smoke's. "Why wouldn't we care about you?"

Smoke's nose brushes mine, before I turn my head to look up at Haze. "Because I seem to be more trouble than I'm worth. I came here to get away from my past. And now, it seems to have followed me, causing your club problems."

"Abby," Haze's hands spin me in place so I'm facing him, with Smoke fitting himself behind me, "you'll never be trouble to us. And you're worth more to us than gold. Don't ever let us hear you say anything like that about yourself again. Do you hear me? Never again."

Looking up at Haze, I hear what he's saying but get lost in his eyes for a minute. They're a mix of copper and lighter brown, and have a goldish hue to them. There's also a ring of dark brown around the outside edge of the iris that gives a stark contrast from dark to the white of his eyes. They're mesmerizing.

"Are you staring into my eyes, beautiful?" Snapping out of my trance, I look down and blink a few times. He lifts my chin back up with his index finger. "There's no need to hide from me. I could look into your raven eyes all day."

"There's that word again . . . raven," I comment. "I don't get it. I have dark black hair and eyes, so what? That's not anything special."

"Yes, it is," Smoke says in my ear. "Everything about you is special. And before you try and argue, it's two against one here. We win."

His attempt at a joke to lighten the mood works, and all three of us chuckle in response.

"If you say so." I lay my left hand over his on my hip.

Standing here, seemingly sandwiched between these two handsome, strong, soul-boosting men, I'm happier than I ever remember being. It's been a week since they began escorting me to and from work, engraining themselves into the very fiber of my days. I can't think of a free moment of my time, whether at home or work, where I wasn't thinking of both of them. Smoke and Haze seem to have put a chink in the armor I tried to carry around with me, and I find myself not really caring that they found a way in.

And that in itself worries me and brightens my day all at the same time.

"We do say so," Haze answers back with a smile. "This last week has shown us that you really are what we've been looking for. No matter the problems with your ex, or the rough road ahead, we care about you more than the trouble. We want you more now than we did the days we met."

"Really?" I feel pressure building behind my eyes, and I blink to try and keep the tears back. I've never heard more simple words pack such a powerful punch.

"Really." Moving slow, I watch as Haze's face moves closer to mine, his eyes looking down at my lips. I know what's coming next. "Tell me if you don't want me to kiss you."

"Please do," I reply without even thinking.

"Such manners our lady has," Smoke purrs. I can feel his entire body shift behind me. His hands grip me tighter, his fingertips pressing into the sides of my torso.

I close my eyes just as Haze's lips touch mine, but they're not forceful or rough. Actually, it's soft and gentle, almost like he's still hesitant. I've realized that Haze is the caring, sensual one of the two, and I'm dying to see his restraint snap. So, I do something bold.

When he pulls back just a fraction to take a breath, I flick my tongue against his bottom lip. His sharp inhale gives me the break I'm looking for, so I lean my chest against his and kiss him like I want him to kiss me.

Our tongues slide against each other's in a battle neither of us can really lose. In a lip-lock like this, we both win.

I feel my skin growing warmer as we pull apart, our eyes locked on one another.

"Damn, that was hot as fuck."

While I didn't forget that Smoke was behind me, because who could with his bulk and weight pressing me forward into Haze, but hearing his voice drags my biggest worry back to the front of my mind. I know it's something the three of us have talked a little about, but until everything is out in the open, I still feel a bit hypocritical.

"I need a second." I let go of my grasp on Haze's arms. I don't remember when I grabbed hold of him like that, and step sideways out of the space between them. Standing beside the bed, I tug off the hair tie that's always on my wrist and pull my hair into a high ponytail. I don't bother with a braid or any updo because I don't have the energy to deal with it right now.

"What's the matter, Abby?" Smoke pushes the chair back to the desk, then he sits in front of where I'm standing. "I can see in your eyes that something's wrong."

"It was my kiss, wasn't it?" Haze sounds worried. His eyes even look a little sad. Haze scoots beside Smoke, leaning his shoulder into him. There it is again. They're touching, even innocently, like it's second nature to them. "I knew it was too soon."

"No, no, no. It wasn't the kiss." I wave my hands. "I more than liked the kiss. Hell, it was me who bumped things up a few degrees there at the end."

"If it weren't for the fact that I snuck in our first kiss earlier, I might've been jealous of the tongue tie you two were just doing." Smoke loops his arm over Haze's shoulders and tugs him closer.

Seeing the two of them so close, knowing they like each other just as much as they say they like me, brings my doubt back to the surface.

"Why do I like you both and not have a problem with it? I mean, I left my husband, the man I was supposed to be married to for the rest of my life, because he wanted a sister wife. My sister. Why am I okay with sharing you two? And, with each other? Isn't that hypocritical of me?"

"I don't think so. What Toby did was wrong." Haze sits forward, so his boots are now touching the floor. "He never once asked you what you wanted, did he? He just told you that's the way it was gonna be."

"And only after you caught him in bed with your sister. That's wrong in so many ways." Smoke shakes his head.

There's something in their words that makes my racing heart slow just a bit, calming me.

I know this situation is different. Both Smoke and Haze were upfront and honest about what they wanted from the start. And I was attracted to them both before knowing they were together.

"I know you're both right." I tuck my hands into the pocket of my hoodie and lean back against the tall dresser, letting it hold me up. My energy has ridden a rollercoaster today and I feel like I'm about to crash. "I just thought all that stuff was behind me."

"And it will be soon, we promise." Smoke has his hands outreached to me, so I stand back up and walk toward them.

I sit on the bed to his right, putting my back to the headboard so I can look at both of them at the same time. "So, what's next. When can I go home?"

"Not 'til we know what Toby's up to," Haze answers.

"We don't feel it's safe for you to be alone or without us. We need you here so we can protect you," Smoke says next.

"I know it's a lot, but this is how we function." Haze rests a hand on my outstretched leg, and I look down at his tan skin against the denim of my blue jeans. "When there's a problem, the club sticks together. We protect our women with everything we have."

My eyes almost bug out at Haze's words. "Your women? You mean I'm yours? Already?"

Smoke chuckles. "While we'd like to claim you and put our cut on you today, we know you're probably not ready for that yet. And we won't rush you. You need to be in this as much as we are, and it's understandable that you're not."

"But what if I am?" I say out loud before I can even think.

"What?" Haze coughs, probably trying not to choke.

"What if I'm ready to be both of yours right now?"

I'm serious. If these two are going to be so supportive when my past has brought drama into their club life, I can't imagine what else they'd do for me. I can't pass this up. I want more.

Smoke stands and pulls me to my feet. "Do you have any idea what that means?"

I'm not sure what he means. Isn't being with someone a simple thing? "Isn't it just that I'm your girlfriend and wear one of those vests like Angel and her sister?"

"Well, that's the start of it, but there's so much more," Smoke says with a smile.

Haze is up and next to Smoke before I can blink, his right hand now holding my left. "And it's not a vest, Abby, it's called a cut. Us giving you our Property cut means you're ours," he points to himself and Smoke, "forever. Like 'til the day all three of us are buried forever."

Looking up at their serious expressions, the light bulb clicks over my head, their words hitting home. "Forever?"

"There's no backing out of being an Old Lady." Smoke lifts our joined hands to his lips and kisses my knuckles.

Haze repeats the gesture, then shakes his head. "Not a way one of us would end up alive, anyway."

"What?" I'm thrown for a tiny loop.

"That's exactly what being an Old Lady means, Abby," Smoke responds. "To put it as simply as I can, it's like a biker marriage without the rings and paperwork. The second we tell the club you're ours and slide our Property cut over your shoulders, it's a lifelong commitment. It's not something we take lightly."

"The dating stage for us would start and stop right then and there," Haze continues. "That's what we told you that night on your porch. It's either all three of us, or just Smoke and me. There are no other options. All in or nothing."

"That's a big commitment."

"It sure is." Haze finally breaks into a smile.

"There's nothing wrong with continuing to get to know each other before taking the next step." I know Smoke's trying to give me an out of my earlier words, but I don't want one.

"Exactly." Haze backs him up. "As much as we'd like to make you ours, we don't wanna pressure you."

Tugging on their hands, I get their attention back to me. "I'd like to give this a shot. I know I'd regret it if I didn't."

"Even with all this fucked up ex-husband bullshit floating around us?" Haze asks.

"I let that man rule my life for six years, and even after getting away, he's still out there trying to mess with me. I need him gone."

"Have you thought about what that might really mean in the end?" Smoke questions, his smile morphing into a frown.

"Like what?"

"Like if he ends up dead," he says with no emotion.

"Dead?" My jaw drops.

"Abby," Haze intervenes, "Toby has crossed some very serious lines with the club. What he did, breaking into our security, is a big problem. We can't let him get away with that."

"You may be new to this, but the rest of us aren't. Before we brought you up here, we had Church and the whole club voted that we're on the lookout for him," Smoke goes on. "We just need you to be prepared for what will most likely happen when we do find him."

"It's not gonna end well for him." Haze's head moves side to side.

I pull my hands from them and back a step away. I don't want what I think they're saying to be real. It seems like a bit much. "You're gonna kill him because he hacked into your security system? Isn't that a little harsh? Can't you let the cops deal with him?"

"Honey, the cops will never even know this happened," Smoke replies. "We don't deal with law enforcement. That's not how we do things."

"But won't you go to jail for killing him? You can't make a body disappear. This isn't some movie where bodies are never seen again." Now it's me shaking my head at them. They sound like serial killers on a *Lifetime* movie.

"That's for us to know and you to never worry about," Haze answers. "If we say he's taken care of, you don't ask questions."

Smoke steps forward, back into my bubble, and takes my hand into his. He really does seem to need to touch me, in some way, at all times. "That's another thing we need to discuss before going any further. If you become our Old Lady, you need to know the ground rules."

I hold up my free hand. "Ground rules? What is this, a game?"

Haze doesn't force his hand on mine, but he does tug on one of my belt loops. "Not even close. This may seem a bit caveman-ish, but as an Old Lady, you're only allowed to know what we tell you. You aren't allowed in Church, and you'll never be in a position of power. You're there for us, your Old Men, and nothing else."

"That's primitive, to say the least." I try not to roll my eyes, but I end up looking up at the ceiling.

"I know it sounds bad, but it's not like that all the time. But it's still something you need to know." Smoke draws my attention back to him. "Because when something happens that we can't tell you about, you can't ask. There'll be things about this club and what we do that you'll never know about."

"There *will* be times when we're called to do something, or we have to go on a run and we won't be able to tell you where we're going or when we'll be back. It'll have nothing to do with you, so we just can't say, and you need to understand." Haze's words sound like he's begging me to understand. He's trying to tell me how things aren't going to be easy, but at the same time, they want to be upfront about the challenges.

"We won't be doing it to hide things from you. It's just how we keep you safe and away from as much potential trouble as we can," Smoke states.

This is so much to take in, I think my brain is frozen. "This is way too much for one day."

"I know we're probably saying all the wrong things, but maybe if you talk to the other ladies, they'll be able to explain things better," Smoke begs, his eyes still looking sad.

"Did any of them say anything to you while we were in Church?" Haze asks.

"No." I shake my head slowly. "Meredith stuck to my side, and I was just watching the room."

Haze kisses my forehead. "Well, now that you're staying here, I'm sure there will be plenty of time to talk more."

I try and jolt back, but his finger on my belt loop doesn't let me move. "Stay here? And sleep where?" I ask.

"You can stay here in my room," Haze answers with a smile and a shrug like it's no big deal that he offered me his personal space.

"But where will you sleep?"

"With me. My room is right through that door." Smoke points at the closed door on the left.

"Your rooms are connected?"

"They sure are." Smoke smiles and winks at Haze, while Haze shoves Smoke with his shoulder.

They both laugh, their happiness radiating and making all my worry disappear instantly. I need to just embrace this and let them take my anxieties away. I told them I wanted them, now it's my turn to let it happen. One step forward. I got this.

CHAPTER NINETEEN

HAZE

"Your rooms are connected?" Abby looks stunned. She's wide-eyed, looking over at the door to Smoke's room.

"They sure are." Smoke winks at me. By the smug look on his face, I know he's remembering how it was his idea for me to move in here so we could be closer together.

In return to his cockiness, I knock Smoke with my shoulder, causing us to laugh at each other. Abby is still standing in front of us, eyes locked on the door like it's a mystery needing solving.

"Wanna see it?" I ask her, tugging her toward the door by her belt loop I still have my finger hooked through.

"If you want." Abby shrugs as she shuffles to follow my steps. "I wouldn't wanna intrude on your spaces."

"Abby, honey," Smoke says as he follows, "if we're gonna really do this, these will be your rooms too. The three of us will share these spaces, and you can do whatever you want with them. We want you to make our rooms your home."

I push the door open and walk into Smoke's bedroom. With the closet and bathroom from my bedroom set between our rooms, there's actually a small hallway between them and the exterior wall of the building. It's private only to us.

As we step into the open area of Smoke's space, he pulls Abby from my grasp and shows her around. Much like my room, he has a dresser, nightstands, desk, couch, king-size bed, and closet, but he only has one door on the far wall leading to his bathroom.

"Are you sure you two actually live here?" Abby turns slowly, looking around. "There's no personal touches at all, anywhere. Do y'all not have family photos or anything?"

"I have one of my mom and me on my nightstand," I answer. It's the only picture I have of my mother. "Well, the only one I had before I found the other copy in Whiskey's office."

"Wait, what?" She stops spinning and steps in front of me. "What am I missing? Why does Whiskey have a picture of you and your mom?"

I thread her hand with mine and sit us on the end of Smoke's bed. "It's kinda a long story, and very new, but a little while back, I found out a man named Brick is my father."

Abby pulls her legs up and crosses them in front of her. "Who's Brick?"

Smoke looks at me, and I nod, letting him speak. This is all so raw and fresh, I don't have it all figured out in my head yet. Knowing he's willing to do some of the explaining for me eases the weight suddenly dropped on my shoulders.

I knew I'd have to explain this all to Abby at some point, but with everything going on with her situation, I honestly forgot my own life-altering news.

"Brick was actually Mountain's younger brother. You see, Mountain and Brick were two of the five original founding members of the Rebel Vipers," Smoke says as he sits on the bed next to me and grabs my hand. "A few years back, Mountain was in a motorcycle accident and lost the lower half of his left leg, so then the President title was passed down to his son, Whiskey."

"A couple months ago, while rescuing Sunshine from a rival club who kidnapped her, Brick was shot and killed." I guess I do have the strength to talk because the words just come out.

"Did you know he was your dad when he died?" Abby pulls my other hand into her lap.

"Nope." I shake my head. "One day, I was in Whiskey's office and was looking at the club pictures on his bookshelf. I found this old envelope and it had a polaroid picture sticking out of it. It was like a beacon calling out to me. I picked it up and recognized it immediately. It was the exact same picture I have in my room."

"How did Whiskey have it?"

"Long story short," Smoke picks up again, "after Brick died, Sunshine and her men moved into his cabin out back. She was sorting through his things and found a family photo album. Tucked inside was a letter written from Haze's mom to Brick, telling him he had a son but that she didn't want Brick to have anything to do with them."

"So, let me get this straight." Abby looks between us, her face getting redder by the second. "Your mom raised you alone? She didn't tell you Brick was your dad? And now that he's dead, you still don't have a dad? What the hell?"

"I don't know, Abby," I say softly. "Please don't be mad for me. I'm still processing everything, but I'm fine. I promise."

Abby shakes her head and jumps off the bed. She starts pacing, fists clenched at her sides. "I don't know why I'm so mad right now. This isn't fair for you. Wait a minute." She stops moving, frozen, staring at me. "You've been in this club for years now, but you only just found out he was your dad. Does that mean you've been around him this long and never knew?"

"Listen to our spunky lady stickin' up for you." Smoke nudges me with his elbow. "I think we got ourselves a good one."

"I know we do."

I stand up, grab hold of her cheeks with both of my hands, then lower my face to hers and show her just how much I appreciate her.

Molding my lips to hers, I press my tongue against the seam of her lips. They instantly part, granting me entry, and Abby lets out a soft whimper. I can feel her hands grip hold of my shirt, tugging on the cotton, holding onto me for dear life.

I continue to cup the sides of her face as we battle each other for breath. I stand stock-still, soaking in and worshipping this woman with every thrust of my tongue.

I probably would keep going if it weren't for my brain registering a knock at the door behind me.

Pulling back, I drop my forehead to Abby's. Moving my hands from her face to her shoulders, I can feel her whole upper body moving up and down slowly.

Wrapping her in my arms, I turn us so I can see who Smoke is now talking to at the door. It's Trooper.

Smoke looks over. "Clubhouse meeting in five. And there's been some new developments."

I nod. "We'll be right down."

Trooper disappears, and Smoke steps behind Abby, wrapping himself around her, his hands landing on my hips. "Let's go get this over with. I'm ready to start our lives together."

Abby turns and kisses him. "I want that more than anything," she says softly.

Heading downstairs, we find an empty couch. Smoke takes the left cushion, I sit on the right, and Abby drops in between us. She reaches a hand out in each of our directions, and we grab hold of hers, showing the entire room that she's ours. We watch the room get fuller as every person involved with the club finds a place to settle in.

Once everyone's here, Whiskey stands in front of the Church doors and explains what's going on. While we

Brothers know from discussing it earlier, now's the time to fill in all the family members and Prospects.

Whiskey talks about the security breach of the cameras at the clubhouse and The Lodge, how Abby's car was stolen by her ex, and how by tracing the IP address, Cypher discovered it was said ex who did the hacking.

He then goes on to explain that Toby is currently missing, basically gone in the wind, and how everyone with available resources is trying to find him. What he did was not only cruel to Abby, but our club doesn't stand for abusive people. He definitely fucked with the wrong MC.

"I got a call a half-hour ago from one of my old FBI connections," Trooper says as he steps forward. "Don't worry, he's not a fed. Just a guy with some very deep pockets and access to some high-power people.

"He informed me that Tobias Moretti, along with several of his religious cohorts, is under investigation by the Kansas state special crimes division of the FBI for several counts of unlawful and underage marriages, along with welfare fraud, amongst a handful of other crimes. No raids have been done yet, but evidence is being collected."

Smoke raises his hand, drawing the room to look at us. "Is this something we need to be concerned about for Abby?"

"Not at the moment." Trooper shakes his head. "Abby's name is on their list, but they know she's not involved in anything illegal. Because of the divorce, she's low on the list and most likely will never be called."

"Thank God." I feel Abby deflate between us. Smoke wraps an arm around her shoulder, and she leans on him while I hold her hand tight in both of mine.

"There's no sign of her car yet, but the search is still on," Cypher says from his perch at the end of one of the long dining tables. "Feelers have been put out to several trusted resources, and I have multiple computer programs running, so fingers crossed something pops up soon."

"And when it does, everybody better be ready to roll out," Whiskey adds as he folds his arms over his chest.

"Not that this isn't important, because it is," Duchess smiles from the couch in front of us, "but what about the Halloween party? I hate to sound like a whiny bitch, but we've got people scheduled to come from Michigan. Are they still coming?"

"I know you want the party, love," Whiskey replies, showing a sad smile for his Old Lady, "but for now, let's put the party on the back burner. If we get this all sorted before then, yes, but I make no promises."

"I called Scar this morning," Steel says, standing beside Whiskey. "The Iron Darkness MC is still slated to be here in two weeks, and they know what's going on. They're onboard to helping if the problem is still going on."

"That's fine. We have all the supplies, so I'm decorating regardless." Duchess and Angel high five, causing the room to laugh, breaking a bit of the tension that's slowly grown as we've been sitting here.

"That's fine," Whiskey says with a wink for her. "We'll take it day by day."

"Any questions?" Steel asks the room.

To my surprise, Abby raises her hand. "When you catch Toby, can I see him before you kill him?"

"What?" I gasp as Smoke's mouth drops open.

"What?" She shrugs, like her question is no big deal, just a normal thing for anyone to ask. "I may not know what y'all do in this club, but I'm getting one hell of a crash course. Not that I'm not appreciative of what y'all are doing for me."

"I like her." I see Kraken standing in my periphery.

"Me too." Mountain chuckles from his recliner, Blue in his lap.

Whiskey approaches and sits on the coffee table in front of Abby. Elbows braced on his knees, he gives her his full attention. "Can I ask why you wanna see him?"

And with the boldness I'm instantly proud of, she looks Whiskey dead in the eyes and says with the power of a warrior, "He deserves a little payback."

"What does that mean?" Whiskey tilts his head in slight confusion.

Abby looks between me and Smoke. "It means the emotional wounds weren't the only ones Toby knew how to keep hidden."

Whiskey sits straight up, shocked. "He hit you?"

Abby nods once. "Yes, sir."

"Well, then," Whiskey growls as he slaps his hands hard on his knees, "I make no promises on what condition he'll be in, but I'll try my damnedest to let you take a few swings at him."

"I appreciate that."

"Anything for a future Old Lady." Whiskey winks, gets up, and walks away, leaving her mouth open wide now.

I can hear the noise around me pick up, but the sounds are muffled in my ears. In the back of my mind, I knew there was abuse, but hearing it in her words brings it to life. When I get my hands on Toby, he's a dead man.

Pressure on my left thigh snaps me back to reality. The room grows loud again with everyone talking around us.

I look to my left and see Smoke's and Abby's heads right next to each other. He's got himself pressed up against her back and his arms are around her waist. At some point, I let go of my hold on Abby's hand, so now both of hers are pressing down on my leg.

"Are you okay?" Abby asks, before she bites down on her lower lip, worried for me.

"I will be." Leaning forward, I kiss her lips. "Just let me process everything. I'll be fine."

"Okay." She sounds unsure but lets it go. Smoke tugs her back to lean against him as he reclines.

I lean forward, elbows on my thighs, resting my chin on my fists. This mess can't be over soon enough. Now that we've found Abby, Smoke and I need the opportunity to show her how good this life can be. Having her start out in the middle of a potential crisis isn't a good thing, even if it's something from her past. Our future is what's important.

"Haze has this thing where he needs to be in his zone to process new information," I hear Smoke telling Abby softly. "His brain is like a supercomputer. Between that and his photographic memory, Haze is a whiz."

Abby gasps. "A photographic memory? That's so cool."

"Me and my photographic memory can hear you two whispering over there." Turning my neck, I smirk at them.

"I'm sorry," Abby whispers, eyes cast downward. The emotion coming off her has suddenly changed.

I sit up and scoot closer, pressing my left thigh against her smaller right one. Lifting her chin so I can see her eyes, I ask her, "What's wrong, raven. Why the sad face?"

Abby wipes a lone tear from her cheek. "If I never came here, y'all wouldn't be dealing with my mess."

"Don't ever apologize for something that isn't your fault." I peck her trembling lips. "None of what happened to you, back in Kansas or here, is your fault."

"He's right, ya know." Smoke leans his head on her shoulder again.

"Wanna know the truth?" I ask.

Abby shrugs. "I guess."

Tucking a wild strand of hair behind her ear, I continue. "I'm sure I can speak for Smoke in saying this, but there's nowhere else we'd rather be than wrapped up in your mess."

"Who better to have your back than us?" Smoke hugs her with one arm, then reaches for my hand with his right. "You've got four very strong shoulders to lean on. We'll be here for you 'til you tell us to go away."

"Which I hope is never."

Abby's smile starts to come back, thank goodness. "I'm starting to see that."

I perk up. "Really?"

"Yea." Abby nods. "This is way super-fast, but I don't know what or how I'd be dealing with this without the two of you. I don't think I'll ever be able to repay you."

"You never have to."

"So, does this mean I'm your Old Lady then?" Abby looks back at Smoke.

I also look at Smoke, and he smiles, then turns Abby to face forward. We both stand, turn to face her, and pull her to her feet.

"How about we put that on the back burner for a hot second?" Smoke kisses her, and it lasts a little bit longer than the first quick one he dropped on her earlier. When they come up for air, he continues. "There's some things Haze and I need to get before we can make it official, but 'til then, I consider you ours in every way that matters."

"So, I'm your girlfriend but will be more soon?"

I nod. "Very soon." I intertwine my hands with both of theirs, creating a circle between us. "We need to make this special for you. Can you let us do that?"

"I don't need anything special. I just want the two of you." Abby has the biggest smile.

"You already have us, honey. Just let us do our thing, okay?" Smoke kisses her forehead.

"We're only gonna do this once. We wanna make it right," I add.

"Okay. I can see this is important to you both."

"It is," Smoke and I say at the same time.

"I just hope I don't disappoint you guys." I feel her hand squeeze mine. "I have a feeling Toby isn't going away so easily."

Smoke lifts the hand he's holding to his lips. "Why don't you let us worry about him? He's caused you enough trouble, and it's our job now to take care of you."

Then, I do the same. "After we find him, you'll never have to worry about him ever again. I promise."

And she won't. I don't know what we did to deserve this woman, but Smoke and I are damn lucky to have found her.

CHAPTER TWENTY

ABBY

As the room begins to disperse from the meeting, Smoke pulls me over to the bar as Haze stops to talk to Whiskey for a few minutes. I don't know what they're discussing, but they keep looking over at me and smiling.

"What are they talking about?" I ask Smoke.

"Nothing for you to worry about, little lady." Smoke pulls me into his chest and kisses the top of my head. "Club business."

I wrap my arms around him and look up, scrunching my eyebrows. "Club business? Is that code for something?"

"Kinda in a way, yea." This time, he kisses my forehead. "Anytime we tell you something is club business, it means we can't discuss it with you. It's all part of the club dynamic. There are just some things we can't and won't say around anyone who's not a patched Brother."

Taking in and letting out a deep breath, I settle my chin on Smoke's chest. "More stuff for me to learn, huh?"

"What are you learning?" Haze appears at my side, startling me, but I instantly settle when I feel his hand on my back. "Sorry about that. I had a question I needed to talk to the Prez about."

I turn in Smoke's arms to face Haze. "Club business?" I ask, raising an eyebrow.

Smoke starts laughing behind me, shaking me right along with him.

"I feel like I missed something," Haze says with a confused look.

I can't help but chuckle. "I'm learning more stuff about the club, is all." Taking a step forward, I hug him, and he wraps me in his arms. "Smoke just explained to me what 'club business' means."

"Ahh, I see," Haze replies as he squeezes me tight. "I have no doubt you'll figure it out and find your place."

"I hate to pop your guys' happy bubble," I turn and see Meredith approaching, "but I'm here to steal your lady."

I turn to face her, my hands settled on my hips, then stick my tongue out at her. "And where do you think you're taking me?"

Meredith laughs as she grabs my hand. "As your new bestest friend, it's my job to give you a tour of this fine establishment."

"Fine establishment?" Smoke cracks a laugh. "Who are you tryin' to fool? The clubhouse isn't the Hilton."

"You hush." Meredith smacks his bicep. "You two go, shoo, and leave us girls be. We'll be outside in a few minutes."

Both of us laughing, I'm pulled away from a pouting Haze and Smoke by my very insistent housemate. We end up standing at the front double doors facing in.

"What are you doing, you crazy woman?" I ask her, my arm looped through hers.

"Like I told the guys, I'm giving you the grand tour." Meredith stomps her cowboy-booted foot on the hardwood floor.

"I may have been carried through it, but I know where the door is." I nudge our connected arms.

"Quit your sassin'. Every good tour starts at the front door."

Meredith proceeds to walk me through the entire main floor of the clubhouse, explaining the purpose and use of every square foot.

To our left is an alcove holding two pool tables, a couple dart boards, and high-top tables. Straight ahead is the bar, which is so long and has so many stools, I can't count with how quick she whisks me by. To the right is the main area, which basically represents the living room of the clubhouse. There are several couches, recliners, and a few coffee tables, all positioned to face a television mounted on the front wall that looks big enough to be in a movie theatre.

Just past the main area is what they call the dining room. There are two long rows of cafeteria-style tables surrounded by a bunch of mismatched chairs.

"The doors there," she points at two closed doors along the wall to the right, "lead to Church. No one is allowed in there except for the Brothers. No women and no kids, ever."

"Why not?"

Meredith shrugs. "No clue. It's just a thing." She then points down a hall. "Down this hall is Whiskey's office on the right, and Mountain and Blue's bedroom to the left." We keep circling and walk past the bar again.

Smoke and Haze are facing the bar, so they don't see us, but I notice how close they are to each other. Smoke has a beer in his left hand, and his right is tucked in the back pocket of Haze's jeans. Haze has his left arm wrapped around Smoke's back and his fingers are under his shirt.

Feeling a little cheeky, I pinch Haze's backside as we walk behind them.

"Hey!" Haze spins around, lunging for me. "You better watch out, my raven. I'm gonna get you when you least expect it."

"Ooohhh, is that supposed to be a threat or a promise?" I jest back.

"Be careful, little lady," Smoke taunts with a half smirk, half smile. "I'm watchin' you."

Meredith pulls me away as we all laugh.

At the bottom of the steps is a normal width hallway to the left and two doors next to that. The hall leads to the club girls' bedrooms, and the doors are bathrooms for anyone to use so they don't have to go upstairs.

And lastly, to the left of the bar, between it and the stairs, is an extra-wide hall that leads to an industrial-sized kitchen on the right, and what I can see is an expansive backyard in front of us.

As we step out onto the covered concrete patio, I find myself speechless. Calling this a backyard isn't enough. It's paradise—only thing missing is the beach.

The backyard is bustling with activity, and there are people everywhere. I know this club has a lot of members—we were all inside just a little while ago—but seeing everyone spread out like this really shows the massive family they have here. It's like a sea of leather and denim.

Almost everyone is split off into groups, some standing in circles, others huddled around picnic tables or lounging in different kinds of outdoor chairs.

Straight ahead is an open expanse of grass, probably bigger than a few football fields, surrounded on three sides by dense woods. There's an unlit firepit a ways out, and a little to the right is what surprises me the most—playground equipment. There are swings, a few slides, climbing ladders, and even an octagon-shaped sandbox that looks like it holds a beach's worth of sand. I guess this place really is paradise.

Then, bordering the right side of the clearing are five almost identical cabins in a row. Each has a slight difference, like the fifth one has a yellow door, but for the most part, they look like they were built off the same plans.

"Who lives in those?" I ask and point as Meredith tugs on my hand, leading me toward what I just noticed is a circle of all women sitting under the overhang.

"Different families live in each cabin," Meredith explains. She pulls two chairs into the circle, and I sit next to her. "I know you've met a few of these ladies, but we'll go around the group and give introductions anyway.

"This is Duchess." She points at the pint-sized, beautiful, red-haired lady holding a sleeping baby in her arms. "She's Whiskey's Old Lady and fiancée. They have Krew.

"Next to her is Angel, her younger sister." Meredith nods at the slightly taller redhead I know as my landlord. "She's with Hammer and they have two boys. Taren is three, and Ace is two days younger than Krew.

"The lovely ray of sunshine to your left is Sunshine."

"Hi." A gorgeous blonde bombshell waves at me with one hand and holds another sleeping baby to her chest.

"Sunshine is Ring and Steel's Old Lady, and she's also Whiskey's sister. She's holding baby Ace." Meredith points out to the yard as two young kids go running past us, shrieking and laughing the whole way. "The girl kiddo running around is Opal. She's Steel, Ring, and Sunshine's daughter."

"Don't be fooled by her looks," Sunshine says with a laugh. "She may be super cute, but she's a handful of trouble just like her Daddy and Papa."

Everyone laughs with her.

"Hi, I'm Sara. I'm Ray's wife." A lady straight across from me with wavy brown hair cut in a long bob smiles at me.

"He's the super-giant of a man out there." She points across the yard, and just like he can sense her speaking about him, a behemoth of a man turns our way and lifts a hand. "Ray is a club hangaround. We just moved here this past spring. Our son, Jamie, is the little boy who just went barreling past."

Meredith continues around the circle, saying everyone's names and who they're paired up with, including two women I work with. "You know Stiletto and Raquel. They may be club girls, but they're a few of the good ones. You know them from The Lodge."

"It's nice to meet you all." I smile around the circle.

"And last but not least is me." Meredith places her hands beneath her chin with a giant smile. "I'm the awesomest roomie ever. And everyone, this is Abby. She's Smoke and Haze's new friend."

"Awesomest roomie ever?" I giggle at her. "If only you would empty the dishwasher when it's done running."

"Hey now!" She places her hand on her chest. "I can't help it if you're OCD about the kitchen being spotless twenty-four-seven."

"I'm sorry, I like a clean house." I nudge her with my shoulder.

"You two remind me of me and her." Duchess nods toward Angel. "This one didn't learn how to do her own laundry 'til she moved out."

"Hush now," Angel says as she flips off her sister. "I clean stuff just fine now. I have a toddler and an infant who don't know the meaning of cleanliness. And neither does their dad."

"So, enough of the messy talk." Sunshine turns in her seat to face me. "Tell us how you got involved with the two newest Brothers. Who saw who first?"

"It was totally unintentional," I start, shrugging a little. "I met Haze at the house when he and Whiskey came by a few weeks back to do the yardwork. Then Smoke showed up out of the blue to give me a ride to work the day my car was stolen. And they seem to have been glued to my side ever since."

"Do you like both of them?" Sunshine asks, switching the baby to lay on her shoulder, rubbing his back.

"I'm starting to. I actually really do." I look around the circle and see nothing but smiles from everyone. Sensing there's no judgment, I barrel ahead with my truth, hoping they'll understand where I'm coming from. After all, most of them are with men in this club too. "But it's all been so crazy fast. Like barely two weeks fast. I got a little girl crushy and haven't been able to look back. They swept in, and I feel like my feet haven't touched the ground since."

"That's what these men do. They run you over, pick you up, and next thing you know, you've got these monsters running around," Sara says, pointing at Jamie and Opal running past again.

I lean back in my chair, letting it take my weight. "What am I doing thinking about getting involved with two men? Am I crazy?"

"Oh girl," Sunshine laughs, "I thought the exact same thing."

"And what did you do?"

"The only thing I could do—I jumped in and held on for dear life."

All the ladies laugh, words of agreement coming from all of them.

"Have they given you the Old Lady talk yet?" Stiletto asks when the chatter dulls.

Looking down at my hands, I pick at my cuticles. "They did."

"And what'd you say?" I look up to see Angel scoot forward in her chair, taking her fussy baby from Sunshine before settling back and giving him his pacifier.

I guess there's no use in lying to these ladies. If I'm going to be with Smoke and Haze, they're all part of that package in a way. "I kinda told them I was ready."

"You did?" Duchess says with a huge smile. "That's so exciting. We need more Old Ladies around here. We're still so outnumbered by all these men, and everyone keeps having boy babies. We need all the girl power around that we can get."

Lifting my hands, I try and stop the excitement. "Nothing is official yet. They said they wanna make it special. I guess there's things they need to get first."

Sunshine reaches over and grabs my hand. "I promise, you'll love what they give you."

"Do y'all know what they meant?" I ask her.

"We sure do." Angel chuckles. "Just let the men have their moment. This is just as important to them as it will be for you. If you're nervous now, just imagine how they must be feeling? Taking an Old Lady is a big deal for any biker."

"Don't worry, honey. It'll all be worth it," adds another beautiful woman who appears seemingly out of nowhere. She's a little older than the rest of us, probably in her mid-forties. She's got dark brown hair with lighter highlights, twisted up into a messy bun on the top of her head. She sits down next to Duchess and takes Krew from her. "BeeGee needs some baby lovin's."

"Abby, this is Blue," Meredith introduces us. "She's Mountain's Old Lady."

"Then who's BeeGee?" I ask.

"I am," Blue says with a smile. "I'm married to Mountain, and Whiskey is his son, which makes this little man my grandson."

"Blue says she's too cool to be called 'Grandma', so Angel and I decided to call her 'BeeGee', short for 'Best Grandma Ever'," Duchess goes on to explain.

"That's so cool." I look between Duchess and Blue. "I call my grandma 'Gram'."

"See!" Blue's smile is even bigger now. "Even grandmas need cool nicknames."

"Enough about you and your silliness." Duchess sticks her tongue out at Blue, making all of us laugh. She kicks off her flip-flops and curls her feet under her. "Today is all about getting to know you, Abby. Tell us where you came from. We wanna know everything, warts and all."

"I agree," Angel chimes in. "I wanna know how you got away from your ex. He sounds like a slimeball."

"I third this motion," Sunshine declares.

"Motion?" Duchess laughs. "What is this? Old Lady Church?"

"Sure! Why not?" Sunshine folds her arms. "The guys get to have Church, so why can't we?"

As time goes on, all the other ladies share their stories of how they came to be involved with their perspective men, and I share my history as well. I think by the time I'm done, I've gotten a hug from every single woman here. They're all super supportive and seem to be welcoming me into the fold like I'm one of them. I can see myself fitting in with these ladies just fine.

At some point, it's decided to have an impromptu cookout, so the grills were fired up and I was shown around the giant kitchen as I helped prepare some side dishes. We had burgers, chips, pasta salads, baked beans, and cupcakes that Duchess and a few of the other Old Ladies had baked yesterday. It was a quick thrown together meal, but everything was delicious.

After loading up my plate, I find myself sitting at a picnic table between Smoke and Haze, with Mountain, Blue, and Brewer, the club's Secretary, on the other side.

When we're done eating, we're just joking and listening to the guys argue about football statistics. I try to hide my fourth or fifth yawn behind my hand, but Haze catches me and asks if I want to go in.

But before I can answer, Smoke butts in, already standing and picking up all our garbage. "I think it's time we head upstairs."

"No, it's okay." I get up to try and pull him back down next to me. "We don't have to."

"Abby, you're dead on your feet." After throwing the garbage in the trash can, he starts pulling me toward the back door. "Good night, everyone. We're gonna make this an early night."

Everyone within earshot calls out their goodbyes and good nights. I wave as best as I can, while still being pushed and pulled inside.

Smoke's the bossy, firm one, for sure, but the more I'm around him, I learn it's just part of his nature. He likes things done a certain way, and I like that about him.

Once we're upstairs and in Haze's room, the guys take their cuts off and hang them on hooks by the door. I stand there and watch them kick off their boots and set them against the wall, under the hanging cuts. Following along, almost like my body and mind are picking up on their routines already, I slip my sandals off and place them next to their much bigger boots, all in a row.

"Why don't you change into something comfy," Smoke suggests as he pulls me in for a kiss. "We can all crawl into bed and watch a movie."

Grabbing some sweatpants out of my duffel bag and digging for a shirt, I stop when Haze appears at my side with a super large black t-shirt in his hand. "You can wear my shirt."

I take it and hold it out, admiring the Tellison Recycling and Salvage logo on the front. "Thank you." I stand on my tiptoes and kiss him before ducking into the bathroom, shutting the door behind me.

I may know that I want both these men in my life, and I've done a share of getting acquainted with their lips, but I'm still a little unsure about undressing in front of them. I guess that will come with time.

Coming out of the bathroom, I freeze in my steps. I don't know why I'm so shocked, but I wasn't expecting this. Both Haze and Smoke are sitting in bed, propped against the headboard, waiting for me. They've both got flannel-looking pajama pants on, but they're naked from the waist up.

Ignoring my awkwardness, Haze pats the space between them. "Climb on up here, our pretty raven-haired goddess. We won't bite."

"Not too hard, at least." Smoke laughs at his own attempt to lighten the mood.

But it works. My feet unfreeze from the floor, and I crawl myself up the bed, then settle between them.

We get the sheet and blanket up over our legs before Smoke tosses the remote to me. "You pick."

"You guys sure?" I ask, looking back and forth.

"Yup," Haze replies. "We wanna know what kinda stuff you like to watch. We're easy to please."

"As long as it's not some runway fashion show or stupid reality dating thing." Smoke dramatically shivers, then wraps his arm around me. "Anything but those."

I snuggle myself into his chest and flip through the channels. And just to push his buttons, I stop when I find a rerun of *Project Runway*. I can't help but laugh when both of them groan at my pretend choice. Laughing as I change the channel, I soak in the day.

It may not have started out very exciting, but the calm and easiness of the evening make me realize this is where I'm meant to be. I'll wait for them to decide how to make me their Old Lady and see what's next for the three of us. Crazy ex-husbands be damned.

CHAPTER TWENTY-ONE

HAZE

We're not a half-hour into some show about two brothers hunting supernatural ghosts or some shit, when I glance down at Abby and see her eyes are closed. Smoke and I are propped up on our pillows, resting against the headboard, while Abby has snuggled herself down between us, flat on the bed.

I snake my left arm over her and find Smoke's shoulder with my fingers. He's engrossed in the show, and he startles when he feels me.

Smoke smiles at me before his eyes wander down. "She's out like a light," he whispers, gently moving a piece of loose hair off her face.

"After the craziness of today, I'm not surprised," I reply.

"Why don't we let her have the bed and head over to my room?"

"But I don't wanna leave her," I say as I look at her face half hidden in the shadows.

"We'll see her in the morning, I promise."

"Fine," I hear myself whine but don't feel any remorse for it. Abby is our woman, and I want to spend every minute with her I can. I understand him wanting her to have her own space, that's part of the reason why these two rooms are perfect for us, but it still sucks.

Not wanting to jostle our sleeping beauty, we slowly slide out of bed, then fix the blankets, making sure she's tucked in all around.

Meeting at the end of the bed, Smoke grabs my hand, and we use the connecting door to enter his room. Once in the small hallway, I push the door closed.

We crawl into bed, me on the right and Smoke on the left. I'm not sure how we'd decided who sleeps on which side, but somehow, it'd been nonverbally declared. Once we're settled under the sheet, my left arm wraps around Smoke's shoulders.

I feel his leg rub against mine as he rolls himself to face me, setting his hand on my stomach. Closing my eyes, I let his calloused hand explore and slide up my torso. But my eyes open not ten seconds later when I feel a tug on my nipple piercing.

"What do you think you're doing, mister?" I growl, sliding myself farther down into the bed. I roll to my side, so we're face to face.

His hand doesn't move, his palm somehow still flat on my pectoral.

"I was treasure hunting."

The room is mostly dark, so I can't see his features very well, but I've been looking at this man every day for the past six and a half years, so I know every line of his whole body.

"Oh really," I murmur as my right hand starts doing some exploring of its own, sliding down his chest, headed for a certain body part I feel moving below our waists. "And what'd you find?"

Smoke's hand begins its trek south just as I wrap my hand around his dick. "I found something shiny, but now, I'm onto something bigger."

While I've become more comfortable with Smoke touching my cock, letting him explore my newfound relaxed limitations, I haven't yet allowed him become intimately close with it. He's jerked me off to completion a couple times, but I haven't let him go any further than using his hand.

We also haven't discussed me letting him take my ass since our first full sexual experience, but the idea has been brewing in my mind. I want that with him. I want him to be able to take me like he so openly lets me take him. But until just now, I hadn't realized I might be ready.

Now, I need to quickly figure out how to tell him before he makes me lose my brain through my dick.

It didn't take him long to work me into a frenzy, and my hips are rocking forward, pumping myself into his hand as he squeezes my cock. My hand on him isn't doing much but holding on, but he doesn't seem to mind.

"Smoke," I say with a groan, eyes pinched shut, "I need you . . . to fuck me."

As soon as the words are out, his hand stops, and Smoke goes still.

Left hand still on my manhood, he props himself up on his right elbow. "You need what? Say that again."

Staring up at him, his long hair falling down the sides of his face, I can't help but smile. This man... this man has become my everything. Well, now half of my everything. While he may have come into my life first, there's a breathtaking, midnight-haired paragon in the next room. Their places in my heart are now equal.

And for someone who just months ago fought this relationship so hard, I'm melting faster than an ice cream cone in a locked car on a hot summer day.

"You, Smoke." I gently pull on his dick, hopefully making him understand my need. "I need you to fuck me. I need you ... now."

To say his smile is stunning isn't enough. His jaw drops, but his cheeks begin to climb higher on his face, and his smile has never been bigger or brighter. The lamp on the nightstand behind me has the dimmest bulb possible, but it provides just enough light for me to see the happiness radiating from him.

"You won't regret this, Haze." Smoke lowers his head, and we lock into an immediate battle for who's in charge of the kiss. Since he's propped himself higher than me, he wins easily.

I've let go of his dick but wrapped my arms around him. One hand on his back, pulling him down, I thread the other into his hair in a fist, keeping it out of our faces.

Using my grip on his wavy locks, I pull him back. His lips seem to have been cemented to mine, with no plans to remove themselves, but my burning lungs require a much-needed breath.

Resting his forehead on mine, we pant, chests heaving against one another. I move my hand down to his cheek, and Smoke's eyes open to meet mine.

"I'm ready," I kiss him once, "but please be gentle with me," I beg, not ashamed of my needs.

"I would never hurt you, Sam." The gentleness of this man knows no bounds. He's perfect. And using my real name, not the road names we've grown accustomed to, makes my heart skip.

"Show me what it's like, Jacob." I return the thoughtfulness with my use of his legal name.

Letting me go, Smoke crawls down to the end of the bed, taking the sheet with him, leaving us exposed to the cool moving air from the ceiling fan above. I feel my entire body break out in goosebumps as he settles himself between my knees and pulls my pajama pants off from my waist.

Once the gray flannel material is tossed somewhere into the darkness, Smoke leans over me, settling his hands beside my head. As if on instinct, my hands find his waistband and push his pants over his backside.

With knees and legs carefully moving, he's naked in seconds.

"Not to be one to look a gift horse in the mouth . . ." Smoke reaches to the side, coming back with a hair tie in hand, then kneeling back to pull his hair into a low ponytail. Once it's out of his face, he's above me again, his face just inches from mine. "Are you sure you're ready for me? We haven't really had time to prep you for this, and I'm not exactly a small man in this department." Smoke rocks his hips, rubbing his shaft against mine.

My legs are spread wide to accommodate his width, knees bent and feet settled flat on the bed.

Setting my hands on his chest, I meet his eyes. "I think as long as you take things slow, maybe a finger or two first, it'll be fine."

"Haze," I feel his whole body ripple as he chuckles, "my dick is a lot bigger than two fingers."

"But with lube—" I start, then recalculate my words to let my truth bomb drop. The last one I've yet to share with him until now. "I may not have let another man fuck me in the ass, Smoke, but that doesn't mean I haven't experimented with things myself."

My words make him sit straight up, and my hands flop to the bed with a *thump*.

"Do you mean to tell me you've been playing with toys without me?" Smoke squints, glaring at me, but his sinister smug smile shows me he's just as excited about those possibilities as he is shocked at my admission. "Have you been hiding things from me?"

Sitting up to mirror him, I grab his hands in mine. "I may have some things hidden in my drawers, but I haven't used them since we got together. I like the feeling, just never trusted anyone enough to do anything for real."

"We'll do this at your speed." Smoke kisses my cheek, rubbing his scruff against mine. Once our eyes meet, he continues. "Why don't you be on top? Then you can control how much of me you take and set the pace. I'm afraid if you let me run this show, I'll get way too excited, and I don't wanna hurt you."

Reaching to my right, I pull a bottle of lube from the nightstand and hand it to Smoke. But before anything else, he sets one hand on the headboard behind me, bringing his face centimeters from mine.

"Last chance to back out, Haze. I don't think I'll be able to stop if we don't stop now."

I tilt my chin up and, against his lips, I whisper, "Take me, Smoke. Make me yours."

"Roll over, up on your hands and knees," he growls back. "I need to get my fingers in your ass, then we'll flip positions."

I flip around and position myself as he requested, dropping my forearms to the mattress. Smoke sets his hands on my hips, I wiggle my knees apart, and the bed shifts as he settles himself between my spread legs.

I'm no stranger to prepping Smoke when I take him intimately, but experiencing it the other way around is a heavy feeling.

I hear the clicks of the lube opening and closing, then see the bottle tossed in my periphery. Looking to the side, I'm distracted but am jolted back to the matter at hand when he folds himself around me, laying his chest on my back. Smoke reaches around my waist and wraps his entire hand around my dick. The coolness is shocking, but the smoothness of his suddenly quickly moving hand distracts me from the temperature shock. Things start getting very warm, very fast.

Fisting my hands and dropping my face down, I stop myself from grabbing my man, flipping us over now, and fucking him instead of letting him take down my last barrier and fucking me.

"Put your fingers in me, Smoke," I pant. "Now."

"Someone's a little impatient," he replies, snickering at my pain.

My dick is at full mast, and every nerve in my body is on high alert. The muscles in my legs are tight, and my toes are curling and flexing with every pump of his slick hand on my cock.

"Impatiently waiting for you to fuck me."

And just as fast as he started jacking me off, he stops. But the sensations don't stop for long. Smoke's weight disappears as he sits back. Tucking my neck to look between my legs, I see Smoke wrap his unlubricated hand around me, pulling my hardness down. His strokes are slow but steady.

That's when I feel the tip of his finger trace down my spine and over my clenched crack. But at his touch, I don't freeze or shut down or push him away. This time, I let my hips drop open, allowing him the entrance he's silently asking for.

His fingers are gentle as his digit traces a circle around my previously forbidden hole.

"Yes," I hiss, feeling the last stone crumble.

"That feel good?" Smoke asks as he presses against my tight ring. I feel my sphincter flex, and his finger slides in on the first push. "There we go. I knew you could do it."

I bury my face in the pillow, letting out a deep groan. "More," I try to say, but it comes out muffled.

"You want more?" I feel Smoke press his finger deeper before pulling it back out. I hear the snap of the lube again, followed by a cool shot against my sensitive skin. "How about two fingers?"

"Please," I beg, desperate for more.

Feeling more pressure against my hole, a sharp twinge of pain runs up my spine when his fingers slide back in. I unlock my knees, pushing my ass back against his invading fingers.

A slap comes down on my left ass check, causing me to push back again, almost chasing his quickly retreading hand. "You want more, Haze?"

"Stop." Pushing up onto my hands, letting my shoulders come off the bed, I resituate myself so my torso is parallel to the mattress. I turn my head so I can see Smoke behind me. "If you don't get your cock in me now, I'm gonna grab it and fuck myself with it just like this." I give my hips a little more of my weight, pushing against him enough to show him how serious and fucking needy I am.

Whether it's retaliation for my harsh words or him being the asshole he is, Smoke's fingers in my ass start moving so fast, I see stars even with my eyes open. Between the lube and his knuckles rubbing against my deepest parts, he has no problem battering me from the inside out, and I'm powerless to stop him.

Knowing I'm about to explode from his fingers in my ass, I bury my face in the pillow, ready to scream because I can feel the tingle running down my spine. I'm stunned when all of a sudden everything stops.

Every nerve in my body feels like it's on fire when Smoke's touch suddenly disappears. The abrupt switch from everything to nothing sends my nervous system into shock. Both of his hands are gone, and I feel him fall to the side of the bed.

Lifting my head, I take a huge breath, filling my lungs with the air I didn't realize I wasn't taking in. I turn to find Smoke lying beside me.

"What the fuck?" I swear, still panting.

"You told me to stop, so I did." His smirk is back in full effect.

"Yea," I slide my knees straight back and flop my weight onto my stomach, "that was before you decided to scissor me from the inside. I almost came from your fingers alone."

"Well, now, I want you on my dick."

I feel his arm moving against my side and I look down to see his right hand wrapped around his dick, slowly pumping the hardness up and down. Fuck, I feel my own cock twitch against my stomach. If I don't get him inside me now, I might actually come from watching him play with himself.

Maybe some other time. Today, I want him inside me too bad for that.

Moving fast, I position myself above Smoke, my knees on either side of his waist. I rest my ass on his thighs as I feel his left hand slide up my flank, coming to a stop on my hip. His right hand is still around his cock.

Growing impatient, I push his hand aside and feel how slick he is for myself. Deciding he could be wetter, I find the lube beside us, tip the bottle on end, and let a fair amount flow down over his cock and my fingers holding it straight up.

Smoke hisses at the cold, but I pay it no mind. My mind is focused one hundred percent on what I'm about to do next.

Once I'm happy with the generous amount of lube that will aid him in finally taking me, I toss the bottle, hearing it hit the wall.

Smoke's hands slide up my chest, flicking my piercings along the way, before settling on my shoulders. He pulls me toward him, so I let go and settle my hands beside his head. "You ready for me, Sam?" he whispers as he draws me closer for a kiss.

I flick his upper lip with my tongue, making him chase my lips before I give in. I press my tongue into his mouth and ravage him. But before things get too crazy, I pull back just as fast.

"I need you to guide me, Jacob," I say as I rest my forehead against his. "Put your cock in me. I'll do the rest."

"Whatever you need."

Spreading my knees to give him room, he slides his hand between us. I look down and watch as he gives himself a few pumps, then pushes down so his hardness is standing straight up behind me.

Feeling his tip at my hole, I push my hips back, the head breaching my sphincter right away. As if hitting a switch, every tense muscle I had left goes loose, and my body gives him entry with zero resistance.

Smoke's hands are suddenly at my sides, holding me tight, and I have full control of both of us. "Fuck me. Goddammit, fuck me," he groans.

Locking my concentration on my lover's face, I lower myself down his length in one non-stop movement until my ass is flush with his hips. I know my mouth is open because every breath I take is a pant at this point, but seeing Smoke's expression makes me feel euphoric. He looks to be even more in heaven than I am.

His eyelids are lowered and his mouth is open slightly, but his teeth are clenched tight. It looks like he's trying not to move a muscle.

Setting my hands on his chest, I let my hips lift, exploring the feeling of him inside me in reverse. And it's just as good, if not better, than before.

Heat flows through my body like a wave crashing over me, and I snap.

"Fuck, Smoke." I sigh as I let my knees and hips set the pace. Using my hands on him to balance, I drop all my weight down onto his lap with each bounce.

Suddenly, his grip on my hips turns painful, though not in a bad way. His fingertips press into my skin as his legs move under me. Peeking behind me, I see his feet flat on the bed, knees bent, then I feel what he's doing under my ass.

On my next slam down onto his cock, Smoke pushes his hips up into me, and I freeze. He takes over, thrusting and pushing up into me deeper than I could've done. My hands lose traction on his sweaty chest, so trying to not fall, I end up with my hands flat on the wall in front of my face. I would've faceplanted on top of Smoke had I not locked my core.

Elbows locked, I hold myself up as Smoke uses my body as his personal toy. He may have given me the time to get acclimated to his girth and length, but apparently, feeling me was too much for him. He's always been a bossy bastard, so I have no issue letting him control me now. Especially with how good he's making me feel.

While on one hand I'm mad I waited so long to experience this feeling, on the other, I'm so fucking happy I waited for this man. The road we took to get here was a rough one, but I would've ridden over a thousand potholes to arrive right where I am now.

"Keep going, like that." I drop my head down, chin to my chest, eyes pinched shut. "Just like that, Smoke. Just . . . like . . . that."

"I'm . . . almost . . . there," Smoke grunts each word sharply.

"Come for me. Come in me," I say between breaths.

Knowing he's about to fill me sends me right to the brink. Left hand braced on the wall, I grab my cock with my right and spread my leaking precum around the tip and down the shaft with every jerk.

Fuck. I've never felt this fucking good in my life. Having Smoke's dick slamming in and out of my ass, rocking both of us with every thrust, it's a whole new experience. If this is how it is every time, we're going to have a battle on our hands as to who gets to fuck who each time we take our clothes off.

There's no way I'm going to last.

This time, he goes so deep, a sensation takes over my whole body. It's more intense than when I fucked myself with my hand.

As weird as it sounds, I feel like my body is in two parts. It's like there's my real body, the one that's on top of Smoke, kneeling on the bed. Then there's the ghost version of myself floating above us. Every inch of my skin is affected by what's happening to me, but I can almost picture myself watching what's happening to me.

"I'm coming," I shout, surprising myself. And I do. I come so hard and so thunderously, I don't recognize the sounds coming out of my mouth. I don't know or care where they come from, or what I'm saying or not saying, I just let it all out.

I blast cum up Smoke's chest and across his abdomen in ropes of white that never seem to end. And I don't stop until my dick becomes too sensitive, and I have to let myself go.

Then, almost like a growling volcano, Smoke explodes right in front of my eyes.

His entire body rumbles as he wraps his arms around my back, forcing me to fall on top of him. Grunts and groans fill my ear as he chases his release and falls off the cliff himself.

Slowly regaining my strength, I move up to my elbows, letting some of my weight off Smoke. I don't get far. His arms wrap around me tighter, not letting a breath between our skin.

"Where do you think you're goin'?" He chuckles, shaking both of us.

"Just tryin' to let you breathe." My forearms bracket his head and I lower my lips to kiss him. "And as good as you feel in my ass, I need to move."

"Kneel up, and I'll let gravity do its thing."

Pushing up onto my hands and knees, I almost buckle when my nerves take another hit as his cock slides out of me.

Luckily, Smoke is three steps ahead of me, because he holds my side with one hand while guiding his dick out of my hole with the other. Once he's free of me, he somehow finagles himself out of my trembling limbs and has me lying on my side. He sits, one leg hanging off the bed.

"You have magic fingers." I roll over, flat on my back, in a daze. Between the life-draining orgasm and the adrenaline rush, my battery is dead.

"In more ways than one," Smoke says with a barking laugh as he flops beside me, causing the bed to shake.

I turn my head and see his lazy smile as he looks back at me.

Although I feel good and don't regret anything, I feel a bit embarrassed about how quickly I came. Any other time, whether with a woman or even with Smoke, I'd been able to hold myself off from coming like that. It's like as soon as he got me going, there was no stopping.

"I'm sorry I came on you like that." I look down at the mess smeared on his torso.

"Oh, this?" Smoke runs a finger down his sternum, collecting my seed on his finger before bringing it to his lips and licking it off. "If that felt half as good for you as it did for me, we're in trouble."

"Why's that?" I ask with a laugh.

"Because no matter who has their dick in who, if we set each other off like that, we'll have to be up all night, going round after round. We'll never sleep again."

Laughter fills the room. His carefree and wild attitude sends all my worries out the window, never to be thought of again. Smoke really knows how to talk me off the ledge and bring my spirits back to him.

"Let's get you cleaned up." Smoke gets up, and I watch his firm, muscular backside shift side to side as he heads for the bathroom. From my position in bed, I can see his reflection in the mirror, so I get an after-sex show too. After wiping himself clean and tossing a washcloth in the laundry basket, he grabs a second wet rag and comes strutting back into the room.

Holding out my hand, he slaps it away. "I can do that myself."

"I made the mess, I clean it up," he replies. "You do the same for me. Now, it's my turn."

Giving in, I lie back and let him wipe me down, being gentle of my sensitive hole. "I don't know why I waited so long to do that. Your dick was made for my ass."

"I'm glad you waited." Smoke smacks my thigh as he gets up. "Your ass will be mine forever."

I can't do anything but chuckle and roll my eyes at him as he tosses the washcloth in the bathroom. When he turns back around, his hand freezes over the switch on the other side of the wall.

Smoke's eyes are locked on something to my left, so I sit up. "What's wrong?"

An evil grin grows, and he says with laughter, "Didn't you close the door when we came in here?"

"Yea, why?"

"It's open."

"The door's open?" That gets me to my feet. I step into the hallway space between our rooms, and sure as shit, the door is open just a crack. Looking back at Smoke, I find him right behind me, my pajama pants in his hand. "Do you think she heard us?"

"I guess there's only one way to find out."

We both get our pants on and head for the mystery hiding behind door number one. I wonder what she heard or saw, if anything, and what she thought about it.

What we were doing wasn't unusual for people in a relationship like ours, but this is all still so new to her. I hope it doesn't scare her away.

Pulling the door all the way open, we step into my bedroom. Abby is lying on the bed, comforter tucked under her chin, eyes pinched shut.

Looking back at Smoke, I see the smirk on his face that mirrors my own. "Someone's pretending," he whispers in my ear.

"Let's see what our raven has to say for herself," I whisper back.

"Abby?" Smoke calls out as he wraps an arm around my waist.

Her eyes open in a flash.

CHAPTER TWENTY-TWO

SMOKE

When we left Abby sleeping in Haze's room earlier, I didn't expect what happened, but I'm so glad it did. Haze let down the final wall he was holding between us and let me fuck him for the first time. But now, knowing that our sweet woman may have witnessed it is sending me into the stratosphere. If I thought being buried inside my partner was heaven, thinking about her watching us is making my dick hard as a rock—again.

Standing in the shadows, I wrap my arm around Haze's waist, and he leans against me. "Abby?" I call out.

The only part of her sticking out of the black comforter is her head, so I see the second her eyes pop open. I know she wasn't really sleeping. I mean, who lays flat on their back, body perfectly straight?

"Were you spying on us, beautiful?" I lean on Haze a bit, and he bumps me with his hip while chuckling.

"I woke up, and you both were gone." Abby sits up, letting the blanket fall to her waist. "Then I heard some noises."

Haze takes a step forward and walks toward the left side of the bed. "What'd it sound like?"

Her eyes drop and she fiddles with the edge of the sheet, not looking at us. "Like moaning."

"And what'd you see when you opened the door?" I make my way to the right side and crawl in beside her.

My question is met with silence. Both Haze and I are now under the blanket with her, scooted as close to her as we can be. If we were any closer, we'd be a pile of bodies.

Although, that sounds like a situation I'd like to get myself into.

"Come on, you can tell us." Haze reaches for her right hand, untangling it from the sheet.

I do the same to her left, holding her trembling fingers in mine. "Did you like what you saw?" I lift her chin. Even in the dark, the only light in the room coming from the lamp on the nightstand behind me, I can tell she's blushing.

She finally peeks up at me. "Yes."

"Then why didn't you say anything?" I ask as I trace my finger down her cheek.

"'Cause I didn't want to interrupt. I felt like a Peeping Tom."

"Oh honey," Haze turns her attention toward him, a big smile on his face, "we would've been even more in heaven had we known you were watching."

"I agree." Oh fuck, do I.

Abby's dark eyes go wide, shocked by our admission. "You do?"

"Maybe you could've joined us." I lean in to kiss her cheek, letting my lips ghost across her skin as my words flow.

Her head tips back, allowing me room to continue down to her neck. "What do you mean, join you?" she asks, ending with a sigh.

Haze leans in as well, his mouth laying kisses on her bare shoulder exposed by the extra-large neckline of the t-shirt she's wearing. "What do you think we meant when we said we wanted you to complete us?"

She turns her head, displacing both Haze and me. "We can do that?"

"We sure can." I instantly don't like not having my lips on her, so I lean in again, this time going for the main prize. Her lips. I watch her eyes close a fraction of a second before mine do.

Her response is hesitant at first, but once I swipe her lower lip with my tongue, she blossoms like a flower in the spring. Abby opens her mouth and, using my tongue, I coax hers out to play. She tastes lightly of mint and sweetness.

The first kiss I laid on her in the main room was purely on instinct. I had no thoughts of right or wrong, I just kissed her before walking toward Church. But this kiss . . . this kiss is methodical. I want her to know this is the real deal. We've got something to prove here.

While sex may not be the most important part of a relationship, I'm a selfish fucking asshole and I need it. I need that connection with my partners. I need to be able to touch and feel them and show them my affection. And I need those same things from them. Touch is almost like my second language—I feed off of it.

While my kisses and roaming hands have turned Abby to face me, I feel the bed shift and know instantly that Haze has positioned himself behind her. I feel his hands brush against mine as he wraps his arms around her. The second she realizes what's happening, her lips stop moving, and I feel her body tense.

Moving my lips to her cheek, then down to her neck again, she relaxes a little more with each kiss. "It's okay, my raven. He's not gonna hurt you."

I think kissing her neck might be her weakness, and I'm more than happy to give it all the attention it needs if this is what it takes to turn her into putty.

"I'm only here . . . to give you . . . everything you need," Haze assures her between kisses of his own.

Sitting back, I watch as Haze pulls Abby's weight back on him.

Seeing her eyes closed, mouth open just a fraction, sighing like she has no care in the world, this is why I want this life. Watching the man I want to spend the rest of my days on this spinning rock with showing his affection to the woman who somehow fell into our lives, this is the start of our lives.

Haze maneuvers himself so he's sitting with Abby between his legs. Her back is to his chest, her head upturned at an angle, and in just the last minute, they've engrossed themselves in a hot, sloppy kiss. I see flashes of teeth and tongue, and I need to get myself more involved in this action.

Pushing the blanket and sheet out of my way, I kneel between four spread legs. Untangling Haze's hands from her waist, I find the bottom of the black t-shirt and start lifting it. Haze leans back, and with his help, we get the material over Abby's head and thrown on the floor.

"Oh!" Abby shrieks, covering her bare chest with her arms.

Settled back, butt on my heels, I pull Abby up by her elbows to kneel in front of me. I trace my fingers up to her shoulders, then down the front of her chest, ghosting her skin as I try to will her arms to move.

"Let me see you, Abby." I lean my head down to hers, drawing her eyes up to mine. "I need to see you. *We* need to see you."

And like the genie emerging from the lamp, Abby lets her arms slowly drop to her sides, and the treasure that is her body is revealed for the first time.

She's absolutely flawless. In contrast to her inky back hair, Abby's covered in milky white skin. The dim light reflecting off her is like a beacon, luring me to her. I want to touch every inch of her.

Tracing up her arms and over her shoulders, then up her neck, I cup her face in my hands and kiss her like my life depends on it.

I take everything she has to give. I wrestle her tongue with mine and don't let go, panting for air between each lip lock, then diving in for more. I won't let any of us breathe again until we're all sated and exhausted.

Tearing my lips from hers, I straighten my arms, holding her back from me.

"Haze," I growl.

"Yea?" He lifts his head from her neck and looks at me. Lucky man has his hands full of Abby's beautiful breasts.

"I need her first." I move my attention to her. "If that's okay with you. If you want this as much as we do."

I feel Abby's forearms flex under my hands, so I loosen my grip and let her move. She sets her now steady hands flat on my bare stomach and slides them up my chest. This is the first touch she's initiated since I basically manhandled her into this position. She's looking up at me with a smile.

"I want you. Both of you." She peeks back at Haze. "I can't promise I'll be any good at this, but if you show me—"

I stop her words with a harsh kiss.

"Never say that again," I growl as I drop my forehead to hers. "You're perfect, Abby. Perfect."

"Let Smoke show you what you deserve, little raven." Haze practically purrs as he turns her head toward him, finger under her chin. "I'll be right by your side."

"Please," Abby says with a sigh.

Between the three of us, we're all stripped down in no time at all. Abby is lying flat on her back, her left knee bent, foot flat on the bed. Her hands are once again flat on my chest, tracing the lines of my muscles.

I've positioned myself on top of her, on my forearms and knees, covering her with my bulk.

Haze has himself lying out at my left, propped up on his side, tracing his hand down her arm.

Hooking her knee in my right hand, I settle my lower half down on hers, our skin from stomach to feet touching for the first time. She wraps her leg around my hip, and I sink that last inch, settling my cock into the valley of her center.

I begin rocking my hips forward, down into her, and Abby responds perfectly. She lifts her pelvis and grinds her hips against mine.

Lowering my head, I trace my nose against hers. "Do you need me to use protection, Abby?" I hate having to ask this question, but whatever makes her comfortable is how we're going to operate. While I'd love to enter her bare for the first time, she makes the rules.

"Please don't." Abby's hands move up to my shoulders and she tugs my chest down to hers. I feel her heat against my skin, and her words cause a shiver to run up my back. "I've got the implant in my arm. I'm safe."

"Thank you for trusting me, beautiful," I say with a kiss. "Are you wet for me?"

"I think so." She sighs, closing her eyes, stretching her neck back.

"I can feel you against my dick." I haven't stopped rocking against her. "You should feel how wet she is, Haze. Feel her."

I lift up, vertical to the bed, separating our chests. Abby's hands slide down and grip hold of my sides.

Haze sits up and wraps one hand around my dick, then works the tips of the fingers of his other hand into her folds.

Abby moans the second he touches her. Using my right hand, I intermingle my fingers with his, finding her hard bud and pinching it.

"Shit," she cries out. "Oh god. More."

"I need in her, Haze," I pant at him as he slowly pumps my girth.

"Then do it. What's stopping you?" The cocky fucker is now kissing up my shoulder.

"I can't put my dick in her with your hand on it." Now wrapping my right hand around his, I follow his movements, just for a second. His grip feels amazing, but I have another sheath I'd like to explore.

"I'll put it in for you if you'd like." Haze snickers in my ear.

"Fuck me." I huff out a hard breath. "You're gonna kill me before we even start."

Haze lifts her left leg to wrap around me to mirror her right. Using our joined hands around my dick, I press down, finding her heat on the first try.

Letting go of myself, I move my hand to Abby's leg, holding her to me, and let Haze guide my tip to her entrance.

And as soon as the back of his hand slides across my hip, I thrust, pushing my cock deep into her pussy in one forward movement.

"Holy shit," I call out.

"Fuck," Abby yells, eyes closed, head thrown back.

There's no going back now. I can't stop. Hips driving forward, harder with each push, I thrust in and out, chasing my personal nirvana. My very own heaven and hell. If I thought fucking Haze earlier was my own personal heaven, this must be my fucking lucky day—pun fucking intended.

I need to be so deep inside this woman, she doesn't know where she ends and I begin. I pound my hips against her, forcing her muscles to recognize I'm the one who fucked her and gave her all the pleasure she's now screaming out.

Abby hasn't stopped crying out obscenities since I started ravishing her. After all we've learned about her in our short time together, I never knew she had the vocabulary of a sailor. We really need to get her to speak like this more often. With every *fuck* and *shit* and *hell* that passes her lips, I dive deeper into her.

Haze has made it his mission to drive her absolutely bat shit crazy by playing with her tits. He has his tongue, teeth, and lips making a chew toy out of her right breast. And his right hand is pinching and twisting the left nipple, making her bud pink, standing out against her pale skin.

The grunts coming out of him draw my attention to the fact that I can no longer see Abby's right hand. When I follow her arm under his side, I see her elbow is moving.

Holy fucking shit, Abby is jacking him off, and I can't fucking see it.

"Haze." Keeping my right hand on her, I use my left to pull up on his shoulder. "I need to see what she's doing."

Haze sits up on his knees, giving me the perfect view of her tiny hand wrapped around his angry, hard cock. I watch as his hands ball into fists, then he grabs hold of my shoulder, balancing himself. "Please tell me one of you is gonna come."

Now that he mentions it, I need to focus on our lady. Left hand sprawled on her stomach, I drop my thumb and find the magical bundle of nerves peeking out of her pussy lips.

Not two rocks of my thumb later, Abby's entire body stretches, goes completely still, and she screams so loud, I wouldn't be surprised if people downstairs heard her explode.

Haze silences her with his lips as he bowls over, bent in half, his hand wrapped around hers on his cock as he climaxes across her chest.

Seeing and hearing their grunting and groaning and moaning sends my endorphins into hyper drive. I kick my hips into a speed I didn't know they could move in and feel my balls pull tight. On the last thrust I can give, I drop my hips down and feel my brain drain out of my dick.

I drop my hands to the pillow, bracketing Abby and Haze's heads, and fold myself over both of them, panting to catch enough of a breath that I don't black out.

"Fuck . . . me." I sigh between breaths.

Haze slides out from under me, settling on his back beside Abby. He looks up at me, smirk already in place. "Give me five minutes and your ass is all mine."

"HA!" Abby starts laughing so hard, she snorts.

I feel her pussy spasm around my dick, and it's too much. I slide my hips back until my pelvis is flat on the bed, Abby's center is against my stomach, then I rest my chin on her sternum, right between her twin beauties. I turn my head to the left and nip at the side of her breast.

"You can't fuck me and Abby at the same time," I mock Haze back, wiggling my eyebrows. Abby giggles again. Needing her lips, I crawl up and dive in. No tongue or aggression needed, I kiss her just because I can. When I sit back, I pull her up to sitting.

One hand resting on my chest, Abby looks at me, then over to Haze, and I watch as his eyes go wide when she tugs him close. She anchors him to her with her hand on the back of his neck. "Will you fuck me now, Haze?"

Her words shock my heart and get Haze and I moving faster than before.

Round two.

CHAPTER TWENTY-THREE

ABBY

"Will you fuck me now, Haze?"

I don't know where I got the gumption to ask that, but with the way Smoke just controlled my body, making it do things it's never done before, I want more. Having my hand on Haze's manhood—holy crap is it huge—makes me want to see if it will fit.

Based on how Smoke's dick felt inside me, I mentally compare the two.

Smoke is hung like a fucking horse, pardon my language. Seeing that his and Haze's hands combined couldn't cover his length, I don't know how he entered me so smoothly.

And while Haze may not be as long, he's really not lacking in that department. But his girth is almost scary. When he was doing crazy things to my breasts earlier, my hand slid down his chest and I wrapped my fingers around him. Or at least I tried, because my fingers didn't meet, he's so big.

Apparently, my question drove them batty, because the next thing I know, Haze is lying on his back, I'm kneeling over him, hands on his stomach, and Smoke is kneeling behind me.

"You don't even have to ask," Haze says, tugging on my hands until I fall over him, settling myself on all fours.

"Fuck, this sight is hot as hell," Smoke speaks up. "Baby, you got one mighty fine ass." I feel his hands palm my butt and squeeze.

"Which one of us are you talkin' about?" Haze lets out a chuckle as he kisses up my neck.

"Both of you." Smoke's hands disappear, but not for long. He folds himself over my back, tugging my head to the side by my braid and sliding his right hand between Haze and me. I can feel him grab Haze's dick. "I may have had your ass earlier, Haze, but the one I just had my hands on is fuckin' phenomenal. Wait 'til it's shimmin' right in front of your dick."

"I look forward to it," Haze mumbles, teeth nipping my earlobe. His hands are holding my waist still, and his hips are rocking below mine, pushing his hardness up and between my folds. I have no doubt if he kept on just like this, he could make me orgasm without ever entering me.

But that's not what I or my lady parts want. We're greedy now that we've had one piece of the pie. I want another piece, and another, until I've had the whole damn thing.

Balancing myself on one hand, I take the other and thread it into the few inches of hair Haze has on top of his head. I lower my face to his and whisper, "Please fuck me, Haze. You can look at my backside later."

"Oh, you asked for it," he says with a snarl. "Smoke, fuckin' put my dick where it belongs."

Smoke lifts my hips with his left hand and guides Haze's dick to my center. And with a not so gentle push forward with his hips, Smoke presses me forward, impaling Haze inside me in one forward thrust.

All three of us groan at the same time.

"Holy fuck, Abby, you're so tight," I hear Haze say.

I have no clue what anything around me looks like anymore. My eyes are closed tight and my head is thrown back, resting against Smoke's shoulder. I also have no control of what's happening to me.

My hands are moved and grabbed and placed by the men around me.

Below me, I feel the bed bounce because the pelvis pressing against my core is thrusting up every other second.

My upper body is wrapped in one arm, a hand bracketing the opposite shoulder. I feel fingers from another hand pushing into my folds, rubbing against a spot that's driving my insides wild. And there are two hands on my waist, but I can't distinguish from who or where they're coming from.

I feel myself floating and moving, and my pussy is having miniature spasms the whole time, but I have no power to stop anything. Not that I ever want this to stop.

There definitely was no need to worry about Haze fitting inside me, because the way I seem to be molded to his cock, it feels like he was made for me.

If it's possible to be made for two men, I've been blessed for sure. There's no way in heaven or hell I'll ever compare or complain about these two gods surrounding me. *They* were made for me.

The hands on my waist grip me tighter, forcing my eyes to open, and I look down to see Haze's fingertips turning white as he holds me to him. His eyes glare up at me, and in a flash, one of his hands grabs my neck around the front, not choking me but forcing me down to him.

I close my eyes as we ravage each other. If I could crawl inside him, I would.

I feel a hand move below me, between my legs, and whatever it's doing, it makes Haze's whole body rumble.

He wraps his arms around my entire body, arms and all, and I fall against his chest with an *oomph*. His knees bend up, feet flat on the bed, and he fucks me faster and harder than before. His last gear is engaged, and I'm the one to reap the rewards.

My spasms turn into fireworks, and I orgasm so hard, I see them behind my eyelids.

I hear myself scream, but there's nothing I can do to stop it, so I bury my face into Haze's neck and let it out. It's muffled a bit, but not much.

Haze's rumbling turns into grunts as he ruts into me, and I feel him pulse inside me. I count in my head every time his lower body jerks, one . . . two . . . three . . . up to eight before he stops moving altogether.

"Ohhhhh, fuck me," I hear Smoke bellow just as something light tickles across my spine. It happens a few more times. He still has one hand on my hip, but as my senses come back online, I can tell from the shaking behind me that he was jacking himself off and just came on my back.

Haze lets go of my waist and threads his right hand into the back of my hair. He tugs until I lift my head and rest my forehead on his. His smile is small, but I can see the joy in his eyes. "You are way more than we deserve. But fuck if we'll ever let you go."

I press a quick kiss on his lips. "I don't wanna be anywhere else," I whisper.

Something soft runs down my back a few times before I feel Smoke's heat cover me. His hands appear next to Haze's head, as mine are now folded and resting on Haze's chest.

"What are you two whispering about down here without me?"

I turn my head and kiss Smoke's cheek. "Just saying I'm happy to be here."

"And we're way more than happy to have you here with us." Smoke's grin is infectious, and I can't help but smile even bigger. He flops over onto his right side, pulling me down along side of him with a hand on my hip.

Haze slides out of me in the move, then rolls with us, his chest pressed against mine.

Over my shoulder, I see Smoke's face appear, and Haze leans up to kiss him. I can do nothing but lie here, watching the two of them show love to each other.

I've seen their affection from many angles, but this one, the one where I'm in between them, under them together, this has to be my favorite by far.

Unable to resist, I lift a hand and trace their sharp jawlines with my fingers. Both Smoke and Haze have beards, though Smoke's is a little longer, long enough to be mussed by my fingers, and he has a mustache. Haze's is buzzed close to his skin, more of a prickle than any length. The textures are different, but neither one is less alluring than the other.

They separate, lips resistant to stopping, and eventually Smoke lies back, chin propped on his hand. "That wasn't bad for our first time."

"Hell no, it wasn't." Haze snickers, twisting a loose strand of my braid around his fingers.

My hair is French braided, but the length allows the plait to come over my shoulder and across my chest.

Their words bounce around in my head, startling me once they sink in. "Your first time having sex?" I'm confused as to what they mean?

When I woke up earlier to find the bed around me empty, I heard faint noises but couldn't tell where they were coming from. The guys showed me Smoke's room, so I got up to see if they were in there watching a movie. Maybe they didn't want to disrupt me since I fell asleep.

As soon as I pushed the door open, the sounds got louder, but I still hadn't realized what I was hearing until I looked around the corner and saw Haze on top of Smoke in the bed. Shocked, I was frozen. I stood there and watched as Smoke held Haze by the hips and they were both moving. I assumed they were having sex.

Instantly embarrassed for invading their private time, I tiptoed back to the other room and crawled back in bed. I tugged the blanket tight to my chin and tried to fall back asleep, but the vision of them naked, skin to skin, continued to play behind my eyelids.

It was hot as hell.

"Our first time sharing a woman." Smoke snaps me from my flashback.

"And I can't wait 'til we get to do it again." Haze has his eyes locked on mine.

It's like I can see our future in his amber-colored eyes. There's so much possibility.

I know that what I'm feeling for both of them is real. I never saw this kind of relationship as a possibility, especially with the way Toby had treated me, trying to add a second wife to our marriage.

But this feels different. Never once during this new sexual experience did I feel cast aside or unappreciated. All of their attention and affection was focused on me. We all participated, but every movement, every decision, every hand seemed to be placed in thought of making it perfect for me.

I turn, adjusting myself until I'm on my back, looking up at both men. "Is it always like that?" I question softly.

"What do you mean?" Smoke links my left hand with his and rests them on my torso, just below my breasts.

"It's never felt like that before for me. Sex always felt like a job, an obligation."

Haze reaches for my right hand, placing my palm under his. "Did you enjoy what we just did?"

I nod. "I did."

"Can I ask what was different for you? If you're okay with telling us." Smoke kisses my temple. "I wanna know how we can make everything better for you."

Staring up at the ceiling fan, I watch the blades spin around, thinking of how to word the way I viewed my marriage. "I'd only ever been with Toby. He was my first. It was never like what we just did. I felt like sex was part of a wife's responsibility." I sit up, and they follow, rearranging to face me.

Again, like whenever one is near the other, they're velcroed at the hip. My knees are bent, legs crossed in front of me, but they've positioned themselves touching from shoulder to waist, legs straight out in front, on either side of me. The sheet has magically reappeared and is draped across all our laps.

"Did you feel that with us?" Haze shifts and leans his shoulder on Smoke's. Smoke wraps his left arm around Haze's.

"No." I shake my head. "With you two, it didn't feel anything like that. It was almost like you both were doing it for me."

"That's because we were," Haze says with a smirk.

"Abby, I'm sorry you didn't have the best past." Smoke rests his free hand on my knee. "But we're going to do everything we can to make the future you have with us the best it can be."

"For us, sex is a two-way street. Well, a three-way street, if you wanna be technical." Haze chuckles.

Their laughs make me feel lighter and happier than I've ever been before.

"Is it always going to be the three of us together?" I ask with a laugh of my own.

Smoke shakes his head. "Not necessarily. Majority of the time, we'll all sleep in one bed, but there might be nights where each of us needs some one-on-one attention."

"But it's not something we keep track of. This relationship is all three of us, and sometimes that might mean we need a connection more with one person," Haze replies. "If someone feels like they need something, we need to be open and upfront about it. If you need some time with just Smoke, tell him. If we all do that, everything will work out just fine."

"And the same goes for Haze and me. That's why this attached room set-up works perfectly for us. There will be times when we need each other," Smoke adds.

"Or I need a night to myself," I comment.

"Exactly," Smoke replies. "I don't think it's something we need to stress on. Let what happens, just happen."

"So, you're both still sure that this," I wave my hand between us, "is what you guys want?"

"You're ours, no questions needed." Haze pulls my hand back into his. "I just wish we'd met you sooner."

"She came just when we needed her most." Smoke pulls Haze in for a kiss.

"I'm glad I found you two." I squeeze their hands. "I'm done doubting myself. This is it for me. I never saw myself as a biker lady. Heck, I never knew that was a thing. But if you say I am, I believe you."

"We always intended to share a woman who we both felt completed us. The woman who completed our knot." Smoke traces his hand down Haze's chest.

"Your knot?" I ask. "What does that mean?"

"See my tattoo, love?" Haze points to the tattoo on his chest that Smoke is tracing with his fingers.

"It's a Celtic cross. Are you Irish?"

"I am, on my mother's side." He nods. "But that's not all of it. Celtic knots have a lot of meaning." I listen to Haze's words and soak it all in. I can tell this is important to him, so I want to learn everything. "They represent eternity because they never end. There's no beginning or end to a knot. They symbolize that life and love and loyalty are all interconnected."

"That's amazing." I untangle my hand and trace my index finger down the center of the design inked into his skin.

"No matter where life takes us, the three of us are one. At the end of every day, we come back to this place, right here, all having each other to lean on."

"And one day, when the time is right, when you're ready, if you want," Smoke squares his shoulders and lets out a big breath, "you and I will tattoo this symbol on our skin to show our connection."

"You want me to get this as a tattoo?"

"If that's what you want," Haze answers.

I don't have any tattoos. I've never really wanted one, honestly. That's not saying I don't appreciate the artwork that some people have, because both of them do and I could stare at them for hours, but I never pictured getting any myself. Maybe it's just because I've never seen a design that warranted being permanently placed into my skin.

The idea, as crazy as it sounds because they just threw it out there, doesn't bother me as much as I think it should. A design like the Celtic cross, on the other hand, would be very meaningful.

"Can I think about it?"

"Of course, you can. We'd never make you do something you don't want to do," Haze says, kissing my knuckles.

"I didn't mean to force that on you." Smoke looks panicked. "Please don't think that."

"Oh goodness no." I kneel, scooting closer to them, and pull our joined hands to my chest, trying to soothe his worry. His tense shoulders drop instantly. "Actually, I find that I quite liked what we did a lot."

"Oh really?" Smoke drawls out.

"Mmhmmm," I hum, winking at them. "And maybe next time, I can actually watch what you two do to each other," I drop my voice to a whisper, "from right next to you?"

"You mean you won't hide in the dark next time?" Haze leans forward and whispers in my ear.

Turning my head, I lean into him. "I think I'd like that."

"As much fun as that sounds," Smoke leans back and slides off the side of the bed, "let's get cleaned up and tucked back in. I don't think me or my dick can handle any more tonight. Between the two of you, I'm dead."

"Aww, you poor thing," Haze gets up and hugs him from behind. "You get your world rocked twice in one night and you're tapping out? What are you gonna do when the three of us all take each other at the same time?"

"Same time?" I gasp, jaw dropped.

"You bet." Haze winks, then slaps Smoke on his ass. "At the same time."

Laughing, they both disappear into the bathroom, then come back out and wipe between my legs with a warm washcloth. I let them manhandle me clean while my brain is running a million miles an hour. Smoke runs another washcloth down my back, then tosses both into the bathroom.

"You mean he and you and me all at once?" I ask when the words finally form a semi-normal sentence. "One of you in my—"

Smoke straightens the sheet and blanket on his side, then slides into bed, pulling me down to lay on his chest. "We'd never make you do anal if you don't want to. Haze just meant that one of us can be inside of you, and the other can be inside of him. Obviously, we do that."

"I've never done that before. He asked a few times, but I always said no." I think back to the whining and complaining Toby always did when I turned down his requests for kinkier things. If my old self could see me now.

Haze lies down behind me, surrounding my back and legs like he's a big spoon. "If you ever decide you wanna try it, we'll be more than happy to help you adjust, but we'll never force you. If you never want to, we accept that."

"Woman," I can feel the growl in Smoke's chest, so I look up at his face, "if the only way I get to feel your tightness is your pussy around my dick, I'll die a happy man." His eyes roll back and he groans.

"Now look what you did." Haze laughs behind me, tickling my ribs until I giggle. "You made the man moan like he's in euphoria."

"Oh, but I am. You felt her. I know you know exactly what I meant. Her pussy was made for us." Smoke rolls so he's facing Haze, me smushed in the middle.

"Alright, stud, enough of that. We need to let our lady rest." Haze pushes Smoke's shoulder, but neither of them budge.

"Wait!" A sudden thought makes me sit up. "I need to shower. You two made me awful sticky."

"You can have one in the morning." Haze grabs my hand, pulling me back down into him.

I roll to face Haze and give him a pouty lip, feeling a little naughty. "I'd let you wash my body."

"You're a minx." Haze kisses me. "I'm too tired to chase your soapy body around the shower."

"I'll make you all bubbly in the morning," Smoke whispers in my ear. "Would you like that?"

"Alright. That's enough, you two." Haze tucks me into his chest. "Why do I have a feeling I'm gonna be the mother hen, pecking you two to keep you in line?"

"Why do I like the sound of that?" I chuckle.

"It's because he's the sentimental one. Our man Haze is a lover, and I wouldn't like it any other way." Smoke yawns behind me.

I yawn too, feeling my eyes getting heavy. "Good night, Smoke." I tug his arm around me, clutching his hand to my chest.

He kisses my shoulder. "Good night, beautiful."

As my eyes close, I feel a kiss on my forehead from Haze. "Good night, raven."

"G'night, Haze."

This is bliss. What's wrong with a little extra love?

If this is how I'll go to sleep every night . . . absolutely nothing.

CHAPTER TWENTY-FOUR

SMOKE

It's been a couple days of life as normal as an outlaw biker can live. Even with the unknowns about Abby's fuckwad ex, some things just have to keep moving in the background. We all have jobs to do, money to make, and somewhat illegal things to take care of.

Whiskey wasn't happy to send a few Brothers offsite, but there was a shipment of guns that needed to be picked up and driven down to Chicago. Between Monty flying down from Canada and Scotty needing the delivery by a certain time to make his own deals, it wasn't something that could be pushed off any longer.

The Brothers who went left before the sun came up Monday morning and rolled in late Wednesday night. They were gone and back in three days, the fastest I think a trip has taken in my time here.

There is one perk of having Abby on the compound all day that I've grown quite fond of. Since I work at Rebel Repairs, and the buildings are so damn close, anytime I can take a break, I run inside to steal a kiss.

Every night since our first time all together, Abby, Haze, and I have gone to bed together and taken our extracurricular activities to another level. The positions we've put Abby in between us rival a big top circus performance. We learned the fun way that our dark-eyed goddess is quite flexible.

It's Friday morning and I've got my hands full of grease and oil, trying to get a stuck piston out of a shovelhead motor, when Whiskey comes running through the big bay door, hollering my name.

"Smoke," he says as he huffs, trying to catch his breath, "Cypher has news on the car. Emergency Church ... now!"

After a quick clean-up, I step outside just as Haze comes running across the parking lot. He was working across the street at the salvage yard, so Whiskey texted him the news.

Heading inside together, I stop two steps in, causing Haze to collide with my back, almost sending both of us to the floor. Whiskey pushes both of us out of his way as he heads to unlock the doors for Church.

Standing like two big dummies, right in front of the alcove, Haze and I stare at Abby. She's sitting on the couch with Angel, holding baby Ace in her arms.

"What's wrong?" Haze asks, stepping in front of me.

Turning him by his shoulders, I show him what I see. "I want that." I point.

"Me too."

Moving to his side, I grab his hand. "You do?"

"Abso-fuckin-lutely." Haze looks back and forth between me and Abby, who's just noticed we're inside. "Imagine her round with our babies."

"We need our cut on her now. Did you talk to Whiskey yet?" I see Abby stand, baby still in her arms, and she heads our way.

"I did, the other day after the clubhouse meeting," Haze whispers. "He said he'd order it for us and gave me the number for the jeweler to get her necklace. But I have to call, then the guy will come here so we don't have to leave."

"I can call if you want," I offer.

He pulls a business card from his wallet, and I tuck it in my back pocket. "That'd be great." His words are rushed because Abby's now right in front of us.

Looking up at us, she sways a little, rocking the sleeping baby. "What's wrong? Why does it seem like everyone's in a hurry all of a sudden?"

Haze folds himself around her side, wrapping an arm around her back. "We've got Church. We'll tell you what we can in a bit, okay?" He kisses the side of her head.

She starts to say something but stops herself, standing a little taller. Head up, she speaks. "Okay. Go do your biker thing."

I tug Abby, the baby, and Haze into my arms. "You're learning, and we appreciate it more than you know," I whisper in her ear.

Haze kisses her cheek as we step back. "Be right back."

"Stay out here with Angel, and we'll find you when we're done." I give her a kiss and head for Church.

Dropping my phone in the box, I walk in and find my seat. The room is filling fast, so once the doors are closed, Whiskey starts talking.

"Cypher found Abby's car at a chain hotel two hours away from here." Unlike usual, Whiskey is pacing the front of the room instead of being in his chair. "We'll send a couple teams to ride out there and check things out."

"Are we bringing the car back?" Haze asks. He's sitting straight up, forearms on the table, and his fists are clenched so tight, his fingers are turning white.

"If it's drivable, I don't see why not," Steel answers. "When you get it here, I'll give it a once-over to make sure it's safe for her to have back."

"Honestly, that car is a piece of shit." I slump back. "I'd rather you put it in the compactor, and we'll buy her something brand new."

"We'll worry about that once it's back on the compound," Whiskey says as he finally sits down. "Until then, let's discuss who's willing to ride the four-hour round trip."

"I'm going!" Haze almost shouts.

"Sounds good." Whiskey nods. "Trooper, that's your team, right?"

"You got it, boss," Trooper replies. "Myself, Haze, Saddle, Cypher, Butch, Tiny, and Diego."

"Alright. Let's also send," Whiskey points to people as he says their names, "Steel, Wrench, Wrecker, Bear, and Buzz. That'll give you an even dozen if something goes fucked-up when you get there."

While I'm itching to go, hoping to find Toby and kick his ass, I know one of us needs to stay here to give Abby some peace of mind. And looking at Haze right now, who's about to jump out of his skin, I know it's me who has to stay. He's not taking the news very well, and I know it's my time to step up and be there for him.

A few logistics are discussed as to who is carrying what extra firepower, and I just sit back in listen. Once Church is dismissed, Steel opens the gun safe in the corner and starts handing out extra ammunition, gun clips, and a few duffle bags to carry everything in.

The guys leaving take a few minutes to say their goodbyes. Abby and I stand next to Haze's motorcycle as he straddles his seat and fires it up. Standing in front of me, my arms are wrapped around her torso as Abby leans back on me, her hands gripping my forearms.

"Please be safe," she calls out as Haze boots up his kickstand.

"I'll be back in a few hours." He blows us a kiss, then waves as he rolls away.

We watch as ten Harleys and the tow truck roll out of the lot, the fence closing behind them.

Wrecker made a last-minute suggestion to make this run look like a repossession to throw off any unexpected questions about why someone is picking up a vehicle that doesn't belong to them. So, the plan is to roll up, put it on the tow truck, and bring it back that way, especially since we don't know if it's in any running condition.

Once the roar finally fades away, I pull Abby inside and leave her with all the other ladies, who've taken over the main room.

I kiss her so long and deep until we need to break for a breath, then I head back outside to stand watch. With this psycho on the loose, I won't let anyone get past me.

Pulling out my phone, I make what has to be the most important call I'll make to date.

CHAPTER TWENTY-FIVE

HAZE

I never knew how much I could miss someone—well, two someones—until just this very moment. I'm currently two hours away from home, a hundred miles from the two people who mean the most to me, and if it weren't for my woman, I would've bowed out of this ride in a heartbeat. But for her, I'd ride through the gates of hell.

Pulling off the highway at the next exit, I follow Saddle and Tiny, Buzz riding to my right, as the road curves to the right. At the stop sign, we turn left and head straight for the four-story hotel where Cypher found the footage showing Abby's parked car.

I've ridden past this town many times before, but never stopped here, so I take everything in. This looks like a nice suburban area. It's just after noon and the sun is out, so there's no dark shadows to worry about danger lurking in. For a pick-up in a strange place, we couldn't have accidentally planned this any better.

The hotel itself sits on one corner of a four-way intersection, a bank across the street, the golden arches fast food restaurant next to that, and a small grocery store on the other. The area looks decently populated, with cars and trucks driving around, and there are houses and businesses branching off in every direction.

But for as nice as the hotel looks, the parking lot is surprisingly empty. There are maybe ten cars in the whole lot, and I spot Abby's immediately. It's backed into a spot right against the side of the building, and there are no other vehicles in this section.

As planned, when we decided to not drive the car back, those of us on our motorcycles pull in and park in a semi-circle, blocking off the area of the lot where the car is. Wrecker drives ahead of us and turns the tow truck around to back up to the car. Once in position, he and Diego hop out, wearing orange reflective vests over their cuts. To make this look as official as we can, ignoring the ten rumbling Harleys accompanying them, they have to at least look like they're doing their jobs.

Cypher and Butch shut down their bikes and head inside the hotel to see if they can get any information on how long the car has been sitting here, or possibly a name connected to a reservation. Not even ten minutes later, just as Wrecker is pressing the lever to roll the car up, the guys come walking back out.

"Room is registered to a fake name," Cypher says, coming to stand beside me. "Butch schmoozed the front desk lady for the key, and we checked it out. It's empty and doesn't look like it was even used. The beds were still made, and none of the towels were touched."

"Then let's get this show back on the road," Trooper calls out. "We'll get back on the highway and stop in the next town for gas before we head back."

In formation, four bikes leading the way, Wrecker and Diego in the truck in the middle, and six more of us behind, we pull out of the hotel parking lot. Lucking out that no cars are coming, we blow through the intersection without stopping. When one truck pulls up just as we fly by, all I do is lift a middle finger to the sky and keep rolling.

Stopping for gas five miles back down the highway, each of us fills up and then pull aside, letting the Brother behind us take his turn.

Just for shits and giggles, I decide to try something that has been bugging me since I saw the car. I get off my bike, walk up to Wrecker, and point at the car five feet off the ground. "Mind if I hop up there and see if this thing will start?"

"Have at 'er." He waves, tosses me the keys, and stands back.

Using the steps built into the side of the truck, I climb up on the platform. Shuffling my feet sideways, I get around the side mirror without falling backward, then open the door. Once inside the car and no longer balancing like a trapeze artist, I put the key in the ignition and turn it a few times but get nothing.

"Maybe the battery's dead," Wrecker calls up.

"Why am I not surprised," I mumble to myself. Getting out of the car, I jump down to the ground, toss the keys back to Wrecker, then head for my ride. "If it happens to fall off on the way home, I won't be sad."

"I'll see what I can do," Wrecker jokingly says with a laugh before climbing up into his seat.

Everyone circles around the lot and heads for the exit.

After another two hours on the road, I help Wrecker get the deathtrap on wheels unloaded. When we got to our neck of the woods, I broke off from the group and turned left into the salvage yard behind the truck while everyone else turned right into the compound. I suggested we park it here behind the privacy fence, so it can't be seen from the street.

As I ride across to the clubhouse, I see Smoke standing on the front porch, so I head straight for him. I back my bike into its spot, then step up in front of him. "How's Abby?"

"She's good." Smoke pulls me in for a kiss. "She's inside with the other ladies. How are you?"

"Fuckin' pissed off," I growl as I hug him back. "We got the car, obviously, but finding Toby was a bust."

"We'll find him." Pulling back, Smoke continues, "Is the car in one piece?"

"Barely. I tried to start it, but nothing, battery's dead." I shrug, then pull his hips to mine, my hands settling around his waist. "We need to get her a new vehicle as soon as fuckin' possible."

"I agree." Smoke rests his forehead on mine, and softly says, "Let's take a minute for you to cool down. Then we'll go find our girl."

"There you two are."

I turn my head to see Abby standing in the front doorway. It looks like she found us first. Knowing she was looking for us makes my heart beat faster, but in a good way.

CHAPTER TWENTY-SIX

ABBY

With Haze gone with a bunch of Brothers to find my car, Smoke left me with strict instructions to stay inside. He volunteered himself for outside patrol duty. I'm not exactly sure what that all entails, but I let him go about his way.

That's not to say he hasn't been keeping an eye on me as well. Every so often, he's popped back inside to check on me. But like the stealth walker I've discovered him to be, just as fast as he appears, he's right back out the door after stealing a kiss or a sweet.

Duchess, Angel, Sunshine, Meredith, Sara, and I have been hunkered down in the kitchen with the kids for a couple hours, getting a whole bunch of pans of tater tot casserole prepped to go in the oven for dinner later. We've also been mixing up some cookie dough to bake cookies for the maybe Halloween party in just over a week. The babies are asleep in swings, set in the corner, out of the way.

My men both tell me they have costumes picked out, but neither will tell me what they are. Since I'm totally not prepared for a costume party, I have no idea what I'm going to wear if this shindig actually goes down. All the ladies offered to let me rifle through their closets if I need something, which I greatly appreciate, so who knows what I'll end up being.

After taking a break to use the bathroom, I pull the door open and step into the main room. Immediately, I'm pushed to the left as Toto runs into me.

"Oh, I'm sorry." I step back. "You just appeared out of nowhere. I didn't see you coming."

"Watch where you're walkin', bitch." She points at the hallway entrance next to the bathroom door. "I was comin' out of my room."

"Like I said," I hold my hands up, "I didn't see you. I'm sorry."

"What the hell are you doin' here anyway?" Toto sets her hands on her hips and starts tapping her way too high heels.

She looks like a stripper Barbie who took a turn through the spin cycle. Her hair is messy, one of her tank top straps has fallen off her shoulder, and her shorts look like they're on backward.

"What do you mean?" She was at the clubhouse meeting last weekend, so she knows exactly why I'm here. "I'm here because the club is keeping me safe."

I don't understand what's going on. I may not like Toto based on how I've had to deal with her at work, but since I've been here, she hasn't said a word to me until now.

"The club may be helpin' you now," Toto takes a step closer to me, "and Smoke and Haze may be givin' you attention, but they'll be back to fuckin' me the second you're gone. So don't get too comfy here."

Not liking her attitude one bit, I step into her space and say with no hesitation, "I know for a fact neither one of them has touched you, so don't even try that with me."

"Is that what they told you?" She laughs. "Men lie all the time. You should just bow out now."

"I'm. Not. Going. Anywhere." I snap out each word.

All that does is make her laugh harder. "Well, in that case, I'll still be here in the background. Maybe since there are two of them, I can help you out. We can share."

"Don't even think about it." My hands are shaking, I'm trying so hard not to slap this whore. "I don't share. Stay away from them, and me."

Toto snickers. "That's not up to you. The Brothers can fuck whoever they want. You're not an Old Lady. You don't have a cut."

"Don't make me tell you again." I'm not touching her, but there's barely enough room between us for a piece of paper. "Stay the fuck away from *my* men."

"*Your* men?" Her eyes go wide, a half smirk on her face. "You couldn't even keep one man happy. What makes you think you deserve two?"

What's she talking about? Not keeping one man happy? I ignore that and focus on the second part, about deserving two men. "Because I fucking said so, that's what."

"I'd like to see you try and stop them from comin' after me." She snarls, and with one finger on my shoulder, she pushes me. I barely move but still lose it.

Stepping back on my own, I ball my right hand into a fist and swing. I punch Toto, hitting her in the left cheek, and she crumples to the floor.

Looking down at her, hands on my knees, I snarl back. "Fuck . . . you . . . bitch."

"What the hell is goin' on out here?"

I stand and turn to see Sunshine and Angel in the middle of the hall.

"Someone," I point over my shoulder at Toto, "tried to tell me we could share my guys."

Angel pulls me over to a bar stool. "Are you okay? Did she hit you?"

"I'm good," I reply, shaking my hand out. "She poked me, but I hit harder."

"Good," Sunshine says as she hands me an ice pack. "Put that on your hand. If the guys see you with swollen knuckles, they're gonna flip their lids."

Resting back on the stool, I swivel to face the bar. "What's so great about club girls? Why are they here?"

"I know you know I used to be a club girl," Angel rests her hand on my shoulder, "but they're all here by choice. No one forces the girls to do anything they don't want. They're here for support for the Brothers who don't have an Old Lady or partner."

"That's dumb." I know I'm pouting like a baby, but I don't care. "I told her to leave me alone, but she just kept going."

"I know you don't like it, and that's okay, none of us do. It's just something we all have to deal with. It's part of the package deal," Sunshine says with a sigh. "If you and your men have an understanding that they stay away from the club girls, I'm sure you'll be just fine."

"Do y'all have that understanding? Your men don't stray?" I ask, looking between them.

"You don't have to worry about cheating or infidelity here. Most of the club girls," Sunshine sneers at Toto as she slowly gets up, "the smart ones anyway, only sleep with the Brothers who want it. And based on how Haze and Smoke look at you, they only want you."

Duchess comes walking around the corner, a baby on each hip. "What's goin' on out here?"

"Abby just had her first run-in with a club girl." Sunshine points to Toto, who's now sniffling, curled in a chair in a corner of the pool room alcove.

"But she took care of it." Angel takes Ace and holds him up, kissing his tiny face. "It looks like your daddy has a run for his money on punching people, Ace. Whadaya think about that?"

"Welcome to the club girl beatdown club." Duchess gives me a high five. "The last skank who decided to talk smack got her face rearranged by the coffee table."

"No shit?" I laugh.

"No shit." She shakes her head. "I was pregnant with little man here, and Whiskey had to pull me off her."

"Let us give you a little advice we all had to learn the hard way." Angel sits on the stool next to me. "Being an Old Lady is probably one of the hardest jobs in the MC. You need to be strong and soft all at the same time. It's a hard line to balance sometimes."

"You'll need to be an extension of your men while still holding your own ground," Duchess adds. "But I promise you with my whole heart, it's so worth it. If you let these mean, burly, grouchy bikers love you, you'll never regret a single day of your life."

A little while later, I'm sitting at the end of the bar with Stiletto, Sara, and Blue. Just then, the front doors open, and bikers start pouring in. The room fills with so much noise in mere seconds, you'd think someone hit the unmute button at a rock concert.

Watching the room for my guys, I see Taren running our way. He steps in front of Gunner just as he turns from the bar, making him almost lose his balance but causing him to drop his beer in the process. The glass bottle shatters, sending dark-colored shards and beer flying everywhere.

"Fuck!" Gunner yells, causing Taren to burst into tears. "Watch where you're goin', half-pint!"

Since I'm the closest adult to him, I scoop Taren up and carry him away from the broken glass and the scary man. He wraps his arms around my neck super tight. "It's okay," I hush him, rubbing his back.

"Hey!" Angel yells so loud, the room goes silent again. "Mr. Grumpy Pants! None of that language around the little ones."

"If the little crotch goblins didn't always get in my way, I wouldn't have to swear," Gunner yells back.

She stomps right up to him. "Did you call my boy a crotch goblin?"

"Did I stutter?" Gunner folds his arms over his chest.

"Okay, that's enough," Whiskey interjects.

"When'd this clubhouse turn into a fuckin' daycare center?" Gunner turns to Whiskey, hands thrown up in the air.

"When'd you get a stick shoved up your backside?" Angel tries to step to him again, but Hammer pulls her back into him.

"I thought we talked about this, Gunner," Whiskey says, pointing at him.

"Well, maybe I don't like it."

"Well, maybe I don't fuckin' care what you do or don't like." Whiskey gets in his face this time. They're both the same height, so the stare-down is intense. "These kids are the future of this club. So, if that's not okay with you, maybe you need to start thinkin' about your future here."

"I'm not leavin' the club!" he roars at Whiskey.

Whiskey grabs the front of Gunner's cut, causing every man in the room to gasp. "If this bullshit continues, you may not have a choice in the matter." He then pushes him away. "Get the fuck outta my sight."

Gunner stomps outside and the room goes back into motion, albeit a little less loud than before.

"Sorry about that." Angel and Hammer walk over to where we're huddled, and Taren practically throws himself at his mom. She holds him tight right back. I've only known her for a little while, but Angel's an amazing mother. "Gunner isn't the biggest fan of the munchkins," she says.

"I can see that. Any idea why?"

"I have my suspicions, but it's not my place to ask." She leans back against Hammer, who takes Taren and holds both him and his Old Lady.

Sunshine walks up with Ace strapped into a sling against her chest. "One day, that man will find himself knocked off his feet by a woman with kids and he's not gonna know what hit him."

"I'd pay to see that," Kraken says as he walks by, making us all laugh.

I look around the room but still don't see where my guys are.

"Have you seen Haze or Smoke?" I ask Hammer.

"They were still outside, last I saw," he replies, pointing to the front door.

"Thanks." I head for the front and push open the screen door. To the left, I see them in the shadows of the front porch. They're holding hands, just leaning their foreheads against each other's.

"There you two are. I was starting to worry."

They both turn their heads toward me. Haze holds out a hand, and stepping forward, I take it and am pulled into the little space between them. I get a quick kiss from Smoke first before I'm spun around and devoured by Haze. I don't know what's wrong, but I let him handle me as he sees fit. And I like it.

After a few minutes of silence, all wrapped around each other, we separate. I'm led to a rocking chair, and they both sit in front of me on a bench.

"What's the matter?" I ask.

"Nothing," Haze shakes his head, "I just needed a moment."

"He got your car back." Smoke leans his shoulder on Haze.

"Really? Tell me everything."

CHAPTER TWENTY-SEVEN

SMOKE

"Unfortunately, there's not much to tell." Haze rests back into the bench we're sitting on. He lays an arm behind me, and I lean my shoulder farther back against his. "Your car was just sitting there, no people around. Had it not been for the other, like, eight cars on the other side of the parking lot, I'd have said the place was abandoned."

Sitting back in the rocking chair, Abby is too far away from us, and I don't like it.

Needing to touch her, I reach forward and pull her up and into my lap. Abby sits on my left thigh, then turns to lay her legs over Haze's.

"There, that's much better." I set my left hand on her lower back, sliding it under her hoodie, or should I say, my extra-large Rebel Repairs hoodie.

"If you say so." Abby giggles as she kisses my cheek, then looks at Haze. "So, Toby wasn't there?"

"He was not." He interlocks her left hand in his right. "At that hotel, you have to give your license plate number to the front desk. The person who checked into the room linked to the car showed a fake ID. And the room hadn't been touched."

"That sounds pretty suspicious." Abby furrows her eyebrows. "Where the heck is he?"

"No clue." Haze shakes his head. "Cypher's still doing his web search thing, and Trooper put another call into his connection, so hopefully, we'll get another lead soon. The sooner we find your ex, the sooner we can get our lives on the forward track."

"But 'til then, you stay here safe with us." I pull her side, silently asking her to lean on me.

We sit in silence for a few minutes, soaking in the closeness. I can hear the voices of people inside, but I ignore them for the quiet of this cool fall afternoon.

"Are y'all hungry?" Abby looks up at me, and I drop a kiss on her forehead. "We made casserole for dinner. It should be just about done."

"I could go for some grub." Haze laughs as he rubs his stomach. "I'm a growing boy."

And as if on cue, my stomach starts to growl. "Food. Yes. Please," I grunt out like a caveman.

"You two are crazy." Abby stands up and holds out both her hands. "If y'all grow any bigger, we're gonna need a bigger bed."

"I can get behind that idea." I really, really can. Haze and I stand, with her pretend help, then pull Abby toward the door. "A California King sounds mighty nice. Plenty of extra room for some nighttime hanky-panky. Hey! Wanna hear a joke about sleeping?"

Abby smiles. "Yes, please. I love your jokes."

Haze rolls his eyes. "Here we go, lay it on us. What goofiness do ya got this time?"

"What did the mother cow say to the baby cow? . . . It's past-ure bedtime."

Abby laughs as Haze pushes me toward the door. I no more have my hand on the handle when there's a loud *BOOM*! An explosion goes off somewhere behind us, and I instinctively pull Abby hard, tight into my chest. Turning my body to the side, still keeping her close, I look just in time to see a fireball lift into the sky and flames start dancing in the distance. It's just starting to get dark, so the trees next to the fence look like they're glowing.

Something exploded over at the recycling and salvage yard, and whatever it was, it was huge.

A roll of thundering boots starts inside the clubhouse behind me, and the doors fly open as a stampede of leather and denim and angry bikers take off running across the parking lot. Holding Abby's hand, we follow Haze, who is moving at not quite full speed but still quickly.

The gate rolls open as Steel comes staggering out of the open fence enclosing Tellison Recycling and Salvage, the business the club owns across the road. He's coughing and trying to catch his breath. Diego is beside him, half holding him up as they stumble into the street.

Haze turns to me. "Keep Abby here," he orders as he and Doc run out to help them, taking the load off Diego.

Between the two of them, they half carry, half lead Steel toward us and then into the clubhouse, each supporting him on a side.

Diego and a bunch of my Brothers go running toward whatever is burning to put out the flames before a passerby calls the fire department. Law enforcement in our area leaves us alone for the most part, but inviting them inside the fence because of a fire would lead to questions and problems the club would rather avoid.

Abby and I follow the group headed back toward the clubhouse. Just as we step inside, Sunshine sees Steel for the first time, with his beat-up, dirty skin and injured hands, and she starts crying. She rushes forward and kneels in front of where he's been placed on one of the couches. Everything nearby is getting pushed out of the way so Doc can check him over.

"I wish there was something we could do to help," Abby says as we all stand back and watch Sunshine and Doc clean the dark smudges on Steel's arms and face.

"I know, babe," I say as I clutch her tight to me, "but he's got all the medical care he needs with those two. Sunshine used to be a nurse, and Doc was a medic in the Navy."

"Well, that's good." I hear her say into my chest. "I just hope he's okay."

"Steel's a tough one for sure." I lead her away from the crowd and lean against the wall, giving us some privacy. "Steel survived a bad prison fight. He can handle a few bumps and bruises, no problem."

"Prison?" I swear her eyebrows disappear up into her hairline.

But before I can explain what Steel did for Whiskey, taking the fall to cover for him, someone calls my name. Turning, I see Whiskey waving me over toward him and Hammer.

"Go see what's up." Haze walks up and pulls Abby in for a hug. "I got our girl."

I follow Ring and Trooper into Church, after Whiskey and Hammer. We all step inside, but the doors stay open.

"Steel's gonna be fine. He's got a few cuts and scrapes on his hands and knees." Whiskey leans back, half sitting on the table, arms across his chest, and folds one boot over the other. "He and Diego went over to take a quick look at Abby's car to see if they could figure out why it wouldn't start. Turns out there was a bomb under the hood."

"A what!" I shout.

"Yup," he sighs, "Steel popped the hood, but as soon as he lifted the latch, he saw some wires that looked out of place and knew something was wrong. Just as he turned to run, it blew. Hence the scrapes he's got. It knocked him on his hands and knees, and he struggled to get up. Diego was moving a little slower, texting his mother, and luckily wasn't close."

"It sounds like it was rigged to go off when the hood was opened," I comment.

"From his maybe three-second glance, Steel seems to think so," Whiskey says as he shrugs.

"Do we have any idea why Toby would want to try and blow up Abby?"

"He tried to blow me up?"

Spinning on a dime, I turn to see Abby standing right behind me.

"Abby—" is all I get out before her eyes roll back and she collapses.

I rush forward to catch her, but by the time I fold to the floor with her in my arms, she's out cold. *Fuck!*

CHAPTER TWENTY-EIGHT

HAZE

I step five feet away to get Abby some water, and when I turn back, she's gone.

"Abby," I hear Smoke say. Looking toward where I know he is in Church, all I can do is watch as her head falls back and her body starts to crumple.

Smoke leaps forward, arms out, and he somehow manages to catch her, folding his knees and sliding down to the floor with her. Landing on his ass, he has Abby in his lap, her head laying against his chest. Her hair is up in a ponytail today, so the long strands are draped over his shoulder like a waterfall.

"Holy hell." I finally get my feet to move in their direction, then fall to my knees in front of Smoke. "What happened?"

Smoke looks up at me with an expression I don't think I've yet to see from him—fear. For the first time ever, Smoke is afraid. "She overheard us talking about Toby putting a bomb in her car and she just fainted."

That makes me fall back on my own ass. "A bomb!"

Sunshine rushes over and kneels at Smoke's side, feeling Abby's forehead, checking her pulse. "Did she hit her head?"

I can't do anything but sit here and let that new nugget of information sink in. A bomb? As Sunshine continues asking Smoke questions, I stare at Abby's pale face. She's not blinking or moving, but thankfully, I see that her chest is moving, so I know she's breathing.

"He's dead!" I growl as I jump up to my feet. As gently as I can, I lace my arms under Abby and pick her up.

"Why don't you lay her on the couch, Haze," Sunshine suggests as she walks beside me, hand on my arm. "Doc is gonna give her a once-over."

Once I have her where Doc points, a couch across from the one Steel is still camped out on, I step back and am almost immediately knocked back over by Smoke. He wraps me in a hug so tight, I feel my ribs constrict.

"I tried to catch her," he mumbles as we hold each other, "I tried." His chest shakes as he takes a deep breath.

"Smoke," pulling myself back, I get his eyes on mine, "I watched it happen. You did exactly the right thing."

"If she's hurt—"

"She'll be just fine." I stop him right there. "Now, what's this business about a bomb?"

Smoke's shoulders deflate like a dead balloon. "Toby rigged the car to blow when someone opened the hood."

"That's probably why the car wouldn't start." I run my hand over my head, thinking about when I tried to start it at the gas station. "Fucker probably unhooked something, so when she tried to start it and it wouldn't turn over, the first thing she would do is open the hood to check the battery."

"Motherfucker," Smoke mutters through clenched teeth.

"Guys?" We turn to see Sunshine waving us over. In our talking about the car, we got distracted from the priority at hand—Abby.

Smoke and I kneel on either side of Doc and watch as Abby's eyes slowly blink, her waking up, thank Hades.

She turns her head into my hand. "What happened?" Her words are a little slurred.

"Baby, you fainted right into Smoke's arms." I tuck a strand of hair behind her ear.

"Don't you ever do that to me again, woman," Smoke adds. "I think I just lost ten years off my life."

Abby reaches her right hand out to him, and he clutches it in both of his, kissing her knuckles.

"Her blood pressure and heart rate are a little high, so keep her calm for the next while," Doc explains as he stands, slapping both Smoke and me on the shoulders, "and she'll be right as rain. Keep these two close, ya here?" He winks at Abby and walks away.

Slowly sitting her up, we climb onto the couch on either side of her. Abby leans back against Smoke, and now, I get her hands in mine. "How are you feeling? I think you need that water now."

A small smile appears on her lips, letting me take my first full breath in five minutes. "Please?"

And as if by magic, as soon as I turn to face the bar somewhere behind us, a bottle of water appears in front of my face. Angel smiles down at us. "Here ya go. I was just about to see if y'all needed anything."

"We're good, thanks, Angel," I reply.

"No problem."

"So, what happened with a bomb in my car?" Abby asks after taking a drink.

"We can talk about this later," I say.

"No," she shakes her head slowly, "I wanna know now." She's got a look of determination, so we fold.

Smoke explains to her what was found, filling me in on some things he learned while talking to Whiskey, in regard to what Steel saw. All she does is blink as her mouth opens and closes like a fish out of water.

Abby looks so lost. "That's crazy."

"Dinner's done," Duchess calls out. "Come and get it while it's hot."

"Why don't I go fix us some plates," I suggest. "You two stay right here." I leave Smoke and Abby huddled together.

A few heaping plates of tater tot casserole and a couple beers later, the three of us are still camped out on the couch, watching movies with a few others. Just as the credits start to roll on the second comedy, Abby sits up and the bottle of water she was holding goes flying into the air, landing on the coffee table.

"If he found me, I need to get my Gram." Abby jumps to her feet, and when she spins back, Smoke and I stand, steadying her. Hands clutched to our shirts, she pulls at the material. "She's not safe in her big house all alone."

Talk about an out of the blue change of topic.

Looking at the clock on the wall behind the bar, I see what time it is. Holy fuck, where did today go? "Abby, it's almost midnight. We can go pick her up in the morning."

"But—"

"No buts, Abby," Smoke speaks up. "She's sleeping, which is something you need to get a few hours of yourself before we venture out to get your Gram. Plus, we need to run this by Whiskey first. He's the Prez, and with what just happened, we can't leave without his permission."

"Fine." Abby looks down, and I know she's sad, but at this point, I agree with Smoke. She needs sleep before she collapses again.

"You two head upstairs." Smoke kisses Abby, then me. "I'm gonna go to talk to Whiskey, then I'll be right up."

Just as I'm helping Abby into one of Smoke's Rebel Repairs t-shirts, tugging it down over her hips, Smoke walks into my bedroom.

"All set for a run to go get your Gram." He pulls her into his embrace. "At nine a.m., we'll head out with a group, along with a vehicle to bring her back. That sound okay to you, beautiful?"

"I guess," she says softly. I watch as she tips her head up and he drops for a kiss.

"Time for bed, you two," I say as I beeline for the bathroom. I need a hot shower after the ride today. Combined with the five hours on my butt and the stress of thinking about the unknown of what we were going to find, my muscles are in need of steam.

After drying off, I put on a pair of boxer briefs and slide into bed next to my woman. Pulling up the sheet, I get a glimpse of the bodies underneath. Smoke is in his birthday suit as usual, and Abby's wearing a pair of my boxers under the t-shirt. Turning her to face Smoke, I snuggle into her back.

"Good night." I kiss her temple before leaning over and kissing Smoke.

"G'night," he mumbles into my lips.

"Night," Abby drawls with a yawn just as I lie down. "I love you both, and I can't wait to be your Old Lady."

Stunned, I straighten right back up. "You love us?"

Abby jackknifes up too, eyes wide open, her head turning left to right. "Oh my gosh. Did I say that out loud?"

"Yes, you did," Smoke says as he slowly follows suit, joining us in our failed attempt at falling asleep.

I turn her head to face me, one hand on each of her cheeks. I tilt her lips up for the lightest kiss I've ever given her. "And you can't take it back. Because I love you too."

"And so do I." I let her go as Smoke tugs her to him, kissing her on both cheeks, then her nose, and finally her lips. "I love you, Abby."

"I really do love you both." Abby takes turns kissing us each once more, followed by a big yawn.

"As much as I'd love to celebrate this moment, we all need some shut-eye," I say, falling back to my pillow.

We lie back down same as before, this time going to sleep for real.

CHAPTER TWENTY-NINE

SMOKE

No more than a minute later, I hear light, soft snores fall from Abby's lips. Our poor woman tries so hard to be strong, but after tonight's craziness, she deserves a peaceful night's sleep. Eyes closed, I kiss her forehead, then lie back.

The covers shift a little under my arm, so I open my eyes to see a hand running up and down Abby's arm. Looking up, I'm met by two golden eyes shining back at me. Something tells me this one's going to have a little bit harder time following his own suggestion to get some shut-eye.

Reaching out my hand, I slide my finger up the inside of his forearm, tracing the lines of his cross tattoo. "I knew you weren't asleep."

"I love you too."

My head jerks up and my eyes go wide. Staring at my partner, I hear the words I've been wanting to hear for a while but was never brave enough to say myself because I felt the smallest worry of rejection. It took Haze so much longer to accept us than it did me, and there's been a tiny seed of doubt floating around in my mind since the very beginning.

"You don't have to—" I try giving him an out, but he shuts me down.

"I love you, Smoke." Haze threads his fingers through mine, which had frozen on his arm at his admittance. "I really do."

Careful not to jostle the princess between us, I prop myself up on my elbow and lean into him for a kiss. There's a bit of tongue, and quite a bit of heat, but we keep our movements slow and just soak in the moment.

Pulling back, I trace along his jaw as I tell him my truth. "I think I've loved you forever."

Hands flat on the shower wall, I brace myself in a battle to stay upright. As the hot water sprays down over me, I push my ass back. With every thrust of Haze's cock fucking me so hard, I'm about to collapse.

My palms slide along the wet tile, so I lean forward, letting my forearms catch my weight. I turn my head and rest my right cheek on the cool, stark white porcelain. With every exhale, I puff out the droplets of water that are rolling down my face.

Not quite what I expected for a morning wake-up call, but holy fucking shit, I'm not going to stop him now. Haze took a shower last night, so I didn't expect a visitor in the middle of mine this morning.

"Fuck . . . me," I grunt, pushing my hips back even more.

"Quit . . . movin'" is grunted back at me. "I'm . . . tryin'."

"Try . . . fuckin' . . ." I push back again, "harder."

Sliding my weight onto my shoulder, I wrap my right hand around my dick, and using the waterfall sliding down my arm, start pumping my length with the tempo of the man sliding in and out of me.

"You close?" Haze asks with a gasp.

"Almost" is all I can say back, my brain cells disappearing at a rapid rate.

"Uuuhhhhhh!" His groan is all the warning I get before I feel Haze's fingertips dig into my sides, pinching my skin. His hips slam against me so hard, I'm forced forward and my whole front is pressed into the shower wall, my arm smushed against me.

I feel his dick spasming inside me, and the warmth of his release fills me so fucking full. Fuck, that feels good . . . so fucking good.

It's so good, in fact, my dick gets that last bit harder, my toes curl, my left knee buckles, and I scramble to stay standing as my cock jerks in my hand. My cum slips over my fingers and down onto the shower floor. My entire body has a small seizure as I fuck my fist, chasing my release to the finish line.

Haze collapses all his weight onto me, and all I can do is lean against the tile. "Am I alive?" he pants as he catches his breath.

I reach my hands back and settle them on his hips. "I certainly hope so," I reply. "Otherwise, it's gonna be a weird morning tryin' to explain to the club how I let myself get fucked by a zombie."

He lets out a laugh so hard, he dislodges himself from my ass. "Shit!" he calls out as he scrambles to find his footing, slipping in the wet tub.

Turning around, I grab his hands, steadying him. "Zombies may not be my biggest worry." I can't help but laugh. "If I have to tell them you cracked your head open after you fucked me, then bled out all over the floor, Whiskey's gonna be pissed at the crime scene clean-up."

"Stop making jokes, asshole." Haze shoves me aside, pushing me out from under the shower head. "Water's getting' cold. Let's hurry up before our dicks fall off."

We hustle through the rest of our shower, then dry off.

As I run a towel over my chest, I ask Haze something I've been thinking about. "Have you had any thoughts on what we should name Abby?"

"I have an idea." Haze leans back against the vanity, towel wrapped around his waist.

Crowding myself into him, I start kissing up his neck. Once my lips are at his ear, I whisper, "Wanna tell me?"

"Raven," he whispers in my ear.

I bite his earlobe, giving it a little tug as I run my hands up his chest and give his piercings a bit of their own attention. Settling my hips against his, I leave my hands on his chest and lean back to see his face. "That's perfect."

Haze wraps a wet strand of my hair around his finger before running it down my shoulder. He smiles. "Should we tell her now?"

I think about it for a second, then stand back on my own weight, pulling him up with me, I push his towel down out of my way and grab a handful of his hard, muscular backside. Our naked bodies against each other, I reply, "Let's wait 'til we get her cut. Then we can surprise her with the name patch."

"I like that idea." Haze reaches for my ass, slapping it. "Now, let's get dressed. We've got a Gram to go meet.'

Coming out of the bathroom, wrapped in towels again, I'm happy to see Abby wide awake.

She showers as we get dressed, then we sit and watch as she pulls her wet hair back into a braid. "I think I need a haircut. This length is getting to be too much."

"But we like it long." Haze almost whines from his perch on the edge of the desk.

"I won't cut it too short." She steps up to him and sets a hand on his chest. "Maybe just to the middle of my back."

"Whatever you want, love," I say as I put my boots on.

"Talk to Angel," Haze suggests as he pulls his cut from the hook on the wall. "She's a . . . what do you call a lady who cuts hair?"

"A barber?" I reply, not sure of the correct term. With my hair like it is, I maybe get it trimmed once a year, so I don't know what the people are called.

"You two are crazy." Abby giggles as she zips up her sweatshirt. "A barber is someone who usually just cuts a man's hair. A cosmetologist or hair stylist is the proper term for a person who works on women."

"See, that's why we need you. You make us sound less stupid." I drop a kiss on her head as I holster my gun and slide my screwdriver into its special holder. Pulling on my cut, I tug on the front, straightening it over my dark green and black flannel. It's supposed to be chilly today, so it's a good day for multiple layers. A wife beater tank top, long sleeve t-shirt, flannel, and my cut will do just fine.

Abby grabs a handful of my shirt and pulls me close. "You're not stupid. You're mine."

I'm too stunned to move as she lets me go, smoothing my flannel down, then she approaches Haze, smoothing down his damp hair. She blows him a kiss as she opens the bedroom door and walks out, booty swaying the whole way. She disappears from sight, and both Haze and I rush to grab the rest of our things.

Phones tucked into our cuts, wallets in our pockets, and sunglasses on our heads, we both run for the door at the same time. We crash out into the hall, the door slamming behind us. It's a race to catch our lady first.

And I'm going to win.

CHAPTER THIRTY

ABBY

There's one thing I've learned to appreciate about these bikers, and that's their keenness for being on time. When they say something is going to happen at a certain time, they're all ready to rock and roll at least ten minutes early.

Last night, Smoke told us we'd be leaving at nine a.m., and according to the clock on the dash of Haze's truck, it's nine-oh-two as we drive out of the clubhouse parking lot. These guys don't mess around with punctuality, and as a stickler for being on time, I like it.

We're on the way to pick up my Gram. I hate that it's been a couple weeks since I've seen her, but with work, then all this crazy Toby drama, I haven't had a chance to visit her.

Haze is driving his truck, one hand on the wheel, the other holding my hand on the center counsel. We're surrounded by a dozen other Brothers, including Smoke, on their bikes along to help and for protection. I don't really understand why Whiskey required so many to come with, but he said it was either this many or we weren't going.

The Brothers had a mini meeting while eating breakfast to decide who was escorting us and where Gram would be staying while she's here. The Prospects were sent on cleaning duty of the empty room across the hall from ours, while Duchess and Sara took on getting it all set up for her.

While it may seem farfetched to go through the trouble to bring Gram to the clubhouse to protect her, because Toby got away, and he knows where Gram lives, I don't know how far he'll go to hurt me.

I called Gram this morning to tell her I was coming to get her, and while she tried to put up a fight, once Smoke got on the phone and told her what was going on, she agreed to at least come stay with us until Toby is found. Smoke saw how frustrated I was getting while trying to convince her, he took my phone right out of my hand and walked away.

Not five minutes later, he handed it back to me and Gram was all on board. Apparently, there's something about a bossy man that you can't say no to, even though you'd like to smack him upside the head.

We're less than a mile from town and approaching an intersection, when a blue truck blows the crossroad's stop sign. Since it's only a two-way stop intersection, and we have no stop sign in our direction, we should've been able to sail right through.

The truck comes to a screeching stop in front of us, and Haze has to slam on the brakes to avoid hitting it broadside.

My whole body flies forward, stopping in a jerk when the seatbelt locks and forces me back. I feel a sharp pain radiate from my right shoulder and down my arm. I try to unzip my sweatshirt, but the seatbelt is in the way, so I unbuckle it.

"Are you okay?" Haze turns in his seat, reaching out for me.

But before I can reply, the world begins to come alive outside the truck. A second vehicle, a black SUV, appears between the blue truck and us, and both driver's side windows roll down. As soon as I see what appears in those windows—guns, big guns—bullets start flying in every direction. It sounds like movie theatre surround sound around me, and I scream.

The windshield starts cracking, round bursts scattered across it, and I fold in half, trying to stay out of sight.

Haze lets out a string of swear words so long, I lose track of what he's saying altogether. He's got the truck back in gear, turned around, and is driving back the way we came so fast, I don't think I had time to blink.

Because I'm not wearing my seatbelt, I end up sliding off my seat and landing on my butt on the floorboard of the truck. My head is tucked between my knees and my right shoulder, still very much in pain, is tucked under the glove compartment.

Haze is driving like he's warming up the tires for a NASCAR race, swerving and jerking back and forth very fast, and I don't think his hands have left the steering wheel once since we turned around.

Staring up at him, I yell, "What's going on?"

"Your ex," Haze yells back, glancing down at me a few times, always quickly looking back up at the road. "The fucker tried to get us to crash."

"Where?" Brain cells dumb from the adrenaline, I'm stupid and try to pop my head up, attempting to see what's going on. I somehow manage to get up on my knees and look between the seats to the what's happening behind us.

But all I see before Haze growls, "Get the fuck down," as he pushes the top of my head back down with his hand, is that the truck no longer has a back window and the back seat is littered with pieces of glass.

CRASH!

Something rams into the back of the truck, knocking my head to the right and into the front face of the dashboard.

I scream again, then bend over, dropping my head to my knees again. Something warm immediately starts rolling down onto my forehead, and it tickles as it glides across my eyebrow, so I use my hand to brush it aside. Figuring it was just my hair, I'm shocked when I look at the back of my hand and see that it's red. Blood. I'm bleeding.

"Haze," I call out, "I'm bleeding." My voice trembles. Tucking my hand into my sleeve, I use the cotton to wipe my forehead again. The yellow section of my tie-dye sleeve turns a dark red.

Still kneeling on the floor, I'm rocked to the right, then back left as Haze slams on the brakes and we come to another quick stop. I look up to see what's wrong, but before I can ask, he starts chanting, "No, no, no, no, no, no," as he's swiveling his torso, looking behind us. "Stay in the truck," he shouts.

Throwing the truck in park, he pulls his gun out of the holster at his side and is out of the truck in seconds. The door is left open, and I see him leaning down a little, aiming the barrel at something.

Using my left elbow, I push myself up and look out what used to be the back window. If I knew what a war zone looked like, this would be what comes to mind. People are running in slow motion, like an action sequence in a movie. You know things happen faster than they show, but everything is slowed way down so you get all the important details.

The front of the large SUV is pushed against the tailgate of Haze's truck, and all four doors are open. A few Rebel Vipers are pointing their guns at the people inside, but the windshield is tinted, so I can't see who's there.

Around us are Rebel Vipers motorcycles parked in the middle of the road, and more Brothers in leather are surrounding the vehicles behind us.

And they all have their guns raised as well, ready to fire. But nothing and nobody is moving, it's eerily quiet. Until it's not.

Something on the other side of the road, a little farther back, catches my eye, and I can't look away as everything starts moving at once.

Haze takes off running toward a motorcycle that's laying on the ground with someone sprawled out on their back next to it, half in the road, half in the gravel.

Behind the motorcycle is the blue truck that had cut us off, and it has a wrinkled front bumper. I know all the information is right in front of me, but I can't seem to put the pieces together to figure out what's going on.

There's yelling and swearing and guns being pointed in every direction. People are being pulled from the SUV and other truck, but all I can do is watch. Something about where Haze is now kneeling on the side of the road is waking up a part of my brain. A thought is needling me deep, and I know I need to find out what it is.

Almost on auto pilot, I flip up the center console and crawl across the bench seat. Once I'm up, kneeling in the driver's seat, I grab the 'oh shit' handle above the door with my left hand and swing my legs out from under me so I land on my butt. To avoid falling, I grab hold of the seatbelt and use it to guide me as I slide down to the ground. The truck is so tall and has no side rails, Haze had to lift me into the truck.

When my feet hit the pavement with a small thud, my body gets jarred, sending another sharp pain from my shoulder down my arm. Now that I think about it, my fingers are feeling a little tingly. I try to lift my hand, but it won't move.

Hearing someone yell my name, I look up, and next to the blue truck, I see Trooper standing beside two men. One man is lying on his stomach, face down, with his arms spread out. It's the second man who makes me lose my breath. Toby.

On his knees, gun pointed at his head, is my ex-husband. He's got his hands up in the air and he's staring straight at me.

"Fuckin' bitch!" Toby yells, his face bright red. It's a look I'm very familiar with. "Look what you did!"

"Is this your ex, Abby?" Trooper calls out. Somehow, I can hear his voice perfectly over the others swarming around me.

I try to speak, acknowledging his question, but nothing comes out. I can do nothing but nod my head fast.

"Perfect." Trooper holsters his gun, pulls out a long-handled black flashlight that's hanging at his side, and hits Toby upside the head. He falls forward, landing face first on the blacktop.

"ABBY!" someone else yells.

I feel like an owl, turning completely around, trying to find the voice, but I freeze when Haze's eyes meet mine. He's sitting on the road beside the man who's still lying on the ground. He has the man's head in his lap and he's running his fingers through the man's long, dark hair.

That's when I realize the man who's been sprawled out on the ground this whole time is Smoke.

Trying to run to him, I immediately realize my arm is hurting worse by the second. Using my left hand to hold my right bicep to my chest, I jog toward the huddle of bikers surrounding my men.

"What happened?" I ask as I try to kneel, but I realize I don't have the balance, so I stay standing, looking down at them.

"What's wrong with your arm?" Smoke mumbles from his perch in Haze's lap. He reaches his right arm up to me, I step closer, and he grabs my leg.

"Don't worry about me," I say as I look down at his half-smiling face. "What's wrong with him?" I look to Haze. His eyes are on an up and down swivel, looking from me to Smoke, and back again.

"His shoulder is messed up hella bad." That's when I notice his left shirt sleeve is shredded, parts missing or dangling by a thread. His skin is dirty and bleeding in some spots. Brewer is kneeling beside them with no shirt on, wrapping his now torn t-shirt around Smoke's forearm.

"And I think he broke his leg, but I'm not sure." His jeans are also ripped down the left leg, his skin torn up and bloody.

Ring, who's had his back to us, turns around, phone in hand. "Doc is on his way with the van. We'll load Smoke up and get him to the hospital." He sees me, arm still clutched to my chest. "You too, Abby." Ring starts talking to the Brothers around us, giving out instructions. "Whiskey is also coming with the box truck. We need to get all these yahoos restrained, loaded up, and taken back to The Pit. And Wrecker and Diego are coming with the tow trucks to get the vehicles and Smoke's bike back."

More members of the club come roaring in to load up the four men they pulled from the SUV, along with Toby and the other guy in the truck who cut us off and hit Smoke.

After getting me settled in the front passenger seat of the van, Doc drives us to the emergency room while Haze sits on the floor beside Smoke.

CHAPTER THIRTY-ONE

ABBY

On the ride to the hospital, I convince Smoke to tell me what all happened from his point of view. When we left the clubhouse, he was riding ahead of us, but the truck Toby was driving cut between him and us, and when Haze turned us around, Smoke rode super-fast to try and get close again.

Just as he got in front of the truck, it sped up and hit his back tire, causing him to lose control and crash. Somehow managing to hold onto the handlebars, Smoke didn't hit the ground too hard. With the bike down on its side, Smoke landed on top of it, hitting his shoulder and lower leg in the process. He did slide along the gravel for a little bit as he let go of the motorcycle, hence the road rash on his arm and leg, but things could've ended so much worse.

The fact he wasn't wearing a helmet scares me the most, but that's an issue I'll bring up with him and Haze at a later date.

The more I hear, the somewhat happier I am with having been stuck down on the floor, not being able to see things go down. Had I watched Smoke crash his motorcycle, and seen him tumble and fall to the ground, who knows how I would be handling things right now.

Once we get checked-in through triage and are placed in adjoining bays, nurses and doctors swarm around Smoke and me, inspecting our injuries. Since we can't say what really happened without law enforcement getting involved, we tell the emergency room staff we were in a four-wheeler accident. I'm not sure if they believe us, but I answer what I can and leave the rest of the talking to Haze.

Turns out, Smoke has a broken collar bone and a fractured fibula, both on the left side, and a good amount of road rash. I have a dislocated right shoulder that hurt like a bitch as two nurses held me tight and a doctor popped it back in.

Despite the nurses trying to give Smoke some pain relief by IV, he refused any medications. He said all he needed was to hold my hand as a nurse sat at his side for three hours, removing the numerous tiny rocks and gravel out of his skin. He looks like he was in a fight with a cheese grater and lost.

Somehow, neither of Smoke's breaks are bad enough or are in places that require surgery. He does have a medical boot on his left leg from the knee down, and bandages and wrappings around his shoulder, looped around his chest to keep everything in place. He did let the nurses put ice packs on his shoulder and front of his chest to numb a little of the pain.

Against several doctors' recommendations, as soon as Smoke heard I was cleared to leave, he wanted to go right away too. I tried to argue with him, to no avail, but Haze assured me that between Doc and Sunshine's medical knowledge, he was okay with him leaving. With the promise he'd force Smoke back if something went wrong, I agreed to whatever they wanted to do.

I think Smoke's more upset about the tears and damage to his cut, from where he slid on the ground, than he is about having two broken bones.

"We'll have someone at the club look at it," Haze assures him again. "Or we'll get you a new cut."

"FUCK NO!" Smoke yells so loud, a young nurse comes running toward us.

"What the heck is goin' on in here? There's a toddler in the next room, and you can't be yelling and swearing like that." She's standing at the end of the bed with her arms folded and hip cocked to the right. This lady means business.

"I don't mean to sound rude, Nurse . . ." Smoke sits up as best as he can, squinting to read her name badge. "Nurse Alason, is it? Cool spelling, by the way."

"Thanks." Her anger is still there, but at least she smiles.

"Totally badass, but anyway, if I don't get out of here by the time the sun comes up, I'm gonna walk out those doors," letting go of my hand, he uses his right hand to point at the doors across from us, "whether you like it or not. I don't fuckin' care what the doctor says. Figure out a way to let me go home."

Her right eyebrow pops up a little. "If you promise to cut back on the sailor language, I'll see what I can do."

"Thank you," I butt in, trying to calm the situation, hoping he doesn't say anything stupid or argue with her.

"But one more f-bomb and it's three more x-rays, then I'll personally come back to draw some blood just for the fun of it." She walks around the bed, approaching his left side, finger right in his face. "And I'll make it hurt." With that, she spins around and walks away.

"Your cut is in that bag over there." I point to a white bag behind the chair Haze is sitting on. "I'll sew your leather back together myself if I have to."

Haze has been camped out in that chair for hours, and since I signed my discharge paperwork, I've sat my butt on the edge of Smoke's bed to his right.

Smoke wraps his right arm around my waist, pulling me close, and kisses me silly. When we break apart, we lock eyes. "I'm so, so, so sorry for letting you get hurt. I know you wanted to go get your Gram, but we should've left you at the clubhouse."

"Arguing with you will do neither of us any good," I say as I smooth his wild hair back off his forehead. "Let's just hush for a bit and wait for that nice nurse to come back. Then we can go home."

"I sure as hell don't wanna piss her off again." Smoke playfully pretends to shiver. "I don't like needles."

"You have huge tattoos." I trace the ghost on the right side of his chest. "How can you not like needles?"

He sets his hand over mine, pressing my palm flat under his. "When I get inked, I lay in the chair with sunglasses and headphones on, so I don't have to see the needles or hear the buzzing. No thanks!"

I can't help but laugh. "You're crazy."

"But I'm your crazy," he says with a grin.

"Mine too," Haze calls out, arms folded and a pouty look making him appear both sad and adorable.

I stand up, kiss Smoke on his cheek, then walk around to Haze. Careful of my right arm in a sling, I sit on his lap and kiss his cheek too. "I didn't forget about you."

"Good." He presses a kiss to my cheek, then rests back in the chair.

After an hour of waiting, Smoke is finally given the green light to go home. He signs some forms acknowledging his refusal of care, but he does it with no reluctance. And with an appointment set for a week away to come back for another x-ray to make sure things are still where they're supposed to be, and a follow-up scheduled for me as well, twelve hours after we drove up to the emergency room doors, the three of us are being driven away. Surrounded by an escort of Brothers, we ride the half-hour back to Tellison and the clubhouse.

The entire way home, Haze goes on and on about how he's going to be our helper, and that anything we need, just say it and he'll get it. According to him, it's his responsibility as our partner to make our lives as easy as possible.

"If you offer to wipe my ass one time, I'm gonna shove this boot up your ass." Smoke glares at him as we walk to the front doors, him leaning on Haze with his right side. "Got me?"

All his threat does is cause the crowd of Brothers, Old Ladies, and friends welcoming us back to laugh.

"I thought you liked when Haze touched your butt," Kraken calls out, which makes everyone laugh harder.

Smoke flips him off but with a smile. "Fuck you."

Hammer and Haze carry Smoke upstairs and get him settled into Haze's room. Even though we have two rooms to float between, it seems like this one has been unofficially claimed as our go-to room. I could care less where we sleep, as long as I'm in a bed with both of them.

"Hey, Hammer?" I ask as he heads for the door.

"Yes?" He turns back to me on my perch on the recliner that was also brought up by Whiskey.

"Could you do me a favor and ask Angel if she could cut my hair when she gets some free time?"

"Sure," he pulls his phone from his cut pocket, "I'll call her now."

"Oh no!" I hold my hand out. "It doesn't have to be now. Maybe tomorrow or something."

"It's no big deal." With his phone to his ear, he turns and starts talking to his Old Lady on the other end of the line.

And not two minutes later, she's walking in, black backpack over her shoulder. "I hear someone needs me and my scissors." She points at Smoke, propped up against a ton of pillows. "Is it you, sir?"

"Oh, hell no," he calls out. "Our raven-haired Rapunzel over there wants a trim."

"Not a problem." Angel sets her bag on the end of the bed and starts pulling out her supplies.

After some discussion between me and Angel, and Smoke and Haze's requests that it doesn't get cut too short, we settle on a length we're all happy with. Cutting it up to a little below my shoulders, I end up losing two feet of hair. My head instantly feels lighter, and I can shake it from side to side without the strands getting caught in my arms. I love it!

Angel slides her shears over my ends to cut in some layers, then runs her fingers through to flip it back and forth a few times. "There," she steps back, tossing her comb in her bag, "all done. Do you like it?"

Standing, I step into the bathroom and look in the mirror. I spin around a few times, taking in a hairstyle I don't think I've had since I was a little kid. I've always had really long hair.

"I love it." Stepping back into the bedroom, I hug her as best as I can with my left arm. "Thank you for this."

"No problem." She zips everything back in her backpack and tosses it over her shoulder. "I'll let you guys be. Have a good night."

Once she's gone, Haze pulls me back into the bathroom, insistent he help me take a shower. After washing my hair, which I didn't realize how difficult it would be with one arm, he rubs my body with soap, tickling me when he can. Once out and dried off and dressed in another of their t-shirts—Haze's this time—he brushes my hair and pulls it up into a ponytail. It turns out kind of messy and has a few bumps, but that's okay. It's the thought that counts.

The entire time we were getting dressed, Smoke was whining and complaining.

"It's so not fair. I wanted to shower with you guys."

"Honey," I say as I slide under the sheet, "you got cleaned up and bandaged at the hospital. You didn't need one."

"Don't even start with me, cranky pants." Haze crawls up the center of the bed on his hands and knees, settling himself into the middle. "With as long as you're gonna be laid up and healing, there'll be plenty of chances for me to rub you down with a loofah."

That gets Smoke's attention. "Really?"

"Yes." I scoot back to sit up against the pillows stacked behind me. "You missed one shower, boohoo. Tough cookies for you." I squint my eyes shut and stick my tongue out at him, totally acting like a child, but not caring.

A pillow smacks me in the face, and I swat it down.

Haze is pointing at Smoke, chuckling. "He did it."

Smoke has his right hand up, palm forward. "I did no such thing. You had your eyes closed, so you can't prove it."

"You two are such children." I can't help but laugh at them.

This may have been a crazy, fucked-up, traumatic day, but it's ending with some very good things.

One, Toby has been found and is awaiting who knows what kind of torture at the hands of the motorcycle club I've found a new home in.

And two, I'm with the men I love.

Minus the injuries, I couldn't be happier.

CHAPTER THIRTY-TWO

HAZE

After a night of surprisingly restful sleep, the three of us are enjoying a lazy morning in bed.

Because of their respective injuries, our sleeping arrangements had to be rearranged. While Abby usually sleeps in the middle of Smoke and me, because of her sore right shoulder, she and I swapped places. Now, she's farthest to the right so no one can bump her arm, I've moved to the middle, and Smoke is still in his normal spot on the left. Which works out well for him, since it's his left shoulder and leg that are bandaged.

Knock knock.

"Sounds like we've got a visitor." I wink at Smoke as I scoot myself down the bed, careful not to shake the sore shoulders behind me.

"People sure wake up early around here," Abby comments as she sits up a little more.

"Someone is always awake, no matter what time of day or night it is," Smoke replies with a chuckle.

Pulling the door open, I'm met with one face I was expecting, and another I wasn't but am not shocked to see—our President and his Old Lady.

Whiskey is standing in the hall, a large, flat, white box in his arms. He holds it out. "I come bearing presents."

"And I brought you breakfast," Duchess adds as she holds a tray of various muffins and donuts.

"You guys didn't have to do that," Abby calls out as I welcome our guests in.

"Yes, we did." Duchess sets the tray on the dresser and gives Abby a gentle hug. "You better get used to my hugs now, 'cause everyone gets them all the time."

Abby looks up at her with a smile. "I think I can handle that."

"Good. Diego brought you up some soda and water," she says as he carries cases in, setting them on the floor against the wall before disappearing.

"And this is for you," Whiskey hands me the white box, "well, kinda." He slaps me on the shoulder, and they head for the door.

"Let us know if you need anything and we'll be up in a jiffy." Duchess then adds, "Is there anything else you need for now?"

"Don't forget you promised me my own cupcake flavor," Smoke replies as he points to Abby and myself. "Remember what you said back when you had your baby shower?"

I see the moment she remembers the conversation,

"I got you covered. I have just the flavor in mind."

With that, Whiskey and Duchess take their leave, and I shut the door.

"Haze, why don't you put that box down for a sec and go get that *thing* from my nightstand," Smoke suggests, nodding his head toward the door connecting our rooms.

"I sure can." I set the box on the desk and head for his room. Going right to the drawer, I pull out what's inside.

Coming back, I find Abby and Smoke have both moved and are now sitting side by side on the edge of the bed. Grabbing the big box, I set it on the bed beside Abby but hand her the small rectangle jewelry box first.

"What is this?" She looks at both of us with an expression of pure wonder. Her eyes are open and bright, her cheeks are rosy, and she's smiling so big.

"Open it and see," Smoke tells her, resting his right hand on her leg.

"I can't open it with one hand." She has it in her left hand, holding it out to me. "Can you do it?"

"I sure can." I take it, turn it to face her, then flip the lid, showing her what's inside.

She gasps like a kid on Christmas morning. "It's so pretty." Abby reaches out and touches it with her finger, almost like she's afraid to break it.

"It's a skeleton key necklace," Smoke explains as I pull it out of the box and hand it to her. "All the Old Ladies have one—Duchess, Sunshine, Angel, and now you."

"Does this mean I'm really your Old Lady now?" Abby turns to him, then me, her eyes still so big.

"This is part of it," I explain. "Do you like the design of the key?"

"I do. I really do." Her hand is flat out, the key laying across her fingers, and she's tracing the swirls with her thumb. "It looks a lot like your tattoo." She smiles at me.

"It's not exact, but it's a Celtic design similar to Haze's tattoo," Smoke tells her.

"We noticed you were a bit leery about getting a tattoo when we mentioned it before, so as soon as we saw this," I take the necklace and place it around her neck, "we knew it was perfect for you."

"I love it." Abby looks down at it lying on her chest, then to me and Smoke. "I love you." She kisses me. "And I love you." She kisses Smoke.

"Next comes the big present." I reach for the box and open the lid. "While normally this is something you'd open on your own, with your hurt arm, I'll open the lid and you can look inside."

Removing the lid, I set it aside. But before I can even turn back, I feel Abby hugging me from behind. The little minx got up and grabbed hold of me with her good arm. Turning myself around, I hug her back as gently as I can.

Tilting her chin up, I see her eyes sparkling. She's crying.

"Oh, beautiful," I whisper, trying to wipe the tears rolling down her cheeks. "What's wrong?"

I look over to Smoke, and he's smiling, holding his hand out to me. Reaching for his right hand, I pull him up to balance on his right leg. Walking Abby backward a few steps, I get her back against his chest, then hug them, using my body to support all of us.

"I can't believe you got me my own cut," she finally answers me with a hiccup.

Smoke leans his head over her shoulder, turning her to look up at him. "We were always going to give you one. We just had to wait for it to get here." Then, he kisses her softly.

"Oh my gosh, Smoke." Abby suddenly nudges me back and turns to face him. "You should not be on your feet. Sit down right now." Holding his elbow, she helps him sit.

"I was fine on my feet for the two seconds I was standing." He laughs as she fusses over him, making sure his sling is tight and that his bandages are still stuck in place.

"Abby," I call out, pulling her elbow, trying to get her attention, "I want you to look at this."

She turns to look at me, then at the box, and traces the stitching on the left side of the cut. "Raven," she says as her fingers move.

Wrapping my arms around her waist, I cradle her from behind. My chin resting on her left shoulder, I explain the name. "It's because of your midnight hair and dark eyes."

"You've called me that before." Abby turns her head to look at me, then back to the box, then over to Smoke. "I just thought it was some kind of term of endearment."

"We'll always call you names like 'gorgeous' and 'beautiful' and 'love'," Smoke illustrates with words that I feel in my heart, "but none of those are enough to describe the right feeling you give us. Giving you a name like Raven is special in so many ways."

"We just don't have the right words to describe how much you mean to us," I continue, the only way I know how. No fancy words, just the honest truth. "We can tell you we love you 'til we're all blue in the face, but this is more. The way we let you know how much you mean to us is by giving you a name all your own."

"From this day forward, everyone will see the name on this cut and know you belong to us." Smoke lifts the leather cut, much smaller than his or mine, and holds out to me. "And that we belong to you too."

Taking it from him, I turn the back of the cut to face Abby. . . no, Raven. . . showing her the patches there. Again, we watch as she traces the letters on the patches, outlining mine and Smoke's names on the bottom rocker.

"Can I put it on now?" Her question is so soft, almost unsure if even asking is okay.

"Of course, you can." I turn it around and hold it open.

Raven turns her back to me and slides her left arm in. Careful of her sling, I rest the material over her right shoulder.

We watch as she turns in a circle, showing us the whole picture. If I could've dreamed this day, it couldn't be much better than this. Broken legs and bones and pulled muscles aside, seeing my name next to Smoke's on a Property cut has got to be my crowning moment. Even more so than the day I got my own cut.

I feel a tug on my hand, and Smoke pulls me to sit next to him. Sliding my hand across his back, I close in on him, inch by inch. His lips crash into mine, and I give back every ounce of love he pours out to me.

Pulling back, he smiles. "We did it," he says with a smile.

"We sure did, love." I kiss his hand in mine. "We sure did."

"What's this?" Turning, I see Raven holding up a bundle of black tissue paper that was in the box.

Shifting in my seat to turn her way, I keep Smoke's hand in mine. "Open it and see," I tell her.

"What did you do?" Smoke teases me, pulling on our hands.

I pretend to zip my lip as Raven carefully tears the paper, only ripping it where the tape is, then unfolds the black frou-frou paper hiding my surprise.

"You don't have to be gentle, Raven, my love," I say. "It'll be going in the garbage when we're done with it."

She pauses her unwrapping and stares at me like I've lost my damn mind. "I don't think so. Are you crazy? Whatever this is, it's obviously important, so I can't tear it to shreds."

"She's the sentimental type." Smoke rocks us together. "Good to know."

When she finally gets the paper unraveled—not easily done, I might add, with only one fully functioning arm—she holds it in her right hand against her stomach and uses her left hand to smooth the paper out on the bed.

Then she takes hold of the contents, one in each hand. I see her eyes volley between both before she holds them out to us. "I'm guessing these are yours?"

Knowing exactly what they are, I grab them both, handing one to Smoke and keeping the other for myself.

In my hand is a white rectangle patch, two inches tall by four inches wide, trimmed in black thread. Stitched in black are the words 'Property of Smoke'. Beside the block letters is the silhouette of a raven on the right side.

The one in Smoke's hand is almost identical, except his says 'Property of Haze' on it.

When no one says a word, I start to get a little worried. I try to explain, hoping to get a positive response. "I called and requested something a little extra."

Smoke finally looks up, and I can tell he's shocked.

Still no words, he pulls me in for a kiss that rivals any we've shared before. While including tongue and grunting and moans, it's also gentle and breathtaking all mixed together.

I try and be careful, remembering his injuries, but I hold him by the back of his neck and soak in the love and affection he's showing me. It's never been a who loves who more competition between us, but right now, I feel the emotion rolling off of him.

After we split and settle back, Smoke holds his patch up. "Where on our cuts should we put these?"

Showing him mine, he takes it, setting it side by side with his on his lap.

"Whiskey said he'd allow them as long as we put them on the right front side of our cuts, opposite our name patches." I tap the right side of my chest.

"I like these." Raven worms her way between us, so I move over to give her room on the bed. She takes the patches back from Smoke and, much like when she handed them to us, holds them out in front of her so we can all see them. "Especially my raven next to your names."

"I like them too." Smoke kisses the side of her head. "They'll be right on the front of our cuts for everyone to see."

Any doubt I had about having them made vanishes.

CHAPTER THIRTY-THREE

SMOKE

Punch! *Oomph*. Punch! "Fuck." Punch! "I'm not tellin' you fuckers anythin'." WHACK! *Uggh*.

"We're gonna kill you," Hammer swings his right fist, "whether you tell us," and then his left, "what we wanna know or not." Finally, he gives Toby an uppercut with his right, before continuing. "So you might as well start talkin'."

It's late Sunday night, only thirty-six hours since our shoot-out and my crash, but we have questions to ask. And those questions can only be answered by a select few people. It just so happens that those six people are currently hanging in the middle of our barn.

The Pit, as we call it, is the barn we use to torture, kill, and dispose of the bodies of the people who do our club wrong. Lately, we seem to be using this hundred-year-old barn quite often, but this is the first interrogation I've been part of since I became a patched member of the Rebel Vipers MC.

I was here and witnessed when Jewel, one of the old club girls, was tortured for information on where Sunshine was being held, but since I was still considered a newbie, I was only involved in the clean-up.

Tonight, we have six men tied up in the barn, all hanging from the I-beam that runs along the rafters. Their hands are bound together and their arms are extended above their heads, hanging from chains attached to pulleys along the beam. With only an inch from their toes to the plastic sheet laid out over the concrete floor, they have no stability while they hang.

When Haze and I and a dozen of my Brothers left the clubhouse a half-hour ago, we left a very pissed-off Raven behind with the other Old Ladies. She really wasn't thrilled about me going, but I gave her no choice. There are just some things that she gets no say in, especially when it's related to club business. That's part of being a biker's Old Lady.

I love saying that. Raven's my Old Lady. Mine and Haze's.

She's also not happy about not being able to see Toby like Whiskey originally said she could. But with her injury, and her being mad at me for coming while I'm injured, it was decided she stay back. I'd rather deal with a pissed-off Raven than an even more emotionally hurt one because of seeing her ex-husband again.

Even though I'm out of commission with a broken collar bone and fractured leg, and stuck with my ass in a chair out of the way against the wall, I refused to miss this.

Haze is angry enough for the both of us, and I have no doubt he'll get his aggressions out before the night's over. He's in prime form, and pretty fucking hot, if you ask me, all worked up and raring to go to get any information from these men about why they came here and tried to hurt our woman.

From the little bit of information Cypher did manage to find online, and what Trooper learned from his connection, we already know Toby got himself involved in a shady religious organization.

When asked, all six men refuse to admit it's a cult, but none of us are fooled. The pieces we know just don't fall onto the legal side of things. Our club should know—we have our toes in a few not-so-legal ponds.

Whiskey paces back and forth in front of the men, then kicks Toby in the shin. "Why did you plant a bomb in your ex-wife's car?"

"A bomb?" the guy third in the row cries out. "I didn't know about no bomb."

Ring pulls a knife from his boot, and standing behind the guy, holds it against the front of his throat. "You didn't know Toby here stole Raven's car and put a bomb under the hood?"

"Uh-uh," he mumbles, trying not to move.

"Well," Haze stops his own pacing and stands in front of guy number four, "what do you idiots know about your dumbass leader here?"

"His wife ran away, so we all came here to help get her back from you," number four says with a squeak.

"You mean his *ex*-wife?" Haze snarls right in his face. "She divorced him a year ago, asshole."

"We didn't know about no divorce." Guy number one, who was silent up until now, looks panicked and starts shaking his head. "Our church doesn't believe in divorce."

"I say since he got us captured," guy number two starts thrashing, causing the chains above him to rattle, "we no longer have loyalty to Tobias."

"Yea," the others call out, all except Toby.

"Well, well," Whiskey laughs as he squares off with the now failed ringleader, "it looks like your sheep have gone astray. What do you have to say about that, Toby?"

"My name is TOBIAS!" he yells at the top of his lungs. "And all these men to my right are traitors of the church and congregation. Y'all will burn in hell when the devil gets his hands on you." He spits toward them, missing by a mile.

Hearing him speak of burning, every one of my Brothers, including myself, busts out laughing.

"Oh, *Toby*," Ring circles in front of him, "if you only knew how true what you just said is."

"What do you mean?" Toby begins looking around, maybe finally taking in his surroundings.

"See that furnace over there?" Ring spins him to face the incinerator in the back corner. "That's where we're going to put your body after we kill you, turning you into ash before we wash you down the drain."

"No, no, no, no, no," Toby starts chanting, squirming his hips, making him start to spin again.

"Oh, yes," Ring stabs him in the front of his leg, "so start from the very beginning and tell us why you wanted to hurt Raven, before my knife decides to start removing your body parts."

The answers I've been waiting for finally start fumbling from his mouth. "I wanted to teach my wife, *Abby,* a lesson because she left me. She embarrassed me in the eyes of the church leaders, and I couldn't let her get away with that. So, I found her grandma's address in a notebook she left behind and came out and put a tracking device on her car."

"How can you be so dumb?" Whiskey is standing back, arms folded, just shaking his head at the stupidity coming from this man. "You're like a blind man trying to get out of a doorknob factory."

"Then, when I saw the places she was driving to, I did some research and realized she was working for a business owned by a motorcycle club." Toby snarls as he says those words. "I couldn't have her around miscreants like all of you, so I had to teach her a lesson."

"Is that what stealing her car was," I speak up for the first time, "trying to teach her a lesson?"

"It was bad enough she worked for filth like you." He glares at me, eyes squinted as he talks. "But when she moved into a house owned by your kind, I knew it wouldn't be long before you got your claws into her."

Feeling a little bit smug about that, I sit back and dig the wound a little deeper for him. "You realize by doing that, you drove her straight into our arms, right?"

"And two of you!" He swings a leg out like he's trying to kick me. Too bad for him, I'm too far away. "She was mad I wanted another wife, and now, she thinks having two thug boyfriends is okay? What a hypocrite!"

I pull my flathead screwdriver out and throw it at him across the barn. It lands exactly where I was aiming, in this leg, right in the middle of his thigh.

Toby screams, thrashing in pain.

Ignoring the drama queen, Whiskey addresses the other five men. "Does anyone outside the six of you know where you are right now?"

"No," guy number five answers. "Our hunts aren't disclosed to anyone outside the brigade."

"What exactly is a hunt and a brigade?" Whiskey asks.

"This isn't the first time we've had to bring back a runaway wife," number three says after Ring points his knife in the guy's face. "Hunters are what we call our congregation's trackers. We're all part of the brigade."

I ask, "While I get that you had a tracker on her car, how did you know about her getting involved with our club? She worked at the bar for months before becoming personally involved with us." I point at Haze and myself.

Toby won't answer.

"We've had a woman on the inside of your gang for a while." Seemingly sick of his leader, the man to Toby's right explains, "She kept tabs for us once Tobias discovered Abby was working for your club."

"I needed to know how much of a slut my wife turned into!" Toby yells. "So, I sent another one of my sluts to follow her around."

Haze stomps in front of Toby, pointing his gun in his face. "Who?"

Again, no answer.

"WHO?" Haze yells as he shoves the barrel under Toby's chin.

"McKenna," he groans the name out.

"You mean Toto? Our club girl?" Whiskey growls, looking around the barn. Everyone looks as confused and pissed-off as he does.

"WHAT!" I shout. I try and stand but don't get far, crashing back down on the metal chair, catching myself before I land on my ass on the floor.

"What does Toto have to do with you?" Hammer comes up to Haze's right and punches Toby in the stomach, causing his body to sway.

"He sent McKenna out here to infiltrate your club once he figured out she was spending time with the two of you," the guy farthest to the left says.

"I wasn't happy she tricked me into a divorce." Toby tries to kick his legs, but Haze's gun still in his face stops him real quick. "But she was less trouble here than she was back home, so I didn't care anymore. I just wanted her dead."

"Gunner, grab Ray and go get Toto from the clubhouse," Whiskey orders. "Bring her back here. She's fuckin' toast."

"Do we kill her before or after these fucktards?" Hammer asks, swinging a punch into guy number five's stomach.

"I say they all die now," Haze replies as he re-holsters his gun before punching Toby in the spot where Ring stabbed him earlier. "Then, when she's brought in, she can see what's coming for her next."

"I'm good with that," Whiskey calls out his approval. "I say one Brother gets one bullet for each asswipe hanging here. Who wants who?"

Since no one back in Kansas knows these men are here, we can't just let them free, not that we would even if they promised never to say a word. That's not how our club works. Once you cross our path and we catch you, we make sure you can never come for us or our Old Ladies again.

After more beatings just for the fun of inflicting pain and passing time, five of my Brothers stand in a row and start going down the line, shooting each man in the head one at a time.

Whiskey takes care of the first man because this is his club to protect and lead.

Cypher is second because of all the extra work he had to do to track these losers down, and because it was his system that was hacked.

Steel goes third because the bomb was seconds away from blowing up in his face. Had he not seen the trip wires, life would be looking very different for him right now.

And that's also why Ring is fourth in line. He said he deserves to kill someone because of the crying his Old Lady did over Steel being hurt. "I hate seeing my woman cry, and I'll kill you because of her pain."

Four down, two to go, Trooper steps forward with one simple line. "I'm gonna kill you because I can."

And lastly, I'm helped to stand so Haze and I can end this whole ordeal with two bullets. I asked that both of us be allowed to shoot Toby because it's our Old Lady he tried to kill.

Whiskey gives us one simple nod, and we pull the triggers. Two simultaneous shots fire at once, and two bullets pass through Toby's skull at the same time.

He's dead, and I feel absolutely no remorse.

Cypher had collected all their electronics at the crash site and shut them off so there was no trace anywhere of them being brought onto Rebel Vipers land. He said he'll use his tech stuff to go through any information there might be on the devices, and after he finishes whatever techno mumbo jumbo he does, he'll destroy it all.

As a few of my Brothers bring the bodies down from the rigging, laying them out on the floor, Ray and Gunner reappear. Just as Toby is being untied and dropped, Gunner walks in with a thrashing Toto over his shoulder, her hands tied behind her back. He tosses her down in the chair I was in before.

After shooting Toby, I refused to sit back down, leaning on the crutches Raven insisted I bring.

Toto, or McKenna, is facing the bodies, and I hear her screams and cries of denial, but I can't look at her. She betrayed our woman, and I never want to see her conniving face again. Turning to Haze, I say, "Let's go back. I need to see Raven."

Whiskey grants our request to leave, so with Haze's help, I get settled into Blue's SUV, which we borrowed because it sits lower to the ground than any of our trucks, and we head for the clubhouse.

With Toby now behind us, and soon to be nothing but ash in the sewers, it's time to move forward.

CHAPTER THIRTY-FOUR

RAVEN

It's been a week since the 'incident'—I don't know what else to call it—and things around the clubhouse are significantly calmer. Well . . . almost.

Each day, Smoke acts more and more like a grumpy, growly bear, not being able to just get up and walk around whenever he wants. For all of our sanities, Mountain was nice enough to lend him his extra wheelchair, so anytime Smoke wants to move around the main room or go outside, he's able to do so freely.

But that's only with Haze's help, of course. I swear that man has made it his mission to follow both of us around like we're blind puppies. Even Teddy, the puppy in the clubhouse, has more freedom than we do.

Speaking of Teddy, he had a visitor on Wednesday. Gram came to the clubhouse to visit, saying since we never made it to her, she now wants free rein to visit whenever she wants. She brought Sampson along, and he and Teddy played and roughhoused in the backyard for hours.

Most of the club knows who Gram is because, unbeknownst to me, it seems Mrs. Nancy Harris is quite a local legend. I knew she took walks around town, but I was only recently informed of her nosy need to know everyone's business. My Gram is a hoot!

Gram fell in love with Haze and Smoke the second she met them. She said Haze's eyes remind her of my Gramps's, and that Smoke is never allowed to cut his hair, ever. Otherwise, she'll never give him a hug again.

She also said she'd gotten her first call from my mother, Diane, in almost five years. The news is that Francesca is in a major panic about Toby being missing and doesn't know what to do. Since she wasn't legally married to Toby, she has no access to his money and she's broke. But get this . . . I do.

It turns out that after I left, Toby hadn't removed my name from his bank accounts or the deed to the house. Gram told Diane that she was going to be of no help to her, so she and

Francesca were on their own, and warned them to never try and contact me. Legally, that money is now all mine.

When I told my guys about the money and house, they said they'd support one hundred percent whatever I wanted to do. Whiskey happened to walk by while we were talking in the main room and said the club's lawyer, Sal, was at my disposal to help figure out my options. I took him up on his offer and will be meeting with Sal in a few weeks.

I went to The Lodge two days this week to catch up on some office work, but Cypher also set me up with a laptop connected to the business's server so I can also do things while at the clubhouse. I'm looking forward to getting back behind the bar, but my men have informed me they aren't comfortable with that just yet.

While I probably should argue that I'm a strong woman and can do whatever I want, I'm enjoying being spoiled by them. I no longer feel like a damsel in distress, but they treat me so well, I'll take this little reprieve to let them dote on me.

Earlier this week, Sunshine shared with me and Haze, in private, the news that she's pregnant . . . with two babies! She's so happy she has Whiskey as a brother, but since it came out that Haze is her cousin, she's gone out of her way to learn more about him. She gushes about how she loves having the family she didn't have growing up. Sunshine said she wanted him to be the first person she told, so not even Steel or Ring know yet.

Haze hugged her and said he's honored and happy he has a family now too. But he made it very clear she better tell Ring and Steel soon, because he sucks at keeping happy secrets and didn't want to spill the beans.

She then asked us to help her set up the surprise. I don't know who's more excited about the plan we cooked up, Sunshine or me. It may be her news, but this is the first big thing that's happened since I became an Old Lady, and I'm happy to be part of it.

For the pregnancy reveal, Sunshine had her ultrasound picture printed on sticker labels, then I had Brewer sneak a few cases of unlabeled beer from Moraine Craft Brewery back to the clubhouse. Last night, while Sunshine kept Ring and Steel occupied outside with a project to build Teddy a doghouse, Haze, Blue, Brewer, Meredith, and I stuck the labels on the bottles, then hid them in Brewer's room until Ring and Steel left for work this morning.

Since Ring is technically my boss, I know his usual work schedule and daily routines. But since I'm not working, I corralled one of the club girls who is at The Lodge today to text me when Ring walks out the door to head back to the clubhouse.

The whole club, minus Ring and Steel, who's out at Rebel Repairs changing the oil on Sunshine's van, are hanging out in the backyard. The women are seated in the circle on the patio, which has now officially become our 'Church'. Everyone else is scattered around, tossing horseshoes, playing cornhole, chasing the kids, or just enjoying the beautiful fall day.

Steel and Ring know we're having a Sunday family barbeque but for obvious reasons were kept out of the loop.

It's just after two when my phone dings with a text.

Jazz: Ring is on his way!!

I show Sunshine and tell the group to get the surprise ready. I follow her inside and watch from the front porch as Ring pulls into the lot. As he parks his Harley and climbs off, I can tell he's a little suspicious of Sunshine, but she keeps telling him to wait. They grab Steel from the garage, and I hold the screen door open for them to come inside.

I follow as she leads them through the main room and out the back doors.

The whole club has migrated into a huge semi-circle and everyone yells "SURPRISE!" when they step outside.

"What the hell is goin' on out here?" Steel asks, looking around.

"I'd like to know the same," Rings adds.

"It's a party, Daddy and Papa!" Their daughter, Opal, starts jumping up and down. We also kept the secret from this little lady, because she would've tattled for sure.

Steel scoops her up, and she hugs him tight. "What's the party for, munchkin?"

"I dunno." Her little tiny shoulders shrug. "Momma wouldn't tell me."

I feel two arms wrap around my waist and look down to see a dark beer bottle in each hand. I take them, kiss Haze on the cheek, and take a step forward.

"I think these are for you two," I say, holding them out to Steel and Ring.

Steel sets Opal down, and he and Ring take the bottles.

It takes them a second, what feels like forever, to comprehend what the labels on the bottles say.

"NO FUCKIN' WAY!" Ring shouts. "Twins? No way! Really?" He grabs hold of Sunshine and pulls her in for a hug, diving in for a kiss that makes her bend backward so far, I'm afraid they're both going to fall.

The long, black label is adorned with the ultrasound picture and bold white letters that say 'Coming Soon X2' and 'Babies Bell-James'. I don't know where Sunshine got the idea, but for someone who runs a brewery, it's so fitting for Ring. And every biker here loves beer, so Steel doesn't seem to mind. In fact, he's still staring at the bottle like he's never seen one in his life.

Steel finally snaps out of his trance. As soon as Sunshine is free of Ring, he does the exact same thing to her, kissing her silly and holding her parallel to the ground.

Pulling back, all on two feet, Steel and Ring each grab one of her hands, beers still in the other, and stare at Sunshine like she's an alien.

"Really?" Ring asks again. "Are you sure?"

"I'm gonna be a daddy again? To twins?" Steel's question is full of awe and wonder.

I've seen how great of a dad he is to Opal, I've no doubt these new babies will be loved just as much.

"It's real, I promise," Sunshine answers, nodding. "I've suspected it for a while, so when I had my yearly check-up last week, they checked and confirmed it. But not even I saw the two babies coming. I almost fainted."

Ring holds out his beer aimlessly, so I grab it before he drops it, and his free hand goes straight to her belly. Had I not known she was pregnant, I wouldn't suspect a thing. She doesn't have a bump at all.

"How far along are you?" Ring asks as he looks down at her.

"I'm fifteen weeks today."

Steel's now holding his cold bottle against his forehead, over top of the bandana tied around his head. "When are you due?"

"On April seventeenth."

Steel gasps, and his smile grows so big, it's infectious and genuine. I know he's heard something that made him even happier. "That's the day before your birthday." Setting his bottle on the table behind him, he wraps her in his arms and lifts her off her feet, spinning them in circles. "We're having twins!"

Sunshine holds on tight, arms around his neck, laughing the entire time. "Put me down, you brute. You're gonna make me sick."

"Put her down right now," Ring orders, grabbing Steel's arm. "You'll make the babies dizzy in there."

Once back on her feet, Sunshine sets her hands on Ring's cheeks and pulls him down for a peck. "That's not how this works, but I love you anyway for thinking of our little apples."

"Apples?" Smoke pipes up behind me, wrapping his arm over my shoulder. "What does you being pregnant have to do with apples?"

Sunshine tucks herself into Steel and turns our way. "To help understand the size of a baby in utero, there's an app you can download on your phone that tells you what kind of fruit it's the same size as. Today they're as big as an apple. Next week, they'll be avocados."

"That's crazy," Ring says in awe. "We've got so much to learn. We didn't know any of this cool stuff when Opal was born."

"And now, we get to do it all times two!" Steel is staring at Sunshine like he's seeing her in a new light. It's so damn adorable.

Sunshine turns to her men, and I can tell this is turning into a bit more of a 'them' thing, so I take my men and step away.

A little while later, while we're all hanging out, Duchess pulls me aside and asks for help with something in the kitchen. She tells me about the new tradition of each Brother getting a special cupcake flavor when he claims an Old Lady. I remember Smoke saying something about cupcakes when Duchess brought us breakfast the morning after our trip to the hospital, so now I understand what he meant.

Each carrying a tray of cupcakes, Duchess and I set them on the bar, and Smoke and Haze both light up like boys who just got brand new bikes for their birthday.

"These are for you, just as I promised. They're S'mores because you need a fire to melt a marshmallow. And fires make smoke, that's you," Duchess says to Smoke with a wink. Pointing to the tray I slid in front of Haze, she continues, "And Haze, you get Mint Chocolate 'cause you're so sweet to our new Old Lady here."

They both dive in, groaning much like they do when the three of us are alone, but I'll let them have this one. Duchess's cupcakes are little round cakes of heaven.

And the day's announcements aren't over. Perhaps the biggest surprise is one even I didn't see coming.

Buzz, the Brother who runs the club's tattoo shop with his dad, Skynyrd, steps forward and whistles so loud, I instinctively cringe at the shrill sound. "I've got an announcement to make. As of about nine o'clock last night, I officially have an Old Lady."

"Wait, what?" Gunner questions.

While every couple's story is different, usually there's some sort of relationship leading up to the actual claiming. And looking around the room, I only notice two faces who aren't shocked by Buzz standing there, announcing he's taken an Old Lady none of them have heard about.

Whiskey, since he's the club President, seems to know things before anyone else, as he should. And Stiletto, one of the club girls, who's standing a little to Buzz's left. When his hand reaches out for her, she threads her fingers into his, and Buzz pulls her into his arms with the biggest smile I've seen from him yet.

Buzz dives into her for a long kiss, and when he lets Stiletto up for air, she stares into his eyes and blushes. The smile on her face radiates like she believes he hung the moon just for her.

Stiletto snuggles back into his embrace and turns to face the group. "And we're having a baby," she says with an unsure smile. Her voice is loud and solid, but her smile, not so much.

There are several open-mouthed, wide-eyed Brothers and Old Ladies around the room, including myself.

"Oh my gosh!" Duchess hands Krew to a still flustered Gunner, who happens to be next to her, and she rushes forward, enveloping the new couple in her arms. "This day just keeps getting better!"

And just like that, the veil of confusion drops, and everyone takes turns congratulating the new couple, asking lots of questions about the new baby-to-be.

Stiletto, whose real name is Amber, is given Star as her Old Lady name. With her fun, sparkly personality, I think Star is perfect for her. Buzz is very adamant that she be called by her new name, just like Angel is, or he'll punch any Brother's lights out.

"I need details, momma." Sunshine pulls Star outside with the rest of us ladies, and we all take the chairs we've claimed as ours in the circle.

It's just now that I notice Star is wearing a skeleton key necklace like the rest of us Old Ladies. Buzz also presented her with her Property cut as she cried happy tears. A lot of us had misty eyes for sure.

When Star was a club girl, she was fully in our circle, but now, there's a pride and happiness in her eyes that I hadn't seen before.

"I'm ten weeks today," she replies, setting her hands on her flat stomach. "Due May twenty-second."

"That's six weeks after me." Sunshine claps. "We're gonna have so much fun planning for these babies. All three of them."

It turns out, unbeknownst to either of them, Buzz and Star's feelings for each other were more than just friendly. But it wasn't until after realizing she's expecting that they'd admitted their secret love for one another.

"Y'all know I didn't become a club girl to snag a Brother," Star almost pleads her case, looking around the group. "I was just here to put myself through school."

"We know that," Duchess says, reaching for Star's hand. "The first day we met, you saved me from skanky Jewel and sat me down, telling me all about the place of a club girl in MC life. I appreciated that so much."

"I don't even know if I can say when everything changed," Star adds, a soft smile lighting her up, "Buzz, he just . . . we just . . . one day, I woke up and it clicked. And I kid you not, a week later, I realized I was two months late."

"Did you get pregnant that night in Sturgis?" Angel asks, laughing so hard she falls back in her chair. "You and your sexy named shots seem to have gotten both of us wild nights in bed."

"Those shots were crazy good, though." Star laughs back. "Too bad neither of us can do anything crazy like that now."

Buzz broke the biker Brother mold, much like Hammer did with Angel, and decided he was claiming his woman and making her his Old Lady.

It looks like I'm part of a very rapidly growing family, and I'm excited to see what's around the corner.

CHAPTER THIRTY-FIVE

HAZE

With our Raven's past turned to ash, she can finally move forward with her life. And by some stroke of fucking luck, Smoke and I are the bastards she's chosen to live that life with.

There are times when I think about what it took to get where I am, and I wonder if I'm worthy of this. But then I think about how lonely I was before accepting the love of a man *and* a woman, and I don't regret it at all. The only thing I wish I still had was my mother. I miss her terribly and would give anything in the world for her to have met Raven and Smoke, but I know she's somewhere up in *na flaithis*, watching over us from the heavens.

Brewer sent me a text message this morning, asking me to meet him in Whiskey's office. I left Smoke and Raven in our room under the watchful eye of Blue, who offered to help with anything they may need, and I'm on my way down there now.

The door is open, so I walk right in.

"Come on in," Whiskey calls out. "We've got a huge favor to ask, and fingers frickin' crossed you can dig us out of a hole."

"Sure," I respond, looking around the office, spotting Brewer in one of the two chairs in front of Whiskey's desk. Mountain is here as well, lounging on the couch against the left wall. "What's up?"

"As you know, I took Brick's position as club Secretary," Brewer begins to explain, "and while the job itself is pretty much smooth sailing, his notes are anything but."

"And what does that have to do with me?" I get that he was my dad and all, but it's not like he ever sat me down and shared club secrets with me.

"All of Brick's notes are written in code, and I can't make heads or tails of anything." Brewer holds up an open notebook so I can see two pages side by side. "I know you've got major math skills, so I'm taking a shot in the dark, hoping you can make heads or tails of this gibberish."

A little taken aback at the thought of having access to past club information, I look to Mountain, pointing to the pile of notebooks on the desk. "Why are you letting me look at this? I'm still new to the club."

"You being new doesn't mean you can't know what happened in the past, it's just that we've never had a reason to go through everything until now. Worst case scenario, you see the jumble we see and we're back to square one. No harm, no foul." Mountain sits forward, resting his elbows on his knees. "But if you can crack Brick's code, we'll thank the heavens."

"And I'll be indebted to you forever," Brewer adds.

"Maybe some of Brick's smarts rubbed off on me." I shrug and drop a small chuckle. "Not much surprises me these days."

"Ain't that the fuckin' truth." Whiskey runs a hand through his hair, tying it back.

"Well, take a look and see if anything pops out at ya," Brewer says with a sigh, holding the notebook he's got in his hand to me.

"I sure fuckin' hope something does. Because while I may have street smarts, those things are alien speak to me,"

Whiskey mutters, fanning the pages as he flips through another notebook. "And Sunshine, well, she's a genius, but after one look at the symbols, she ran for the hills . . . no pun intended."

"I guess none of those super smart Hill family genes passed down to you two." Mountain laughs. "Sorry, son."

"Thanks for that." Whiskey flips him off, laughing while doing it.

"Get comfy. We might be here for a while." Mountain nods to the empty chair beside Brewer.

Taking a seat, I flip through the green notebook I grabbed from Brewer. A few pages in, the wheels start moving and I see a pattern. "Sure shit, Brick was one sneaky fucker. I think there's a code." Laying it open, flat on my lap, I grab another notebook and start turning more pages. Stealing a pen from the coffee mug on Whiskey's desk, I begin making notes in the margin. "Holy fuckin' lightbulb, I see it. But I either need to find the key, or figure one out to decipher everything."

"How the hell did you pick up on that so fast?" Brewer jumps up and looks over my shoulder. "I've been looking through these for months and all they do now is make my eyes hurt."

"I noticed this repetition of letters here and realized it's a sequential pattern," I say, pointing to a chunk of four letters repeated several times to show him what I found. "Smoke says my brain works like a computer," I shrug and scribble a few more notes, "and I've got a photographic memory, so puzzles are kinda my thing."

"You do?" Mountain puffs up, his eyes open super-wide. "Brick did too."

"Just one more thing we shoulda seen from the get-go. I still can't believe the clues about you bein' family have been here the whole damn time and it took Brick dyin' for the secret to come out." Whiskey picks up a stress ball and tosses it in the air, catching it and throwing it again. "It fuckin' sucks."

"Hey, Haze, can you put that down for a sec?" Mountain pulls my attention from the notebook. "Now that we know you've at least got an idea of what we're dealin' with here, what do you think about a promotion of sorts?"

Closing the notebook, I set it and the pen on the edge of the desk. "What do you mean?"

"Well, now that the club is well into its second generation of members, I think it's time we have someone step up as a historian of sorts." Mountain points to the stack of notebooks again. "In addition to going through all this stuff, I think we should have someone start making note of the big important dates we have going on."

"You mean like the sudden influx of Old Ladies and babies that are popping out of the woodwork?" I ask, making all of us chuckle.

"Exactly," he says with a nod, then points behind me. "Those boxes are just a portion of the stuff we have. There's a fuck-ton more in the storage room. If Whiskey doesn't mind splitting your time between this stuff and over at the recycling yard, I think you've got a few years of translating work ahead of you."

I spin in the chair and see a stack of file boxes I didn't notice when I walked in. if the eight in here are just the tip of the iceberg, it looks like I'm going to be swimming in letters and numbers for a very long time.

"I'd be honored to take on this job." Turning back to the room, I take in the three faces looking at me with very hopeful expressions. "As long as the boss is good with rearranging my schedule, I'm onboard."

"It's fine by me," Whiskey replies, hands knotted behind his head. "Until you get this key or deciphering thing you need to get figured out, why don't you make this your focus? Then once you reach a point where you feel comfortable just translating everything over, we can sit down and make a schedule to work around both the yard and this."

"I say we put it to a vote at Church on Friday." Brewer jumps up and starts moving the notebooks from the desk to the open box on top of the stack. "Not that I think any of the Brothers would have a problem with it, but being the Secretary, I need to make sure we make it official. And since I'm in charge of writing everything down, I need to make sure from now on, everything's up to snuff so our new *official* club historian doesn't have to decode my shit one day."

"You're too much sometimes, Brother," Mountain stands up and knocks his elbow into Brewer, "but we wouldn't trade you in for nothin'."

"You couldn't get rid of him if you tried, old man." Whiskey tosses a crumpled piece of paper at his dad. "Brewer would hog tie you with the ropes he uses in his kinky shit, and you'd never be able to untie the knots."

"Oh, fuck you, son." Whiskey is kicked back in his office chair, with his boots up on the edge of the desk. Mountain quickly pushes his feet down, causing Whiskey to scramble to avoid falling over backward. "I still got some spring left in my step. Just ask your aunt."

Whiskey finally stops flailing and stands up. He shakes his shoulders in revulsion. "There's just some things a guy doesn't need to know about his parental units. Yuck!"

"That's enough outta you," Mountain says back. "Now, excuse us while I take Haze here and go give him that thing we talked about earlier."

"What thing?" I ask, looking back and forth between the two sassing Hills.

"I'll show ya in a second. I gotta get it from my room." Mountain heads for the door, and I follow.

Once out in the hall, we hang a right, then an immediate left at the door to Mountain and Blue's room. While I know it's his room, and I've been in it once, it's still weird invading someone else's personal space.

Mountain walks over to a desk against the wall to the right of the door. Above the desk is a big picture window facing the backyard of the clubhouse. Seeing it from this point of view is actually really cool. The window has a privacy film on the outside so no one can see in, but it looks crystal clear from in here.

He opens the top drawer and pulls out a cluster of keys. Twisting a ring off the bunch, he holds a set of three keys on one keychain to me.

I take them and twist the ring around my finger. "What's this?"

"Those are the keys to Brick's house," Mountain says, making my jaw drop. "Well, actually, the house is in both our names, but he's the only one who's been there in the last dozen years or so."

"And what do I need these for?" Whatever he's trying to tell me by handing these over isn't clicking. I'm going to need a bit more information.

"Let me explain." Mountain sits on the edge of the desk and points toward another chair by the wall. I pull it over and take a seat. "You see, before we started the club, our parents, your grandparents, owned a farm about an hour away from here. After my dad passed, and I came home from the Navy, Brick and I ran it for just about a year. When it was decided to sell, we kept the house and five acres for my mom to live on."

"Is she still alive now?" I ask, never having heard of her.

"Sadly, no," he says as he shakes his head. "She passed a few years back. She would've loved to know about you and Sunshine."

"I'm sorry I didn't get to meet her."

"Well, that's part of why I'm giving you those keys." He points to my hand. "Those were Brick's set, and I know he'd want you to have them. I'll give you the directions. Why don't you take Smoke and Raven out there for a few days of R and R? I'm sure with everything that just went down, the three of you could use some time away from the craziness of the clubhouse."

Thinking about it for a few seconds, I realize he's got a point. While Smoke and I are used to the hustle and bustle of clubhouse living, we've yet to discuss what our future living situation is going to be. Raven still technically lives in Duchess and Angel's house in town, but we need to talk to her about moving her stuff in here.

And as far as using this offered home for a vacation of sorts, I sure could use one. Other than going on long distance runs or when we went to the rally in Sturgis, I haven't left the clubhouse for any reason. I haven't taken any time for myself since I started Prospecting and could use a few days to be with my two people.

"Thank you for offering this to us." I stand and hold out my right hand. Mountain reaches out and we shake. "I appreciate it more than you know."

"Not a problem. The house is yours to use whenever you want." He writes an address on a piece of paper and hands it to me. "There's a caretaker who comes in once a month to clean and make sure it hasn't fallen down. Otherwise, all you'll need to do is maybe open a few windows to air it out."

He goes on to explain that behind the house a little way sits a huge lake that it has access to. When they sold the surrounding farmland to the two farmers on either side, they made the property line specifically so they all had equal access to the water.

The farmers have built a few houses around it over the last few years for their kids and families, but everyone still has space and privacy if needed.

"Hey, Mountain?" Before I go, I ask about the one thing that's been on my mind for a while. "Do you mind if I have that letter my mom wrote? I've read it a few times since the day I found it, but now I kinda wanna sit down and show it to Smoke and Raven before I pack it up and tuck it away for safekeeping."

"Absolutely," he replies with a nod. "It's in the safe in Whiskey's office, so just let him know you want it, and he'll get it out for you."

"Thanks."

"Anything for family." Mountain slaps me on the shoulder as we walk out of his room. "Now, go find your people and tell them about the vacation you're about to go on. You're more than welcome to take Blue's SUV, so Smoke doesn't have to climb in his truck with that dumb boot he's wearing."

"We just might take you up on that. Since Raven's car is nothing but burnt metal, not that it was much to begin with, and my truck is filled with bullet holes, we need a vehicle I can tote my injured people in."

"I get that." He chuckles as we walk into the main room and stop by the bar. "When I lost this damn leg," he kicks out his left boot, showing the prosthesis under his jeans, "it took me a while to suck it up and realize I couldn't just jump up in my truck whenever I wanted. Now, I hafta think before I move."

"Thank God, Smoke's only got a fracture, but with his broken collar bone, climbing up isn't the easiest."

"I get it. When you decide to go, we'll swap Blue's keys for Smoke's truck, then she'll have something to drive 'til you get back. No worries."

"Sounds like a plan to me."

I know Raven loves the club, and the people here, but I owe her so much more than I've been able to give her recently. It seems like every Old Lady who's been claimed lately, minus the surprise of Buzz locking down Star, has done so in a catastrophic way, so we deserve a reprieve.

Duchess came here looking for her lost sister and ended up being abducted from our own backyard.

Sunshine was looking for her long-lost father, and someone broke into her house, knocked Ring unconscious, and took her.

And Angel was kidnapped not once but twice by people trying to mess with our club.

Now, Raven came into our circle by escaping a shitty past, but it followed her and wouldn't let go until we took it out.

If you asked any of us men if we regret the trouble we went through to claim our Old Ladies, I know the answer would be a resounding "Fuck no!" but that doesn't mean we wouldn't wish it had been easier on them.

But now that we have nothing but our future together ahead of us, a few days away is just what the doctor ordered. A week of privacy to spoil and dote on my partners sounds like a good way to start our next chapter.

CHAPTER THIRTY-SIX

HAZE

As we pull up to the Hill family farmhouse, I'm blown away. Mountain said it was a big house, but big doesn't begin to describe its size.

The two and a half story house sits at the base of a small incline, and the steps up to the front porch are massive and wide. There's a wraparound porch with white picket spindles holding up a natural wood railing.

"What is this place?" Raven stands at the bottom of the front steps and stares up.

Since the back of the house is on flat ground and is accessible if we were to walk around it, I try to convince

Smoke we should go inside that way, but he refuses. I'm holding his right arm as he hobbles and takes the steps one at a time.

"When Mountain said it was big, he wasn't kidding," I reply as we finally make it to the top. Leading Smoke over to a chair, I get him situated, then head back to the SUV for our bags.

"No wonder Brick didn't share this place with any of us," Smoke says with a chuckle. "If he'd brought our rowdy group here, it probably woulda fallen down years ago."

"You got that right." I fish the keys out of my pocket and open the front door. Raven and I step in and we both freeze. Looking at her, her jaw is dropped and her eyes don't stop moving. "Whoa!"

"I think I'm never going to want to leave," she whispers in awe.

While the outside is beautiful with its stark white siding, black shutters, and porch swings, the inside is immaculate. The wood floors are gleaming, the windows are already open and there's a nice breeze floating in from the huge patio doors straight ahead, and there's enough furniture in this house to probably seat about half our club.

I shit you not, there are six couches lined up in a giant U shape around a coffee table that looks like it's built out of old railroad ties. There are also a few recliners, some regular wood chairs, and a bench seat built into the bay window that faces the front of the house.

I hear Raven squeal with excitement. "You guys gotta come see this!"

"Don't leave me out here!" Smoke calls from where we left and forgot about him on the porch.

I rush out and lead him inside. "Let's go see what has our lady so excited."

Walking past a dining table with a dozen chairs around it, we push through a swinging door and walk into a kitchen full of stainless-steel appliances to rival a restaurant. The counters are made of white marbled stone, and the same material creeps up the walls, leading to open shelves and glass-front cabinets.

The floor is the same hardwood that flows through the entire first floor, and there's a second smaller table in here that fits under the window looking out over the backyard.

That's when I get my first look at the lake Mountain told me backs the property. What I failed to get, and he didn't explain, is that the lake borders what I guess to be the *entire* property. It's huge!

"Can we move here?" Raven appears at my side, snapping me out of my trance.

"I wish we could, love, but this is too far away from the clubhouse for an everyday commute." I drop a kiss on the top of her head. "But I can promise that we'll visit whenever we have time. The keys are ours to use."

"Maybe we can bring Duchess and Whiskey with us next time," she says while clapping. "Oh, and Angel and Hammer and all the boys. I bet they'd love swimming when they get a little bigger."

"We'll talk to them when we get back home." Leaving Raven standing to enjoy the view, Smoke and I walk back into the living room and plop down on one of the couches. "I think I'm gonna like it here."

"Dude, it's gonna take a world-ending event to get her out of here." Smoke laughs. "I almost regret grumbling about leaving the clubhouse."

"You're too much sometimes," I pull his face in for a kiss, "but you're *my* too much."

"And don't you forget it."

"I'm gonna bring in the cooler so Raven can get the food put away. Then go on a hunt to find a room for us for the next few days. Once we're all unpacked, we can start on dinner. I'm starving."

Standing, I offer Smoke my hand to pull him up.

"Knock that off." He pushes my hand away, and with his good arm, uses his crutch to stand on his own. "If I'm supposed to be here to heal, you gotta let me do some shit on my own."

"Fine, fine." I step out of his way and start backing to the door. "Be right back."

As I carry everything inside, I think about the last year and how I got here.

While I've known of my attraction to Smoke for quite a while, I never would've guessed he'd ever feel the same way.

And I never would've imagined that we'd be so lucky as to find a woman who loves us both.

I drop an armful of duffle bags on the king-size bed in the master bedroom and turn around to see a family portrait hanging on the wall above a long, wide vanity-style dresser. Based on the four smiling faces, it's Mountain, Brick, and their parents, but the faces I recognize are much younger than I've ever seen them.

And the eerie thing about seeing Brick as a teenager is that I see a lot of myself in him. He's tall like me, but lean and lanky like I was before my muscles grew in. There's this tilt to his chin, a little to the left. Thinking back, I can picture him sitting in Church, head tilted to the side as he scribbled in his notebook. And I do the same thing when I'm in deep thought. My head tilts to the left and I prop my chin on my fist and get lost in my thoughts.

Thinking back to the day Brick was shot, all I remember was seeing the man lift his gun and shoot two bullets into his back. Brick fell face first into the grass, and that was the last time I saw him move.

Bullet, the Chaos Squad fucker who shot him, saw me and took off running. I called out for help but ran after him on my own.

I managed to catch him, tackling him to the ground, and used my long legs and arms to wrap myself around him so he couldn't escape. I got him in a chokehold, and Trooper handcuffed his arms behind his back. Once I was sure he was unconscious, we left him lying face down and rushed over to the huddle of Brothers around Brick.

It was only then that it really sunk in that he was dead.

At some point, he was rolled onto his back, and Ring was trying to do CPR, but it was too late. Doc said he was gone, and Mountain was sitting beside him, holding Brick's hand in his. His blood brother was gone.

Now that I know I'm part of that blood, I feel a sense of pride being in this home. I've almost broken Brick's code, I'm a Brother in the club he helped build, and I'm standing in the very place where he and his family lived for many years.

This place is just one more way to feel connected to the man who helped give me life.

Walking down the hall, I hear laughter floating from the kitchen. One voice, the deep timbre of one-half of my heart, Smoke, and the other, a lighter giggle belonging to the second half of me, Raven.

Before we left this morning, Raven and Smoke had their first check-ups since leaving the hospital. While we were all excited for some time away, I agreed to leave right away only if they saw a doctor first. Sunshine pulled some strings with her hospital contacts and got them both appointments immediately. We packed our bags and planned on heading north as soon as they got the all-clear.

Smoke's leg is stuck in the walking boot for six more weeks, then, depending on how it heals, he should be good.

He may be a stubborn fucker, but Smoke knows messing up a healing leg isn't a smart idea, especially since he's already bitching to get back on his Harley. While I know he wants to get up and do as he pleases, resting is the name of the game right now. I follow him around, driving him crazy, but I don't care. I won't let him do too much, no matter how many times he threatens to punch me or never suck my dick again.

His collar bone requires him to wear a sling to keep his arm close to his chest. He's allowed to take it off to shower and do a few stretching exercises twice a day, but when we get back, he has to make an appointment with a physical therapist for a longer-term treatment plan.

I'm really not looking forward to the grumbling that will come with that, but if he ever wants to ride again, he needs a full range of motion. One more thing to help him with, so I have no complaints.

Raven's healing super quick. While she still has some tenderness in her shoulder and upper arm, she's resilient and a warrior, for sure. I have no doubt she'll be back to her liquor bottle slinging ways very soon.

But regardless of their physical limitations, one thing is definitely not off the table—sex. I may have two banged-up and broken lovers, but if I have to, I'll whip out the Kama Sutra book to find a position to put all three of us in.

"Holy fuck," I try and say through a groan. Smoke has my dick so far down his throat, I'm not sure if he can breathe.

After a dinner of grilled steaks, twice-baked potatoes, and enough dinner rolls to rival a Texas Roadhouse, we all crashed on the couch to watch a movie. But we barely made it through the opening sequence before Smoke shoved his hand down my pants and ordered me to strip.

Somehow, I pieced together a few brain cells and managed to convince him to move our activities to the bedroom, so here we are.

Smoke is lying flat on the bed with his feet pointed toward the headboard. His head is balancing at the very edge of the bottom, and he's got a pillow under his shoulders, neck, and head to keep him elevated.

Raven is straddling his waist, riding his cock, rocking her hips front and back in a steady but slower pace than usual. Jostling Smoke too much would be bad on his shoulder, so she's doing all the work. Her face is right in front of mine, and I'm trying to concentrate on kissing her, distracting myself from blowing my load too soon, but it's hard. His mouth and tongue feel so good on my cock, I think he's trying to killing me.

I'm standing at the end of the bed with my right knee propped against the end of the mattress, my hips angled over Smoke's face, and my left foot is flat on the floor. My left hand is holding the side of Raven's neck, keeping her kisses on me, and my right is on Smoke's right shoulder, steadying him as best as I can.

And just when I think I have the upper hand, that it's my hips pushing my cock down his throat, Smoke turns the tables. I feel his hand touch my stomach, and his fingers start sliding up my chest.

CHAPTER THIRTY-SEVEN

RAVEN

If Haze's kisses weren't distracting enough, the dick I'm rocking back and forth on would do the trick. In an effort to make Smoke as comfortable as possible, without missing any of the fun, I suggested he lie out flat and let Haze and I do all the work. He can participate but not do any moving. Great idea in mind, but functionally, that's starting to get away from me.

The way my clit is rubbing against his pelvic bone is hitting all the right places. All I can do is try and focus on the face in front of me, and hope by keeping my lips locked to Haze's, that I don't lose control of myself and fall on top of Smoke in an out-of-control orgasm.

Apparently, self-imposed orgasm denial is a real thing, and I'm not sure if I'm a fan or a hater yet.

While chasing my tongue with his, Haze is doing two jobs at once. He's holding my head steady, keeping me upright with one hand, and his hips are angled over Smoke's face, getting a blowjob. And based on the sounds coming from Haze's mouth, groaning and grunting into mine, Smoke is driving him crazy.

Needing to take a breath, I pull back from Haze's lips and rest my forehead on his shoulder. This gives me a straight down look at Smoke's chest and where his right hand is starting to move toward.

Smoke sets his hand flat on Haze's stomach, then begins sliding it up higher with every pump of Haze's dick in his mouth. I feel Haze inhale a deep breath, causing his shoulders to shudder, and Smoke starts playing with his nipple piercings, twisting one, then fumbling across Haze's chest to find the other.

And like they're his hot button, which I know from experience that they are, a few twists from Smoke's fingers and Haze climaxes.

"Holy . . . fuck . . . me," Haze swears through his panting. His eyes are rolled back, and I watch as he chases his release. His grip moves from my neck to my shoulder as he grunts and swears.

Feeling Smoke's torso rock under me, I listen as he struggles to swallow and watch as Haze unloads in him, but he never once tries to tap out. His right hand is gripping my hip, but not in a painful or panicked way, just holding on, taking what he's being given by Haze.

I hear Smoke take in a deep breath as Haze shifts his weight to the side.

Before pulling away, Haze sets both his hands on my shoulders and rests his forehead on mine, catching his breath. "It's your turn, Raven." His eyes open and his smile grows, almost wicked.

Oh hell, what does he have in that evil mind of his?

My hips still rocking, feeling Smoke's dick hit every nerve ending I have inside of me, I can't concentrate on much else or I'll lose control and come.

Watching Haze climb up on the bed, he settles himself, kneeling to my left. He slides one hand up my back, into my hair, and grabs hold of my head, tilting it backward. His lips caress my neck as he kisses and licks and nips at my skin.

His left hand sprawls across my abdomen and tickles me as his fingers begin a journey down. Haze slides two fingers into the folds of my pussy, finding the bundle of nerves immediately and pinching them. The shock wave that hits me throws me off my rhythm, and I grab hold of his forearm, trying to keep my balance.

"Yes, yes, oh heavens, yes," I chant each time I spasm, my eyes pinched shut, seeing stars.

My fingernails pinch his skin as I clench my core tight in an attempt to stay upright. My orgasm washes over me like a rogue wave out of nowhere, drowning me with no air to breathe, and takes all of my energy.

And just as fast as I skydived off the edge, I come floating back from the ether, feeling Smoke grab my hips before he explodes too. Groaning through his release, his legs tremble under my thighs as he growls.

It's like my orgasm triggered his and we ride the wave together. Staying perfectly still, using Haze as my support, I do everything I can to not jostle Smoke too much.

Once we've all gone silent, Haze is the first to speak. "Is this heaven?"

Smoke and I start laughing so hard, I fall to the right, sliding off of him so I don't bump his arm or leg. I roll until my feet find the floor, then I lean back on the mattress on my forearms, my head next to his.

Haze collapses, lying next to Smoke on his good side.

"I think you sucked his brain out his dick, Smoke," I mumble through a giggle as I kiss his cheek.

He turns his head toward me and traces his nose along mine, kissing me back. "He's done it to me enough, turnabout is fair play."

"Give me a minute and I'll move and get us turned back around the right way," Haze says, finally looking at us. "I just need to let my brain get back into my skull."

The room again fills with laughter. If anyone were close enough to the house, they'd probably think whoever was here is a crazy bunch of lunatics.

In a way, we are. Falling in love with two men, two bikers . . . two bikers in an outlaw motorcycle club . . . even I think I'm a little crazy sometimes. But that doesn't stop me from holding on to the love they show me every minute of every day in return. I thought I had fallen in love once before, but that was nothing like this. Not even close.

Ever the responsible taskmaster caretaker that he's become, Haze forces Smoke and I to take our medicine before our adrenaline crashes. Simple over-the-counter anti-inflammatories are all Smoke will take, so we each kill a bottle of water before we clean up, rearrange, and all crash in bed.

It's lights out as I hold Haze's hand and my eyes drift closed.

CHAPTER THIRTY-EIGHT

SMOKE

"Yarrrrr, shiver me timbers," I croon in my best, and worst, attempt at pirate speak. "Would ya look at the booty on that hippie lass!"

Haze turns his stool around and takes in the mighty fine sight in front of us. "Hot damn, she's got one hell of a booty, alright."

Today is October thirty-first, and the Halloween party is in full swing. While the sun was still shining, all the kids and families were running amok, eating candy and holding babies, and having fun appropriate for the eyes of children under the age of thirteen. But what's happening right now is far from child appropriate. In fact, it's downright naughty . . . and hot as fuck.

Our Old Lady, along with Duchess, Angel, Sunshine, and Sara, are all gathered in a circle, dancing to some sugar song that's blasting from the clubhouse speakers. They're swinging their hips, arms waving in the air, tits shaking for our enjoyment. I don't know if they care that we're watching, but even if they did, I can't keep my eyes off the flash of tie-dye in front of me. Sugar? Yes, please indeed.

Raven's costume for today is a hippie. She's wearing one of her tie-dye shirts from The Lodge, but she made a few adjustments to the standard t-shirt design. Cutting slits in the chest, her cleavage is out in full force. The sleeves are gone altogether, and she removed a good foot of material from the bottom, so her toned stomach is on full display.

She's wearing a hip-hugging blue jean miniskirt, tan knee-high heeled boots that are covered in fringe, and big, round green-tinted sunglasses. Her hair is pin straight and she has a tie-dyed bandana folded and wrapped around her head. As she shimmies and spins, her hair flows around her in a curtain of inky black waves.

Since Raven didn't have long to prepare for the party, everything but the boots and sunglasses are hers. She borrowed the boots from Angel's insane closet, and the sunglasses were a last-minute share from Blue, who saw what she was wearing, then ran to her room and came back with the finishing detail.

For something just thrown together, she looks stunning.

I decided this year I wanted to dress as a pirate. Last year, I was just a Prospect and didn't dress up because I wasn't sure if we were allowed to, but not this year. I went all out.

Under my cut, because even with a costume, we still have to wear them, I have a white long-sleeve, billowy shirt. My ass is wrapped in tight black leather pants and I'm rocking these killer black boots, on my right foot at least. I'm stuck wearing this almost knee-high medical boot contraption for a few more weeks, but at least I can put some pressure on it and walk a few steps at a time without falling over.

Much to my dismay, my hair has been poofed and gelled, making my normally wavy hair all curly and styled. I never take the time to do anything to my hair other than leave it wild or tie it back, so when Angel insisted on styling it for me, I folded and let her do whatever she wanted. Happy Old Ladies make life so much easier, even if she's not *my* Old Lady.

So, with a red strip of fabric tied around my waist, another chunk holding my bum arm tight to my chest, and my trusty screwdriver wielded like a sword, I'm a damn pirate.

Ever the sneaky fucker, Haze wouldn't let me see what he was wearing until he was dressed and ready to go. When he opened the bathroom door, I knew the idea behind his costume instantly. He dressed up for me.

Wearing a blue t-shirt almost sculpted to this chest and abs, baggy straight-legged black pants with a yellow and white reflective stripe down the sides, big black boots, and bright red suspenders, my man is one hot firefighter.

"Since you had to chase me down, I figured I'd chase the smoke this time," he said with a wink.

Sitting on the edge of our bed, I'd pulled him between my legs and kissed him until we both needed to breathe.

At some point, he lost the stuffed Dalmatian dog he had tucked into his pocket to Opal, along with the kid-sized plastic helmet he had on his head to Jamie, so here we sit, watching the women get their groove on.

The Iron Darkness MC from Michigan got in early yesterday, so our clubhouse is chock-full of bikers in all sorts of costumes.

Scar and his Old Lady, Ivy, and those who came with their club, are dressed in cowboy western themed costumes. Not that it's much different from *standard* biker wear, but there's a lot of denim and leather around, in addition to fringe, cowboy hats, and even a few lassos.

A few of our family groups decided to dress in themes as well.

Ring and Steel are dressed as bees, wearing yellow and black striped t-shirts and black jeans. Sunshine is a beekeeper, because, in reality, she's the one who keeps those two yahoos in line. And before she was corralled to Angel and Hammer's cabin for a sleepover with all the other kiddos, Opal was dressed as the *queen bee* in a sparkly yellow top, black tutu, yellow and black tights, and a headband with flashing antennas and a crown with glitter on it.

Ring is wearing a headband with wobbly antennas on his head too, but Steel refused. His are sticking out of his back pocket. I'm just surprised they got Ring to wear something that wasn't all black, so I'd call this a win.

Whiskey and Duchess are sharks. Whiskey's wearing a dark gray hoodie under his cut, but the hood has a fin on it. His sleeves may be pushed up to his elbows, but he's still rocking the hood up. Duchess is in a full-body light pink onesie, and even Krew had on a tiny gray onesie with a hood like a shark's open mouth, teeth and all.

Second year in a row, Hammer's wearing his glow-in-the-dark skeleton shirt. But going with the theme, Angel worked her magic. She, along with both their boys, is dressed like a skeleton as well. She's got a little more skin showing with her black tank top and high-waisted Daisy Duke black shorts, but her painted-up face is actually really cool.

By some miracle, the club girls all agreed to dress in a coordinating theme. I didn't know dressing like a crayon was a thing, but there's no cattiness or bitching happening, so whatever floats their boats. But they're all slutty crayons, each dressed in a different color, all wearing headbands with pointy cones on their heads that look like the tip of a crayon.

Jazz is in green, Raquel is yellow, and Cinnamon is red.

I hadn't realized until now that our club girl numbers have been dropping like cement shoes in the harbor. Not that I have a need for them anymore, but I feel kind of bad for the single Brothers. Hopefully, for them, some new girls come around soon.

"What's a pirate's favorite letter?" Brewer, in a white baseball uniform with blue and yellow letters spelling his name across the front, hops up on the stool to my right.

"I don't know, Brother. What's a pirate's favorite letter?" I take a swig of my beer as I wait for his answer.

"You'd think it's AR-rrrr," he croons, "but it's the C-eeee he loves."

While I'm usually the one with the jokes around here, that was a good one, and I almost snort my beer out my nose. "HA!" I laugh over a cough. "You got me there."

"I got one," Haze joins in on the fun. "A pirate walks into a bar and the steering wheel from his ship is stuck to the front of his pants. The bartender hollers, 'Hey man, your steering wheel is down your pants.' The pirate replies, 'Yarrrr, it's drivin' me nuts!'"

Our laughter draws the attention of everyone around us, and next thing I know, my Raven is in front of us, her hands sliding up both our legs. "What's so funny over here?"

"These two chuckleheads," I nod at Brewer and Haze, "think they can tell funnier jokes than me."

"Oh really?" she remarks, a tiny curl to her smile. "Can I try?"

"If you think you got what it takes," I tease her.

"Where's Kraken?" She looks around the room. "I think he'd like this one."

I spot him over in the corner by Link, Scar, Whiskey, and Bear. He happens to look over, so I wave to get his attention.

Kraken wanders through the crowd before stopping behind Raven. "What's up?"

"Raven here has a joke to tell you," I explain as she turns around.

"Whatchya got for me, little birdie?" He smiles down at her from his foot-and-a-half perch above her head.

Her shoulders go back and she stands up tall. "How many tickles does it take to make an octopus laugh?"

Kraken scratches the side of his beard and stares off, thinking really hard. His brows crunch down and he appears confused. Finally, his eyes go back to her. "How many?"

"Ten. 'Cause he has *ten*-tacles."

I don't think I've ever seen or heard Kraken laugh so hard, and the whole room goes silent as he bellows out at the punchline.

Kraken pulls Raven in for a hug so tight, she almost disappears in his muscles. He kisses her cheek as he lets her go. "You, little birdie, are my new best friend. That's the funniest thing I've ever heard."

When Kraken grabbed her, Haze had jumped to his feet, ready to pull her back, but with a hand set on his shoulder, I stopped him.

Now free of our sea-loving Brother, Haze tucks Raven under his arm and growls at Kraken. "Keep your filthy tentacles off our Old Lady, you cue ball headed jailbird."

Kraken is dressed like an old school prisoner, wearing a black and white striped jumpsuit. He had a plastic ball and chain wrapped around his ankle when the party started, but when people kept tripping over it, and someone accidentally crushed the ball with their boot and cracked it, he improvised and draped the chain over his shoulders.

Needing to win back the joke telling trophy from all these yahoos who think they can best me, I toss out one I've been saving all day.

"Why can't ghosts have children?" Looking around our circle, everyone stares back at me in confusion.

"Why?" Brewer finally asks.

"Because ghosts have hollow-weenies."

And it works! Everyone busts out laughing, and I even earn a kiss on the cheek from Raven. I say my joke was a success.

As the night wears on, and we drink a little more than we should, everyone starts getting a little handsy with their significant others, so I decide it's time for me and mine to take the party somewhere a little more private.

As we follow Raven up the stairs, I lean on Haze and finally get to use the joke I've been wanting to say all day, I'd just been waiting for the right moment.

"Are you a firefighter?" I nip his earlobe and growl through my teeth. "Because I need someone to help hold my hose."

CHAPTER THIRTY-NINE

RAVEN

We spent a total of five nights at Brick's house, relaxing, healing, and learning more about each other. Being around my guys is so easy and carefree, I oftentimes find myself forgetting that our love is still so new. It's been only a few months since I met them, but my heart feels like it's finally found its home.

When we woke up Sunday morning, and they realized it was October thirty-first, Haze and Smoke begged me to agree to go back home to the clubhouse. We'd lost track of what day it was, and when they thought we were going to miss the club Halloween party, they offered to do unspeakable things to me until I saw things their way.

Truth is, I was kind of sad we might miss it, having left when we did, so I was as excited as they were. It didn't take much, only two screaming orgasms, one from each handsome devil, before I caved. I would've said yes before Haze rolled me over and buried his head between my thighs, but we don't need to tell them that.

We got back to the clubhouse just before noon and the festivities were already in full swing. After digging through my bags, I decided on my tie-dye hippie outfit, then left the guys to get ready. Angel offered to straighten my hair for me, so by the time I was dressed and ready to get my groovy on, Smoke and Haze were all decked out.

Seeing all the kids dressed up was so much fun, and the late-night adult party got to be a little bit wild, but I'm glad we got to be a part of it.

Opening my eyes, I wake up to an empty bed and go searching for my men. Much like the night I witnessed them in a much more intimate act, I hear noises coming from the adjoining room. Not sure what I'm going to walk in on this time, I try and stay quiet, tip-toeing into the connecting hall.

As I peek around the corner, I see my whole world cuddled together in a mix of muscular arms, tanned, tattooed skin, and messy hair.

Haze is lounging back with Smoke leaning back against him. Smoke's booted foot is propped up on a chair in front of the couch they're snuggled on, and both of them are sporting full smiles as they discuss whatever is pressing business at seven o'clock in the morning.

They look so happy, I almost don't want to interrupt them. But before I get the chance to slink back into the shadows, they sense me and look up.

"Come here, Raven," Haze calls out, holding his free hand out to me.

As they shift to let Haze untangle himself from around Smoke, they share a sweet, soft kiss. They each scoot a bit to the side, making a space just for me in the middle.

I sit and am immediately snuggled between two warm bodies, Smoke to my left and Haze on my right, and I'm surrounded by heat and muscles and just pure masculinity.

"Good morning. How'd you sleep?" Smoke asks as he hooks my chin with his finger, turning my face to meet his.

"Good." I start to say more but get interrupted when his lips press against mine.

Not three seconds after Smoke lets me go, Haze pulls me into his arms next. His kiss is a little more urgent, and I can feel his heavy breath against my lips. He reluctantly pulls back and tucks me into our jumbled embrace of arms and legs and love.

I can't wait to let him show me what has him all worked up, but just for these few minutes, we lie against each other. If it's anything like every night, and afternoon, and morning since our love began, I'm in for quite the ride.

Like a moment straight out of a fairytale, I know we're going to get our happily ever after.

I woke up this morning having the best dream, and now that I'm in the arms of my two loves, I know I couldn't be happier. It's all perfect.

My head resting back against Haze's chest, I slink down into the cushions. Smoke lifts my feet onto his lap, and I just listen as they pick up their conversation of whatever they were discussing before.

As they keep talking, I start to doze off, letting my dream take me back under.

I'm sitting on the end of the pier at the lake behind the farmhouse. My legs are dangling over the edge, toes skimming the water as I swing my feet.

The sun is just coming up, the light brushing across the lake as the sky starts to shift from black to gray to purple, then pinks, oranges, and yellows follow next.

I slip into the water and float on my back, watching the sky come to life above me.

Then, just as the first shade of blue peaks over the horizon, a low-lying fog covers the water, almost like I'm being surrounded by a cloud emerging from its morning swim. I reach up, trying to grasp the fading droplets, but they lift higher as the sun rises.

My life feels a little like my dream. I was lost in the dark, not knowing where I was going to end up or if I'd ever feel safe again. But one day, the sun came up and everything took a turn for the better. It's hard to believe it's only been a month since the day I woke up and decided it was going to be a good day, and it may not have gone like I'd expected, but what came after has made the journey to get where I am right now so worth it.

I found the love of two handsome, wonderful men, and they spend every day making my life better than I could've ever dreamed.

So, I'll continue to dream for more amazing days, soaking in the calm of my dream, almost like I'm floating in the middle of a smoke-filled haze.

THE END!

EPILOGUE

BLUE

Looking down at the handsome little man sleeping in my arms, I can't help but think back and imagine how different my life would've been had I been able to give birth to the baby I lost.

Would he be a strapping young man, a spitting image of his father, and following in the footsteps of his big brother?

Or would she be a beautiful woman, just reaching the age where she wants to spread her wings and driving her Pops crazy with talk of boys and college and what color she wants her bedroom painted?

While there is very little I regret in my life, not giving my husband another baby is right there at the top of my 'what if' list. I'd never admit it to anyone, but the weight on my heart is sometimes too heavy.

That's a big reason why any time I'm near my grandbabies, whether they're related by blood like tiny Krew I'm holding now, or not like Angel's boys Taren and Ace, I give them all my love. I scoop them into my arms and soak up all the young, innocent love they have to give. They know none of the wrong or mean or hurtful parts of life yet, and I want to keep them wrapped in that cocoon as long as I can.

"What do you think?"

I look up and am transformed back to the brightly lit bridal store I've been sitting in for the last hour. Duchess is standing up on a pedestal, trying on her wedding dress for the last time before she takes it home.

I'm here with all the ladies who are getting married next week, getting to see their dresses for the first time. Due to offering to watch the babies, I didn't come along when they came in to buy them last month. But between Duchess, Angel, Sunshine, and Star constantly begging me to come today, I couldn't say no.

They all look so beautiful in the dresses they've picked, but there's something about Duchess that makes me lose my breath. I don't know if it's that I feel a stronger connection to her because she's marrying my nephew, or because I'm holding her adorable son in my arms, but I start tearing up.

"Oh, Duchess," carefully standing, holding Krew to my chest, I step forward to take in the details on the front of this ivory-colored dress, "you look radiant."

This dress looks like it was designed just for her. The sweetheart sparkly beaded neckline leads down into a fitted bodice, then at the waist, the material flows out into a skirt covered in lace. And the fit is perfect, like a second skin.

"Isn't it pretty?" she whispers as she runs her hands down the sides.

"That dress is more than pretty. Whiskey isn't gonna know what to do when he sees you."

She looks up, eyes already brimming with tears. "You think so?" Duchess picks up the sides of the skirt and turns to face the three-way mirror behind her. She turns this way, then that way, but her eyes never leave her reflection.

"I know so." I nod. "Do you want me to take a picture for you, so you can remember what it looks like?"

"While I'd love that, if I have any evidence of this on my phone, you know Whiskey's bound to find it and ruin the surprise," she replies with a giggle.

"Then I'll take it on my phone but not send it to you 'til after the big day." I set Krew down in his car seat and pull my phone from my pocket. "Anytime you wanna see it, you come find me."

"Deal." I snap a few pictures, then sit back and watch as Sunshine, Angel, and Star come out of the back room and go to check out.

Since everyone is so close, it was decided amongst the four couples that they wanted to share a wedding day. The ladies are all super excited, and their men will do anything for them, so there was no turning back. The date was set. There will be a giant wedding at the clubhouse on Christmas Eve.

Things are already well in motion, turning the clubhouse into a winter wonderland, and everyone is on board with the transformation. I just wish I could be there to see it, but life doesn't always let us have everything we want.

"What are you going to wear on the big day?" Sunshine asks as she drops onto the couch next to me, snapping me back to the present.

"I have a black dress at home I'll wear." Not able to be completely truthful with her, I cover my real plans with a white lie. "This is your big day, no one will care what I wear."

"That's a bunch of baloney," Duchess calls out from behind us. "You need a special dress too. I don't know why I didn't think about it sooner."

"I don't need—" I try to insist but am cut off.

"Yes, you do." Sunshine pulls me to my feet and leads me over to a rack of dresses that has something of every color of the rainbow. She starts pushing dresses to the sides before settling into the blue section. She pulls out one that's covered in lace and such a light blue, it almost looks silver. "I think you need to try this on."

She practically shoves it into my arms so I take it and am led back into a fitting room.

Knowing I'm not going to be allowed to leave the store unless I sneak out the back, because let's face it, the Old Ladies of the Rebel Vipers MC are almost as crazy as the Brothers, I give in.

I fold and set my clothes aside, then step into the dress. Lifting the material up, it ends mid-calf, and I slide my arms into the sheer, lace sleeves. Looking at myself in the mirror, I'm instantly transported back to the planning of my own wedding and the excitement I experienced all those years ago. I remember the dreams I had, the plans I was making, and all the wishes I had for our future.

The recent wedding planning has brought up lots of memories of the events around my big day. While many of them have come true, there's always been a small worry in the back of my mind that Mountain may regret having rushed into inviting me into this life.

I wonder, if he knew how the following few years would turn out, would he have still wanted me?

And with the way he's been acting lately, I wonder if he still wants me now.

TO BE CONTINUED ...

ACKNOWLEDGMENTS

Mr. J – Thank you for giving me the extra time I needed to get this one done. All my late nights, not crawling into bed until three or four in the morning, you never once complained when I woke you up. I love you to the moon and back!

Rebecca Vazquez – My book fairy godmother. #DoubleTrouble took the win on this one for sure. I wrote up to the wire, but you cheered me on the whole way. Let's do another one! #TeamRebelVipers

Jackie Ziegler – Thank you for swooping in at the last minute to help. It is greatly appreciated!

My KM Alpha friends – Kay, Becca, Olivia... Heidi, you've been waiting for your troublemakers for a while, and I hope you love their yummy abs as much as Raven does.

Charli Childs – I say this every time, but this is my favorite cover so far! The green is spot on!

And last, but definitely not least, YOU! THANK YOU, READERS! Thank you for reading Smoke, Haze, and Raven's story. These two sneaky dudes are definitely troublemakers, because when I started the series, I had no intention of giving the Prospects a story. They were supposed to be these funny guys who floated around in the background, making everyone laugh with their silly antics, but when they decided to couple up, everything changed in a flash. Hopefully, you enjoyed their welcome into the club!

Coming next is a mix of a trip down memory lane and a catch-up from the original Rebel Vipers MC President, Mountain, and his lovely Old Lady, Blue. Grab those handlebars tight, you're in for twists even I didn't see coming.

ABOUT THE AUTHOR

Jessa Aarons was born and raised in the frozen tundra of Wisconsin. She has had her nose buried in books for as long as she can remember. Her love of romance began when she "borrowed" her mom's paperback Harlequin novels. After experiencing a life-changing health issue, she had to leave the working world and dove back into books to help heal her soul. She would read anything that told a love story but still had grit and drama. Then she became a beta reader and personal assistant to another author.

Jessa is the boss of her husband and their castle. He really is her prince. Thanks to his encouragement, Jessa started putting pen to paper and creating new imaginary worlds. She spends her free time reading, crafting, and cheering on her hometown football team.

SOCIAL MEDIA LINKS

Facebook Author Page

FB Reader's Group

Instagram

Twitter

Amazon

Goodreads

Bookbub

Pinterest

Spotify

TikTok

OTHER WORKS

<u>Rebel Vipers MC</u>
A Mountain to Climb
Whiskey on the Rocks
Ring of Steel
Hammer's Swing
A Smoke Filled Haze
Top of the Mountain

<u>Standalones</u>
Pure Luck – cowrite with Kay Marie